JEWEL

"You'll have to teach me, Ross," Stephanie said in a small embarrassed voice. He gave a tender smile, lying on his side and gazing down at her, as if to drink in every vestige of her alabaster skin with his eyes.

"Do you think I don't know that or that it will give me the greatest pleasure to do so?" he murmured back. "A man's desire is to have a bride that has known no other than himself. And it is just as important for her to know that he will take no other wife," he added.

For a moment, Stephanie sensed that his thoughts were far away then. They were somewhere in that other realm, where Prince Hali Ahmed could have his choice of concubines. But this was England, and this was her marital bed that she was sharing with her husband, who belonged to her and whose only desire was to pleasure her now.

DANGEROUS GAMES   (0-7860-0270-0, $4.99)
by Amanda Scott

When Nicholas Barrington, eldest son of the Earl of Ul-
combe, first met Melissa Seacort, the desperation he
sensed beneath her well-bred beauty haunted him. He
didn't realize how desperate Melissa really was . . . until
he found her again at a Newmarket gambling club—being auctioned off by her father to the highest bidder. So,
Nick bought himself a wife. With a villain hot on their
heels, and a fortune and their lives at stake, they would
gamble everything on the most dangerous game of all:
love.

A TOUCH OF PARADISE   (0-7860-0271-9, $4.99)
by Alexa Smart

As a confidence man and scam runner in 1880s America,
Malcolm Northrup has amassed a fortune. Now, posing
as the eminent Sir John Abbot—scholar, and possible
discoverer of the lost continent of Atlantis—he's taking
his act on the road with a lecture tour, seeking funds for
a scientific experiment he has no intention of making.
But scholar Halia Davenport is determined to accompany
Malcolm on his "expedition" . . . even if she must kidnap
him!

Jewel

Jean Innes

Zebra Books
Kensington Publishing Corp.
http://www.zebrabooks.com

ZEBRA BOOKS are published by

Kensington Publishing Corp.
850 Third Avenue
New York, NY 10022

First Printing: April, 1998
10 9 8 7 6 5 4 3 2 1

Printed in the United States of America

One

As the evening wore on, the raucous sounds of male voices from the salon below became more noticeable. Stephanie was aware of them long after she had retired to her room to write up the day's events in her diary. And she was far too curious to be able to resist creeping along to the one-time musicians' gallery above the male preserve, where the fragrant smell of expensive cigars drifted upward to tease and tantalize her nostrils.

She had been banished all day to an elderly cousin's home in the country, while her stepfather entertained a party of what Cousin Claire disapprovingly called his more sophisticated friends, several of whom would undoubtedly not leave until after tomorrow morning's breakfast. Stephanie was still resentful at having to spend a boring time with a relative who seemed to disapprove of anyone remotely young when she would much rather stay up in town, where she belonged.

She knelt as silently as she could behind the elegant, chased oak panels on the first-floor gallery of the London townhouse, her figured silk gown rustling annoyingly as she did so. But no one was likely to have heard her. There was far too much noise and tension going on in the salon below, where the gaming tables had been set up, and where her stepfather was by now blustering and puce-faced, as he flung the dice in a fury across the green baize cloth. A score of male heads craned forward to see the result.

"It seems you lose again, my lord."

Amid the gasps from the gentlemen crowding around the table, she heard the drawl that was commanding everyone's attention. The well-educated voice had a pleasingly rich timbre. It stated the obvious so pleasantly to the loser that the words were almost insolent. And Stephanie knew that her stepfather was not a man to take losing calmly, despite the fact that his gambling fortunes fluctuated alarmingly.

She tried to see the face belonging to the unknown voice, but for the moment, she could not. There were still too many craning necks below, waiting to see how Lord Buchan would react. Among them were undoubtedly those who predicted that he would eventually become so enmeshed by his need to gamble, and his hopeless luck, that he would one day lose everything.

"I'm not a fool, Kilmarron," she heard her stepfather said tetchily. "I can count the numbers on a dice as well as yourself."

"Then what do you say to a final throw to settle all?" the man called Kilmarron went on, as cool as before.

Stephanie's stepbrother intervened wildly now, his fleshy face almost as contorted as his father's.

"Father, no! I beg you not to risk everything on a single throw. Think what you're doing, for God's sake!"

The older man brushed aside the boy's restraining arm on his sleeve.

"For *your* sake, you mean, you little pipsqueak. Your only concern is that I'll gamble away the house and its contents, and you'll be left without an inheritance—but there's plenty in the coffers yet."

"And why would I not be worried?" Percy demanded peevishly. "It's mine by right."

"Not yet, it's not!" Lord Buchan bellowed. "And not ever, by God, if you don't mind your manners!"

Stephanie assumed that the company below would be well

used to hearing such displays between the two of them, shameful though it was to be so vulgar in public.

The day her mother had married *that man,* as she always referred to him, was the worst day of her life. It had given them both security, but the marriage hadn't been a happy one. It had eventually sapped her mother's strength, and she had died before Stephanie was fully grown. But now she was well able to stand up to the bullying ways of the male Buchans.

She risked raising her head as the gentlemen seemed to move back a little from the central table, and she saw the tall, dark-haired figure of someone mockingly tossing the dice from hand to hand as he waited for the fracas to die down. A figure who stood head and shoulders above the rest of the self-indulgent company who normally frequented these occasions, she thought swiftly. A figure of powerful proportions and the kind of rugged countenance that spoke of many hours spent outdoors in a hot sun. Which made Stephanie even more curious, for not even the best of English summers was the place to acquire quite such a tan.

While the wrangling went on below, the man suddenly looked up. Maybe he had caught a movement of her pink silk gown, or the sheen of her extraordinary silvery hair. Whatever it was that caused him to look directly into her eyes, it had the effect of making her bob down quickly behind her gallery shelter, her heart beating wildly. But for just one startled moment, she had the odd sensation that their two gazes had met and locked, and flashed an unspoken message.

She knew such a feeling was totally absurd, for what possible message could a handsome and wordly young gentleman be sending to a girl of twenty summers who was naive enough to crouch down behind a gallery panel? She seethed at her own assessment of herself, for she didn't consider herself naive at all. On the contrary, her quick wit and quicker tongue usually had her stepbrother Percy raging against her, as he came off the worst in their verbal battles.

"I've no wish to deprive your father or yourself of your inheritance, young man," the stranger said in a patronizing way that Stephanie knew would have the boy squirming. "But I have the right to call for one more throw of the die, and to suggest a wager to our mutual agreement."

Stephanie didn't fail to notice the pile of promissory notes in front of the man now. He was on a winning streak all right, and her stepfather would be a fool to risk much more.

"He's right, Lord Buchan," a fellow gambler put in. "Your honor depends on it, no matter what your opponent demands. Otherwise, you'll be taken for a welsher."

Buchan scowled. "Do you think I'm not aware of that? And when did you ever know me to welsh on a bet? So, Kilmarron, what is your wager? My pipsqueak of a son requests that you leave the house intact," he added with heavy sarcasm.

"I've no desire for your house. I've property enough of my own," the man said insultingly. "But you do have something that appeals to me."

"Name it, man," Lord Buchan said irritably. "A painting, perhaps? Or a carriage and pair?"

As he spoke, Stephanie saw Kilmarron's eyes stray toward a fine oil painting on the salon wall. Her heart began to beat painfully fast as he studied it for long seconds. It was not a valuable Old Master, such as her stepfather coveted and hoarded. It was a delightful portrait of a young girl with her long silvery hair loose and unpinned. She was seated on a chaise longue, and her delicate fingers caressed the petals of a long-stemmed rose.

The artist had captured a remarkable mixture of innocence and sensuality in the pose by allowing the girl to lean backward and sideways so that the curves of her breasts and her raised hip were pronounced. In contrast, the fall of her silvery hair, the clear blue of her eyes, and the hesitant smile on her generous mouth betrayed the virginal quality of her tender years.

Stephanie looked away from her own portrait, but she didn't miss the way Kilmarron's glance swept momentarily upward to where she crouched. And she knew that he was fully aware of her presence.

"I'll take your stepdaughter," he said calmly, and at the outraged gasps of the onlookers, he held up his hand for quiet. His powerful personality made them all fall silent.

"As an added incentive, Lord Buchan, I will wager all that I've won here tonight, and a sum of ten thousand pounds besides, for the girl."

He looked toward the musicians' gallery once more, while Stephanie reeled back on her heels. Such a sum was the ultimate in vulgarity, she raged. For all his educated manner, he was shameless enough to be virtually buying her, unless, of course, her stepfather refused the outrageous bid altogether. But she knew he would not refuse. Even from here, she could see the way his eyes glittered with greed. She could almost read his devious mind.

His fortunes had been so bad tonight that surely the tide must turn, and he would win back all that he had lost, and so much more besides. Stephanie found herself holding her breath, not sure which of them she would choose to be the winner. She despised them both.

But she was virtually a prisoner in this house, hating the male Buchans to whom she was bound by her mother's unfortunate marriage, and restrained at every turn. Lord Buchan didn't want her here, and saw her as an irritation, no more. But if Kilmarron's outrageous wager was to be won and honored, the alternative would seem to be to exchange one prison for another in the company of a stranger. It was a prospect that didn't please her at all.

"By God, I accept, sir!" she heard Lord Buchan say, just as she had known he would. "The girl's of marrying age, and 'twould save me the trouble of looking for a suitor if you were to take her off me hands. Not that you're going to win, mind, for I aim to relieve you of that ten thousand pounds you mention, as well as all your other winnings to-night!"

Kilmarron smiled politely, and it was the smile of a hunter biding his time, Stephanie thought. She knew she should get away from here right now, and not be witness to this degrading bargaining. But something was compelling her to stay, and she couldn't resist peering through the gaps in the gallery panels as the ritual of the wager began. First, there was the drinking of a glass of port before any major bet. The two opponents raised their glasses to each other, and then to the surrounding company.

Such politeness was all so false, Stephanie thought, when each was planning how they could outfox the other. A servant handed each man a damp cloth to wipe his hands, and another on which to dry them before the die were thrown. It was all so farcical, so ritualistic, so stupidly *male,* Stephanie raged. They were like children, teasing each other, each of them trying to undermine the other's confidence in a battle of nerves.

But there was nothing childlike in the way Kilmarron had gazed at her portrait, she thought with a shiver. Nor in the way those dark, seductive eyes had held her gaze for a breathless moment. She knew enough to recognize a look of blatant desire in a man's face when she saw it. But what made her more uneasy than anything else was *why* Kilmarron should have made such an extraordinary wager. Such a charismatic man could surely have any woman he wanted. Why should he choose Stephanie Wheatley Buchan? If they had met before, and the wager had been premeditated, it would have been more understandable. If it was said on a whim, then the chances for a comfortable future seemed to Stephanie to be precisely nil.

"Come, sir. Let's see if your luck holds out. I suspect you've had too good a run for it to continue," Lord Buchan was saying now, fortified by the port and the urging of his supporters. He flexed his fingers aggressively.

Kilmarron smiled politely. "Loser goes first, I believe, for the best run of the cloth," he said.

Buchan scowled. He picked up the die and threw them onto the green baize. One rolled quickly to show the six spots uppermost. The other teetered for a moment, and then toppled over to reveal the face with five spots. A polite cheer went up from Buchan's supporters.

"You'll need a perfect score to beat that, Kilmarron," he said with satisfaction.

"I always aim for perfection," the man retorted. "Which is why I see your fair stepdaughter as the perfect foil to myself."

While Stephanie was still seething at such blatant arrogance, he threw the die almost nonchalantly. Two perfect sixes landed squarely. And as more cheers went up, Kilmarron raised his head and looked directly toward the musicians' gallery with a half-smile on his lips, and to Stephanie he was darkly satanic at that moment.

She fled into the sanctuary of her bedroom, nerves taut and her entire body shaking. And trying to come to terms with the fact that a short while ago she had been safe in the protection of her stepfather, however much she loathed him, but because a wager would have to be honored, she was to be thrown to the wolves in the shape of someone called Kilmarron, whose given name she didn't even know.

It was impossible to sleep, no matter how hard she tried, in order to avoid imagining all the possibilities of the future. But the images wouldn't let her restless mind relax. She didn't even know if the man intended to marry her or to keep her as his servant. His insulting statement that he would take the girl could mean anything, and her stepfather had been as unconcerned about her feelings as ever to establish the facts before the wager commenced.

Once she was out of his protection, her new keeper could

do anything he liked with her. She licked her dry lips, as wild thoughts of selling girls into slavery flitted in and out of her mind.

She awoke to a tangle of bed clothes and bathed in perspiration. In her worst nightmare, she had been sold to the highest bidder in an eastern brothel, after living on her wits in the shady bazaars and back streets of some unknown country filled with infidels. But it was even worse when she had been captured and sold, for above the white flowing headdress that hid the face of her owner, were Kilmarron's dark eyes.

"I'm being a fool," she said loudly, as if the sound of her own voice would reassure her that the reality was this comfortable bedroom in a large house on the corner of a leafy London square and that all the rest was fantasy.

"Are you ill, miss?" She heard the voice of the maid who had come to draw back her curtains.

"I am not, Maisie, nor do I intend to stay in bed one moment longer."

She leapt out of bed, and the maid looked at her dubiously.

"There's no need for you to be hasty, Miss Stephanie, for you'll be the only one up and about. After the gentlemen's late night, Cook had orders not to prepare breakfast until eleven o'clock and it's barely half-past nine o'clock."

"Well, she can prepare some for me right now," Stephanie declared. "What my stepfather does is his own business, but there's no need for the rest of the household to starve, is there?"

"No, miss," Maisie grinned, used to this kind of reply. "I've brought your washing water for you, and I'll tell Cook directly."

As she drew back the curtains completely now, she let a stream of sunshine pour in. The motes of dust in the air danced and gleamed in its rays, and to Stephanie it was far too good a day to be lazing about in bed. She loved the sun, even though she knew better than to let her skin remain uncovered in it for too long. Her complexion was so fair that she burned easily, and it was unfashionable to display reddened flesh. Queen Victoria and the little princesses were always careful to carry parasols whenever they went outside in the summer months, and it was wise to follow their lead.

Obviously, such things didn't apply to gentlemen, Stephanie thought as a flash of memory surged into her mind. Kilmarron was as tanned as she had ever seen a man. For just one second, no more, the thought slid into her mind to wonder if that tan extended to more of his body than was on show last night. Then, she had only seen his face, and his large hands, tossing the die between them in an oddly sensuous way, as if he caressed a woman.

She swallowed, wondering if she was going mad with thoughts about a man she had never seen until last night but who was destined to figure largely in her life in whatever way he chose. She didn't *want* to think about him, nor to contemplate the future with him. His manipulation of her was still an outrage, and as she began her morning ablutions, she caught sight of her large, scared blue eyes in the mirror above her washing stand.

By now, she had dismissed the slavery fantasy as absurd. But the fact that he was a sophisticated man was very evident. So what *did* he want of her? If it was marriage, then she would come to him as an innocent, and he would naturally assume as much. Was that what he wanted? she thought with hot embarrassment. In one of his more vicious moods, Percy once taunted her that some men would give their souls to marry a virgin and that she had best keep herself pure for the highest bidder. She had never thought how prophetic those words were going to be.

She attended to her washing quickly, as fastidious as ever. But for the first time in her life, she was unable to resist wondering how other eyes would regard her body and how it would feel when other hands reached for her breasts and fondled the secret parts of her that had never known any attention other than her own. And that, only in the necessary daily routine of keeping herself clean.

As if drawn by an irresistible curiosity, she touched her breasts as if it was Kilmarron's hands touching them, half closing her eyes and imagining that those tanned fingers were caressing and circling the nipples . . . and at their sudden responsive erection, coupled with an exquisitely sweet new sensation surging downward toward her loins, she dropped her hands in a fright, wondering if she had inadvertently done herself some damage.

Scarlet with shame, she turned away from the reflection of her own sensual expression, dressed quickly, and went downstairs in search of breakfast, glad of this time alone to compose herself from all the new and unnerving happenings, both in herself and her future life.

In the dining room, she stopped abruptly, her heart thudding wildly as the lone figure there turned to greet her from the breakfast hot plates that had already been brought to the side tables. He was as darkly handsome in his day clothes as in the evening wear of the previous night. And to her chagrin, she saw that her only breakfast companion so far was the man Kilmarron.

"Good morning, Miss Buchan," he said gravely. "I trust you slept well?"

Stephanie knew she should answer politely, and supposed that she should also go through the ritual of pretense with this man, until she was summoned to her stepfather's study to hear her fate. But reason didn't enter into her feelings right then. All she saw was a smiling predator who could change her life by a single throw of the die. And all she felt was a raging anger.

"And I think you know that I did not, sir!" she said, her eyes blazing. "I think you know very well that you caused me a very uncomfortable night indeed!"

If she expected him to be taken aback by her outburst, and mutter some apology for the ill he had done to her, she was very much mistaken. To her astonishment she saw that he was laughing. His face altered considerably when he laughed. It was younger, more open, and not so intense—and just as devastatingly attractive as when he was serious.

"Oh, my poor Stephanie, I do know it," he said, ignoring her gasp at his free use of her name. "But since there's no help for it now, I suggest that you and I try to get along as best we can, for it will be a miserable kind of marriage if we're always at loggerheads with one another."

She didn't speak for a moment, and when she did, her voice was strangled.

"You do mean to marry me then?" she said.

He came to where she stood rigidly by the dining table, not yet able to move toward the hot plates from which the family always served themselves at breakfast. Food was the last thing on her mind right now.

Kilmarron moved with an elegant grace for so large a man, and again, she had the illusion of the hunter stalking his prey. The tiger or the wolf. Before she knew what he intended to do, he had taken her pale hands in his own, and the contrast of light and dark created a potent imagery in her mind. They complemented each other, but she mustn't think of such things now. She must keep the sense of outrage uppermost, and not be swayed by the very charisma of the man.

"What else did you think I had in mind, my sweet girl?" he said softly, a faint northern accent creeping into his hitherto correct manner and making her shiver with an unbidden reaction to the unexpected charm of it.

"How was I to know? Your exact words were that you would take the girl—" She bit her lip, for now he would know, if he didn't already know it, that she had heard everything, and that she knew exactly why she was being offered up as a kind of sacrifice.

"And so I will," he said, his voice conveying a slightly different meaning to the words. "And I promise that you won't be disappointed in the taking."

Stephanie snatched her hands away. He went too fast, and he spoke of things she didn't yet know. But he would be anticipating all those things with a lustful pleasure, she thought, wishing bitterly that Percy had never put the unsavory thought in her head. *Some men would give their souls to marry a virgin.* But Kilmarron hadn't had to go that far. He had wagered a pile of promissory notes and ten thousand pounds, but he had got her for nothing. In effect, she was worthless.

She lifted her chin as the hateful thought entered her head. She wouldn't be bought. She would rather take her chances on the streets, but even as she thought it, she knew she would not. She had seen the wretched creatures who hung around London's back alleys, ready to lift their skirts for a copper, and risking all kinds of disease and humiliation. But perhaps she could still reason with the man.

"I can't think why you should want to marry me, sir. You don't know me, and I'm sure you wouldn't even want to know me when I'm in one of my worst moods. My stepbrother calls me a wildcat, and I'm sure no gentleman would wish to have such a harridan for a wife!"

She paused for breath, only to see that the laughter was back in Kilmarron's eyes again. Damn the man, she fumed. Did he have no scruples at all? But obviously, he did not, if he could resort to finding a wife in such a despicable way.

"I've no objection to taming a wildcat," he said, humoring her. "In fact, I shall take the greatest satisfaction in doing so, and in pleasuring you."

Stephanie ignored the thrill that the seductive words sent through her veins. She spoke vigorously.

"Your reason for marrying me is merely to crown your victory at the gaming tables! Mine for marrying you will only be because I am forced into it, and for no other reason. You have my word on it that you will not find me a willing wife, nor a subservient one, sir!"

"Then I thank God for that," he said briskly. "I've never

relished the thought of bedding a woman who lies beneath me like a log."

Stephanie's mouth dropped open. She had never heard a gentleman speak so freely about intimate matters in her life, especially when they affected her so personally. She felt her delicate skin flood with color. And the prospect of what marriage with this man would mean was swiftly taking precedence over all else.

"Then you mean this to be a full and proper union?"

"Naturally," Kilmarron said. "Don't you believe in the sanctity of marriage?"

"Of course I do—"

"And in the procreation of children?"

Stephanie stared at him. The words were said almost carelessly, but something told her instantly that he wanted children. And perhaps that was the only reason he had made this absurd wager, to save himself the trouble of finding a suitable mother for his children by having to go through the usual courtship rituals.

"You want me to be a breeding cow, is that it?" Stephanie said sarcastically, knowing she would scandalize half of Victorian London by her frankness, but finding nothing more scandalous than having to face up to this man who thought he half owned her already.

But she saw that she had not shocked him at all. Nothing seemed to do so, she raged. Whatever she gave out, he gave back in full measure. In that, she thought, with a tiny frisson of alarm, perhaps they were not so ill matched after all. But she didn't dare begin to think in that way. She must keep up her defensive barriers at all costs.

"Why not? If our dear queen can produce so many children for the royal nursery in so short a time, why shouldn't her subjects do the same?"

"I hardly think you should speak so about the queen," Stephanie said indignantly. "But perhaps one can't expect a person from the north of the country to have the same respect for the monarch as she deserves."

"Lincolnshire is hardly the far north, and I've long since severed all connection with the county. But perhaps you mean to imply that we're a wilder breed than you southern folk," Kilmarron said with a slight smile. "And coming from a wildcat woman like yourself, I don't think you need bother your head about such matters, Miss Buchan. I've a feeling that we shall be an admirable match for each other."

It was damnably near to her own thoughts, but she didn't care to acknowledge it. She wouldn't give him an inch of encouragement. As for his comment about the sanctity of marriage, it seemed that precious little of such sentiments would apply to this particular marriage. Their proposed union shamed the very word.

"I'm hungry," she said abruptly. "If you will excuse me, I shall help myself to some breakfast."

"Of course. I like to see a woman with a good appetite, and some flesh on her bones."

She flushed anew as his gaze lingered over her, and it was almost as though he stripped her naked with his eyes. At the same time, he ran the tip of his tongue slowly around his lower lip as if savoring something very sweet. And she felt again that peculiar, surging sensation in her loins that she had felt earlier that morning. How could such a powerful sensation be aroused by just a look? she thought tremulously.

"I would be grateful if you did not stare at me so," she said in a low voice, suddenly thrown into confusion, her usual confidence ebbing away.

"You're a very lovely woman, and a man always wants to stare at lovely things."

"Especially those that he owns, I presume," she couldn't help saying.

She heaped scrambled eggs onto her plate, slamming a piece of toast on the side, as if to imply that if she became as fat as a suckling sow, she wouldn't care.

"Especially those," Kilmarron answered gravely, and she was immediately stumped by the seriousness of the man. She could rail against his teasing, storm against his outrageous remarks and sexual innuendoes, but she was helpless at this seriousness that sounded so sincere, when she knew it couldn't possibly be so. She tried to gather herself together as she sat down at the dining table and proceeded to eat her breakfast. As Kilmarron joined her, he spoke again, still in that grave manner.

"I've offended you, and it was the last thing I wanted to do. I wish we could have a lengthy courtship so that I could prove to you that a gambling man is not all bad," he said with that sideways smile that made her heart turn over. But it was not only his smile that did that. It was also what he said.

"Why can we not? Have a lengthy courtship, I mean?" She was confused even as she spoke, since it sounded as though she wanted to experience that state of prenuptial bliss . . . or even worse, that she was quite prepared to rush into a hasty marriage with a stranger.

"Are you so anxious to get back to wherever it is you live?" she added, the thought starting to appall her, as she saw herself immersed for life, away from everything she knew and loved. The city might not appeal to everyone, but it was all Stephanie knew, and she loved every weathered stone of it.

"I must get home at some stage, but business keeps me here in London for the present," he said with some regret, his tone and his words taking her by surprise, and she was unable to resist showing her relief. "Does that please you? Do I take it that you're not enamored with the thought of country life?"

"Not altogether," she said, as he confirmed her suspicions. But she answered cautiously, knowing how sensitive and hot-headed people could be on such matters, and she had already deduced that Kilmarron was no fop. She went on hurriedly.

"So will you be staying in London for a considerable while then?"

She was even more thankful when her stepfather and several house guests arrived in the dining room, allowing the tension between the two of them to ease a little.

"For a short while, yes. But not for much longer. I intend to return to Egypt while the climate is still kind enough for our British skins to bear, and you will come with me, of course. The marriage will be arranged with all speed, since my ship sails for the Mediterranean in a month's time, and from there we go to Alexandria."

Two

As she stared at him in shocked silence, taking in all that he had said, her stepfather joined them.

"Kilmarron is an archeologist, Stephanie," he commented, as if taking a personal pride in the man's achievements. "He's been responsible for some very fine discoveries in Egypt that have won him the praise of the governments in both countries."

Her temper rose quickly at the prospect ahead of her, and Stephanie found it very easy to ignore the splendor of the man's achievements, even when he put in more modestly that he was only one part of an expeditionary team.

"You surely don't think I'm going to travel to some hot, dusty desert country with you, do you?" she spluttered.

"As my wife, I shall naturally expect you to accompany me," Kilmarron said, as if there was no question about it. "I understand that you're an accomplished artist, for a woman, so you will be an asset to me in my work. My assistant takes all necessary notes and collates them, but it will be unique to have a woman's touch in sketching the artifacts and relics in our discoveries. And, of course, it will be safer for you to be by my side while we travel," he added.

The reference to her safety passed almost unnoticed. Insultingly, it seemed to be added as an afterthought, Stephanie raged. His male arrogance left her speechless, but not for very long. She had never been one for holding her tongue when something needed to be said.

"I've no desire to go to Egypt at all, let alone be an asset to you, which I'm quite sure I would not!" she snapped. "I know nothing of antiquities and I've no wish to be connected with your work in any way! If we must continue with this farce of a marriage, then I suggest that you leave me here in London, while you get on with it."

She looked at him hopefully, knowing that it was a vain hope that he would agree to such a thing, and she heard her stepfather begin to bluster.

"Now then, my girl, I see that you're fully aware of what's been arranged, but you'll do yourself no good by insulting my guest—"

"I'm not insulting him, just reminding him that I'm not his chattel yet, sir!"

And never will be, she added silently. She saw the slanting smile cross her future husband's face again, and her heart leapt sickly. Why did he have to be quite so attractive? she thought savagely. Why was there a devil's heart hiding beneath that devastating smile?

"I'm hardly likely to take myself a wife, and leave her alone while I go on my travels," he said in his lazy drawl. "What kind of a husband would do such a foolish thing, especially when he has such a lovely and desirable bride?"

Stephanie felt her mouth go dry at the insinuation in the words, and in the way his gaze continued to rake her body. Evidently, such blatant innuendoes were of no concern to Lord Buchan and the type of people who frequented his gaming parties, for none of them raised an eyebrow at Kilmarron's remarks. Which only went to show that they were no gentlemen, and neither was he.

"I would probably become ill in the first few hours in such a hot climate," she said suddenly. "My skin is very fair, and I wilt easily. You would probably have a corpse on your hands if I had to stay there longer than a day."

She challenged him with her eyes, and it was as though there were no others in the room besides herself and this handsome stranger. In any case, the others were minding their own business, and getting on with the more important task of filling their bellies with breakfast, rather than bothering about these two. But at her own words, she felt a hint of warmth come into her cheeks, for despite her delicate coloring and seemingly fragile air, Cousin Claire had frequently informed her that she was as strong as an ox, and disgustingly so. Cousin Claire always deemed it quite unladylike for a young girl not to have the vapors at the least provocation.

"Then if you become ill," Kilmarron said softly, so that only she could hear, "it will be my pleasure to nurse you back to health with all tenderness."

She shivered at his tone, knowing she had little option but to commit her life to this man, but before she could think of some pithy reply, he turned to her stepfather.

"Since the young lady is already aware of my plans, do I have your permission to walk with her in the grounds, Lord Buchan? There are certain things we have to discuss."

"Of course you may." Lord Buchan waved them away dismissively, confirming to Stephanie that he would be very glad to be rid of her, without all the bother of finding her a husband and the necessary expense it would entail. For all his wealth, he had a very mean streak, and there was none meaner than selling her off to a stranger.

But she went out into the sunlight with Kilmarron without further demur, and once they were in the shade of the rose arbors, she turned to face him.

"I'm sure I don't know why you made that extraordinary wager, sir, but I have to tell you—"

She gasped in midsentence then, as she was suddenly caught and held in his arms. His face was very close to hers, and on his skin there was a musky scent of exotic lotions whose perfume she didn't recognize at all, but which was very sensuous indeed. She could see the texture of his skin, well weathered by the hot desert suns, but still taut and supple enough for a man at the height of his virility.

"I think you talk too much," he said, and the next moment his mouth was on hers, shocking her into submission as his lips parted hers with a determination she was unable to resist. She felt his tongue touching the tip of her own, then circling it with a delicacy that belied the possessiveness of his embrace. The intimate caress sent swift spirals of desire coursing through her veins, and without knowing what she was doing, the movements of her tongue were matching his in a simulated ritual mating. When he broke slightly away from her, she stood in a kind of daze, and when she felt his tongue circle her moist lips, her mouth involuntarily parted again, inviting him in.

"I think I shall be well pleased with my virginal bride," Kilmarron said with quiet pleasure, and as she felt the pulsing of his body against the softness of her belly, she gave a gasp and tried to spring away from him. She rubbed at her desire-swollen mouth, but he still held her fast.

"You've no right to behave in this way—"

"Yes I have, my sweet one, but I promise you that this was only a taste of the delights we have in store for us. Very soon, I shall have the right to all of you, the same as you. Marriage should be a two-way pleasure, so do you like what you see, and what you feel?"

He was the challenger now, and her face was hot with embarrassment as he pressed against her in a way that was totally uninhibited. With a great effort, she ignored the darting thrills that every movement of his body gave her, and stared at him in icy displeasure.

"You disgust me, sir," she said simply. "If I have to marry you, I will do so, but I shall never enjoy it, and you will never have my love."

"I don't recall asking for your love," Kilmarron said, and his irony wasn't lost on her. "We both know that this marriage is not a love match, although many an arranged marriage has proved to be as successful as any other kind. All I require of you is your obedience as my wife, and that you accompany me on this one last expedition in Egypt. After that, I shall return to my estate in Oxfordshire, where I plan to write a detailed account of my work for publication, and you may go where you will."

Stephanie looked at him in astonishment. She had quickly discovered just how passionate and powerfully sensual he could be, and yet there was another side to him also, if he could react in this coldly clinical manner. He probably had everything mapped out to the last, calculating detail, and she was but an incidental part of those plans. But he had told her a great deal in those last few sentences.

"You don't intend to enslave me forever then?" she said insultingly.

Kilmarron laughed, letting his hands run gently down her bare arms in the morning dress that she wore, and his touch on her skin was enough to make her shiver once more.

"I've no wish to enslave you at all, sweetness. But I'll wager that a time will come when you'll be begging for my kisses. And despite what you say, I promise that you *will* enjoy our life together, for I'll take you to places and show you treasures that you never dreamed of."

She couldn't deny that her imagination was caught by the vivid images he evoked, and she burned to ask him more about these treasures and places unknown. But she wouldn't give him the satisfaction of showing too much interest too soon. As she sat down abruptly on one of the stone seats in the fragrant rose arbor, he sat close beside her. His gaze never left her face, and she became embarrassed by so much close scrutiny.

"Please stop looking at me in that way," she muttered, lowering her eyes.

She felt his hand cup her chin and hold it still, until she was obliged to look into his eyes. His words took her by surprise, as so much else about the man did. But she couldn't miss the soft seduction in his voice.

"I spend enough hours looking at the dead treasures of another age. Right now, it's far more agreeable to look at a living, breathing woman who's so soon to be all mine."

Stephanie swallowed. There had been other ardent young men that her stepbrother had brought to the house. They had flirted with her, and one or two had tried to kiss her, but she had rebuffed them all. None of them had been man enough to stir her senses in any way. But she was quickly realizing that this man only had to lift his little finger, and she responded in a way that was almost frightening. And common sense told her that she would be very foolish indeed to think she could ever fall in love with him, for love clearly wasn't in Kilmarron's plan of things. He intended to make her beg for his kisses, and she would die before she did so, she vowed.

"Will you please tell me something?" she said in a low voice. "And will you be completely honest with me?"

He removed his hand, his gaze steady and cool now.

"I've always considered myself to be an honorable and an honest man."

She was very tempted to comment that most people wouldn't consider gambling on a young girl's future to be honorable or honest, but for the moment she let it pass.

"Please tell me exactly why you want to marry me. I can't believe it was a premeditated wish, since we have never met before. How can you have taken such a sudden decision on a matter that's normally taken very seriously by two people who wish to spend the rest of their lives together?"

She tried not to let her voice break, for she had always believed that marriage was the highest and most emotional state on earth for those who loved each other deeply, and this union that Kilmarron was forcing her into was no more than a shameful sham.

"I assure you I am taking it very seriously," he replied,

and then he gave a sigh. "But I see that you have a mind of your own, and if I don't tell you now, you'll find out when we reach Shaladd."

"Who or what is Shaladd?" Stephanie said suspiciously.

"Shaladd is a lush but isolated desert princedom where my old friend Hali Ahmed resides in the royal palace, and the place where we begin our expedition into the desert."

Stephanie stared at him. He spoke of things of which she had no comprehension, but her schoolroom learning about noble princes and royal palaces had not been confined to the London establishment where Queen Victoria and Prince Albert and the royal children lived. But it was an entire world away from a desert princedom, from people and places with strange-sounding names, and expeditions into the desert. Despite her qualms, Stephanie felt a shivering excitement, because it also sounded like the adventure of a lifetime, one that few young English ladies had the chance to experience.

"I see that I've caught your interest at last," Kilmarron said with some amusement, bringing her dreaming eyes back to the present.

"But you still haven't explained what I most want to hear. Why do you want to marry me?" she said bluntly. "And why me, or would anyone have fitted your requirements?"

Immediately, she wished she hadn't asked the question, for to her fury, she knew she didn't want to hear him say that anyone would have done. She wanted to hear him say that he'd fallen in love with her portrait, or her character, or her beauty . . . and just as angrily, she knew how unlikely such a response would be.

"My first intention was to pay someone to act as my wife," she heard him say, shaking her to the core. "It's vital that I have such a lady by my side when I return to Shaladd. But there was always a risk that the woman would easily succumb to the many other pleasures Prince Hali might offer, and if the truth then came out, I would be shamed in his eyes. The result would not bear thinking about. So there was no help for it but to actually find myself a wife and be done with it. I was still debating how to go about it when the opportunity offered itself."

Stephanie didn't *intend* to hit him. It wasn't the done thing for a young lady of good character to hit out at a guest in a gentleman's house. But right at that moment, she felt nothing like a lady and Kilmarron was no gentleman to go about things in such a despicable way. He shamed her entire sex by his callous words, and before she could stop herself, she had leapt to her feet and put her whole weight behind the lashing, open-handed blow she sent to his cheek.

"You little vixen!" Kilmarron said hoarsely, catching at her wrist with one hand, while nursing his painful cheek with the other. "If you couldn't take hearing the truth, you should never have asked for it!"

"I didn't expect to hear something so barbaric!" she snapped. "Nor to find myself regarded as the next best thing to a whore!"

The hated word slipped from her lips, and she hated herself even more for using it. But while her breasts heaved with her fury, she realized that Kilmarron was adept at asserting control over his emotions, and was calming down more quickly than herself.

"I would never treat you like a whore. And you will be treated more like a princess by everyone at Shaladd. You will be showered with jewels and precious ornaments, and you'll be bathed in asses' milk and dressed in the finest silks and be waited on by eunuchs. As my wife, you will be accorded every respect that the royal palace can offer."

As the wanton images he described flashed into her mind, she conceded that he made it all sound dazzlingly and alluringly erotic. Again, she thought it was the kind of once-in-a-lifetime adventure that a woman might only dream about in her wildest flights of fancy. But still she looked at him with the utmost suspicion, sure that there was still more here that she didn't know.

"But why do you need a wife at all, if these people already know you and so obviously respect you?"

"I suggest that we sit down again, and then I'll tell you, providing you promise not to strike me again," Kilmarron said with a faint smile. "You look as though a breath of desert wind would blow you away, but thankfully, I can see that it will not."

After a moment, she sat down, folding her arms across her chest and sitting well away from him. She stared into his eyes, and waited for his explanation, promising nothing.

"On our last expedition into the desert, we were caught in a violent sandstorm," Kilmarron said, as if such an occurrence was no more than a minor nuisance. "Prince Hali had accompanied us, since he frequently decides to join in any of our European treks into the desert. We rely heavily on his patronage and goodwill, to say nothing of the guides and camels and provisions that he supplies, so his entourage is a necessary accompaniment."

To Stephanie, it was as though he was describing some fabled Arabian story, about a place as distant from an English garden in fashionable London as the moon.

"As it happened, the storm turned into something very fortuitous, for the mountainous dunes thrown up by the wind also revealed the edges of a tomb. It was during the first excavations into the tomb that Prince Hali slipped and fell into what seemed like an abyss. I won't bore you with the details, but he came dangerously close to being killed, and I happened to be the one to get him out before the sides of the ancient passageway caved in."

"So you saved his life!"

Kilmarron gave a twisted smile. "So I did, and because I've a fondness for the prince, I was more than thankful to do so. But that's where my problems began."

"What problems? Was he badly hurt?"

She could hardly believe she was asking such questions, for this was surely all fantasy. None of it seemed remotely real to her. If it hadn't been for the seriousness in Kilmarron's voice and manner, she would be sure he was simply playacting.

"His pride was hurt, but nothing more. But to a desert prince with unimaginable riches, Stephanie, repaying the gift of life to someone is to heap rewards on them to the extent that no ordinary mortal can credit. I could have jewels and horses, a desert residence of my own, or anything that I named. Rather than offend him, I accepted what I considered a reasonable reward, but to Hali, it still wasn't enough."

"So what extra gifts did he insist on giving you?" she said, too intrigued to leave the story unfinished now.

"It's what he intends to give me when I return to Shaladd that's the problem," Kilmarron said grimly. "And why I had to tell him that I must reject his most generous offer, since I was already betrothed, and that my bride was eager to return to Egypt with me to meet him."

She felt the slow rage begin to boil up inside her again. So many lies, and one would seem to spawn another.

"So this *was* a premeditated plan?"

"I certainly needed to find a wife," he said shortly. "Otherwise, when I return to Shaladd, there will be six of Prince Hali's harem concubines at my disposal, and a multiple wedding will be arranged. Shaladd law is a law unto itself, although such a union would never be recognized in England, of course. But I suspect that Hali hoped I'd be content to remain in his jeweled stronghold forever. He has a habit of ignoring the things he doesn't want to hear, and God knows how much of the arrangements are already under way."

Stephanie felt crazily as though the earth was shifting beneath her feet. She had never heard such a wild tale in her life before—and yet, she knew instinctively that Kilmarron was simply stating the facts. This fabulously rich desert prince was offering six of his own wives to Kilmarron, who would be expected to take them or risk deeply offending his royal friend. She ran her tongue around her dry lips.

"What would be the penalty if Prince Hali knew you had been inventing a bride all this time, or if the lady exposed you for the liar that you are?" She spoke fearlessly, daring him to deny it.

"Execution by the sword," Kilmarron said briefly. "Arab emotions are very volatile, and while friendships are strong, betrayal is stronger, and he would consider I had shamed him by refusing to take his wives."

The visual image of execution by the sword was too much for Stephanie to contemplate. "So you were quite deliberately looking for a wife in order to resist taking a harem yourself?" she said huskily.

"Quite deliberately," he said. "And if I haven't quite shocked you into virtual silence, you may tell me what a prize bastard you think I am."

"Does my stepfather know any of this?" she said instead, finding the very thought humiliating.

"Nobody knows of it but yourself. As I said, it's Shaladd law, and Prince Hali is a very powerful man in his own world. But I hardly think the news would be welcomed in English court or political circles."

"And what if I were to tell?" Stephanie said.

He looked at her steadily, and again, those dark, penetrating eyes held her almost spellbound. He didn't beg, or plead, or become angry or threatening. Instead, he drew her slowly into his arms again, and as the erotic perfumes on his skin drifted into her nostrils, she seemed helpless to resist. She felt the touch of his lips on her own once more, and he spoke softly against them.

"I'm offering you the chance of a lifetime, my sweet one. You will be my desert princess, for the luxury heaped upon you will be no less than that, and in every way you will be worthy of the name. Your beautiful hair is the color of moonlight, and you'll be as a gleaming star among the dark-skinned beauties of the harem."

He touched her silken hair as he spoke, and she was both

captivated and enchanted by his words. They were reminiscent of the words in the old fables, she thought faintly, and
she guessed that his long association with the Arab world
had resulted in this elaborate manner of speech.

"I seem to have no option," she murmured, and the mouth
that was touching hers so erotically was suddenly bruising
it in a wanton kiss of unbridled desire.

Her mouth was forced open, not so much in brutality as
in passion, as his tongue roamed around the yielding inner
flesh, and she found herself responding with a fervor she
didn't know she possessed. She felt his hand brush against
her breast, palming it with a gentle touch that was more
evocative than if he had crushed it. She felt her breath
quicken, as she recognized the swift reaction of her treacher-
ously responsive body.

When they broke away, he cradled her in his arms for a
long moment, and she felt extraordinarily cherished and safe.
And she knew it was the oddest way to feel toward a stranger
who was about to take her to a new and alien world, no
matter how exotically he described it. But short of screaming
and scratching and putting herself in total disgrace with her
stepfather, she knew the truth of her own words. She had
had no option since the moment Kilmarron had chosen her
for his bride. He had wagered and won, and in his arrogance,
he had never once considered losing.

They continued strolling around the gardens to allow her
fevered face to cool down, and as she tried to breathe more
slowly, and to forget the shivering anticipation of the new
life ahead, she remembered something else he had said.

"What are these eunuchs that you mentioned before? I
never heard the name. Are they special servants?"

He laughed, tucking her hand in the crook of his arm as
if to show that now that he had claimed her, he was never
going to let her go.

"You could say that. They live well enough and are protected by their masters, though by western standards they're the poorest of wretches, and there's not a man in Christendom who would change places with one of them."

"Why not?" Stephanie said in bewilderment.

"Because, my sweet innocent, they're castrated before they're allowed to be employed in the harem. Do you know what that means?"

She did not. The very word sounded unpleasant enough, and Kilmarron's tone added to the certainty that she wouldn't want to hear this. But as she hesitated to admit her ignorance, he went on matter-of-factly.

"Castration means that they have their testicles removed, so that they're unable to lie with the concubines," he said. "Their masters can then confidently leave their wives to be bathed or dressed or fed by these half-men, knowing that no eunuch can take what belongs to him alone."

Again, Stephanie felt as if the world was spinning away from her. What kind of men were these, she thought faintly, who could mutilate others for their self-gratification? But the so-called masters obviously saw no reason to deny these eunuchs the sight of the unclothed concubines. And even Stephanie, with no knowledge of the ways of men or the enticements of women, could agree that the eunuchs were poor wretches indeed to be subjected to such daily frustrations.

And there was even more that she did not know. How could she, having been sheltered and raised in a gentleman's house, and protected from all contact with undesirables? Her despised stepbrother had never spoken of such things in his frequent tauntings of her innocence. The anatomy of a man's body was never discussed until a girl was on the brink of marriage, and then only in the vaguest terms by an older female relative. In some cases, particularly where the relative was an elderly unmarried lady, she would know as little as the girl herself.

"Forgive me for asking," Stephanie said humbly now. "But what are these testicles?"

He stared at her, seeing the delicate pink color steal across her velvety skin. For a moment, she thought she saw a frisson of shame pass across his face, but it was quickly gone, and she thought she must have imagined it. But his words were a long time coming, and when they did, they sounded as if they were being dragged out of him. But he was frank to the edge of brutality.

"My God, but I have truly got myself a treasure. Have you never had any instruction on the evils of fornication or the necessity of procreation? Nor any indication of the joys of married lovemaking?"

All the words he used made her flinch. The blush deepened as she shook her head, assuming that her education had been sorely lacking, and feeling utterly inadequate compared with this worldly man who was so soon to be her husband.

"My dear girl, there's no need to look so abashed," she heard Kilmarron say softly, seeing the shine of tears on her long, silky lashes. "I've shocked you unnecessarily, and I promise that your initiation into the marriage bed will be painless and pleasurable."

Painless? Why should it be otherwise? Stephanie thought nervously. The very words he used to reassure her put a new anxiety into her mind. She was well aware that very soon now her stepfather would have been seeking a suitable husband for her, if she was not to end up on the spinster's shelf. And her dreams of marriage to a loving and caring husband had been the rosy-hued dreams of the very young. She would live in a similar house to her stepfather's, and be launched more confidently into the social life that London offered, with her husband by her side.

She had never contemplated marriage with a stranger who hinted, however obscurely, that certain rites of the marriage-bed could be painful. Nor that she would be whisked away to a part of that dark and mysterious African continent that was only acceptable to English ears in fable and story. She shuddered, wondering just what the future held, and thankful that she could not see into it.

"You still look afraid, but I promise you there's no need," Kilmarron was saying now. "I shall go slowly, and you will learn that there is more than one way to make love. A thousand and one ways, if the Arabian nights tales are to be believed," he added, in an attempt to make her smile.

She tried, but it was a feeble attempt. Instead, she diverted him from this all too intimate conversation.

"If I am to marry you, sir, would it not be a good idea if I were to know your given name?" she said huskily. "Or am I to call you Kilmarron for the rest of my life?"

With his laugh, the tension was released between them, and she saw how his dark eyes sparkled when he was amused. It would be very easy to fall in love with such a man, she thought swiftly, and to give her heart to him unconditionally.

But she must never forget that he had wanted her for one reason alone, and that reason wasn't love. It was to ward off the gifts of this Prince Hali Ahmed, whom she half hated already, simply from the sound of his lifestyle, and his all-powerful presence. No man should wield that much power over a tiny desert realm, she thought uneasily. But as Kilmarron raised her hands to his lips, she forgot all about such trivial matters, and concentrated instead on the man to whom she was so soon to entrust her life.

"My full title is Captain Ross Kilmarron, late of Her Majesty's Highland regiment serving in India," he said with an unmistakable pride. "The military wasn't my first choice, but I joined my father's old regiment as a courtesy to him. When I was injured to the point of death in a skirmish, I decided to buy out and follow my own desire to explore the desert, having done my duty regarding the family honor."

"I see!" He surprised her again. "But you are not Scottish, I think?"

"I was born there, but I lived in Lincolnshire from the age of two, where both my parents died."

She heard the hint of pain in his voice, and guessed that it explained the fact that he had severed all connection with the county, and never wished to return.

"Does that tell you enough, my sweet? Or do I need to produce any further credentials to persuade you to marry me?" he said, reverting to the seductive manner she was beginning to know only too well.

"You already have my stepfather's word on that, so you hardly need mine—"

His finger lifted her chin, and she drew in her breath at the intensity of his dark gaze.

"But every man is desirous of a loving wife, Stephanie, and obedience in all things."

She swallowed, for although he spoke lightly, it seemed that she could almost hear the echo of another, darker presence in his voice. The echo of the all-powerful Prince Hali Ahmed, perhaps, who demanded servitude and obedience above all else from his underlings. But not from a young English lady, Stephanie vowed, more than ever determined never to be an underling to anyone.

Three

Kilmarron was invited to stay at the London house until the marriage, which was to be arranged six days before they set sail for Alexandria. To Stephanie, everything seemed to be taken out of her hands, and was moving far too swiftly. She had no say in things, and Cousin Claire was also summoned to move into the house to attend to all the female details, as her stepfather referred to them. But she was no more than an irritating replacement for Percy, who had returned to his college and was thankfully not around to continually bait her.

By the end of two weeks, when she and Kilmarron had been seen in public so many times in the company of her insistent relatives that she had begun to feel like a puppet in a marionette show, she put her foot down.

"Will you please give me time to breathe!" she raged at Lord Buchan, when he and Cousin Claire were planning the most advantageous seats for the proposed theater visit that evening. Kilmarron was away for the afternoon on business of his own, and the other two behaved like vultures. They weren't the ones who would be devouring her personality and sapping her will in that other hostile country, but it seemed that they intended to get their pound of flesh before she left English shores.

"It's necessary that you appear in public with Captain Kilmarron as often as possible," Cousin Claire snapped. "Whatever the circumstances of this marriage, you must be seen to be enjoying the attentions of your future husband."

"And why should I do that? It's more than likely that everyone in London knows the circumstances of this farcical marriage by now, if the scandal sheets have had anything to do with it," Stephanie snapped back, uncaring if she offended the woman, since she would so soon be rid of her scratchiness for good.

It was one thing in favor of moving away, but it was also small compensation for the enormity of living in Egypt and the unknown Shaladd, which was unnerving her more and more as the day of the marriage drew nearer.

"Well, since we don't allow such rags into the house, we shall never know," Lord Buchan said sharply. "And you will do as you are told, miss, and put a good face on it. I demand some gratitude for all the years I've kept you in comfort since your mother died. I could have put you out on the streets, and don't you forget it."

"It's a pity you didn't, and then I wouldn't be going to marry a man I don't even know," she muttered, but she wilted a little, knowing she *had* been dependent on his patronage, however much she despised him.

But what she said wasn't quite true. In the two weeks since the outrageous wager had been made and won, the man she was now to call Ross had wooed her relentlessly. It was as if he intended to make everyone believe that this had been a true love match after all, however whirlwind the courtship, and that any talk of a shameful wager was all moonshine, since the handsome captain seemed to besotted with his betrothed.

And as for Stephanie herself—no young woman could help being dazzled by a visit to the most prestigious jeweler's establishment in London, where her future husband purchased a beautiful betrothal ring for her finger. Despite her pleasure in the jewels, it seemed to seal her fate.

Who would not have her romantic head turned by having a roomful of flowers delivered to the house the day after the wager had been won? And to find nestling among each bouquet and floral basket arrangement a little trinket made of gold, or amethyst, or sapphire, to attach to a bracelet of charms for her wrist? That Captain Ross Kilmarron already had riches at his disposal was very evident, and if Stephanie still felt suspiciously that he was buying her, she tried to dismiss the feeling, for there was nothing on earth that she could do to prevent it, short of killing herself. And she was not so driven as to contemplate such a wicked thing.

Besides, by the end of those two weeks, she was driven by far more primitive and basic feelings. She discovered that she was enjoying all of Ross's attentions, the way his hand pressed hers in the dark seclusion of a theater box . . . and the way they drove together in a carriage to their various outings, as an affianced couple . . . and the way he was left alone with her when the older Buchans had retired to their beds, and never failed to take advantage of the fact. By now, she knew she wasn't averse to those times. If she was totally honest, she eagerly anticipated the moment when the door closed behind her stepfather, and Ross took her in his arms, whispering the enchanted, strangely erotic words with their eastern influence, "At last, my dove."

It wasn't Ross who annoyed her, but the constant plotting and planning by the Buchans of where next to show her and Ross off to best advantage, when they could very well manage their own courtship without any help from them. Lord Buchan might pretend not to take notice of the scandal sheets, but if it became too widely known that he had bargained with his lovely stepdaughter, his honor would be sadly dented, and Stephanie knew that was the real reason for pushing these visible meetings to the limit.

But she was having no more of it. Soon now, the ceremony would take place in the drawing room of this house, since she had begged not to have an elaborate affair. The minister had agreed to it, and there would be few guests. She had insisted on a quiet wedding, but perversely now, she almost wished she had asked for a great ceremony in St. Paul's Cathedral or Westminster Abbey, and left her stepfather with the staggering cost. It would serve him right for all his manipulations. And such a display would also show the world that one of them was marrying for love, if not the other.

She got to her feet while the older relatives still argued over which flowers would be most suitable to adorn the table for the wedding breakfast. Her heart hammered in her chest as the thought of loving Ross Kilmarron surged into her mind. She pushed it quickly away, not even wanting to acknowledge such a thing to herself, knowing that love didn't enter into his scheme of things. Her hands were clenched tightly at her sides, and she saw Cousin Claire look up in astonishment as she spoke.

"I assure you that Ross and I can manage our own affairs for these last few days. I thank you both for all that you've done, but please, will you leave us both *alone?*"

Lord Buchan folded up the sheet of paper on which he was writing, and stood up in a huff.

"If that's all the thanks I get, then I'll leave you women to sort out the final arrangements, for I can't abide hysterics. I daresay Claire will be wanting to advise you on certain female matters."

He stormed out, and Stephanie sat down again stiffly. She rarely saw eye-to-eye with Cousin Claire, and the last thing she wanted was a red-faced discussion on marriage from a elderly woman who had never known the state herself.

"He means well, Stephanie," Claire said after a long pause. "It's been difficult for him to have a young girl growing up in a male household, without the benefit of her mother to guide her."

"Don't you mean I've been an embarrassment to him, when he'd much prefer to carry on with his gaming parties and his male pursuits?"

"That, too," Claire said with surprising calmness. "But a

woman must always be tolerant of male pursuits, as you will learn when you're married."

Stephanie concentrated on studying her clasped hands in her lap. She desperately needed to know what was expected of her, but how could this barren woman possibly explain the glories of a loving relationship that was supposed to surpass all others? She heard Clare sigh.

"We've never got along very well, Stephanie, and I know you think I've no understanding of your feelings right now. But many years ago, I was confidently expecting to be married, until a bitter campaign against Bonaparte at Waterloo put an end to all my hopes."

As Stephanie looked up, startled, the woman gave a twisted smile. "I was not born old, girl. There was a time when I was as vital as you, and as capable of loving."

"I'm sure everyone has that capacity, and I'm sorry I never knew of your misfortune," Stephanie murmured.

But at the unexpected softening of her cousin's usually hard eyes, she took advantage of the situation, and went on in a little rush.

"Will you explain to me the evils of fornication?"

As soon as she had said it, she knew she had made a mistake. A look of horror passed over Claire's face, to be replaced at once by a red-faced withdrawal, and Stephanie knew that the time for confidences was over.

"Wash your mouth out with soap, miss," Claire snapped. "Whoever put such a word into your vocabulary should be horsewhipped. It was one of the servants, I daresay, and I shall have words with them at once."

"It wasn't one of the servants!" Stephanie said hotly, "and if it's something so terrible, I think I have a right to know, so that I don't make the mistake of mentioning it in polite society."

She knew this was guaranteed to extract a reply, and, tight-lipped, Claire proceeded to add to her education.

"It's a word that describes the connection between a man

and a woman without the benefit of marriage," she said pompously, as though reading it from a learned text.

Stephanie knew at once that she should have guessed, and she felt briefly sorry for putting this straitlaced woman through the ordeal of explaining something so obviously abhorrent to her. In her nervousness, she plunged on.

"You mean, like street women?" *Or whores?*

Cousin Claire immediately pointed a scrawny finger toward the door without looking at her.

"Soap, miss."

Stephanie fled upstairs to her bedroom, where Maisie was changing the sheets on her bed. She looked on in astonishment as Stephanie obediently splashed cold water onto her burning cheeks, and scrubbed at her teeth with a bar of soap before spitting the horrid taste away into her ablutions bowl.

"Whatever's wrong?" Maisie asked in bewilderment. With her hands on her ample hips, and her cheeks scarlet from her exertions, she looked more like a doxy than a servant in a gentleman's house, Stephanie thought fleetingly, and on an impulse, she put the same question to her. Her mouth was already foaming with soap, so a little more probing wouldn't harm her sensibilities.

"What do you know about fornication, Maisie?" she asked.

The girl burst out laughing, then clapped her hands to her mouth as Stephanie reddened.

"Oh, beggin' your pardon, Miss Stephanie, but you fair took me by surprise."

"Well?" Stephanie demanded in annoyance, thinking that even servants knew more about the world than she did, cloistered as she had been all her life with an austere governess until a year ago, and no confidante since then. It hadn't occurred to her until now how lonely her life had been.

"Well, miss, I don't rightly know as it's suitable for your tender ears," Maisie said doubtfully.

"If I'm so soon to be married, I have a right to know all

there is to know about men and women, and since no one else seems prepared to tell me, you'll have to do. And you're not leaving here until you do so," she said, locking the door behind her and slipping the key into the neck of her dress.

She sat on her chaise longue and folded her arms boldly, knowing it was an action that was frowned upon in ladies' circles, and quite uncaring. She was more irritated by the fact that the lower orders always seemed to have knowledge of the things that were considered taboo for a young lady's delicate ears.

"Well then, miss, if you really want to know, then I'd best be telling you," Maisie said, sitting on the edge of the bed, and with her eyes starting to gleam.

In the next half hour, she elaborated in words and gestures and demonstrations that left Stephanie reeling. Why had no one warned her of all this? she raged. How dare they let her go into marriage with a man without knowing the most basic and terrifying things that were to happen to her?

"And you say it's meant to be pleasurable, this joining?" she said suspiciously, choosing to ignore just how Maisie knew quite so much about it.

"I should say so, miss—depending on the man, of course," Maisie said with enthusiasm. "Some are too rough, and only interested in getting their oats, but you'll have no trouble with a proper gent like Captain Kilmarron. He'll be very considerate, I'm sure."

"Thank you Maisie. You can go now."

"But I ain't finished the bed yet—"

"Then come back and do it later," Stephanie snapped.

She unlocked the door and the girl went out, grumbling, and she leaned against the door panel, her head buzzing. And not only her head. In Maisie's explicit telling of the various acts of pleasure, she had been aware of a tingling deep inside her, and a spreading sense of erotic pleasure as the girl had passed her hands over her own body to show where a man liked to fondle and kiss and look.

Stephanie shivered, aware that there was a sensuality in her own nature that she had never even suspected before now. It had been there all the time, dormant in the sterile atmosphere of her stepfather's house, waiting to be awoken and explored, much as those ancient sand-covered ruins of Egypt waited to be awoken and explored. And by the hands of the same man.

She closed her eyes, and instantly, Ross Kilmarron's image was there in her mind. His face was close to hers, his mouth no more than a whisper away. His arms were holding her, his hands running over her body, learning her as if to commit every pore of her to memory. She breathed in the eastern perfumed essence of his skin that seemed to put him half in that fabulous world of which she had no knowledge as yet and half in the normal, everyday world of the European gentleman.

She slowly opened her eyes again, knowing how badly she yearned to know all these mysterious things of which Maisie had been telling her. Knowing that she was ripe and ready to be a woman, and Ross Kilmarron's wife. And into her bemused mind came the echo of a biblical phrase from her religious lessons that she had always thought so beautiful: *Whither thou goest, I will go.* It seemed more apt now, than anything else in her life.

The wedding day dawned brightly. Late September was balmy in London, and Captain Ross Kilmarron was at his most handsome as he moved to stand by the side of his bride, approval in his eyes. She was dressed in a shimmering gown of pale-blue silk, and her silvery hair was swathed up on top of her head in a coronet interlaced with pale-blue and white flowers. She carried more flowers in a posy, and long, delicate lace mittens rather than gloves so that her bridegroom could slide the gold ring onto her finger without hindrance.

Stephanie listened to the words of the marriage service in

a kind of stupor, still wondering if this could really be happening. She heard herself promising to love, honor, and obey, and as she raised her eyes to gaze into those of Ross Kilmarron, she saw his imperceptible nod, and knew that he would insist on her obedience in all things. She gave a small shudder, wondering just what lay in store for her on this new journey. It was more than a journey to an unknown country—it was the journey she was embarking on with a man who was not of her choosing that was just as unnerving.

And yet would she not have chosen him if she had had the option? If they had met in any other circumstances, would he not have charmed her into falling headlong into love with him? She couldn't take her eyes away from his face now as he repeated the final words of the ceremony, and then she felt the wedding ring slide onto her finger, and it was as symbolic a gesture as if he slid into her, in the way Maisie had outlined so graphically.

She almost snatched her hand away, but she couldn't do so, since Ross was holding it so tightly. And the minister was beaming at them now, as if this were truly the love match of the century, and urging Captain Kilmarron to kiss his bride.

"Do you object to a chaste kiss in front of this company?" Ross murmured close to her lips. "The time for passion will come later, I promise you."

He didn't give her time to answer, merely put his hands lightly on her tense shoulders and pressed his lips to her cold mouth. Behind her, she could hear the polite applause of the wedding party, and she broke away from Ross in some embarrassment as one and another moved forward to congratulate Kilmarron on his beautiful bride and to wish her happiness for the future. With her arm tucked firmly in his arm now, and the unfamiliar gold ring on her finger being a symbol that her life now belonged to this man, Stephanie's feelings were a turbulent mixture of delight and dread.

She was thankful when the wedding breakfast was over. By then she had had to suffer the smirks of her stepbrother, home from college for the occasion. He had always been jealous of her, and enjoyed bullying her, and he cornered her before the newlyweds left for Ross's Oxfordshire estate, to spend the first days of marriage before embarking for Alexandria.

Percy had stood with his arms folded, barring her entrance to one of the anterooms adjoining the drawing room.

"You'd best be a dutiful wife, sister, or he might decide to dispose of you. Take care you don't end up in one of his old tombs, wrapped in a shroud like an Egyptian mummy," he sneered. "They say the Arabs treat their women like dogs, and I understand that your husband has lived with them long enough to absorb their ways."

"At least I'll have the pleasure of not hearing any more of your pathetically stupid remarks," Stephanie retorted.

Percy's face darkened, but his eyes glittered.

"Enjoy your freedom while you can," he jeered. "You'll be as much a harem wife as those desert women, whose opinions count for less than camel dung, and if you dare to speak to your masters before you're spoken to, you risk having your tongue cut out!"

Stephanie pushed past him to rejoin the other guests. She didn't believe a word of it, but she knew Percy must have been talking to others to have gleaned this information, however garbled and misinformed. And he scared her.

But the feasting had finally ended, and at last she and Ross were seated in the nuptial carriage, leaving London and heading for the rolling, verdant countryside of Oxfordshire. And Stephanie tried to give no more thought to the hateful Percy Buchan. She was more struck by her husband's odd silence. He sat remotely away from her, as if lost in thought, and after initially inquiring if she was quite comfortable, he had said nothing for a considerable part of the journey.

"Have I done something to displease you, Ross?" she said with a timidity that was unlike her. But even as she spoke, the image of someone having their tongue cut out for daring to speak was vivid and terrible in her mind. Her senses swirled

for a moment, and then she saw Ross smile at her and reach
for her hand, and the world seemed to right itself again.

"You have not, my dove, and forgive me if I seemed a
little distant. My mind was far away on future events, and
I'm the one who should be apologizing for such neglect on
our wedding day."

It should have satisfied her, yet somehow it did not. His
words were said with that strange inflection again, as if he
still stood half in one world and half in another. It was vital
that he must eventually choose, she thought intuitively, for
it was surely a situation that was impossible. No man could
be a part of two diverse cultures and remain sane.

He suddenly came to sit beside her in the swaying carriage,
and his arm went around her shoulders.

"I don't care to see that troubled frown on your lovely
face, Stephanie. Is it the breaking of the maidenhead that
frightens you?"

She flinched visibly. Until that frank talk with Maisie, she
had not even heard of the word. But now she knew it, and
what it implied, and her throat was dry with shock that a
man could talk openly of such intimate female things.

"I—I'm afraid of everything," she whispered, even while
she despised herself for her feebleness. But if he wanted the
truth, he would hear it, and she *was* afraid, so very afraid
now, of her life ahead. The great sense of adventure had
temporarily deserted her, and she wished desperately that
she had never heard of Captain Ross Kilmarron.

She felt his arms tighten around her, and he nuzzled the
side of her neck. He had given her a pair of gloriously translucent pearl ear studs for her wedding gift, and she felt the
dig of the pin in her flesh as his lips gently pulled and nibbled
at her lobe for a moment. The tingling thrill of this unexpected intimacy was tempered by the prosaic hope that the
small sharp pain of the pin wasn't prophetic also.

"My darling girl, you have no need to be afraid of me, or
anything else in this world while I'm here to protect you,"

he said softly. "And if anything troubles you, then you must always tell me."

"Is that allowed then?" she said with a touch of bravado. "Can I be sure I'm not to have my tongue cut out for speaking before I'm spoken to, or risk being wrapped in a shroud like a mummy and thrown into one of your old tombs?"

All the fears that Percy had put into her mind spilled out of her, and she heard Ross begin to laugh.

"I assure you nothing of the kind is remotely likely to happen, my sweet! And just who has been putting such wild ideas into your head?"

She relaxed against him as his fingers stroked her cheek sensuously. For good or ill, she was bound to him, and she had to trust him.

"No one of importance," she murmured, and she was rewarded by being folded more tightly into his arms and kissed to the rhythm of the clattering carriage wheels.

Stephanie was not unused to entering a mansion with the obligatory lineup of servants, such as those who waited to greet the returning captain and his bride. In any case, her nervousness had given way to weariness. The traveling had taken some hours, and dusk was already falling when they reached the place simply known as the Kilmarron Estate.

By then, she was hot and dusty, and glad to be shown to the master bedroom, an opulent room with a thick Persian carpet covering the floor and costly velvet draperies and furnishings. In the center of the room was a very large four-poster and lace-canopied bed, from which Stephanie averted her eyes for the moment, preferring instead to look through the large windows at the vista of undulating green hills and the darker green of a distant forest.

While she was still trying to contemplate the fact that eventually this was to be her home, she felt her husband's arms encircle her from behind.

"Does it all please the captain's lady?" Ross said softly. As she involuntarily leaned back against him, his arms slid upward from her waist to cup her breasts, and she gave a sharp intake of breath.

"It's all beautiful," she said unsteadily. "The house, and the grounds, and these lovely views—"

"And do I please my lady?" he said more seductively, his fingers starting to gently tease her nipples into searing points, as a flame like desire enveloped her.

"You do," she whispered.

He suddenly turned her round into his arms, and looked deep into her luminous blue eyes, filled now with a sensual longing that had never yet been fulfilled. She felt the hard, masculine proof of his own desire pressing into her through their outer clothing, and the thrill of excitement overcame any thought of fear.

"But you cannot yet answer the question fully, my darling one. I've given orders that we're not to be disturbed until I send downstairs for a late supper to be brought to our room, so I suggest that we wait no longer before finding out."

She wasn't sure what he meant for a moment, until she felt his fingers removing her traveling coat, and then tugging at the fastenings on her bodice. His hunger for her added to the sense of soaring excitement that was filling her now, and her own fingers helped him to strip away her garments and then his own. It was Ross's intake of breath that she heard then, as he took in every curve of her firm young body, as white and unsullied as that of an innocent child, yet with all the nubile allure of a young woman, ripe and ready for love.

"We should bathe first," he said huskily. "But I cannot wait so long. I must have you now, Stephanie, and I promise you that our joining will be as sweet as if we were doused in attar of roses or the finest musk oil."

She listened as if in a dream, and when he lifted her in his arms and carried her to the bed, her hands clung around his neck and she marveled at the strength and power in his body, and the proud potency of it.

She lay inert where he placed her, not knowing if she was expected to do anything at all. If there was a finesse to love-making, it had never been part of her instruction, she thought in some frustration, yet knowing an instinctive urgency to please him as much as she knew he intended to please her. But she didn't know how.

"You'll have to teach me, Ross," she said in a small, embarrassed voice. He gave a tender smile, lying on his side and gazing down at her, as if to drink in every vestige of her alabaster skin with his eyes.

"Do you think I don't know that, or that it will give me the most profound pleasure to do so?" he murmured back. "A man's greatest desire is to have a virgin bride who has known no other but himself. And it's just as important for her to know that he will take no other wife," he added.

For a moment, Stephanie sensed that his thoughts were far away then. They were somewhere in that other realm, where Prince Hali Ahmed could have his choice of concubines to warm his bed. But this was not some distant desert princedom that was a law unto itself. This was England, and this was her marital bed that she was sharing with her husband, who belonged only to her, and whose only desire was to pleasure her now.

As his fingers began stroking her down the length of her body, he interspersed each caress with small kisses that pulled and tugged teasingly at her flesh. Unknowingly, Stephanie arched her back a little, and gave a long, sighing breath of pure joy. As if at a given signal, the sensual kissing went lower, over the rounded swell of her belly, to tease at the inviting silvery triangle below. She could hardly breathe for the hot, intense pleasure that his hands and mouth and tongue were imparting to her now. It rippled through every part of her, as if every nerve in her body had a will of its own, and was individually responding to the caresses and kisses that were being heaped upon her so relentlessly and so sensuously.

She felt one of his hands leave her flesh for a moment and guide her own to where the potent stalk of his desire throbbed and swelled. She gasped at the sheer magnitude of it, wondering for one fearful second how such an instrument could ever break through her membrane barrier and enter that most secret core of her body. But even as the fear trembled through her, she heard Ross whisper against her flesh.

"The resistance will be but for a moment, my dove, and then you and I will be as one."

Even as he was speaking, she felt the spear of his finger pierce her flesh, but she was so aroused, and so ready for him, that no more than a small moan escaped her lips. And then he had taken the stalk in his own hand, and was guiding it to where she awaited him so moistly.

Seconds later, she felt the fiery tip gently penetrate her, and he paused to kiss her mouth and caress her breasts as if to take her mind away from any hurt that occurred. Gradually, he began to move into her more surely, deeper and deeper, until it seemed as if the whole of her body was filled with him. She had been so sensuously prepared, and her own desires were so alive, that she could only glory at the wonder of it all, for never had she known such sensations as those that were suffusing her so quickly so that she was gasping with the almost exquisite torture of it. She didn't understand what was happening, only that her husband seemed momentarily overcome by her response.

"My sweet one," she heard him breathe at her unbidden writhing beneath him. "My own, beautiful one!"

She was breathing so heavily she could hardly speak, and yet she had to speak, to break this spell of enchantment that was almost too perfect to bear.

"Do I please you, sir?" she said hoarsely.

"More than if you had given me all the stars in the sky," he said, surprised by his own feelings.

And then, as her muscles began to relax from their clench-ing sweetness, she felt him begin to move within her again, slowly and rhythmically at first, and then with a thrusting urgency that sent her excitement soaring anew. And when he finally gasped out her name, and spilled his hot seed into her, she felt again that clenching, spreading sensation of plea-sure. A sensation that she thought must surely take two lovers closer to heaven than anywhere else on earth.

He felt a sudden guilt. He was taking everything from her, and giving nothing in return except his name and an unknown future. It had been no more than a whim to take her as a gambling debt, and his first instinct on returning to England had been to find a woman to act as his wife and then pay her off. But then he had seen Stephanie Buchan.

She was a very tolerable bride, and surprisingly sensual, he admitted now. It was easy to be fond of her, but although love did not yet enter into his thinking, she was now his re-sponsibility, and he had promised before God to cherish her.

It was a somber thought, and one that did not sit too easily on his mind. He had always believed himself to be an hon-orable man, and she was stirring his conscience.

They had had no time for a formal courtship, but he con-soled himself by a pretense of courtship by his use of the flamboyant speech he had learned from Prince Hali. He was acting a part, but being an English gentleman, such deception did not go well with him.

He was also pleasantly surprised at how very compatible this young woman was toward him. To a man who had taken his pleasures in less salubrious places, to find such a wife was a bonus indeed. And that was something that only added to his feelings of guilt.

Four

"Tell me more about Shaladd," Stephanie said lazily.

She lay back prettily in a narrow punt on a lake, which she had delightedly discovered in the grounds of the Kilmarron Estate. She wore an afternoon gown of delicate lemon taffeta, and held a matching parasol over her head to keep out the rays of the afternoon sun. Ross poled the punt around the lake in a leisurely fashion, and his hot eyes told her he had never seen anything more delightful.

Stephanie felt her cheeks flush, knowing she must look the epitome of the seductive woman, lazing in the afternoon sun with the afterglow of love still surrounding her. Last night, in the early hours of the morning, and again on waking, she had known the tenderness and sensuality of her husband's lovemaking. She shivered, wondering how anyone could exist endlessly on such a high plane of ecstasy, and knowing instinctively that they could not.

She also knew she should never forget the outrageous reason for this marriage, and how Ross had told her of Prince Hali Ahmed's wish to give him six of his harem women. His marriage to Stephanie was merely to prevent the unwanted gift so that the Arab prince would not feel insulted by Ross's rejection of the women. He might—and certainly did—feel lust for Stephanie, but she had no way of knowing whether or not it was love. And the more she learned of this harem life, the more she knew that a man could make love to many women without ever loving them. To Stephanie, it was a sad and humiliating thought.

But she didn't intend to allow such introspection to dispel this lovely day. There was a special glory about knowing they were entirely alone on these first intimate days of their marriage, and that even if there had been prying eyes, she and Ross had every right to be here, to be sharing this bliss, with the overhanging willow trees trailing their branches right down to the water's edge where they were about to disembark for their afternoon picnic.

"What do you want to know about Shaladd?" Ross said, expertly sculling the pole to bring the punt right into the bank and securing its rope to a tree stump.

"Everything!"

He laughed, stepping out of the punt and making it rock alarmingly. Then he was holding out his hand to her, and pulling her safely onto the grassy bank that led to a leafy and secluded copse.

"Everything will take a little longer than one delightful afternoon, my dear girl, and besides, we have more interesting ways to spend our time than merely talking."

"So we do," she said, feigning innocence. "We have the delicious food your cook has prepared for us, and the flask of wine and the fruit to enjoy—"

She paused as he pulled her none too carefully into his arms. "And we have each other to enjoy," Ross said with a world of seduction in his voice.

Stephanie gave a small gasp as his lips tugged gently and provocatively at her mouth.

"You don't mean to ravish me out here in the open, I trust, sir!" she teased him back, finding that the daring words she used gave her an unexpected frisson of pleasure.

"Would you disobey my wishes so soon after promising to love, honor, and obey me in all things, woman?" he demanded, his eyes dancing with amusement.

His arms circled her waist, and his hips thrust very firmly

against her, leaving her in no doubt that he meant every word he said. And while she thrilled to his mastery, there was still the nagging semblance of something not quite right here. It was almost as if, despite his undoubted desire and delight in her, he was driven on to put her completely and irrevocably under his spell. Somehow, she sensed that there was more urgency in him than even the powerful urgency of lust, and it was something to make her uneasy.

But Ross Kilmarron wasn't a man to leave a woman wondering for long. He scooped her up in his arms and carried her to where the copse opened up in an intimate carpet of green, dappled by the sunlight through the tall trees surrounding it.

"This is an admirable place for seduction, I think," he said softly.

"Does a man still need to seduce his wife then, when she is always available to him?" Stephanie said hesitantly.

He ran his finger under her chin in the way that she found so sweetly erotic.

"The man who does not do so is a foolish man indeed," he said gravely. "And the greater the man, the more skilled in the artistry of love he should become."

"A man such as Prince Hali Ahmed?" Stephanie asked, mesmerized by the darkening of Ross's eyes as he looked deep into hers.

"Especially such as Hali Ahmed," he agreed. "His Highness's aim is to give every wife the greatest of satisfaction and pleasure, while demanding and expecting the ultimate in servitude and supplication from her.

Those were not words that Stephanie would have chosen to hear. An English bride naturally expected to serve her husband in all things, but supplication was an alien word. Coupled with the word, the intensity in Ross's voice as he said them began to alarm her. But then he smiled again, and the moment of anxiety passed.

"You need not concern yourself with such things. Wait

while I fetch the blanket and the picnic basket, and since you seem so eager for fortification, I shall feed you with grapes and wine in the way of the ancient Romans."

"At their orgies, do you mean?" Stephanie said without thinking, and Ross laughed again.

"Why not? We might just have an orgy of our own," he said in a wickedly suggestive voice that left her no doubt he meant to do exactly that.

And why not? She was his wife, and they were on his land. He could demand whatever he wanted of her, and she could not refuse. She began to realize that she was as servile in this civilized country as any concubine tied in bondage to a powerful desert prince. And while the thought of it revolted her, it also gave her a tremendous drive of excitement. Here, in this isolated place, they could be anything they wanted to be. Ross was her prince, and she was his slave.

By the time he returned with the blanket and picnic basket, she was standing motionless, as if her whole being was somehow taken over by these all-consuming needs. He spread the blanket on the soft ground, and opened the basket. Then he looked at her.

"This is women's work."

He spoke mildly, but he left her in no doubt that he meant what he said. No gentleman of Ross Kilmarron's stature would bend to do such a menial tasks as serving a picnic spread, any more than a fabulously wealthy desert prince could be expected to do it.

She leaned forward quickly, knowing she was allowing her fanciful nature to get the better of her. But in her mind, for long, mesmerizing moments, she knew that the unknown Prince Hali Ahmed and Captain Ross Kilmarron were becoming alarmingly one and the same. This was no longer a patch of green in the quiet English countryside, but somewhere beneath the heat of a shimmering desert sun.

She knelt to her woman's task, spreading the pristine white damask cloth on the blanket. Then she removed the cloth-wrapped dishes of fruit and sweetmeats, the flask of wine cooling in an earthenware pot, and the exquisite glasses and china from their safety clasps inside the basket. Ross watched her silently all the while, and gradually, far from being resentful of the tasks she was performing in such a docile manner, Stephanie was aware of a new excitement in being observed so closely.

Unconsciously, and then more deliberately, she began to use provocative and sensual movements as she removed the items from the picnic basket. She spread the damask cloth as sensuously as though she smoothed a lover's skin. She unwrapped the bunches of succulent black grapes and caressed them for a moment before laying them on a serving platter. She ran her fingers around the rim of the two matching crystal glasses, and matched the action by leisurely sliding her tongue around her lips. She fastened them securely in the holders provided for them, and then gave a little cry as she was suddenly seized from behind. Ross's hands were roving over her buttocks, and then moving surely upward to caress the lush curves of her breasts.

"You may be unversed in the ways of love, my darling, but you're a very willing pupil," he said with a hoarseness in his voice that told her instantly of his mounting desire. "I could take you here and now, and to hell with food and wine, but since you play the concubine so instinctively, you should learn some of the subtler pleasures in the art. We'll satisfy one appetite first, and the other appetite will be sated all the more sweetly for the waiting."

He took his hands away from her body then, leaving her trembling. He spoke so strangely at times, still half in that other culture that was so alien to her. For a second, she wondered again if she would be wise to request that she stayed in England while he went on his expedition. And just as quickly, she knew that it was the last thing she would want, even if he agreed to it, which she knew he would not. Wherever Ross went, she would follow, even to the ends of the earth.

But his mood had changed now, as he plied her with the juicy black grapes so reminiscent of the Roman orgies she had read about. For a while he dropped each perfect piece of fruit into her mouth and followed it with a kiss. Then his kisses teased the inner softness of her mouth and took the fruit from her to eat it himself, while she laughed and demanded that he stop, for fear that she would choke.

He poured them each a glass of cool, sparkling wine that made her head spin at first, and then filled her with a sense of relaxation and lethargy. She could almost imagine there had been something in the wine to arouse all her senses . . . but there was no need for drugs or potions, for it only needed Ross himself to arouse her.

"The game-playing is over, and I can delay no longer," he said finally, sweeping the entire picnic cloth and its contents away from the blanket with one gesture. "I must have you now, my sweet one."

She looked at him dumbly. She was so wild with passion for him that she would have complied with any demand he made. But she wasn't sure quite what he wanted of her, and she sat back on the blanket, awaiting instructions. *In the manner of a concubine,* the thought flashed into her mind. She knew she should be irritated by it, but she was too dazed with desire to heed it.

"I want to see my woman unclothed. Remove all the trappings, Stephanie," Ross went on in that soft, seductive voice she was beginning to know so well.

She shivered at the look in his eyes. He demanded, and she must obey. And again, it was as if she was in the midst of a desert mirage, and this might no longer be a leafy hidden copse on the privacy of a gentleman's land, but the glowing sensuality of a harem, where she must do the sultan's bidding or be slain.

Slowly, she unfastened all the buttons and hooks on her

dress and undergarments. He didn't attempt to help her, and she knew he was taking pleasure in seeing her trembling movements. She was entering new and untried territory, and the excitement of it mingled with a sense of adventure and daring. The summer air was cool on her flesh, and a small breeze rippled over her breasts as the last confining bodice was finally discarded. Her nipples were ripe and ready for love, and she heard Ross's small intake of breath as he acknowledged the fact.

She knelt back on her haunches, never taking her eyes from his face as his gaze slowly devoured her nakedness, and then his hands began to trace their own way over the curves and hollows of her body, pausing where they chose, and drawing small, primitive sounds from her lips. Her thighs parted involuntarily as his hands brushed the mound of bright hair, then those questing fingers reached their ultimate goal, and her eyes dilated at the swift sensation of eroticism as they invaded her moistness.

"So, is my woman is quite ready for me?" Ross asked unnecessarily. She opened her eyes, and forced herself to answer teasingly, if only to break these almost unbearably intense moments of pleasure.

"I think you know that your woman is more than ready," she whispered. "But it seems that my man is not."

He looked at her in surprise, and with a dart of displeasure in his face. She went on hurriedly.

"I don't doubt my master's readiness in certain areas," she said delicately. "But is it some kind of male superiority to take a woman when you are fully clothed?"

She knew she was risking even more of his displeasure. She knew so little about him, really. If she sometimes feared him, there was an excitement in that fear. She had long craved for some excitement in her life, knowing she had been confined for too long in her stepfather's world. She had wanted for nothing, except love. Even so, she understood how a woman and a man could make love without ever being in love. If that were so in this case—but now was not the time to question it.

She heard Ross give an amused laugh, and he began to remove his own clothes with sensual slowness. By the time he was as naked as she, his eyes were dark with passion.

"My woman of spirit pleases me very well," he said softly, and then the time for talking was over. She was pinned beneath him on the blanketed ground, and she gasped as she felt the familiarity of his deep penetration. Without thinking, she threw back her arms behind her head and lay in total abandonment as he thrust into her.

There was a strange new pleasure in making love like this. She felt totally at one with nature and the elements, and with the very existence of God Who had created Adam and Eve and all things that were beautiful. And *this* was beautiful, this same thrusting passion that those first lovers on earth had known, and which was still the most perfect expression of love.

Stephanie's eyes slowly opened as she felt Ross withdraw from her slightly, and raise himself up from her. He knelt astride her, his hands molding and caressing her swollen breasts, the tip of his manhood just moving slowly inside her in a shallower penetration. In her bemused mind, she expected to feel a desperate longing for him to plunge deeper, but there was a different kind of eroticism in these small, tantalizing movements. They became brisker and shorter, and had her gasping with pleasure as they pressed against her swollen nub of acute sensitivity.

And then she was writhing and twisting beneath him, and crying out his name as she clung to him. She was in a state of almost trancelike euphoria as the clenching spread of heat in her loins began to envelop her. And, sensing it, Ross drove into her as his climax coincided with her own, and he clasped her possessively to him as if he would never let her go.

* * *

The couple who returned to the Kilmarron Estate some while later epitomized decorum itself. The demurely dressed captain's wife, and the handsome captain himself, solicitously helping her out of the punt onto the small landing stage at the edge of the lake, gave no indication of the vigorous and abandoned lovers they had so recently been. Stephanie found a delightful piquancy in the game they played, so correct in public, so recklessly shameless in private.

She wished such an idyll could go on forever, but she knew it could not. Even though they would be married forever, she thought, crossing her fingers as she did so, they could not be alone like this forever. They must meet other people, enter into social activities, and for Stephanie, at least, be indoctrinated into another way of life while they were in the desert princedom of Shaladd.

It was only later, when Ross was ensconced with his lawyer and his new young assistant, and discussing the final details of the trip, that she realized he had still told her virtually nothing more about Shaladd, nor even the ways of the concubines. And she was becoming ever more curious to know more about these poor creatures who were obliged to share a husband. It was not the British way, Stephanie thought fiercely, and she thanked God for being born into such a civilization, rather than into the Arab culture.

At the dinner table that evening, Stephanie discovered that while the lawyer had gone back to London, the young assistant had accepted the invitation to eat with them. His nervous presence took away the closeness between the newly married couple, and there was such a correctness about Ross in the gentleman's company that made her marvel that he could ever be so abandoned as to make love in the open.

"Mr. Davey agreed to dine with us, in order to take a message to your stepfather and your cousin, Stephanie. He'll inform them of the time of our departure from Tilbury if you wish it," he told her. "I daresay they may wish to come to the boat to see us off."

"I'm not sure that I do wish it," she said at once. "There's been no love lost between myself and any of my relatives, and I see no point in putting on a show of false affection for any curious onlookers."

She saw the lawyer's face grow a little puce as he choked slightly over his wine. He was very young for a lawyer, even a junior one, Stephanie thought. She was more used to the grizzled features of the man who frequently gave her step-father much-needed financial advice. This Mr. Davey was fresh-faced, and clearly not expecting to hear such a forceful reply from a new bride. To her relief, she heard Ross laugh.

"You'll see that I was right in my observations, Davey," he said lightly, and Stephanie realized they had already discussed the matter. "My wife has a mind of her own, and has no wish to be associated with those who have done her wrong."

Stephanie flushed, for he should remember that it was Ross Kilmarron himself who had done her the most wrong, in offering to marry her for such despicable reasons of his own. It was on the tip of her tongue to say so, but she bit back the words. No matter how much Ross baited her, she wouldn't give him the satisfaction of knowing she could be reduced to indulging in a bitter tongue-match in front of a guest.

"I only meant to offer my services, ma'am," Davey said, so anxious to please that Stephanie wondered how on earth he behaved when faced with a strong-willed client like Ross Kilmarron, let alone be brave enough to don the wig and gown in a court of law!

"Thank you, Mr. Davey," Stephanie murmured. "But if any of my family wish to come to Tilbury, I'm sure they can discover the time of our departure for themselves. I wouldn't want to cause them any embarrassment by making them feel obliged to come. We've already said our good-byes," she added, lest he should think her an uncommonly unfilial woman.

"Davey himself is thinking of marrying in the spring of next year, my dear," Ross went on smoothly. "Do you have any advice to offer his bride on the newness of marriage?"

She went hot to the roots of her hair and the ends of her toes. She couldn't think why he was doing this. He was embarrassing her, and more than embarrassing this young man, who was practically squirming in his chair now.

"The only advice I would give is never to listen to other people's advice about marriage," she said sweetly. "Each couple must find their own happiness, and learn from their own mistakes. In your profession, wouldn't you agree that such sentiments apply in all walks of life, Mr. Davey?"

"I would indeed, ma'am," he said, pathetically grateful that she had taken the sting out of the question, and answered it so calmly. She glanced at Ross and saw him raise his glass to her, and she felt as though she had won a small battle, without ever knowing she was involved in one.

Later, when the lawyer had departed, she rounded on Ross in the drawing room where they took their coffee, and her husband took his glass of brandy.

"Why on earth did you suggest that I could give any advice to poor Mr. Davey's bride?" she blazed at him. "It embarrassed the poor man terribly—"

"It did, didn't it?" Ross drawled. "The man's an idiot, and I've no time for idiots. I doubt that he'll last long at the bar, if he even makes it that far. Any red-blooded counselor worth his salt would have been able to shrug off the discussion and turn it to his own advantage with a few comments of his own, the way that you did, my dear."

Stephanie stared at him, recognizing a cruel streak in him that was often associated with a man used to wielding power over others. Maybe it came from the job that he did, living with danger every day in an alien land and having to make quick, often life-saving decisions, and maybe it was from his association with that self-imposed dictator, Prince Hali Ahmed. Whatever the reason, Stephanie didn't like it.

"So was it all some kind of test, to prove that I, too, could fend off unwanted questions?" she demanded.

"Something like that," he said. "You conduct yourself very well, Stephanie. You please me in many ways."

If his words were intended to pacify her, they failed. She began to feel more and more like an object merely chosen from a vendor's shelf for its beauty, for which the buyer was finding ever more uses, and was continually congratulating himself on his purchase. She should never forget that any other woman would have suited his purpose just as well.

"But you don't love me, do you?" she heard herself saying bitterly before she could stop herself. And at the guarded look in his eyes, she clenched her hands to her sides and sprang to her feet.

"Oh, don't bother to pretend, Ross. We both know why I wear your ring on my finger. I'm no more than a convenience to you, am I? No more and no less than one of Prince Hali's concubines. I doubt that he's spared one of them a single moment's love, once they've satisfied his lust."

"That is their purpose," Ross replied stiffly. "That, and to be the vessels to provide him with sons to prove his virility."

Stephanie stared at him sickly. Every word he said about the unknown Prince Hali Ahmed made her dislike him more. He was a monster, she raged, to use women in such a way. She couldn't imagine how they must suffer at his hands, and it seemed ludicrous to recall how Ross had said he was afraid that any female companion other than his own wife would be lured into the desert way of life at Shaladd. No decent, respectable, confident European woman would ever dream of entering voluntarily into such a humiliating existence.

"I see that I've shocked you," her husband said briefly now.

She gave a twisted smile. "Why should you worry about such a thing? You shock me all the time with your tales of barbaric practices and slavish rituals. You shock me with the realization of how little I know you, and I'm shocked into wondering just how disastrous my future life is going to be, now that I have to entrust it to you."

"You are remarkably eloquent—"

"For a woman?" she finished for him. "Would you prefer it if I was silent and subservient like the desert women? That *was* the word you used, I believe?" she said, all sarcasm now.

"I would not," he snapped. "Anything less like one of Hali's women, I cannot imagine you to be. And I've no desire for an angelic creature such as one of them for my wife."

"Is that how you see them?" she asked. "And are you sure you wouldn't care for me to be as docile as you suggest to me that they are?"

For some reason, she wanted to keep this argument alive, to try to probe that enigmatic mask that came over his face whenever she got too close to finding out more about the desert princedom.

"Strange as it may seem to you, my dear, I would not. Too much sugar can begin to cloy even the most receptive of palates, and a little bit of spice now and then is a refreshing change."

"I see. Then you don't object entirely if I speak my mind when it pleases me?" she challenged him.

"Nothing you do in the privacy of our own domain will ever annoy me," he said, though she doubted that such a remark was strictly true. But his choice of words intrigued her, and warned her that there was more to come. And she was unable to resist putting the final question to him.

"And at Shaladd?"

She realized she was holding her breath as she awaited his reply. When it came, it was almost as if she had known it all along.

"At Shaladd, we do as Prince Hali dictates. We will be his honored guests, but even the most revered of guests must abide by the rules of the prince. You will take care not to voice your opinions forcefully in public, Stephanie, for if I'm obliged to reprimand you, I will lose dignity. Should an argument then ensue, I would be obliged to put you in chains for a while until you come to your senses and grovel publicly before me for forgiveness."

All the while he had been speaking, Stephanie's mouth had dropped open wider and wider, until finally all her saliva had dried, and she swallowed painfully. She couldn't believe what she was hearing, and yet, she *had* to believe it. Ross delivered the words in such a sepulchral voice, and with such a remote look on his handsome face, that he could only be speaking the truth. And all her brave spirit left her.

"What kind of a devil's hole are you taking me to, Ross?" she whispered.

He started, and looked at her sharply, seeing how all the color had drained from her face, and he came toward her swiftly. He sat beside her and took her cold hands in his own.

"Dear God, I didn't mean to frighten you so. What I described is only done in extreme circumstances—"

"But it has been done? Have you seen it done?"

He nodded reluctantly. "I've seen it done, when a concubine has stepped over the line of civility toward Hali or a visiting nobleman. You must realize, Stephanie, that we will be entering a culture where women are treated very differently from the way they're treated here. If Hali visited my home, I would expect him to abide by the etiquette of Oxfordshire. So when we are in Shaladd, we must do him the courtesy of behaving according to his rules."

"But you wouldn't really ever put me in chains, and expect me to grovel publicly to you for forgiveness, just because of a small argument?" She tried to smile at the absurdity of the thought, but was totally unable to get the image of such an appalling humiliation out of her mind.

Ross gave a small smile, and leaned forward to kiss her lightly on the mouth. His lips were as cold as her own, and she gave a small shiver as he moved away from her to pour himself another glass of brandy.

"Don't give me any cause, and you'll never know, will you?" he countered.

The prevarication told her more certainly than anything else that if such an act ever became necessary, then he would do whatever was required, even to the extent of humiliating his wife in public. She hated the all-powerful Prince Hali and all he stood for, but she vowed to be very careful indeed not to be seen to argue with her husband in his presence.

"If you want to go to bed, Stephanie, don't let me detain you," he said a short while later, when she sat in quiet despondency, contemplating the future. It had once seemed so bright, and now it seemed beset with dangers, the like of which were only just becoming known to her.

And what of the so-called luxury and fabulous treasures of which Ross had spoken that were to enchant her so much? It seemed that these wretched concubines knew very little of any of it, and that they were simply prisoners of Shaladd. If they had to watch every single word they said, it seemed they were also virtually mindless creatures whose only duties were to be bedded by the prince and bear him sons. Otherwise, they might as well not exist at all. The emptiness of their plight began to affect Stephanie very deeply, and she took a deep breath, uncaring now whether she angered her husband or not.

"Since you are sending me to bed, do I take it that you've had your fill of me for one day? Am I to be relieved of my duties for the present and allowed some sleep?" she said waspishly.

To her fury, Ross looked at her in some amusement. He pretended a mock assessment of her anger.

"Unfortunately, I have business to attend to in my study before I retire. But I think five lashings and one hour in chains would be a suitable punishment for such insolence, and then you may crawl to me naked for forgiveness, while I decide what further punishment to give you."

Horrified, she made to rush toward the door, but he restrained her just as quickly, his arms holding her in a viselike grip.

"I'm teasing you, Stephanie," he said, suddenly angry. "Do you think I would willingly harm one inch of your beautiful body?"

"I don't know," she said frantically. "I don't know anything any more. I just feel very afraid—"

His mouth was warm on hers then, stilling her words.

"Sweet Stephanie, I promise that no one will do you harm while I'm there to protect you—"

"But who is going to protect me against *you?*" she said tremblingly, betraying her innermost feelings.

He let her go so suddenly that she stumbled heavily against the door, which just saved her from sprawling in an ungainly heap on the floor. She clutched at the door handle and opened it, fleeing upstairs to the bedroom they should be sharing. But the night lengthened, and still Ross didn't come to join her, and despite all that he had said in his attempt to reassure her, she had never felt so desperately alone in the whole of her life.

Five

The days seemed to rush by until it was time for them to leave England, and it was then that the reality of it all began to undermine Stephanie's confidence. At first it had seemed like such a wonderful adventure, but who knew how it would all end? But then, how could anyone know what the future held? All of life was an adventure, and a person could only make the best of it. Even as she thought it, she chided herself, for didn't she think she already had the best of it, with Ross?

"Why do you look so gloomy?" he asked her as the swaying carriage took them back to London en route for Tilbury docks. "Are you regretting everything already, Stephanie?"

"Should I be?" she countered.

He gave a half-smile. "I hope not. Our marriage didn't come to pass through normal circumstances, but I see no reason why it shouldn't be a successful and harmonious one."

Stephanie avoided looking at him. It suddenly sounded so cold and calculating. A successful and harmonious marriage . . . The words were supposedly meant to be reassuring and optimistic, but they could just as easily be applied to any business partnership. She felt unaccountably depressed, just when she should be at her most radiant, the way a new bride should be.

She felt Ross's hand cover hers for a moment.

"I can promise you the adventure of a lifetime, Stephanie, and after that—"

"After that?" she said dully. What was he implying? That they could go their separate ways? Once before, he had intimated as much, but no mention of it had been made since. And by now she knew that she couldn't bear to spend the rest of her life without him.

"After that, we shall return home, where I shall write up the story for the rest of the world to read, and you will illustrate it. We'll make a good partnership, Stephanie."

The fact that he evidently meant their association to continue after the trip to Egypt didn't mollify her at that moment, and she spoke caustically.

"Wasn't it fortuitous then, that when you were looking for a wife, you found one with artistic talents?"

"I had already seen the evidence of your sketches and drawings. Your stepfather was not averse to crowing over his charge's accomplishments, and gave me several of your sketches. I was impressed by your attention to detail. You may have any amount of drawing materials that you wish, my dear, to indulge in your hobby as well as helping me in my work."

"Thank you," she muttered, somewhat taken aback. Drawing and sketching had been one of the ways she had managed to forget that she was so beholden to a relative she despised and to keep out of the way of her bullying stepbrother.

"What is Prince Hali like?" she asked, changing the conversation. "Is he old and fat, and hideously ugly?"

She shivered visibly then, pitying all the lovely young women he chose for his harem, for surely none would be able to refuse him. From what Stephanie had heard and read by now, they risked losing their lives if they dared to anger him in the slightest way. And to refuse a prince was to insult him beyond measure.

She realized Ross was laughing, his voice full of amusement now.

"I hardly think Hali would relish being accorded with such a description! He and I are much the same age and stature. In Shaladd he's revered as a god among men, not only for his position and wealth, but for his good looks as well."

"I wonder that such a paragon can really exist!" Stephanie said, oozing with sarcasm. Far from attracting her to Prince Hali, such male arrogance only made her loathe him more. She felt Ross take hold of her wrist and grip it hard.

"You'll do well not to show off your English snobbery so blatantly, my dear. In Shaladd, Hali is known as The Great One, and he who dares to mock his way of life risks losing his own," he said, confirming her fears.

"Or hers?" Stephanie said through stiff lips.

"Or hers," Ross said. "And don't think that being my wife makes you immune from respecting the culture of our hosts. You'll be entering a different world, Stephanie, but a very beautiful and exotic one."

Quickly, she turned her thoughts away from the unpleasant idea that the harem women might as well be bound and shackled, no matter how beautiful the surroundings.

"If you've seen some of my sketches, you'll know that I enjoy drawing pastoral scenes as well as still life. Will I be permitted to sketch Shaladd as well as the artifacts from the desert tomb?" she said, not wanting to dwell on such thoughts.

"Perhaps. I will ask Hali's permission when the time is ripe."

"Why can't I just ask him myself?"

His eyes were icy. "Because you cannot! Women do not speak unless they are invited to do so, and to make such a request is not permitted unless a special audience in the Golden Chamber is granted. You must heed my advice, Stephanie, if you're not to commit an unwitting insult to our host."

"So I see." She spoke faintly, for with every word he said, he unnerved her more.

She felt his arm slide around her shoulders, and then she savored the warm pressure of his mouth on her own for a moment.

"I've alarmed you unduly, and it was never my intention to do so. Just follow my lead, and keep in mind that eastern ways are not our ways, and all will be well. And remember something else, Stephanie . . ."

"What's that?" she asked, as he paused.

"Remember that you have a husband by your side. You will not be entering this new country alone."

It was said to comfort her, but frustratingly, it didn't. If only he'd said that she had a husband who loved her, who would do anything to protect her against all the evils in the world, she might have been comforted.

But how could she expect love to grow so soon, if ever, even though she knew she could easily love him? This was no normal marriage. She had been bought on a gambler's whim, and as a foil to prevent a generous prince showering Ross with the gift of his harem women. *She* should be pitied, too, thought Stephanie bitterly, for the concubines were no more demeaned by their lot than she was herself.

They stayed at an inn on the night before they sailed from Tilbury. Stephanie fully expected Ross to take her in his arms and make love to her, but he seemed far too preoccupied with the forthcoming trip. While she lay sleepless in the uncomfortable bed the inn provided in their room, Ross sat near the window long into the night, poring over documents and files until the candlelight spluttered and died.

Only then did he come to join her in the bed, but although she snuggled up against him, he merely told her to try and sleep, and she had to be content with the closeness of his body, the steady sound of his breathing, and his hands resting lightly on her breasts. And she wondered if he could possibly know how the nearness of him was affecting her. She had been a child before, but with those marvelous hands and body he had made her a woman, and she wanted him.

He was awake and dressed before her in the morning, while she lay lethargically, almost reluctant to move. Once she did, they would be starting their journey, and once the ship set sail, there would be no turning back.

What on earth was wrong with her? she thought angrily. Why could she not see all this as a wonderful chance to explore destinations unknown that most people never saw in their whole lives? Why did it all seem such a letdown? But she knew the answers only too well.

It was because she had expected too much. Despite the circumstances of this marriage, she had still gone into it wearing rose-tinted glasses, believing that in the intimacy of marriage, Ross would surely fall in love with her. And it simply hadn't happened. He would rather spend time on his old books, than with her. And to a romantic young woman of not yet twenty-one summers, with her head and her heart still full of dreams, it was like a slap in the face.

"If you don't stop scowling, your expression will stay like that," Ross's voice said lazily from the other side of the room. "I'll wager that some well-meaning female dragon has already told you as much."

"Must you wager against everything?" Stephanie said, sudden anger making her sit bolt upright in the bed. Her shining hair cascaded like a silver waterfall over her shoulders and nightgown as she glared at her husband. "Is betting the only yardstick you know?"

"And a grouch in the mornings as well," he remarked, refusing to rise to her bait. "If this continues, I'll have to see to it that you're kept well out of Hali's way until the middle of the afternoon, by which time I trust your temper will have cooled."

"Oh, so you intend to hide me away until required, like his harem women, do you?" she said witheringly.

"Only if you behave like a child. As long as you behave like my wife, I shall be proud to have you by my side."

Her eyes stung. Sometimes he said some of the very things she longed to hear, but it never went far enough. It was as if he always held himself in check, for fear of revealing his true feelings—whatever they were. She hardly knew. He could be the most ardent lover, but a man could lie with any woman and be roused, as she very well knew by now. It wasn't the same as loving her. And she wanted so badly to be loved by him, more than she had ever thought possible.

For some reason she remembered Ross's strange words about the reason for a man like Prince Hali Ahmed needing so many concubines. "To be the vessels to bear him sons."

"Do you want children, Ross?" she blurted out without thinking.

She saw his eyes narrow, and immediately she felt humiliated at asking such a naive question. In any ordinary marriage, it would have been a perfectly natural question for a wife to ask a husband, but this was no ordinary marriage. Stephanie wondered now if he thought she asked him the question because of an ulterior motive.

Perhaps he suspected that she wished to become pregnant at the earliest opportunity, in order to keep him. Perhaps her innocent love had already become transparent to him. Or perhaps he saw her for a schemer who would seize the opportunity to continue the soft life as Captain Ross Kilmarron's wife, even when her usefulness to him was done.

"Every man wants a part of himself to live on in his children," he said shortly. "Isn't that so of women as well?"

"Of course, though not every woman is so keen to be tied to domesticity on a husband's whim," Stephanie retorted, hurting herself by her own words, and hardly knowing why she did so. They were such a denial of the way she really felt, knowing that the idea of holding Ross's child in her arms had suddenly filled her spirit with intoxication.

"A husband's whim," he said thoughtfully. "Is that how

you see the consummation of marriage then? Perhaps I've underestimated your sweetness, if you can talk so blithely of the pleasures of the marriage bed, and the fundamental need to procreate."

Stephanie flushed, gazing at him in consternation. Somehow this breezy conversation had turned into something ugly, and she knew it was all her own fault. As he looked at her without blinking, she turned away from that penetrating stare, feeling oddly transparent, and again unable to look at him.

She hardly knew he had crossed the room to the bed, until she felt his arms go around her. She drew in her breath as he held her fast against him for a long moment. She could feel the steady beat of his heart, and wondered if he registered the erratic throbbing of her own. Then he held her away from him slightly, and tipped up her chin with his finger. His eyes were soft and gentle now, with none of the gambler's ruthlessness she knew they could display so quickly.

"My poor sweet," Ross said in a voice that held no hint of passion. And yet it had the power to set her toes tingling. "Is it going to be so very distasteful to you to be married to a man you don't love?"

The words brimmed on her tongue, but she had too much pride to say them. It wasn't the done thing for a lady to confess love to a man who didn't love her. It was humiliating, and put her at a disadvantage . . . She hesitated as the thoughts swept through her head, and finally she knew they meant less than nothing. She longed to tell him how desperately she was learning to love him, but she had paused too long, and she heard him give a rueful laugh and shook her gently.

"Don't try to pretend, my sweet. It doesn't become you. But I promise I shall try to make life tolerable for you, even when it doesn't have the excitement of Shaladd."

And how could she tell him now, that being with him was all the excitement she would ever want?

But the moments passed, and he released her abruptly as a voice outside the door announced that the breakfast he had ordered was awaiting them. Stephanie covered herself quickly, as he called to the girl to come inside, and the tray of food was placed on a side table. Stephanie didn't miss the envious glances the girl shot at her, and thought how little she deserved them. She was a bought bride, and she couldn't get the thought out of her head, no matter how much she tried. But the intimacy of taking breakfast in their room didn't escape her, and she joined Ross at the small table, donning her robe over her nightgown. It felt deliciously decadent.

And it was one more sweet memory to take out and remember in the dark days when this farce of a marriage was over, she thought with new cynicism. For of course it couldn't last. They were poles apart in every way. Once she had served her purpose, there was no reason why she should stay, and even less reason why Kilmarron would want her to.

All roads leading to Tilbury docks were crowded with a great crush of people from all walks of life as their hire carriage took them toward the waiting steamship *Princess Maria*. There was an obvious division between the lower-class passengers and the servants, and others, like themselves, who would be using the best cabins and mostly making the Grand European Tour.

"Are you a good sailor, Stephanie?" Ross inquired, once they had been safely ushered on board. She swayed slightly, the ship rocking gently beneath her as it bumped against the barnacled dockside.

"I hope so," she said fervently. "I've heard tell of the storms in the Bay of Biscay, so I shall do my best not to disgrace myself if we encounter one."

"It's unlikely," he assured her. "We travel at the best time of the year, and the weather's set fair. But we shan't be leaving port for some time yet, so we may as well get acquainted with our cabin."

This was another intimacy, Stephanie realized, when a young cabin boy had shown them to the cabin on the upper deck.

"I hadn't realized it would be quite so small!"

Ross grinned. "Did you imagine we'd have a bedroom like the one at home?" he asked.

The use of the word "home" sent a little glow through her veins, and she smiled back.

"I'm not that stupid. But I thought there would be enough room to—to—"

"To get away from one another? I'm afraid not, my dear. Though it will pain me to sleep separately from you even in so cramped a space. I've become accustomed to the feel of you beside me."

Stephanie felt herself blush as she looked at the two narrow bunk beds, one on either side of the small cabin. If this was luxury, she thought fleetingly, what on earth could the lower quarters be like!

"A penny for your thoughts," Ross said softly.

"They're not worth the telling," she said.

"Then let me guess. You're wondering how we shall manage to make love in such cramped conditions for all the days and nights of the voyage. Am I right?"

"You are not," she said crossly, because it was exactly what she had been thinking.

He laughed out loud. "Then you disappoint me, my dear, because I was thinking exactly that. But no doubt we shall use our ingenuity."

"Or remain celibate for the duration of the voyage," she flashed back at him.

He put his arms around her, his arms spanning her waist and pulling her close. He gently rubbed his slightly roughened chin against her cheek, and she caught her breath. She could smell the musky scent of him, and her throat was dry as she saw the hunger for her in his eyes.

"I think not," he said softly. "I suspect that such close proximity will arouse my need for you even more thoroughly, and I promise you that lust will find a way."

Lust. Not love. She mourned his use of the word. Coupled with love, it was exciting and sensual. Alone, it made her feel incredibly lonely and used. And he could surely not have made it plainer that his desire went no further than that of a man for any woman who was ready and available, and belonged to him through the ties of marriage. But what was a marriage without love? Stephanie suddenly felt like weeping at the futility of it all.

"You've got that blank look on your face again," he said suddenly.

"Have I?" her voice was a husk of sound. "I was always told that my face betrayed my feelings too readily."

"It was one of the alluring things about you, Stephanie," Ross said, to her surprise. "But already you're learning to mask your feelings. Don't grow up too soon, my darling."

She gaped at him, half in anger, half in surprise at his admonishment.

"And please don't treat me like a child," she snapped. "I'm a woman and a wife—"

"You needn't remind me of that," he grinned, but if she thought he was about to kiss her or put her words to the test, there was a perfunctory knock on the cabin door, and the cabin boy appeared with all their baggage. When he had gone, Stephanie looked at it in exasperation.

"Now we have even less room! Can't they store it all somewhere until we reach Alexandria?"

Ross grinned again. "How quickly you learn to play the lady, too! No, sweetness, they cannot store the baggage anywhere else, but you may leave it to our steward to hang our clothes in the closets once we've seen the last of England.

Shall we go up on deck and watch the rest of our traveling companions come on board?"

She agreed, though privately she would far rather have stayed in the cabin and sorted out their belongings herself. How stupid she was, not to have realized there would be space for hanging things, however small it seemed. Ross was so much more knowledgeable and wordly than she, and she was determined to learn from him. She didn't want to let him down, and she didn't want to appear an ingenue in public either.

But the Channel breezes were refreshingly cool on deck, and Stephanie felt a sudden tug of nostalgia as she noted the late-summer haze above the crowded buildings of the distant city. It would be many months before she saw England again, and the seasons would have come full circle or beyond. It made her feel strange inside, and she gave a small shiver.

"Having second thoughts?" Ross murmured, as he had done once before. She turned her clear eyes toward him.

"No. I was just wondering what will have changed by the time I step ashore on English soil again."

It was an obscure remark that could have meant anything. A downfall of government, national catastrophes, a royal marriage, or more personal affairs, such as her stepfather's health deteriorating. Even as she thought it, Stephanie realized there was still some feeling for her benefactor, despite all. She was too soft-hearted to feel bitterness toward him forever. And besides, however inadvertently, he had given her her heart's desire.

She found herself wishing now that she had agreed to the family coming to wave them good-bye. There were so many family farewells between the ship and the dockside as the *Princess Maria*'s engines began to throb beneath them. So many tears and smiles and good wishes. It was the right and proper thing to do.

And then, she wondered if she had truly conjured them up, or if she really was seeing the angular proportions of

Cousin Claire, and the more robust shape of Lord Buchan as they hastened along the dockside, trying to pick out two familiar figures on deck. And it occurred to her that Ross wasn't surprised at all as he waved and called their names, and held Stephanie's hand tightly.

"Did you arrange this?" she said huskily.

He shrugged. "It seemed appropriate," he said. "No bride should go off to foreign parts with her new husband without a proper send-off."

Without thinking, she threw her arms around his neck, regardless of the amused glances of the fellow passengers clustered around them for a last glimpse of family and friends. They were so obviously newlyweds that it hardly mattered, and one embrace among the excited travellers drew little real attention. Except from Ross himself.

"Why, Stephanie, if I didn't know you better, I'd have said that was a kiss of real affection," he drawled. "I must remember to give you more little surprises if it results in such a delightful lack of inhibitions."

"Don't make fun of me," she said. She was still breathless, but more because of the quick response he had given to her kiss than from anything else.

"I wouldn't, not ever," he said gravely, and then she gave all her attention to her stepfather and cousin, who were waving quite frantically now, as if they were genuinely fond of her and sorry to see her go. How extraordinary, thought Stephanie, when she had always believed she was only part of the Buchan household on sufferance. She waved back just as enthusiastically, but all the same, she was thankful that Percy hadn't come down to see her off as well. That would have been far less of a spontaneous gesture.

But finally, all the farewells were over, the ship's hooters were blaring, and the *Princess Maria* was easing away from her moorings and moving out into the English Channel. And the group on the dockside grew smaller as the ship steamed out into deeper waters, and the breeze freshened. Stephanie was tempted to go below, but she was reluctant to lose the last glimpses of England, and she remained leaning on the ship's rail until they were in mid-Channel, and there was no more than a hazy outline of the edge of the land.

"Pardon my interruption, sir, but are you not Captain Kilmarron, the renowned archaeologist?" said a masculine voice behind them. Stephanie recognized the faint burr of a Scottish accent, similar to Ross's own.

She heard her husband sigh, and guessed that this kind of recognition happened from time to time, and that it could be irksome. But he turned at once, then, as they both saw the young man with the pretty girl clinging to his arm, she heard Ross give a great burst of laughter.

"Good God, what are you doing here, man? I thought I'd seen the last of you out east!"

But from the way he pumped the young man's hand, Stephanie understood that he wasn't displeased. She wasn't sure how she felt. Jealous wasn't quite the word to use, but the natural camaraderie with which the two men greeted each other was borne out of long friendship and a background knowledge of each other. The kind of knowledge she and her supposedly nearest and dearest hadn't yet acquired. She gave a faint smile to the young woman standing beside the stranger, and noted the bump on her left hand inside her glove, which denoted the presence of a wedding ring.

"Ross, old laddie, I was almost sure it was you," the stranger went on more warmly. "But I thought I'd give you a fright and pretend I was one of the admiring hangers-on you always seem to attract."

Ross shook his head slightly, clearly amazed and pleased to see the man again.

"You exaggerate as always, Gordon. But let me introduce my wife—"

"You're *married!*" The other man's good-looking face colored, and he spoke apologetically to Stephanie. "Pardon me, ma'am, for my incivility. It's just that we never thought Ross would get married, being more devoted to his work than to any woman. Though the whole regiment knew that if it ever happened, it would have to be to an exceptional lassie, and we were obviously proved right."

He gave a gallant little bow, clearly hoping to retrieve the situation.

"All right, you old rogue," Ross said with a grin. "This is Stephanie, my wife, and I'm sure she'll forgive you. This reprobate is Captain Gordon Fraser, my sweet, and I daresay he'll eventually introduce us to his lovely companion."

Sheer red jealousy swept through Stephanie's heart now. Unreasonable, unnecessary, and overwhelming. And all because her husband, who had married her out of necessity and not out of love, was openly complimenting an old friend's wife.

"It seems that we've both been fortunate, Ross," Gordon Fraser said with a smile. "This is Jeannie, and we were married yesterday."

"So you're on your honeymoon! How wonderful!" Stephanie said swiftly, digging her hand into Ross's arm in a mute request for him to remain silent.

Because not for worlds could she admit to this couple, so blatantly head over heels in love, that they, too, were newlyweds. Not when the circumstances were obviously so vastly different. Love shone out of Jeannie for her husband, and she still gazed at him lovingly, even while she spoke shyly to Stephanie and Ross.

"We're doing the Grand Tour," she said with an attractive Scottish lilt. "We want to see *everything!*"

And it probably wouldn't matter a jot if they never saw a single monument or museum or ancient treasure, Stephanie thought, with an envy so sharp it was almost painful. They had eyes only for each other. It only emphasized the hollowness of her own marriage. A marriage of convenience was so shameful, compared with the trust and love shining out of Jeannie Fraser's blue eyes.

"So when did this event occur, Ross?" Gordon was saying now.

"Oh, a while ago now. We're an old married couple, compared with the two of you," he said to Stephanie's great relief. "But this calls for a celebration. I suggest that we meet for dinner in the dining room this evening, unless you intend to spend every minute away from all human contact."

"Ross, you'll make Jeannie blush—"

But the other couple took it all in good part, and it was clear that the gentlemen had known each other very well at some stage of their lives, and found it just as easy to pick up the friendship again.

"That would be fine, Captain Kilmarron," Jeannie said at once. "I've heard so much about you from Gordon. He's very proud of you, you know."

"Good God, don't tell him that, you'll make him swollen-headed," Gordon said with a wink, and then he patted his wife's hand. "But we're away now to get unpacked, and we'll see you both later."

Stephanie and Ross were silent as they watched them make their way to the companionway, then disappear from sight. The silence lengthened, and Stephanie was aware of the constraint between them. And she found herself wishing desperately that Gordon and Jeannie Fraser had chosen some other ship to go traveling on their Grand Tour. Not that she objected to company, just the company of newlyweds who made her own situation seem so dreadfully inadequate and unreal.

"Thank you for not telling them," she murmured when she finally felt bound to say something.

"Did you think I would? I've no wish to let it be known that I wagered for your hand."

Stephanie felt her face redden with anger. "I wasn't meaning that. I meant thank you for not telling them we were just married, too. I couldn't bear them to know that things weren't all that they should be between us."

She felt his hand close over hers. "I'm sorry, Stephanie. I'll make everything as easy for you as I can. It's not my way to force a woman into doing anything she doesn't want to do."

She bit her lip, knowing he couldn't see the irony in his words. She didn't want him to go easy on her in certain respects. She wanted him to love her, and ravish her, and to make her feel a woman in every sense of the word. But his last sentence made her realize anew that Ross Kilmarron had known many women before her. Maybe even some of the experienced concubines at Prince Hali Ahmed's court. He must be finding her a complete innocent compared with them.

She should hold her head high at the thought, for hadn't her despised stepbrother taunted her with the words that every man sought a virgin for his bride? But she hadn't considered the other implications of those words. A man sought and expected a virgin bride, but he could dally with as many whores as he pleased before he came to the marriage bed. And afterward as well, perhaps?

She didn't realize that a small gasp of distress had escaped her lips until she heard Ross's voice close to her cheek. Although he sounded considerate, she didn't miss his note of exasperation, either.

"Now what have I said to displease you? Does it upset you that a man talks so freely to his wife? You must get used to it, my dear."

"Of course not, and I'm just being silly. It's just that I've always been disturbed by any mention of force, however innocently it was said," she invented quickly. "I truly appreciate your concern for me, Ross."

"Then I trust you're not going to shout or become argumentative whenever I come near you. We both made a bargain, Stephanie, and you know my reasons for bringing a loving wife to Shaladd."

"And a submissive one," she couldn't help saying.

"And that, too," he said calmly. But the words were oddly menacing, reminding her anew of the bargain that had been struck, even though she had no say in it at all. But she knew she must abide by it or suffer the consequences. And in the masculine stronghold of Prince Hali Ahmed's Shaladd, she didn't dare guess what those consequences might be.

Six

They bathed separately in the small hip bath allocated to the first-class cabins, refreshing themselves in time for dinner, and then joined the other young couple in the dining room that evening.

For Stephanie it was sweet agony to see how Gordon constantly gazed at his Jeannie, as if he couldn't bear to take his eyes away from her. There was an aura of happiness surrounding them, as tangible as a warm blanket. Stephanie envied them so much, because theirs was clearly a marriage made in heaven, while hers was made in shame.

"You seem to have lost a little of your sparkle this evening," Ross said coolly. "Is it the motion of the ship that's upsetting you?"

She looked into his dark eyes that were watching her so steadily, but with none of the adoration of the other man for his wife. Ross's eyes were coldly assessing her, she thought with a shiver. Wondering if she was going to live up to his expectations, or if he had made an infuriating mistake in choosing her, she guessed cynically.

"I'm quite well, thank you," she said. "I was taking note of Jeannie's attractive accent. A nonaccent is so boring, don't you think?"

As soon as she had said it, she knew she had made an appalling error. The last thing she had intended was to be patronizing, but somehow that was the way it sounded. She saw the tinge of color in Jeannie Fraser's cheeks, and the other girl spoke too fast. She was clearly embarrassed, but she spoke with a soft dignity.

"Not at all. It's far more boring to be stamped immediately by our place of origin, and to be put into little boxes because of the way we speak, don't you think?"

"I daresay it is," Stephanie said at once. "But, Jeannie, I genuinely love the way you speak, and I could go on listening to you all night."

She heard Gordon Fraser give an indulgent laugh. "You'll not get the chance for that, lassie. Jeannie and me have other things to do that are far more interesting than just talking. We might just take the time for a stroll around the deck with the two of you if you've a mind for some fresh air before turning in. A *short* stroll, mind."

"Gordon, please, you'll make me blush!" Jeannie said, but the glow was back in her eyes, and the awkward moment had passed. And the repartee between them was so artless and so open, that it served to underline how careful Stephanie and Ross must be, especially when the conversation turned to how the couples had met, and how long before they were wed.

By the time they were taking coffee and brandy, they were all on easy and sociable first-name terms, helped by the old military acquaintance of the two men.

"I fell in love with Stephanie's portrait," Ross said, to her complete and utter fury.

"How romantic!" the soft-hearted Jeannie said at once. "And was it love at first sight for you as well, Stephanie?"

At the girl's clear-eyed look, Stephanie forced a smile. "Well, not quite. My first sight of Ross was from a distance. I confess that I thought he was a very dynamic and single-minded gentleman, and there was definitely something about him that evening that told me we were destined to be together."

Her eyes challenged him to deny it. She went as far as she

dared to taunt him, and only the two of them knew that her thoughts on that degrading evening were far from romantic. She couldn't forget the way he had glanced up toward the gallery in her stepfather's house, perfectly well aware that she was eavesdropping on the shameful wager he made for her.

"And was it a whirlwind courtship?" Jeannie persisted, and then gave an embarrassed laugh as her husband chided her for being too curious. "Oh, forgive me, both of you. But Gordon and I have known one another since childhood, and it always seemed that we were just waiting to grow up before we fell in love. It's fascinating to hear how other folk can fall in love at first sight."

Stephanie felt Ross's hand cover hers as it lay lightly on the pristine damask cloth on the dining-room table.

"You could definitely say that once we properly set eyes on one another, there was never going to be anyone else for either of us," he told the starry-eyed young bride. "Does that satisfy your romantic wee heart, Jeannie?"

"Oh, it does indeed!" she said, delighted, while Stephanie managed with a great effort not to snatch her hand away from the fingers imprisoning it.

It was all so farcical, she raged. But now that they had met the other two, who were obviously intending to become attached to them on the voyage, she could only hope that all such talk of meetings and courtship were ended. It was against her nature to prevaricate so much, and to talk in innuendoes. But it was clear that Ross had no such difficulty, and was far more adept at bending the truth than herself. But so he would be. Any man who could sink to such depths as to bargain for a wife in the way he had was an out-and-out rogue.

She kept telling herself as much all the while they strolled around the deck in the cool of the evening. The ship was well into the English Channel now, and steaming steadily toward the coast of Cornwall and then south along the coasts of France and Spain. The two ladies were glad of their evening shawls around their shoulders, and the gentlemen's protecting arms about their waists. They looked the epitome of a happy traveling foursome, Stephanie thought, and no one could have guessed at the circumstances surrounding one of the couples.

The blackness of the night sky was studded with stars now, and a great yellow moon had risen high above them, seemingly motionless. It was a night that was surely designed for lovers, and her breath caught slightly in her throat as she felt the warmth of Ross's body close to hers, keeping out the chill of the evening.

Rogue and a cheat he might be, even forbidding at times . . . unpredictable, enigmatic. He was all of those things, but still she knew she could truly love him.

"I think we've had enough strolling, so we'll be saying good night to you both," she heard Gordon Fraser's voice come out of the darkness.

And because Stephanie had become more attuned to the nuances in a man's voice now, she recognized the need in it. He wanted to make love to his wife. And at Jeannie's breathless good night, Stephanie knew that she wanted him, too. They had been long enough in company, and all they wanted now was to be together. She and Ross leaned against the ship's rail after they had gone, watching the scudding white waves as the ship cut through them.

"It's getting cold," Ross said at last. "It's time for us to go below, too."

"As you wish," she said, her lips dry. The evening had been very pleasant. The company had been lively and entertaining, and now it was over, and she felt unaccountably depressed. Everything was flat and gray, and she didn't know how to lift herself out of the gloom.

"You might show a little more enthusiasm for bedding, my sweet," Ross teased, not realizing how her spirits were plunging.

"Why? Do we have to continue this farce of happy families in private as well as in public?" she snapped before she could stop herself.

She felt his hand grip her wrist. His voice changed to the taunting one she knew so well.

"Is it so difficult for you? You've shown remarkable aptitude for it so far, even in the open air—unless you're a far better actress than I believed."

She felt her face grow hot. Why must he remind her of the way she had been so sensuously abandoned at their picnic hideaway? And how dare he suggest that she was pretending. And yet, perhaps it was exactly what she should make him believe. Anything, rather than let him think how passionately she was under his spell.

"It seems as if you've found me out," she said in a noncommittal voice that took all her strength to deliver.

He said nothing for a moment, and then, to her astonishment, he took her slowly into his arms and forced her mouth to succumb to his in a long and seductive kiss. She was helpless to resist, and if he noticed how ardently she was kissing him back, it seemed of little concern to him. When he finally let her go, she was almost drained of all emotion.

"So," he said in a low, mocking voice, "if my wife is such an experienced actress in the art of loving, then it's time the play commenced."

He pulled her with him toward the darkened companionway. There were few other people strolling the decks now, and none that glanced their way. Had they done so, Stephanie thought, in acute humiliation, they must surely have wondered why a gentleman of Captain Ross Kilmarron's stature should be hauling his wife so unceremoniously toward their cabin.

"Undress," he ordered. "And then we'll see just how accomplished an actress you really are."

He began to frighten her. There was only a dim light in the cabin, the flame safely encased in a thick glass globe that had been lit by their steward earlier on. It threw just enough light to see across the cabin, throwing eerie shadows all around them. In the gloom, it seemed to Stephanie that Ross suddenly assumed monstrous proportions.

"What do you want of me?" she whispered as she struggled to rid herself of her clothes, knowing that she had no option but to obey.

"I'll have you as Prince Hali has his women," he said coldly. "Then we'll see whether or not you see yourself as one of his concubines."

"I never suggested that I would—"

"Nor that you wouldn't. But you needn't look so alarmed, my dear. This will only be a brief initiation into the delights of the harem. I don't expect you to bathe in asses' milk and color your hair with henna, nor paint your eyes with khol and entice me with perfumes and spices—"

"I should think not!" Stephanie spluttered as the imagery he evoked seeped into her brain.

"But you'll supplicate yourself to me as a concubine does to Prince Hali," he instructed mockingly.

Stephanie felt the tears start in her eyes. This was a different Ross, one that she didn't know, and one that she feared. She put out a tentative hand to touch his arm.

"Why are you doing this?" she whispered. "Can't we just forget all this nonsense? If I've displeased you, I'm sorry, but I'm truly so tired—"

It was true. She was nearly dropping with sleep, and if it wasn't for the tension between them, the throb of the ship's engines could quickly induce a sense of lethargy in her. Ross shook off her fingers.

"A concubine doesn't approach her master until commanded," he said. "Finish disrobing and stand at the foot of the bed."

She obeyed numbly. She thought for a moment that she

had detected an apologetic note in his voice, but it was as if once started on this ridiculous act, he was determined to see it through. But she decided she must have imagined any regret, for he stood motionless while she removed all her garments and stood shivering where he instructed her.

And then it was his turn. She watched as his clothes were removed one by one, to fall into the small space between the narrow beds. The silent actions began to stimulate all her senses, and she was aware of a tingling arousal in her loins as the contours of his body were revealed in the dimness, and she finally drew in her breath in awe as she realized that he was magnificently ready for her.

She took a hesitant step forward, but he raised his hand to stop her and slid between the covers. He pointed a finger to the bottom of the bed.

"Lift the coverlet, and crawl to meet your master's pleasure," he ordered.

Stephanie felt her eyes dilate. What devilment was this? she wondered. She was shaking all over by now, from cold, from fear, but also from an undeniable feeling of sensual excitement. The titillation of what was happening was starting to invade every pore of her body, and without a word, she dropped to her knees in the confined space of the cabin and lifted the coverlet.

It was warm and dark beneath it, and the first thing she encountered was a pair of feet. Ross's feet. She felt utterly stupid for a moment, and then she allowed her hands to grasp his ankles, and felt the twitch of his flesh as she touched it. He was not so immune to her then, the thought flashed through her mind.

Very gradually, she let her hands move upward, to caress his calves and then to circle his knees in the way that he palmed her breasts, slowly and sensuously. And without exerting too much pressure on him, she was gently pushing his knees apart and crawling upward in the bed, in the way she imagined a concubine would do.

Everywhere her flesh touched his, she felt the tingle of excitement rush through her. Was this truly the way the concubines were schooled to please their prince? And could they possibly be so immune to the sensuality of the occasion that they were not stimulated, too, the way she was already stimulated and aroused to the point of near ecstasy?

She felt Ross's hands tangle in her hair and caress her cheeks, and she heard his indrawn breath as she reached the hard evidence of his desire. His hands pulled her head gently over him, and her mouth opened to receive him. She heard his tortured gasp as she tasted the hard, taut flesh, and her tongue circled it delicately.

He allowed the intimacy for just a moment, and then she was pulled away, and he was twisting her around so that she lay beneath him, and the familiar, remembered invasion of her body began. She was so ripe and ready for him that she writhed immediately beneath him, moaning softly in her throat as he thrust into her, his hands kneading her breasts and pearling the nipples in his fingers to enhance her desire.

There was no finesse, and yet no cruelty either. His need for her was matched by her own vibrant need for him. His lovemaking was hot and vigorous, and her desire rose to meet his, causing her to cry out as she felt the spurting heat of his climax. He slumped against her, damp and spent.

And then she heard him groan against her cheeks, as if the words were torn out of him.

"Forgive me, my darling. God knows what made me subject you to such humiliation. I promise you it will never happen again."

She stroked his head, finding a poignant need to comfort him.

"It's all right," she whispered, knowing that the dampness on her own cheeks came as much from the sensual pleasure of his lovemaking as from gladness that he had reverted to gentleness now.

"It's not bloody well all right," he muttered. "I shamed

you, in the way the harem women are shamed every time they're called for service."

Stephanie winced at these words. They were crude, and probably justly deserved in the context he used, but she didn't want to hear them. She wanted to hear the words of love that he had never yet spoken to her. She shifted slightly beneath his weight, and he moved at once. Immediately, she wanted to draw him back to her, but she knew he'd left her mentally as well as physically.

He bent his head and kissed her very gently on the mouth. It was so tender, so oddly vulnerable, that it stirred up all her emotions and made her weak.

"I'll never subject you to such degradation again, Stephanie," he said quietly. "You deserve so much more."

Swiftly, he eased himself out of the narrow bed and pulled the coverlet over her. The bed was still warm from his body, and this was the bed he had chosen for himself, but he left her in it and crossed to the other one, where the bedding still held the chill of clean linen. She appreciated his thoughtfulness, but she mourned the fact that a ship's bunks were far too small to accommodate two people for very long.

Ross said good night, and blew out the light. A long while later, sleepless, Stephanie found herself wondering just how Gordon and Jeannie were managing. They were so blatantly in love, so eager for each other, and she doubted whether either of them would find any problem in sharing a bed that was far too small.

The next morning, she discovered that Ross was already awake and dressed before her. At some time, their steward had left a breakfast tray outside their door, and Ross was already pouring out tea when she struggled to open her eyes. For a minute or two she couldn't think where she was, feeling the odd motion beneath her suddenly disturbing. She sat up in the bed, looked down at herself and gasped at the sight of her nakedness. Quickly, she pulled the coverlet up to her neck, disregarding Ross's amused glance at the action. Memories of the previous night flooded into her mind, and she could hardly bear to look at her husband.

According to his own words, he had degraded her, and she supposed that he had, and yet she knew there was a wildness in her soul that had responded to all that he asked of her. An eagerness for new experiences and sensations, that he had fulfilled.

In the life of the harem, perhaps it was degrading. For one man, however regal and privileged, to have a succession of women performing the supplicating, sexual acts that Ross had demanded of her last night, *was* degrading to western ideals. But for an adoring wife to participate and enjoy the acts of love in any form her husband chose was surely not wrong. No one had ever suggested there were any rules in love, other than fidelity. She might be young, but she had already worked that much out for herself.

"What's going through that brain of yours right now?" Ross said. "You've been staring at a speck on the porthole for the last five minutes."

She spoke quickly. "I was hoping you'd have the decency to leave me to dress in private once we've eaten. I feel silly with only the coverlet wrapped around me."

He burst out laughing. "Good God, woman, it's a little late for modesty, isn't it?"

Stephanie flushed. "Not at all. You must allow me some feminine privacy, Ross. It's part of a woman's mystery."

"All women are a mystery to men," he said good-humoredly. "But you're probably right. We'll eat the toast and preserves and then I'll take a turn on deck for half an hour. Will that be long enough for your titivating?"

"That will be adequate, thank you," she said, refusing to rise to the bait of implied vanity.

She couldn't eat much breakfast anyway. The excitement of the voyage, the start of a brilliant new morning with the sun streaming in through the grimy porthole, was making her eager to be up and about. She had never been one for wasting half the day in bed, despite the fact that a young lady of quality wasn't expected to be alert in the mornings.

But in half an hour, she had washed and dressed and attended to her hair. She didn't need the attentions of a maid, either, having always scorned the need for a second person to do what she could do perfectly well for herself. Once they reached Shaladd, she knew things would be different. There, she would have to accept the hospitality of Prince Hali Ahmed, and, according to Ross, there would be servants to attend to her every whim.

Far from pleasing her, it made her feel more claustrophobic than even this small cabin. She even began to think of the voyage as the last stage of freedom before being swallowed up in a strange new world and she tried to shake off the feeling, knowing it was absurd. For hadn't Ross told her repeatedly that he would show her fabulous things, the like of which she couldn't even imagine? And most women would be enchanted to be waited on hand and foot.

But it was impossible to rid herself of uneasy thoughts, and she turned thankfully when Ross reentered the cabin. On an impulse, she ran to him and caught at his hands.

"I was afraid," she said simply at his startled look. "I don't know what will be expected of me, and I'm sure I shall do many things to displease you. I ask you to be patient with me, Ross."

He folded her in his arms, and her rapid heartbeats were steadied by the nearness of his body.

"Just be yourself, and everyone will be charmed by you. You'll be a shining jewel among all the rest, my darling. And there's no reason for you to afraid, because I'll always be there beside you. Remember that, Stephanie. You'll never be alone again."

Never? She longed to say the word, but she dared not. Not while he was being so considerate and so gentle with her.

She leaned against him briefly, and she felt his hand smooth her hair.

Why couldn't it be love that he felt for her? she thought passionately. *Why couldn't they have met under other circumstances, and not beneath the shadow of a gambling wager?*

"Are you ready for a stroll around the deck?" he said more briskly. "Our new friends are already up and about, but you'll need something around your shoulders, because the air is quite fresh."

So the sweet, poignant moments were over. Stephanie reached for a shawl from the cabin closet, and allowed Ross to place it around her shoulders. She thought she felt the touch of his lips on the nape of her neck, but she couldn't be sure. Instead, she told herself that she mustn't expect too much. He had married her to suit his purpose. She had accepted it, however grievously it insulted her, and she must just try to enjoy the traveling experiences and adventures, and not ask for anything more. The thoughts were noble enough, but she wasn't at all sure that she could live up to them.

Once the ship had left English shores, the voyage closely followed the coasts of France, Spain, and Portugal, through the straits of Gibraltar and into the Mediterranean Sea, steaming steadily onward to the Egyptian port of Alexandria. As they voyaged, the air became steadily hotter and drier, and the sun was a constant golden orb in a cloudless blue sky.

As the ship began to edge into their final destination, the passengers crowded onto the deck for their first glimpse of the city, with its tall, thin minarets soaring skyward among the lesser buildings and meaner dwellings. Only in the center was there any real sense of an important city. What struck Stephanie most of all was not so much the sights as the smells, in the overpowering yellow dust-laden heat. Some were decidedly unpleasant, but permeating all was the aromatic aroma of spices bound for foreign parts. Their perfume hung heavily on the air, enticing and exotic.

By now, the two young couples on board had become firm friends, but as if by silent agreement, they made no plans to renew their acquaintance at a later date. They would go their separate ways once the Kilmarrons disembarked at Alexandria, while the Frasers traveled farther on their Grand Tour. But as they made their farewells, Stephanie knew she was going to miss the companionship of another young woman.

"Never mind. I shall look forward to seeing your illustrations in the book Ross is going to write," Jeannie told her. "And I shall feel as proud as Gordon to be able to tell my friends I knew you both."

"We'll be sure to send you a copy," Ross replied.

And then there was no more time for hugs and handshakes, for the Alexandria passengers were already starting to leave the ship. The dockside was alive with dark-skinned workers in long, flowing robes, hurrying and scurrying with baggage and offers of help, along with dozens of small, huge-eyed children, all frantically stretching out their hands toward the affluent Europeans.

"Baksheesh . . . baksheesh . . . baksheesh . . ."

The same cry seemed to emerge from every throat, and Stephanie asked Ross quickly what the children were saying.

"They ask for gifts," he said shortly. "They're beggars—"

"Oh, but shouldn't we help them?" Stephanie said at once, and he put his hand firmly on her arm.

"If you offer a gift to one, you risk having a thousand more on your heels. It's best to ignore them, believe me. Resist their appeals at all costs."

To Stephanie, it seemed heartless, but at the teeming throngs of children converging on the arrival of the ship from every entrance to the dockside now, she allowed that he was probably right. She averted her eyes from the closest children, snatching her skirt away as small hands clutched at it. She was suddenly frightened by the sheer mass of them.

"Away!" Ross shouted at them, and then shouted louder in words she didn't understand, but which the children clearly did. It didn't deter them completely, but with the help of several baggage carriers, they managed to push their way through the crowds to a small hooded carriage, pulled by a miserable-looking donkey.

"My brother, he takes you to your hotel, Sidi," the man said, obviously proud of his broken English. "The name of it, if it pleases you."

"The Cleopatra," Ross said shortly. "And as quick as you can, man."

"Of course, of course." The first man stood with his bare foot on the board of the carriage, his hand on the donkey's reins, and clearly not intending to move until Ross had given him a *baksheesh*. Ross flung some coins in the man's direction, and he leapt away at once, to disappear into the crowd, having no further interest in them.

The carriage lurched forward, its large wooden wheels doing nothing to lessen the discomfort of the journey between the port and the hotel. Stephanie clung to Ross for dear life, certain that their baggage was about to be flung into the crowd, and that she would never see any of her belongings again. Her mouth was full of dust, and she coughed and spluttered, holding her hand across the lower half of her face.

"It will be better once we're away from the port," Ross told her. "The driver is taking a shortcut, but I promise you the hotel is the cleanest and best in the city."

She couldn't answer right away, wondering just what standard of cleanliness was applicable here. Already, she was appalled by what she was seeing as they trundled through the rough tracks that passed for back streets. Groups of male Arabs sat huddled in doorways, seemingly doing nothing, while dark-clothed women sat outside their hovels peeling vegetables in the sunlight.

In the streets themselves, dogs ran wild, and there was excrement everywhere. There was no sweet aroma of spices in this area, only the stink of filth, and a vicious mixture of unwashed bodies and stale vegetation.

"What have you brought me to, Ross?" Stephanie gasped, the bile rising in her mouth at the sight of a raddled old man spitting and hawking into the street.

His arm slid around her shoulders, holding her tight.

"The damn driver should never have come this way," he said angrily, "but it's not far now. Look above the rooftops and you'll see a large building ahead of us. That's the Cleopatra Hotel. We'll be meeting some of our English team there tomorrow."

The building he pointed out looked large and solid enough, and a world away from the mean hovels through which they were passing now. Stephanie had never thought herself a snob, but she felt the strongest urge to draw in her skirts as far away from these people as possible, and she had to pinch her nostrils to keep out their smells. She was ashamed at the thought, but she could no more help it than she could stop breathing. She was not one of these people, and never could be, and the great adventure was becoming more of a nightmare by the minute.

And this was only her first initiation into Egyptian life! Was she completely spineless? she asked herself. Then, for a moment, a suspicion ran through her mind—had Ross known all along that the driver would bring them through these dingy places? Had he even instructed him to do so, to alarm her and to make her appreciate the stark contrast between here and the lush, oasis princedom of Shaladd? It might be a foolish suspicion, but it wasn't allayed by the fact that Ross could converse so fluently in the Arab tongue. He could be saying anything and she would never know.

She sat silently for the remainder of the journey, simply closing her eyes to everything else that they passed, clamping her mouth shut and refusing to acknowledge the smells that assaulted her. She didn't even notice when the movement beneath the carriage wheels became less bumpy, or that they had entered a moderately wide street. It was only when the motion of the carriage stopped altogether that she opened her eyes cautiously.

She gasped again, but with relief this time. Up close, the hotel was far more splendid than she could have imagined, built of red brick and with white marble colonnades at the front entrance. White-robed hotel staff came hurrying down the steps as soon as the carriage stopped, and greeted Ross warmly in English.

"Welcome back, Sidi Captain Kilmarron. It's good news to be seeing you again," one of them said.

"And you, Calid," Ross answered. "And I've brought my wife with me this time."

Stephanie stepped out of the carriage with his help, and smiled faintly at the Arab. During the entire voyage she had had no hint of motion sickness, but this short ride in that awful carriage was threatening to make her disgrace herself. Mentally, she kept a rigid hold on the contents of her stomach.

"It's an honor to meet you, Saïda Captain," Calid said gravely. "You honor our humble hotel with your beauty."

"Thank you," she murmured, wishing only that they could go inside out of the heat. Her head throbbed, and she longed to immerse herself in a long, refreshing bath—if the hotel had such a thing.

She soon discovered that it did, and that Ross hadn't lied to her about the Cleopatra's comforts. The hotel staff were well used to European visitors and their requirements. Their room was light and airy, with an adjoining bathroom, and considering that this was Egypt where everything moved at a leisurely pace, they settled into their temporary abode in a remarkably short time.

By the time they descended to the dining room for dinner that evening, Stephanie's fears were lulled into the background, and the growing sense of adventure was back. After all, this was the experience of a lifetime, and she was sharing it with her husband. It was a thought to lift her spirits more than any other since they had landed in Alexandria.

Seven

That night, they slept as soon as their heads touched the pillows. For Stephanie it was sheer bliss to lie in a proper bed again, one with cool white sheets and the width to accommodate two people cozily but comfortably, instead of the cramped quarters of the ship's cabin. When she awoke next morning, she stretched leisurely, and her hand encountered bare flesh. She went to snatch it back, but Ross's hand captured hers and kept it stilled on the taut expanse of his broad chest.

"Why so modest, my sweet?" he said softly. "This is hardly the way for a bride to behave, now that she's known the sweet fruits of love."

The words were strangely formulated, and to Stephanie's ears it was almost as though he was again absorbing the flowery speech of a desert prince. She gave a small shiver, wondering anew just what she was letting herself in for in allowing her whole self to be so enveloped in this man's life. Was she completely mad?

She realized how close his face was to hers. She could feel his breath on her cheek, warm and caressing. She could see his eyes, dark and hot with a passion that she sensed he was holding in restraint. She could feel the trembling inside her as his free hand moved seductively down the length of her body over her nightgown, pausing in all the right places to make her tingle and all her senses were suddenly on fire, anticipating the loving that could be sweet or savage, and was just as exciting either way.

Ross's mouth covered hers in a demanding kiss, while his palm rested lightly over the part of her that most craved his attention. She felt her lips part, as though that other part of her was repeating the action, but she quickly realized that the loving was not to be. Not now, in the comparatively cooler morning air of the shady hotel bedroom, and she was conscious of a swift disappointment.

"Much as I would love to ravish you right now, sweetheart, I have other commitments," Ross said reluctantly. "You may languish in bed all morning if you wish, but some of my team will be arriving during the morning, and will expect me to be alert, and not drowsy from too much loving."

Stephanie was very tempted to say that in her experience of him, he was never drowsy after loving. *Invigorated* was more the word she would use, but it would be unseemly for her to say as much. For a moment, she wondered if normal brides in normal marriages felt less inhibited than she did. As the thought came into her head, she felt herself blush. Inhibited in passion she was not, as she and Ross had both discovered! But in words . . . Oh, yes, in words, she still held back something of herself.

"I shall not languish in bed all morning," she said somewhat crossly, annoyed at the image of the pampered young lady he suggested. "If we are to be in Alexandria for so short a time, I would prefer to see something of the city—"

She gave a small cry as his hand clamped over her wrist. He was never aware of his own strength, she thought fearfully, nor how those strong masculine hands could bruise a woman's delicate skin. Or maybe he was, she thought with a shiver.

"You will obey my instructions, and not leave the hotel without me to accompany you, Stephanie. It's not safe for an English woman to venture out alone, and I would prefer not to have to chase halfway across the desert to bring you back from any barbarians who think you a luscious prize to capture."

She stared at him for a moment, wondering if he could possibly be serious. And because it all sounded so unlikely, she laughed out loud. Somehow she managed to shake off his restraining hand, and rubbed at her tender wrist.

"How melodramatic you make it all sound! Barbarians in the midst of a city, indeed—"

"Don't take my words lightly, Stephanie," Ross snapped. "I know this country, and while many places might be perfectly safe, others are not, and a city is no less a dangerous place because it has fine hotels and wide streets."

"You needn't tell me that," she muttered. "I saw some of them yesterday, didn't I?"

The remembered smells of that shuddering ride from the ship to the Cleopatra Hotel could still make her nauseous.

"Then think well of the narrow winding alleyways that seemed to disappear into darkness. And think well that you're a novelty here, a prize that many an unscrupulous Arab gentleman would welcome into his abode. And don't think that all villains are foreigners. There have been tales of young English girls vanishing off the face of the earth, after an apparently eager young Englishman has offered to escort them around the city. You will steer very clear of strangers, Stephanie. I insist on it."

He spoke at such length, and with such authority in his voice that she could only nod dumbly. He evoked such a feeling of terror in her that she would as soon rush straight back to the haven of the *Princess Maria*, and be taken back to England. But there were reasons why she could not, of course. For one, the ship was continuing on its voyage for those passengers taking the Grand Tour and for another, Ross would never allow such a thing to ruin his plan of producing a wife for the benefit of Prince Hali Ahmed and the most vital of all was because she couldn't bear to be apart from him now.

He had moved away from the bed, and she watched him go to the adjoining bathroom, lithe and handsome, and her heart swelled with love for him. At the same time, it was sweet torture to be so much in love with him, when she knew very well he had only married her because she suited his purposes. She was constantly frustrated by the knowledge.

It was a mockery to Stephanie that her own beauty, acknowledged by so many others, and destined to bring her abiding happiness in marriage, was the one thing that had condemned her to a liaison with a man who didn't love her. Presumably this desert prince, who knew Ross so well, would never have accepted a bride who wasn't as beautiful as his English friend deserved.

"Don't look so downcast," Ross threw over his shoulder, on hearing her involuntary sigh. "You may take as long as you like to attend to your toilette, and then take a stroll around the hotel grounds or explore the fine library here for the relaxation of visitors. You needn't be bored, my dear, and once my initial business is done, I shall find you and you may meet our companions for the journey down the Nile."

It would sound pleasant enough—if she were fifty years old and a spinster companion accompanying a magnetic personality abroad. Sometimes that was exactly how she felt, she thought irritably, no more than a useful addition to a flamboyant gentleman's entourage. She would feel it even more, knowing she was to be the only woman traveling to Shaladd with his expeditionary team.

She pushed aside her uneasy thoughts and sprang out of bed. No fifty-year-old rheumatics for her! She walked across to the window, and drew back the drapes to peer through the slats of the shutters. The day was spectacularly beautiful, their room overlooking gardens where fountains played and exotic blooms filled the scene with vivid color. She ached to sketch it all. She felt her spirits lift, and knew how foolish she was to be on such a seesaw of emotions. She was here, and nothing could change that. She was with Ross, whom she loved, she finally admitted, and nothing could change that either. And the future could take care of itself.

An hour later, she was strolling through the fragrant gardens of the Cleopatra Hotel and breathing in the scents of highly perfumed flowers and shrubs that were new to her. Her parasol shielded her from the rapidly advancing heat of the day, which was pleasantly tempered by the cool spray of water from the fountains. In the small round lake at the foot of each one, brilliantly hued fish darted among the green water foliage like golden rays of sunlight.

It was hard to believe that the hotel was in the middle of a teeming Egyptian city, for its atmosphere was calm and quiet, and reassuring. If the palace of Shaladd was even one iota more luxurious and exotic than this, Stephanie thought, it would be paradise indeed.

She felt a small leap of her heart as she heard her name being called in a voice she didn't recognize, and knew that despite her apparent calm, she was still aware of Ross's warnings to her. She turned quickly, and then smiled with relief as she saw one of the young Arab duty boys of the hotel walking toward her. He bowed effusively.

"Please pardon this interruption into your reverie, Saida Kilmarron," he said, with obvious pride in his carefully rehearsed English. "Your husband requests that you join him in the tea lounge forthwith. It will be my pleasure to show you the way."

"Thank you," Stephanie murmured, thinking she would far rather have lingered in the garden, or visited the hotel library that she hadn't yet had time to investigate. But she recognized a command when she heard it, and knew she must follow the young duty boy into the hotel once more.

As he stood aside for her to enter the tea lounge, she saw Ross in animated conversation with two European men, and she felt her heart give an unexpected stab of jealousy. For, from now on, their intimate honeymoon would be at an end, and these strangers would accompany them wherever they went.

The expedition was Ross's real reason for being here, of course, but for a while it had been easy to forget that. It had been even easier, at times, to forget their reasons for marrying, and to let herself believe that theirs was one of those idyllic happy-ever-afters that romantic young girls dreamed about.

But maybe this was the real Ross after all, she thought. This vital man, so rapt in the sketches and plans the other two were demonstrating to him now, so much a part of this male preserve of adventure-lust, and so apart from her.

Stephanie stepped forward, wanting to break into their closeness, even while she hated herself for being so foolish. She spoke with an imperiousness that would have made her sneering stepbrother proud of her.

"You sent for me, I believe—sir?"

Ross looked up from the papers spread out in front of him at the table, and a little warning look came into his eyes. Or perhaps she had imagined it, for it was gone in an instant, and he was moving swiftly toward her, drawing her into the circle, his arm loosely around her waist.

"I requested your presence, sweetheart, since it must be all of an hour since I last saw you," he said easily, with all the teasing nuances of the new husband. She saw the smiling glances of his companions, and sensed at once that they had known nothing of Ross's own plan to bring back a wife to Shaladd. She must be a great shock to them.

She began to believe that Ross had not even considered such an outrageous plan himself until the time drew nearer for him to return to the oasis. And that his plan hadn't been truly formed until he had been winning handsomely at Lord Buchan's gambling tables, and seen the comely features of his stepdaughter.

But however shyly she faced the fact that these large, sunburned men would all see her as the new, blushing bride, it was far preferable than having them know the truth. She couldn't have borne that. In a moment of devilment, she traced her finger down Ross's cheek, her eyes dancing mischievously at him as she answered him in like manner.

"Sixty-five minutes to be exact, my love, and never has the time passed more slowly."

She felt his fingers press into her waist and she gave a little gasp. The strangers might believe that this was a private, intimate little moment on the part of newlyweds, but she knew Ross was well aware that she was mocking him.

"Come and meet your traveling companions," he said more briskly, and the moment was over. She turned in some relief to the burly men, whom she acknowledged as Mac and Dawson. She couldn't be sure whether these were first names or surnames, but since they both addressed her as Ma'am, it didn't seem necessary to ask.

"We'd like to offer our congratulations to you and the captain, ma'am," the one called Mac said expansively. "We were certain sure he'd find himself a wife one of these days, and if it ain't a liberty to say so, I reckon he's done well for himself."

The other man agreed with nods and mutters, and Stephanie sat down awkwardly, wishing they'd just get the formalities over and behave more naturally. Though she couldn't be sure how the presence of one woman was going to affect their previous relationship. For the first time she wondered if Ross had been so wise after all, in bringing a wife on the expedition.

With relief, she saw the duty boy bring in the tray of tea and thin, spiced wafer biscuits. He poured the brew for each of them into the tea glasses, offering them sugar or lemon, but no milk. At Stephanie's look, Ross spoke a mote impatiently.

"You should try it with one or the other, love. You'll find it refreshing. You may even prefer to take iced tea."

"I will not! Tea is meant to be made with boiling water and left to brew for the proper amount of time, not served up as cold as charity!" she said without thinking.

The men grinned. Dawson drawled his agreement. "Just what my old mother used to say, ma'am. But you may have heard the saying that when you're in Rome, it's best to do as the Romans do."

But they were not in Rome, and she ignored the man as she asked the duty boy to bring her a small jug of cold milk.

"You'll not find milk in the desert, ma'am, unless you've a mind to milk a camel or two," Dawson added.

Stephanie shuddered at the thought, and stubbornly refused to drink the glass of pale-colored tea until the jug of milk was ceremoniously brought to her. She thanked the duty boy, and poured the required amount in her glass herself. The taste was a little odd, but that could be due to anything—the brand of tea, the water, or the fact that it probably hadn't been boiled or brewed properly in the first place. Only when she had drunk a quantity of it did Ross inquire how she liked camel's milk.

It wasn't ladylike to splutter, but she had a job to avoid it right then. She glowered at him, well aware that the others were hiding sympathetic smiles at her discomfiture.

"Why didn't you warn me? Is that what this is then?" she said, realizing that there was a sweetness in the tea that couldn't be attributed to sugar, since she didn't care to take too much of it.

Ross gave a sudden laugh. "Oh, Stephanie, you're too beautifully gullible, and I'm too cruel."

"What do you mean by that?" she almost snapped.

"It's not camel's milk, my love," he said, far too smoothly. "They don't serve camel's milk in good hotels."

"Thank goodness for that!"

"It's goat's milk," he said calmly, and she clattered the glass down on its little saucer, just as affronted.

"My dear Ma'am, I'm afraid you'll need to get used to

all kinds of different tastes in Egypt," the man Dawson said. "You won't always get the sort of refinements you're used to in England, except at Shaladd, of course. But the captain will have told you all about that, I daresay."

She decided she didn't care for him much. He said more than Mac, and he didn't seem particularly well educated, yet he managed to sound superior in everything he said. He made her feel that she knew nothing—and as far as Egypt went, it was perfectly true. But it didn't help her equilibrium to know that he was well aware of it.

"Have you finished your business?" she said coolly to Ross. "I'd like to take a look in the library if you don't mind. I find I'm not in the mood for tea-drinking after all."

"We've near enough finished," he said. "You can have about half an hour, and then we'll be on our way."

Stephanie stared at him. "Today, you mean? Are we moving right away? I thought we'd be staying at the hotel for a few days. At least I thought we were going to see something of Alexandria!"

"We're not here for sightseeing, Stephanie, and the sooner we start on the next part of our journey, the better."

She felt cheated and annoyed. He didn't give her time to draw breath—not that breath was easy to draw in the stifling atmosphere of this country. And this was only the northern tip of it. Heaven help her when they went south, and into the desert. She thought wistfully of Gordon and Jeannie Fraser, continuing by ship on their leisurely Grand Tour. She envied them so much. Why couldn't fate have decreed that she and Ross could have been another pair of voyaging lovers?

"Then I'd best find the library at once, or I shan't even be allowed the time to open a single book," she said, with barely contained sarcasm.

She turned and left the men to their refreshment, still with the sweet, tangy taste of goat's milk in her mouth. She didn't find it altogether unpalatable, but it was different, and it took time to adjust to different tastes.

Still ruffled, she reflected that it took time to adjust to being married as well, and to appreciate the feelings and opinions of another person. She didn't think Captain Kilmarron had taken any of that into consideration when he'd got the wildly preposterous idea to take a wife back to Shaladd, fully intending to dispose of her afterward.

She felt her heart give a more uncomfortable lurch now, and wished those exact words hadn't entered her head. For, of course, he was too much of an English gentleman to cast her out in the cold, or *dispose* of her in the way an unscrupulous villain would. He must have wanted her a little.

Stephanie caught her breath, as the pictures in her mind suddenly swept through her. Oh, yes, there was no doubt that there were times when he wanted her and hungered for her, and when he couldn't resist a man's need for a woman. But she was convinced that he didn't love her. Otherwise, he would surely have said so by now. She reasoned it out with the young, innocent reasoning of a girl who had never been in love before, suffused with frustration at not having everything spelled out in black and white.

"I won't think about him anymore," she muttered crossly to herself, putting a well-used childhood dismissal into operation. If he didn't love her, then she simply wouldn't love him!

She pushed open the door to the hotel's small, airy library, ruefully aware that in the world of adult emotions, such childish pettiness had little effect. But for a while, at least, she would forget everything but the joy of being surrounded with the musty, distinctive aroma of books and the clean, pungent smell of leather armchairs. Here were books in several languages, for the pleasure of the Cleopatra's guests, and with a sense of anticipation, Stephanie took down an English-language, illustrated book of Egypt's treasures.

As she opened the pages, the ancient pyramids suddenly

came to life for her, as did the temples, and the fantastic mazelike interiors of the tombs. The weird hieroglyphic writing adorning every wall was explained in careful detail. But what attracted Stephanie most were the drawings on the temple and tomb walls, depicted in vivid color in the pages of the book, each sequence telling a story of gods and goddesses, kings and queens, sons and daughters, and burial rites.

Such things had always fascinated her, and she had never thought to see any of it for herself. Thanks to Ross she would do so, and she felt a deep gratitude to him for that, despite his own devious reasons for bringing her here. Without him, she would never have been on the brink of this marvelous adventure, and her spirit began to revive.

With it came the urge to use her own artistic gifts and draw these exotic Egyptian women, painting in the gorgeous kohl-rimmed slanting eyes and curving figures, adorned in the beautiful bronze colors that seemed to be favorite, and especially the heavy, beautifully elaborate jewelry and headdresses.

To Stephanie, the illustrations were incredibly sensual, and since they were said to be a true representation of the finds in the temples and tombs, those ancient women were presumably just as sensual. Or at least that was the way the artists had seen them. She found herself wondering about those times. It was a world she couldn't even dream about, and yet still a world where men and women made love, had children, died and mourned. Times changed, but human emotions remained the same.

She was so lost in her reverie that it was only when a dark shadow fell across the page of the book that she looked up with a start to find Ross gazing down at her.

"Are you planning to sit here all day?" he said with a smile that was neither condemning nor mocking. "What have you found that intrigues you so much?"

She wanted to share her joy with him, even though he

would have seen it all before. She wanted him to feel her elation at the thought of touching those ancient walls, painted thousands of years ago, by some artist who would never know that a young lady living in Queen Victoria's England acknowledged the love of his craft and envied it.

She looked at him with shining eyes and showed him the page of the book where the goddess Isis stood in profile, dressed in a glittering sheath of gold cloth.

"Isn't she beautiful? Oh, Ross, I can't wait to see it all. She and her brother Osiris look so perfect together, and the story about them says that they once ruled Egypt as king and queen."

"You should have read on a little more, my sweet, and learned of the incestuous relationship between your perfect god and goddess, and the evils of their brother."

Stephanie felt her face flush. "What incestuous relationship?" she asked, hating him for ruining her pleasure.

Ross sat on the arm of her chair, turned a few pages in the book and pointed to a far more aggressive-looking male figure with a mask over his head. He carried a dagger in one hand and a long spear in the other.

"This is Set, the brother of the other pair, and the god of deserts, storms, and war, and a very nasty individual. He murdered Osiris and cut his body into pieces." He paused as she flinched. "Shall I go on?"

"Why not?" Stephanie said. "You've spoiled everything for me now."

Ross shrugged. "I just don't want you to get a false idea of it all. Anyway, I'm surprised you haven't read the gruesome details in the book already."

"I've been studying the illustrations—and before you say I'm not intelligent enough to read the text, I've been studying them with an artist's eye. You *do* want me to sketch things for you eventually, I believe?"

"That was part of our arrangement. And I wouldn't dream

of calling you unintelligent," he said with a grin. "So, do you want to hear a bit more before we join the others?"

"Yes."

Anything to keep him by her side, she thought. Anything to have him leaning toward her, one arm loosely around her shoulders, the warmth of his thigh against her shoulder. She could even rest her arm on his upper leg if she dared—but she didn't dare. Instead, she listened intently as he told her more of the story of these strange god-people.

"Osiris and Isis had a son, Horus, which involves the incestuousness relationship, though the ancient Egyptians saw nothing wrong in their brother and sister gods and goddesses mating, since it kept the line pure of human influence."

Stephanie had never heard this kind of talk before, and she was very glad there were no other listeners in the small library that morning.

"After Set killed Osiris, Horus fought and defeated his uncle Set, spearing him from his boat, since Set had by now disguised himself as a hippopotamus—"

Before he could go on, Stephanie had begun to laugh.

"This is a fairy tale," she protested. "I can't believe a word of it!"

He took his arm from around her shoulder, and turned the page of the book until he found the illustrative drawing, with the caption beneath saying exactly what Ross had said. Her eyes met his in disbelief, and he spoke quietly.

"Don't argue with things you can't disprove or understand, Stephanie. And especially don't mock the ancient ways of Egypt while you're at Shaladd. Every man has a right to his beliefs, and these illustrations don't depict ordinary mortals. They're gods and goddesses, and it's still believed by many that they could transform themselves at will."

"And do you believe it?" she asked, wondering how anyone with a Christian background could be so gullible.

"What was written in stone can hardly be ignored," he said without giving her a direct answer. "I'm merely relating an ancient story to you, and since you'll assuredly hear many more, I'm advising you to act with caution in the country of your hosts."

"Well then, if Set came to an untimely end as a hippopotamus," she said, finding it hard to keep a straight face as the imagery filled her mind, "what happened next?"

He looked down at her thoughtfully. "I'm not sure that I should tell you any more."

His tone annoyed her. She felt an impatient urge to stamp her feet as she had done as a child, when grown-ups had a secret that they considered her too young to understand. And she wanted to know now. She had every right to know, if only so that she didn't make a terrible faux pas at Shaladd, and she said as much. Ross gave a small smile, as though he had known very well she would want to hear the rest of it, she thought suspiciously.

"Forget about Set for now. The important god in all this was Osiris, who was one of ancient Egypt's most popular and influential gods. So into the story now comes Anubis, the god of embalming."

This time, Stephanie's stomach balked. She knew she shouldn't have pursued this, but Ross went on relentlessly.

"Anubis helped to collect the pieces of Osiris's body, fitting them together again and bringing him back to life—"

"I don't want to hear any more," she said immediately.

She jumped up from her chair, afraid that at any minute there would be some other horrible tale connected with Anubis, the embalming god. She gave a great shudder, and felt Ross's arms around her.

"I've frightened you, and I'm sorry," he said. "But you seemed so intrigued by it all, and you need to know that not everything in ancient Egypt was beautiful, any more than life is now. Everything has its ugly side, Stephanie."

"Even Shaladd?" she said, staring at him with wide, unblinking eyes.

He shrugged again. "I suggest you let Shaladd speak for

itself," he said, which told her nothing. "But we've spent enough time in here, and we should prepare to leave. I'm sure you'll want to return to our room to refresh yourself first."

The restraining hand that she put on his arm suddenly trembled.

"Ross," she said, a world of pleading in a voice that was newly husky. "It will be all right, won't it?"

Although they were in a public place, they were as isolated from the rest of the hotel as it was possible to be, here among the rows of bookshelves. He cupped her face in his hands and tipped it up to meet his own. He bent and kissed her lips, and it was a kiss as sweet as summer. And she told herself how pathetic and guileless she must be, if such an innocent kiss could stir her heartstrings so much.

"Everything will be all right, and you will always have my protection," he said.

But from the stiffness in his voice, she couldn't help remembering how his first intention had been to hire an actress for the role of his wife.

Whatever tenderness he showed her could well be no more than acting on his part, too, since he had to convince Prince Hali that they were lovers as well as husband and wife—and she would be wise not to forget it. And she shouldn't forget, either, that he had found something special in her, since she had been a virgin when they wed. Whatever she owed him for the chance of an adventure, he owed her far more. And he had still not said that he loved her, she thought wanly.

There were sounds of other guests approaching the library, and his arms dropped to his sides as he led the way out of the room and into the marble foyer of the hotel. Their traveling companions were seated, quietly discussing the journey ahead of them.

"We'll be with you directly," Ross told them. "Have you arranged for transport to take us to the river, Mac?"

He nodded. "It's all taken care of, Captain. As soon as you say the word, we can leave."

Stephanie wondered again just how much the two of them had known of Ross's intention to find a wife quickly. And the reasons for it. Were they aware that he would have been offered six wives on this visit, and that it would have been a gross insult to refuse? And if so, were they also aware that she had been married in haste, not only to a man who didn't love her, but who had won her hand in a wager? It was too burningly humiliating to think about, and also something she simply couldn't get out of her mind.

The moment they reached their room, she rounded on her husband. By now, their main baggage had been taken down, and all that remained there was her small personal toilet bag, her bonnet, little lightweight cloak, and parasol.

"How much do they know?" she demanded at once.

"About what?" he asked to her fury, when she knew very well he must guess at once what she meant.

"You know what! Are they aware of the circumstances of our—our farce of a marriage?"

"Is that what you call it?" he asked.

"What else should I call it?" she cried, suddenly hurt beyond measure at his seemingly careless attitude. "You don't love me, and I was brought up to believe in the sanctity of marriage, and that those who married did so for love, and with the intention of having children—"

She stopped, seeing the sudden amusement in his eyes. He brought her hands swiftly to his lips, and smiled wickedly into her eyes.

"If it's children you want, my dearest, it will be my pleasure to gratify your whim at the earliest opportunity. In fact, if we weren't in such a hurry right now—"

"That's not what I meant!" she said, hot with embarrassment. As she snatched her hands away from him, he turned to fetch her belongings from the wall closet and handed them to her.

And she hadn't missed the mocking note in his voice when he mentioned wanting children. Of course he wouldn't want her to have a child if his intention was to abandon her once this trip was over. He had merely said it because he thought it was she wanted to hear.

And so she did, of course, she realized. She might not have thought of it until this very minute, but in any normal marriage, children were the fruit of a couple's love. The urge to bear Ross's child was as primitive as the urge to weep in frustration, knowing that their circumstances were very far removed from that of any normal marriage. It was something else she shouldn't allow herself to forget.

Eight

The transport was nothing like Stephanie had expected, but she was fast beginning to accept that this was to be a continual journey of surprises. It consisted of a large cart, with thinly upholstered seats for the passengers, and a seat for the driver at the front. There was a space at the rear for the assorted luggage of the four passengers, and the vehicle was drawn by a team of scrawny-looking horses.

The whole thing looked highly uncomfortable to Stephanie, and as the day progressed it proved to be so, especially as there was only a canvas cover above them to keep out the heat and glare of the sun, and she was still obliged to keep her parasol open at all times to keep from fainting clean away.

But in an amazingly short time they had left the winding alleyways and environs of Alexandria behind them, and ahead of them there seemed to be nothing but vast, open desert scrub. Away in the distance, and appearing to go on endlessly southward, were what looked like mountains, but Ross told her they were no more than desert dunes.

"How long is this going to take?" she muttered through dry lips, when they had been traveling for several hours, and seemed to be getting nowhere.

She couldn't imagine how the driver knew where he was going, for there seemed to be no proper route at all. Occasionally they passed another vehicle, usually a broken-down affair with a dozing Arab driver seated astride a plodding donkey. There were sometimes small groups of Arabs on foot or leading laden camels, and Stephanie wondered in some horror if they were planning to walk the entire distance between Alexandria and the Nile River.

Sometimes a lone donkey would appear, heavily laden with bundles of reeds across its back, and the Arab driving him on with a whack of his stick would wave cheerily to them, and shriek out a greeting in Arabic. But by now, Stephanie was simply too fatigued to comment. In any case, Ross had already told her not to respond to any greetings, since it wasn't a woman's place to do so. She was beginning to think uneasily that women had little place in this wilderness at all.

Ross answered her question briefly. "With luck we should reach a small village fairly near to the river by sundown, where we'll stay for the night, and then we'll transfer to the felucca at first light."

"And where do we stay in the village? Or are you planning for us to sleep in the cart all night?"

It wouldn't surprise her. Nothing would surprise her now, or so she thought.

"Not at all. We'll stay at the house of an old friend of mine."

"An Englishman?" she asked hopefully.

Ross smiled sympathetically as she passed a weary hand over her brow. "I'm afraid not, but you'll find Omar and his wife very agreeable. You should try not to be quite so insular, my dear. There are rogues in this world, even among Englishmen."

It was on the tip of her tongue to tell him she knew that only too well, for wasn't she sitting beside a prize rogue at this very moment! But she bit back the words, knowing it would only stir up the interest of their three companions if she were to denounce her husband so shamefully.

But she wouldn't always be so reticent, she vowed. She

was no wilting violet to be overpowered by a man's dominance—though a wilting violet probably described very well the way she was feeling now. She felt as if the heat was draining all her color away, and she found herself swaying with the motion of the cart, and leaning more and more against Ross's side.

She made no objection when his arm went around her, and she settled more comfortably into the lee of his body. And her eyes felt so heavy, she simply had to close them, and to let the parasol lie against her head in whatever ungainly way it would.

When she awoke, it was to find that the heat was a shade less fierce. She struggled to sit up straighter, stiff and awkward, and she pushed the bonnet back onto her head from where it had flopped over her face. She must look a terrible sight, she thought, giving in to a moment's vanity.

She couldn't see much for the dust that was swirling all around them as the horses pawed the ground. There were a few miserable-looking dwellings, and surely—yes, there was definitely a hint of moisture in the air. The river couldn't be too far away then. And when the dust cleared a little, she could see the welcome greenery that must also indicate a more fertile region than the desert.

"Have we arrived?" she said through parched lips.

"We have," Ross said. He jumped down easily from the cart as though he hadn't just sat through an endless journey, Stephanie thought irritably, while she was stiff and aching in every muscle. He turned to assist her, and she gazed around her in dismay. Was this—this *hovel*—the friend's house where they were to stay? It seemed as though it was. And before she could say more, their two companions had bidden them farewell until morning, and had disappeared from sight. Stephanie neither knew, nor cared, where they were to stay for the night. It couldn't be anywhere worse than this!

"Put your snobbish English eyes back in your head, my

sweet," she heard Ross say evenly as her face betrayed her feelings. "Remember that we're guests in this country, and if life here isn't the way we're used to living it, we must accept it graciously."

For a moment, Stephanie remembered the pampered life he visualized for her at Shaladd. There could surely be no greater contrast between there and this mean little place. But she took heed of his words, remembered her manners, and lifted her head high.

"I assure you I shan't let you down," she said. "And I'm looking forward to meeting your friend and his wife."

It would be good to talk with another woman, she realized. She was already missing Jeannie Fraser's company. Even as she thought it, she prayed that Omar's wife wouldn't be subjugated and veiled, like the few other Arab women she had seen so far. She gave a deep sigh, and stumbled slightly over the dusty ground. Ross wasn't there to hold her arm at that moment, as he was instructing the driver to unload their overnight baggage only.

"What's happening now?" she asked as the cart trundled away in a cloud of dust.

"Mac and Dawson will continue to the boat with all the baggage and ensure that our supplies and camel handlers will be ready from our local source when we touch land again. It will take us three days to reach Shaladd from the landing point, and we'll have Arab guides to escort us."

"Why couldn't we have traveled overland all the way from Alexandria?" she said, not understanding this logic.

Ross was holding her elbow now, and leading her toward the shabby-looking dwelling, while a grinning young urchin carried their overnight baggage and ran alongside.

"It's too dangerous a route regarding some of the desert tribes," he said simply. "It's far safer to sail down the Nile and take the safe route to Shaladd."

Her heart skipped a beat, but she took his word for it. She was too tired to argue anyway. She yearned for the comfort of a soft bed, but she doubted that there would be European home comforts in the dwelling they were approaching now. As they reached it, a handsome young Arab appeared at the door, his arms outstretched. To Stephanie's complete shock, he embraced Ross warmly, kissing him on both cheeks, and gabbling what was obviously a greeting to an old friend.

For several moments, the two of them spoke rapidly, and she might as well not have been there at all, Stephanie thought with growing annoyance. She was hot and tired, and right at this moment, she was being made to feel very much the inferior. When Ross finally made to include her, she was ready to snap at him, but the dig of his hand in her arm just enabled her to resist.

"My dear, this is my good friend, Omar, who bids you welcome to his humble abode."

The man gave a small bow, and spread his arms toward Stephanie. For a startled moment, she thought he was going to kiss her, too, but she should have known better, for of course, he would not do such a thing. He didn't touch her, and merely embraced the air.

"You are welcome, wife of my friend. Please, you will enter and take some refreshment, for you must be tired. My wife has prepared a bed for you, where you may retire when you have eaten, leaving my friend and myself to enjoy our talking."

It sounded very much as if she was going to be dismissed as soon as she'd had a meal, Stephanie thought indignantly, leaving the two men alone. She couldn't ever compare this journey to a real honeymoon, but in her eyes there were aspects of it that were becoming more ludicrous than companionable. But if the two men were to be closeted together for conversation, why couldn't she and the Egyptian wife do the same?

She soon discovered the reason. Minta didn't speak one word of English. Moreover, apart from a shy response to Ross's inquiry after her health and that of her father, said in

Arabic and English for Stephanie's benefit, the wife seemed to melt from their sight into a back room that was presumably the kitchen. A very strong smell of garlic and spices emanated from the room, and in a short time the meal was brought to the table.

It consisted of chicken pieces well marinated in a garlic sauce, with vegetables of various kinds, including carrots, turnips, and potatoes. There were others that Stephanie didn't recognize, but all were doused in the same thin garlic sauce. While she liked a little of the strong flavor, too much of it was starting to make her nauseous, and she found herself pushing the food around her plate.

"Eat it all," Ross said to her beneath his breath. "To refuse it is to insult your host."

And what if she were to vomit all over the place? she thought. Wouldn't that insult him even more? But she gritted her teeth and got down as much of the food as she could, more than relieved to wash it down with a light, heavenly-tasting concoction of honey, crushed fruit, and rose water, which Omar assured her would rest the throat and take away the taste of the garlic. Stephanie smiled weakly, praying that it was true.

"My wife will show you to your room," Omar said, once the meal was over and they had drunk their hot, bittersweet coffee. At once, Minta rose from her seat at the foot of the table and moved toward an inner sanctuary.

Stephanie followed her, as if in a dream. She wasn't really here, she thought dazedly. She was safely at home in her stepfather's house, and none of this was really happening. But she had to admit that the hovel wasn't a hovel inside. It was adequately comfortable, with many rugs on the floors and walls, and the soft light of lemon-scented oil lamps in every room.

And Minta was a sweet-faced young girl who could hardly have been more than fifteen years old. When she lifted her head briefly to look at Stephanie, her skin was smooth and golden, the dark eyes large and beautiful, and rimmed with kohl. Apart from her clothing, which was far more modest than the glittering sheaths depicted in the illustrations of the tomb paintings, she could have been a queen or a goddess— and at the thought, Stephanie knew that tiredness was letting her imagination run away with her.

"Thank you," she said when the girl indicated the rug-covered bed on which their overnight things had been placed. Minta inclined her head and made to leave, and Stephanie stopped her quickly. "Oh please don't go. I'm sure we can talk somehow. Won't you stay a while?"

The girl looked at her blankly, shook her head, and glided out of the room as silently as she had entered it. Stephanie felt completely isolated and frustrated, and it was a far from pleasant feeling. Though she had to admit it would have been very difficult trying to carry on a one-sided conversation, and she was probably better alone.

But she didn't want to be alone. She wanted Ross, and she didn't like this feeling of being pushed into the background in a man's world. It wasn't what she had been used to in the home of an English gentleman. Lord Buchan might not have been the ideal parent, but she had never wanted for anything, nor felt anything less than a young lady. Here and now, she felt like nothing.

By the time Ross joined her, it was as black as pitch outside. She had undressed and got into bed, but she was totally unable to sleep, and she was in a wild rage. If she hadn't been so conscious of the close proximity of their hosts, she would have lashed out at him in no uncertain manner. As it was, she could barely manage to be civil as she railed at him in a loud stage whisper.

"How could you leave me alone like this! I'm scared, and I'm ill—"

She felt his hand cover her mouth, and just resisted the urge to bite his fingers.

"If you're really ill, I'll get some help for you. Or is it just that you ate too much and too well at suppertime?"

He removed his hand, and she snapped out an answer.

"Well, if that's not just about the limit! I was forced to eat food I didn't want, and now you imply that I was being greedy!"

"Hush, sweet thing," he said, and hearing the grin in his voice, she guessed that he and Omar had been indulging in wild male talk all this while. He turned down the oil lamp and slid in beside her, and she knew at once that he was naked.

"I will not hush . . ." she began, and then his mouth covered hers, and she had no option but to still her words.

"Then I must think of some other way of distracting you," he said softly against her lips. "For I'll not lose dignity with my friend by letting him think that my woman is not fully satisfied with her husband."

"Why should he think anything of the sort?" she said, feeling his hands begin to roam over her body and inch up her nightgown until he encountered bare flesh. "Ross—you don't—we're not—oh please no, I shall be so embarrassed in the morning—"

"And would you insult a friend by letting him think we do not care to make love in his house? Your eyes will show it in the morning, I promise you."

"You make these things up," Stephanie muttered, but she was finding it hard to resist the stroking softness of his fingers against her skin, and in the end she gave a little sigh and relaxed her tense muscles.

"I assure you I do not," Ross whispered. "But even if I did, is it so hard to believe that I want to make love to my beautiful wife?"

He gave her no more time to answer. So smoothly that she hardly knew how it happened, he was covering her with his body, and she was opening up for him as naturally as a flower opening to the sun. From his sudden rapid breathing, she knew he wanted her badly, and oh, she wanted *him* so much. She felt the first hot wild thrust of him, and then he had filled her, and she was soaring with him toward the realms of delight that only he could give her.

He gathered her into him, and she realized he was muttering in her ears and her hair. She couldn't understand a word of it, for it was in a language she didn't know. He could have been saying words of love, or lust, and she would never know. But if this was his way of loving her, then it had to be enough, for now.

They reached the peak of desire together, and she clung to him, the words she, too, was unable to say bursting out of her soul, but remaining unsaid. And even when they finally relaxed together, spent and sated, he reached for her and continued to hold her close in the unfamiliar bed.

"Tomorrow your eyes will tell the world that your husband has made love to you," Ross murmured against her neck.

And far from affronting her, the words gave Stephanie a safe, warm feeling of belonging. And as she drifted into sleep, she thought weakly and naively that perhaps making love and being in love weren't so very different after all.

They left Omar's house early in the morning, before the sun had climbed too high into the sky. By then, Minta had already gone to the river to wash the clothes, and it was only Omar who wished them well in their journey, and all good fortune in their findings.

"How do the Egyptians feel about people like you coming here and seeking out their past treasures?" Stephanie said curiously, when they were walking the short distance from the house to the river. It had been too dark last evening to gauge how close they were, but now she could see the myriad white sails of the felucca boats, and it was as busy a waterway scene as any English city full of traffic.

Ross shrugged. "There have been tomb robbers through

the ages, but an authorized archeological team treats the artifacts with respect, and is acknowledged in the same way. We tread softly, with no intention to desecrate those who still sleep beneath the desert sand."

His words charmed her. "You really do have a sense of empathy with this land and its past, don't you, Ross?"

"I wouldn't be here if I didn't," he said simply. "There's an old saying that the man who doesn't love his work should look to other things, or he'll never give of his best. I believe that's true. I could never desecrate any finding in a tomb, and nor could any of my team. I choose them carefully, and any man who wants to join me merely for greed is looking to the wrong company."

Stephanie thought that for a man who could play for big stakes at the gambling tables, he had a curiously fine sense of integrity. And the more she learned about him, the less she thought she really knew him. She shook her head slightly.

"Do you doubt me?" he said at once.

She answered without hesitation. "Not at all! I was just thinking how complex you can be. Just when I think I know you, you say something to surprise me."

Ross laughed. "A man should always be able to surprise his woman. When the element of surprise has gone from a relationship, there's no longer any relationship."

"Is that another old saying, or did you just invent it?" Stephanie asked.

"I'll leave you to decide that for yourself," he said with a grin, and then they turned a corner from the dark alleyway through which they were walking.

Stephanie gasped with pleasure and delight. The wide waters of the Nile River were dazzlingly blue in the sunlight, and to her already sand-weary eyes, it represented life and renewal, as it had done for eons of years to these people. The river was alive with craft of all descriptions, from mean little fishing boats, so flimsy they looked as though they would surely founder if their owner drove their poles too hard against the sides to the graceful, white-sailed feluccas gliding up and down in majestic splendor. Although not huge by the *Princess Maria*'s standards, they seemed to carry the life-blood of the river between them, transporting cargo and food supplies, as well as people of all descriptions.

While Stephanie was still contemplating the busy river traffic, she heard Ross's name called, and looked to where their companions of yesterday were already aboard one of the craft, moored alongside the river. Between the boat and the bank there was a narrow plank, and even as Stephanie watched, she saw several of the young workers skimming barefooted across the plank without even looking down. Her stomach rebelled at the thought.

"We don't have to do that, do we?" she said, the charm of the voyage diminishing rapidly.

"We do, unless you prefer to swim out to the boat," Ross said shortly.

"But surely there's some other way! Why can't they bring the boat closer to the bank? Or why not provide a wider plank? It looks terribly precarious to me!"

They were beside the felucca at the riverbank now, and Ross looked at her in exasperation.

"My dear girl, if you're going to protest at something as simple as walking a dozen steps on a plank, you're clearly going to be little use to me in the desert."

Her mouth dropped open in surprise and then fury. How dare he speak to her in such a way! And when other people were within earshot, too. She could see the grinning Englishmen's faces, and guessed that they thought her a very fine miss indeed, if she could react so prissily.

Before she could think further, she had picked up her skirts, and accepted the grizzled hand of the boatman waiting to assist her on board. Before she knew it, she had covered the dozen steps on the wobbling plank, and was stepping on board the boat, with Ross close behind.

"Well done. I thought a few well-chosen words would rile

you enough to make you forget your fears," he murmured in her ear.

She turned sharply. "Then you don't think I'm going to be entirely useless to you in the desert?"

She spoke before she could stop herself, knowing how very important it was to her to know that he needed her. She felt his arm go lightly around her waist.

"I think you know how much I appreciate your presence by now, sweet thing," he murmured.

She flushed as they moved farther down the side of the boat to where their companions awaited them. Such archness wasn't what she had meant, nor wanted right then, but there was no time to demand his assurance that he thought of her as a useful artistic assistant for his proposed book.

There was no room for anything on board the felucca, but the squashed presence of passengers, baggage, and cargo. They and their two companions were the only Europeans on the boat. The others were all dark-skinned, all wearing the long Arab style of dress, and all were male. They all conversed in their own language at nineteen to the dozen, and from the various glances she received, Stephanie was quite sure that she was very much the topic of conversation.

"How long will it take until we reach the landing stage?" she asked Ross.

"You seem to be obsessed with time," he said, and then, at her look, "We should be there well before sundown—"

"You mean we have to drift down the Nile like this for the whole day?" she said, appalled, as the boat began its slow meander into the middle of the river.

"It will pick up speed once the boatman gains more control," he said. "Meanwhile, I suggest you make yourself as comfortable as possible, since there's nothing else to do but enjoy the sights as we pass them."

She looked to where he gestured. The river seemed to stretch ahead into the distance. On either side there was a strip of greenery, and occasional groups of hovels similar to

Omar's, amid patches of habitation. Beyond that, on either side, was the desert.

"What sights?" she said bitterly.

"Sit on the baggage and rest a while," Ross advised. "The time will pass more quickly if you doze."

But Stephanie had other thoughts in mind. She realized how her fingers itched to sketch it all, wanting to commit it all to memory in the best way she knew how—and it would keep her mind off the varying smells from the mass of humanity all around them, their spices and their garlic, and the baskets of fish and other commodities.

She sought in her bag for her sketching pad and crayons, and without making any comment, she began to draw some of the scenes, including the gnarled faces of the Arabs. She soon had a crowd of interested onlookers around her, and as she finished each rough sketch, she was rewarded by loud applause.

She offered several portrait sketches to the fishermen, and they were almost embarrassing in their bowing gratitude. But long before they had journeyed any distance, she had collected a montage of sharply observed sketches to remind her of this voyage, knowing she would never see its like again.

"You've impressed them mightily, my dear," she heard Ross's mocking voice say awhile later. She was intent on detailing the vegetation along the banks of the Nile and incorporating a group of washerwomen into the scene.

"It passes the time," she said with mild understatement, for by now she was greatly enjoying herself. She was in her own world, doing what she liked best. She had skills of her own, and wasn't altogether spineless in being forced to accept marriage with a stranger.

Until now, she hadn't recognized the extent of the resentment she had felt because of it. It affronted her femininity to be bought like a slave.

She must have assumed a downcast look at the thought, for she heard Ross's voice again, more gentle now.

"My poor sweet. All this is so much less than you expected, isn't it?"

Stephanie looked at him sharply, wondering if she had really heard the concern in his voice, or if she had merely imagined it, simply because she wanted to hear it so much. But his hand was abruptly removed from hers, and he was answering queries from his men, and she regarded them with almost savage jealousy for taking the moment away from her.

Why must they be here at all? she thought resentfully. A newly married couple should have time to be alone, to explore each other, to learn each other's personalities and revel in the abandonment that love brought. She felt a blush stain her cheeks, for she was romancing in the way a real bride should feel. And she was not a real bride. She was bought and paid for, and must remember Ross's real purpose in wanting a wife and bringing her to Egypt.

The fact that he enjoyed the pleasures of a wife should add to the humiliation of all the rest. But it was to her shame that she considered it so rarely now. Instead, she craved his attention and his love more than she had believed possible. She had been an innocent virgin when he married her, but now that she had known the pleasures of love, she wanted more, and needed more.

"Are you felling unwell?" she heard his voice as she drew in her breath sharply. "You can hardly say the motion of the felucca upsets you."

She could not, for there was very little motion in the boat. It glided along with its tall sail billowing, and the two experienced boatmen guided it effortlessly toward its distant destination. Stephanie gave a more relaxed sigh, unexpectedly finding the graceful mode of travel quite sensual. At least it would have been but for the crush of passengers on board. If only it were possible to forget them, and see only Ross.

He heard the sigh, and misread it. His voice became sharper. "It becomes an Egyptian wife to remain silent at all times, Stephanie, but when I ask a question, I expect an answer."

"I wasn't aware that it needed an answer," she said snappily. "I'm not feeling upset in any way. In fact, I was quite enjoying the peacefulness of the travel, until I was so rudely interrupted."

He gave a sudden grin, and it seemed to imply that he preferred her snappy to a docile creature.

Her eyes flashed dangerously. "And the good Lord preserve me from a man who is impossibly overbearing and arrogant," she added for good measure.

She was suddenly aware that some of the Egyptians closest to them had fallen silent, their dark eyes watching her unblinkingly. She quickly deduced that they saw her as a bad woman now, for daring to argue with her man in public. A ripple of apprehension ran through her. If these comparatively lowly men thought themselves so superior to women, what must the attitude at Shaladd be like, where Prince Hali Ahmed was the undisputed ruler of a desert princedom?

She glanced at Ross, but he seemed unconcerned by her words, and apparently hadn't noticed the Egyptians' dark looks. It was for his sake, to save his dignity, she told herself, that she suddenly put a hand over his, and looked into his eyes in a more abject manner.

"Forgive me, please," she said softly. "I know I have a lot to learn about the ways and customs of a new country, and of a new husband, too."

He looked at her suspiciously, but her changed manner had apparently satisfied the onlookers, and they turned away to talk amongst themselves. It had all transpired in less than a moment, and maybe Ross was unaware of it, but to Stephanie, it had begun to open up a new feeling of unease about the world into which she was being enveloped.

She put away her drawing materials, and dozed on and off all day. From time to time she felt the coolness of water slide down her throat as Ross held a water bottle to her lips, warning her not to drink too fast. They had hard biscuits and succulent fruit to eat, which slaked her thirst a little more. The felucca floated into the bank of the river whenever required for passengers to alight and for new ones to board. And still the Europeans continued southward, and, in Stephanie's mind, toward the blazing heat of the sun.

Ross had fastened her parasol behind her head by attaching it to the side of the boat, but she was still hot and tacky, and longing for the bliss of a warm bath. Not that there was any likelihood of that for days, she thought dismally, and she vowed fervently never to take such simple luxuries for granted again.

By now, she knew that during their journey to Shaladd in the camel train, their shelter by night would be in canvas tents. The charm of sleeping in such close proximity to Ross couldn't even lift her weary spirits anymore, until at last he roused her, and pointed ahead to where the boat was drawing toward the bank and the outlines of a small town that was little more than a hamlet by English standards. But their journey down the Nile was at an end, and the desert beckoned.

Nine

Stepping onto firm ground again after the gentle movement of the felucca was both welcome and strange for a few moments. Stephanie declined to make any comment about negotiating the plank onto the riverbank again, and simply breathed a sigh of relief when she was safely ashore. Nearby, there was a group of camels sprawled out on the ground, aimlessly chewing, their drivers sitting cross-legged on the ground in deep conversation. This attention to conversation seemed to be a continual occupation with them, Stephanie thought.

Then, as if by a given signal, the men rose together and whacked each of the camels on the backside. Grunting, the animals got to their spindly legs, and the men began to haul loaded canvas packs across their backs.

"This is our transport, I presume?" Stephanie asked dryly, hoping desperately that Ross would say no, and knowing full well that he wouldn't.

"You won't find camel transport too uncomfortable," he told her. "It may make you slightly nauseous at first, but the secret is to let yourself go with the motion of the beast, and the two of you will find your own rhythm. A bit like making love," he added.

It was said so blandly that Stephanie wondered if she had heard the intimate words at all, and if she had, then she was thankful that the other men were going about their business.

It was hardly the time or place for such comments, and she decided it was best to pretend that she hadn't even heard it.

Instead, she viewed the camels with mistrust. She certainly had no enthusiasm about using this mode of travel, especially since the animals seemed so much larger and smellier at close quarters, and she had a strong suspicion that their coarse coats were flea-ridden.

She had also hoped to sleep somewhere half decent for the night, but it seemed they were to start the last part of their journey at once.

"You'll find it more comfortable to travel after sundown," Ross told her. "And on our first night, we always try to get some distance inland before we make camp near a water hole."

A water hole sounded rather less glamorous than an oasis, Stephanie noted. But it seemed she had no option but to seat herself carefully on the back of the animal, and with Ross's help, she did so with much trepidation. There was no genteel sidesaddle here, only the thick padding of a saddle cloth, and the ungainly animal's own hump to cling on to. And once the beast rose up on its spindly legs, the horrible swaying motion it produced threaten to curdle the contents of her stomach, and she clung on for dear life.

"You'll very quickly get used to it," Ross said from what seemed a very long way below her. Seconds later, he had swung onto the back of a second camel, and was alongside her.

There was a kind of harness attached to each animal. In no way could it be described as competent as a horse's reins, but it was adequate enough to hold on to. Stephanie also realized that the Arab guides were attaching each harness to the next one, so that they were safely linked together. It was reassuring—providing she didn't let herself think that if one beast bolted, they would all bolt.

There were nine camels in all: one for each European, themselves, Mac and Dawson; another three laden with supplies; and two for the Egyptian guides who would lead them safely to Shaladd. In a moment of sheer panic, Stephanie wondered if they would ever reach it, or if it was an unattainable star, forever out of reach.

She heard the weird piercing sound of the muezzin then as the priests called the faithful to worship to the mosques. But surely there were no mosques in this shambling little collection of riverside hovels? Even as she thought it, she glimpsed the soaring minaret of the building, glinting richly in the golden rays of the dying sun.

However mean their other buildings, the mosques always shone like jewels among the squalor. And regardless of the differences in religious persuasions, she was oddly comforted by the thought that there must be good people here, and she mustn't let herself be frightened by wild tales of brigands and desert rogues, or the slavery of the harem.

"Do we go now, Captain Sidi?"

She heard the leading guide shout back to Ross for instructions, and he was immediately given the assent. The next moment, all the camels had followed their leader, and they were underway, led by the two guiding camels, then Ross himself, riding ahead of Stephanie, and then came the supply camels. Behind them were Mac and Dawson so that she was safely cushioned between them all. Ross continually turned to ask if she was happy and comfortable, and she gritted her teeth and said that all was well. Not for worlds was she going to admit that it was the most appalling, miserable ride she had ever undertaken. And they had three days of this.

Instead, as they traveled westward, she concentrated on her first real sight of the desert at sunset, and as she watched the spreading colors in the heavens turn from gold to crimson and finally to blue, she knew she had never seen anything so beautiful, or humbling, as though everything else in the world was brought into perspective by this nightly spectacle of nature. The sun was surely larger here than anywhere else on earth, and seemed to encompass the whole universe in its enervating warmth.

And then there was the desert itself. If she had ever believed it to be no more than a flat expanse of sand, her eyes were opened anew, even in the twilight. Or perhaps especially so at this time, for the constantly shifting and rippling patterns of the sand seemed to be touched with gold. Way ahead of them were massive dunes, in all their fantastic shapes and sizes, some like great sleeping, golden cats, some like impassable distant blue mountains. And already she could believe that the desert was vast, and limitless.

"Does it please you, Stephanie?" She heard Ross's voice come back to her, carried on the wind.

"It's more beautiful than I believed it could be," she said honestly. "But perhaps I'm seeing it at its best in this soft light, and I'll be disillusioned when I see it in daylight."

She heard him laugh. "Anyone who doesn't find the desert constantly alluring and fascinating has no eye for beauty, and I can't believe that of you, my love."

They were well on their way now, and the life-giving waters of the Nile seemed a long distance behind them. They were now traveling what was presumably their safe route to Shaladd, and Ross shortened the length of attaching rope between their two camels to ride alongside her. The other men were divided from them by the supply camels, and there was a sweet intimacy in riding together into the desert sunset.

She could almost forget that there was anyone else with them at all. She could almost imagine that they were completely alone in a magical world of their own. She drew in her breath, and felt Ross's hand reach out to take her own.

"Was that a sigh of regret?"

She shook her head quickly. "It was not!"

"Then why the sigh?" he persisted, and she was glad of the swift tropical darkness that came so suddenly after the twilight, and was already almost on them.

"It's hard to explain. But I've always been moved by natural beauty that hasn't been made by man, but fashioned by a far greater force. And now you'll think I'm an artistic fool for becoming so emotional over a desert sunset, when you must have seen so many."

"But never with you. And that's what makes this one so special."

She bit her lip. There were times when he made *her* feel special, too, when she could almost believe that he loved her. Perhaps he did, a little, since their intimate times had proved to be so spectacular, but she needed him to love her for herself, and not just because she was to serve a very useful purpose in his life.

"Don't you believe me?" he said gently, just as though he could read her mind.

She gave a wry smile. "I believe you could turn even the most stubborn woman's head by your talk," she said.

He laughed. "I thought I'd already succeeded in doing just that, my dear!"

"I don't recall being totally stubborn when I agreed to marry you!"

"But that was because you were virtually forced into it, wasn't it? I wonder what your reaction would have been if we had met under other circumstances, and I had courted you in a more leisurely way?"

She gazed straight ahead, to where she could just see the swaying outlines of the leading camels now. If he couldn't see that she was wild with love for him, and would always have been so, then she must be a better actress than she thought. She realized he was loosening the rope between their camels.

"It was an unfair question, and one that I hardly expected an answer to. I'll leave you to ponder on it, while I check on how far we have to go to reach the water hole.

She watched him go, tall and skilled on the ungainly animal. What a complex man he was. A gambler, of course, like many wealthy men were in these times, and a charmer, of that there was no doubt. A reckless philanderer? Hardly so, or why would he not have accepted Prince Hali's gift of his concubines? A man in love with his wife? How dearly she would like to believe it, but she could not forget that she was here for a purpose. Which led her to wish that things could have been different. If only he had wanted her for herself, and not as payment for her stepfather's stupid gambling debt.

She hated Lord Buchan's gambling habit, yet she wondered if she and Ross would ever have met if it hadn't been for those very circumstances. It wasn't a pretty thought, but it tempered the anger she felt against her stepfather in a small way. It also made her despise her own weakness in knowing that her love for her husband had grown since she had known him.

He had come back to her side now and rejoined the rope between their two camels. She tried to forget her disturbing character analysis of him and studied the changing scene all around her. The sky was dark now, but a great yellow moon had replaced the sun, and a myriad stars hung low overhead. Between them the light from the moon and the stars was almost turning night into day. The shadowed shapes and contours of the dunes were more subtle and seductive now, and it was truly a night made for lovers, Stephanie thought again. She wondered if Ross thought the same, or if the eagerness he had always shown whenever he held her in his arms, was solely directed now in reaching his destination.

"We're nearly at the water hole," he told her eventually. "We'll make camp in a few minutes, and have some soup and bread before we turn in for the night."

Stephanie felt her mouth water. Soup and bread might be the plainest of meals, but it sounded so welcome, and so normal. She would be so relieved to get off the camel's back, too. She was stiff and aching from her awkward position on the animal. It would be good to place her feet on the ground again, even if there was shifting sand beneath them.

But the welcome dark shape of the water hole was close by now, and the camel train came to a halt. Stephanie quickly registered the nature of the place. It was no lush green oasis, but a welcome respite all the same, with just some sparse scrub and a few scrawny palm trees to give shelter. Ross helped her slide down from the animal's back, and she stumbled against her husband after the several hours of riding. She felt his breath, warm on her cheek, as his lips brushed her skin.

"I wonder why you can't always be so compliant in my arms, sweetheart," he said with gentle irony. "But such delights must wait, and I suggest that you rest by the water's edge while we get the tents erected."

Despite her stiffness she had become almost lethargic with the plodding motion of the camel, but she was alert now, and there was no reason why his words should irk her so. Yet they did. They placed her in a servile female position, and while she had no wish or intention to help in erecting the tents, she felt oddly useless, when everyone else had a job to do and was suddenly busy.

And they were clearly very efficient at setting up camp with all speed. A fire was lit, and the aromatic if undefinable smell of soup began to waft across the desert air. Stephanie did as she was told and wandered to the edge of the water hole, but without any intention of sitting down to rest. She had done enough sitting for one day.

Apparently, the camels didn't need to take their fill of water. They squatted or stood about nearby, but the sight of the refreshing water was too much for Stephanie. She knelt and scooped up a handful of it, splashing it over her face and neck, and giving a sigh of pure bliss at its coolness.

She couldn't have said exactly what happened next. One minute she was kneeling over the edge of the water hole. The next, she was sent floundering into the shallow water, screaming and thrashing.

She heard a cracking sound as she was hauled ignominiously out of it, and wondered fearfully if they were being set upon already by tribesmen. And then she turned in a fury as she heard Ross and the others laughing at the state of her. She realized the cracking sound was one of the guides, still whacking his camel with a stick, and she glared up at Ross as she shook herself free, bedraggled and humiliated.

"I'm glad you're all enjoying this so much!" she snapped. "And which one of you thought it so clever to push me into the water hole? If this is one of your pathetic little games to keep yourselves amused, I don't think much of it!"

"Don't be ridiculous, Stephanie," Ross said, barely able to keep a straight face. In the fireglow and the light from the moon, she couldn't mistake it. "Do you really think any of us would be so childish?"

"Well, I didn't just fall in! I was pushed! I trust you're not about to tell me some ghoulish tale of a desert demon who pushes unsuspecting travelers into water holes!"

Her voice was heavy with sarcasm, but she felt a shiver run through her all the same, and wished the unlikely thought hadn't entered her head. But *something* had pushed her, and if it wasn't anything human.

"There's your culprit," Ross said dryly, pointing to the camel that was still getting a whacking. "You shouldn't present such a delightful rump to a playful animal, my dear."

"No one could possibly think of a camel as a playful animal—and I'll thank you not to be so crude," she snapped, thankful that Mac and Dawson had drifted away to the cooking fire and couldn't hear him.

"Nothing that occurs between a husband and wife is crude, Stephanie, and you should know that by now," he said in a more intimate tone. "Come to our tent and I'll help to dry you, then we'll have some hot soup."

"Thank you, but I'm perfectly capable of drying myself," she retorted.

But she couldn't object to him escorting her, and feeling more than ridiculous in her damp dress and straggly hair, she followed him to one of the canvas tents. Inside, there was barely room for two people, but by now she knew that these were only the transient tents. When they began the real expedition, she was assured that the mobile accommodation would be far more comfortable.

She had no idea just how comfortable that might be, but she eyed the blanket inside their present tent with indignation. There was apparently nothing more for them to sleep on, and Ross was well used to roughing it in the desert. Even though his English home was so elegant and genteel, he was clearly very adaptable.

Here, their baggage was simply placed in one corner, and she had no choice but to forage for a clean dress and undergarments, struggle out of those she was wearing and start to dry herself with the towel Ross handed her. After a moment, he took it from her hands and ran it over her damp body.

"You're so beautiful," he said softly. "Is it any wonder I find it so difficult to keep from touching you?"

"You don't seem to be trying very hard," she said in a husky voice as his hands palmed her breasts. The towel was between her skin and his hands, but it did nothing to lessen the sensual effect his touch was having on her. She felt his mouth touch hers, and she had a job to restrain herself from throwing her arms around his neck.

"Have I ever told you how much I love your mouth?" he went on in that soft, seductive way.

"No—" she said faintly.

"Then that was very remiss of me, and I'm telling you now," Ross said, slowly circling the lusciously full red curves of her lips with his tongue, in a way that made her knees go weak. Dear Lord, did he mean to ravish her here and now, while the others were around the campfire taking refreshments? And if it *was* his intention, could she ever resist?

Ross suddenly bent his dark head, letting the towel drop a little way from her breasts and kissing each swollen tip as she arched toward him. Then he had covered her again, and his voice was oddly rough.

"If I don't leave you to finish dressing, I may not be responsible for my actions, and I don't care to entertain our companions by the noisy evidence of our lovemaking at this precise moment. Come to the fire as soon as you're ready, Stephanie."

He was gone, and she was left staring at the tent flap. She touched her fingers to her lips, remembering his words. *He loved her mouth.* It wasn't the same as saying he loved *her,* and while it had filled her with a momentary excitement, she was left frustrated and resentful now. He had built her up, only to let her down.

She felt a sudden sob rise to her throat. She might be vulnerable where he was concerned, but she was basically strong, and she would be strong now. She pulled the clean dress over her head and fastened it with savage fingers, tidying her hair as best she could, and walked out to the cooking fire with her chin held high.

"Would you like some soup, ma'am?" Dawson said. He was polite enough, but Stephanie was certain he was still laughing at her beneath his breath.

"Thank you, yes," she said with quiet dignity, "and since you've all had your funning, I would be obliged if you would now consider the camel incident closed."

"The captain's already requested it, ma'am," Mac assured her. "Consider it forgotten."

She glared at him suspiciously, quite sure he wouldn't be forgetting it in a hurry. Not if the provocative imagery Ross had evoked were fixed in his seedy little mind. Presenting a delightful rump to a playful animal, indeed!

But, despite herself, she felt her own lips quirk. She wasn't lacking in a sense of humor, and if it had been anyone else being tipped so ignominiously into the water by a camel . . .

"All right," she conceded calmly. "I'm sure it was very

funny, and I suppose I can't blame you for enjoying the sight of it. But I promise you I'll be more careful in future!"

"And we'll be sure to warn you of any likely hazards, ma'am," Dawson went on, his face cracking into a friendlier smile than usual. Stephanie smiled back, accepting the mug of hot soup from his hands. Knowing that they had to be traveling companions for the foreseeable future, there seemed no point in always being at loggerheads. Perhaps she had been a little stiff and unbending until now—and she could hardly blame the two men for resenting the sudden appearance of a woman into their all-male preserve.

The soup and bread was as welcome as the finest repast, and just as appetizing. Stephanie felt totally replete when she had finished, and Ross suggested that they all turn in and get some sleep, since they would be on the move again at dawn, and rest during the hottest part of the day. This would be their usual pattern of travel in the desert, he told Stephanie as they retired to their own tent, since it conserved energy as well as their own body fluids.

She presumed the phrase was meant to be an objective one, but she felt her face grow hot on hearing it. Because it was perfectly obvious to her now, that despite the few hours sleep they were to get, Ross had every intention of making love to her now. And she was more than ready for him.

They sank down together onto the blanket that covered their bed of sand. His hands removed the dress she had so lately put on, and her own hands eagerly reached for his clothes, and helped to strip them from his body.

For a moment, she had a strange feeling of watching herself as if from a distance. Such a short while ago, she had been an innocent. In many ways she still was, for there was still much to learn about the ways of men and yet, she was innocent no longer. She knew a man's body as well as she knew her own, the scent and the shape of it, the sight and the feel and the taste of it. It was erotic and wonderful, and

the bonding together of male and female was still a source
of wonderment and pleasure to her.

"Why do you stare, my sweet?" she heard Ross say softly,
as she seemed to lie motionless on the blanket and to gaze
unseeingly above her. Her eyes focused properly on her husband again, knowing she had truly come a long way from
innocence if she could lie here in nakedness and feel no
shame or embarrassment. She spoke in a low, husky voice.

"Please don't laugh if I tell you. I was pondering on the
awesomeness of the Being who created man and woman to
fit together so perfectly," she said, and she felt herself blush
furiously at putting such thoughts into words. If Ross mocked
her now, she would feel utterly mortified, but when he answered, his voice was tender, and she knew he had understood.

"Then let's not disappoint this great giver of earthly delights, my darling girl," he whispered against her mouth, and
she felt the warm, familiar weight of his body covering hers.
She moved beneath him, opening up for him, and not wanting
to waste a precious moment of this short night, and sighing
with an exquisite sense of oneness as she felt him enter her.

She could forget all else but him. No one else existed but
the two of them, merging into one, out here beneath a shimmering desert moon. Ross made love to her slowly, and then
with mounting passion, fulfilling all her wildest dreams of
ecstasy. And when the moments of climax came, her eyes
teared with the deep and abiding pleasure he gave her.

"Sleep now, little one," he whispered in her ear, wrapping
them both in the blanket and settling her into him. "Daylight
will come soon enough, and no night in the desert will ever
be like the first one, so savor it all."

"No other night could ever be as beautiful as this one,"
she murmured back, but she was already so drowsy and longing for sleep, that she didn't even know if she said the words
aloud, or if they remained in her head.

* * *

She awoke to sounds of activity outside, and a feeling of hardly having been asleep at all. It was a struggle to open her eyes, and when she reached out for Ross in the cloying warmth of the tent, she discovered she was alone.

At once, the sense of closeness that had been forged between them last night seemed to disappear from her mind. She had half expected soft words, tender glances, and a slow, leisurely beginning to the day, and even as the thought tumbled through her head, she knew it was no more than an illusion. Ross had told her they were to be on the move at dawn, and it must surely be dawn now.

She lifted the tent flap, to be met by a glaring shaft of sunlight. The sun was only barely over the horizon, but its brilliance promised the dawn of a relentlessly hot day. With a feeling of unease, Stephanie prayed that she would be able to cope with such a climate. The heavy, confining clothes of an English lady were hardly suited to it, and with a sudden firm decision, she decided to abandon most of her undergarments, wearing just one petticoat beneath her lawn day dress, for modesty's sake. Older European ladies might be scandalized by the action, but rather than faint clean away from the heat, it seemed the most sensible course to take.

And it felt remarkably good to be so unrestricted. She could almost envy the Egyptian women in their long loose robes and their bare feet. And then she recalled how subservient they had appeared in Alexandria and all along the banks of the Nile, where the women seemed to be constantly toiling, and her brief sense of envy disappeared.

She had washed in the small bowl of water Ross had apparently left for her, and was fully dressed when he came back to the tent.

"As soon as you're ready, I'd be glad if you'd leave the tent so that it can be taken down, Stephanie," he said with a hint of impatience. "We've no time for dawdling."

"Are we allowed time for breakfast, or are we supposed to go hungry for the whole day?"

She couldn't stop the sarcasm in her voice, but Ross appeared not to notice it, or her baleful look.

"Breakfast consists of hard biscuits and tea, since I prefer to be on the road as soon as possible. We'll have a cooked meal when we make camp this evening," he said. "By then we shall be more than halfway to Shaladd."

He was obviously eager to reach this so-called fabled princedom she was beginning to resent more and more. In her mind, Prince Hali Ahmed was no knight on a white horse, the way Ross seemed to envisage him. Hali Ahmed was a procurer of women, who sought to persuade his English friend to join in his indulgences that reduced his harem women to little more than slaves waiting on his every whim.

And presumably the concubines thought it a great honor to be rewarded by a summons to Hali's bedchamber. But what if any of them were truly in love with the prince? How must it feel, knowing she had to take her turn, and was only one of a number of women from whom Hali could take his choice?

Stephanie shuddered at the thought. And this was also the man who had wanted to reward his English friend by presenting him with six of his favorites. At least Ross had resisted the temptation. And at least he had made no secret of his reason for marrying.

She could have stubbornly refused, challenging her stepfather's threat to throw her out. If he had been cruel enough to do it, she could have gone into service for some titled person, or become a nursery governess. Too late, she knew that there *had* been choices for her, however difficult her life might have been from her old one.

She had taken none of them, because she had simply been too young and naive to question the will of two strong men— her stepfather and Captain Ross Kilmarron.

But she, too, could be strong, and if it was in her power at all, she would let this Prince Hali Ahmed see that the marriage between one man and one woman could be beautiful and fulfilling, with no need for any other, yet even as she thought it, she wilted, wondering if Ross Kilmarron really saw it like that, too, or if she was merely fooling herself. How was she to know whether or not he took a willing harem girl to bed, which was very different from having six of them offered to him as a gift to take home to England!

She knew she was torturing herself, and her head jerked around when the tent flap was suddenly thrust aside once more, and Ross was snapping at her.

"The guides are smothering the fire at any minute, so if you want some hot tea, I suggest you get it now," he ordered. "You're not ill, are you, Stephanie?"

"No, I'm not ill," she muttered. *Just sick at heart, because a once-golden dream of finding love and happiness with the man of her heart, was fading so fast.* Physically, they were so often as one, but in every other respect, she hardly knew him at all.

She pushed past the three men and walked to the fire, where the Arab guides bowed respectfully to her. She took the mug of hot sweet tea and drank it quickly, biting into the hard biscuit with little taste for it, but knowing she should eat something if they had a long day of traveling through the desert ahead of them.

Already, the sun was rising in the sky, and the remaining soft colors of the dawn were merging into the harsh relentless blue of the day. All the pearly golds and delicate pinks had gone, and to Stephanie's fanciful mind, it was like the contrast between dreams and reality. Desperately, she pushed such gloomy thoughts aside, remembering one of her cousin Claire's old sayings. She had made her bed, and she must lie on it. Never had it seemed so poignant as it did right then.

Once the tents were down and the overnight baggage packed, the camel train was on its way. Glancing back toward the water hole, Stephanie saw how a small welcome breeze was already scattering the sand over the evidence of their camp. The roughened surface of the ground was becoming newly ridged with the vagaries of the wind, and within a very little while, no one would know that they had been there at all. It was ominously frightening.

Ten

By the end of three days traveling across the desert, Stephanie felt completely disoriented. The long hours of riding on the camel's back became alternately soporific and excruciatingly painful. She lost her appetite, but was always desperately thirsty, and drank eagerly from her leather water bag, despite Ross's caution to drink more slowly.

She began to think her mind was becoming affected by the mere sight of the endless desert that was fast losing its charm. It would be easy to concentrate on the glittering sand so hard that one lost all sense of time and distance. By now, she was filled with resentment toward Ross for bringing her here at all. It was no place for a woman. She tenderly rubbed at her bruised hips on their last morning, and told him so in no uncertain terms.

"You won't say that when you see Shaladd," he said shortly. "I've always promised you it will surpass your wildest dreams."

She couldn't even answer. Her eyes were gritty, and strained from the constant glare of the sun. So much sand was stirred up by the camel's feet that she had long since discovered the value of winding a silk scarf around her face. Even so, she tasted sand and breathed sand, and the few enjoyable times she had been taken to the English seaside as a child were but a distant memory. Such gentle activities as making sand pies had quickly lost all their appeal.

An hour or so later, she decided she was definitely hallucinating. There was a shimmering white dome on the far horizon, and it seemed to glint with gold wherever the rays of the sun struck it. She told herself it was a mirage, no more, and if she blinked her eyes a few times, it would surely go away. As her camel plodded along behind Ross's, she closed her eyes firmly, glad of a brief respite from the sun.

She determinedly held her parasol over her head to stop her skin from burning, and kept her arms covered at all times, but it was difficult enough to do so and hold on to the camel's reins as well. But by now, she realized she was actually becoming quite adept at the balancing act of riding on the animal's back.

Her eyes were still closed, and she was wondering just how long she dared keep them so, when she felt Ross's hand on her arm, and realized he had once more drawn back to ride alongside her.

"You disappoint me. I thought you'd be overjoyed to see your first glimpse of Shaladd," he said now.

Her eyes flew open then, and she saw that he was pointing toward the distant white dome.

"Is that it?" she echoed, not sure whether to rejoice or be truly disappointed that it certainly didn't resemble a desert stronghold, in the way Ross had described it to her. One building didn't make a city.

He laughed. "When we get nearer, you'll see that Shaladd lies in a fertile valley in the desert, almost hidden from the outside world by the dunes ahead. The dome that you see is merely the crowning glory of Prince Hali's golden palace."

His choice of words alerted her. "It's not really made of gold, is it?"

"To a man of such fabulous wealth, it could hardly be anything else," he said dryly.

Stephanie's mouth dropped open with the shock of this statement. It was said with such conviction she knew it could only be the truth. She closed her mouth again as the dry taste of sand immediately invaded it, and hastily adjusted the silk scarf around her face.

"There's nothing to be alarmed about, Stephanie," Ross went on. "Hali will be enchanted with you—but not too much so, I trust."

"What do you mean by that?" she demanded.

"Nothing at all," he said, far too blandly for her to believe it. There had been something behind his words, but for the moment she couldn't fathom what it was. Unless . . . The idea that came to her then was too absurd, and too unsavory to even think about. But having thought it, she couldn't get it out of her mind. *Prince Hali Ahmed would surely not look covetously on his friend's wife?*

"Tell me more about the harem," she said with sudden huskiness in her voice. "Are the women completely bound in slavery?"

Ross glanced at her. "It depends what you mean by that. They are not bound hand and foot or kept in chains. And they're not slaves, except that they obey the prince's every desire, but they are grateful and humbled to do so. Their most fervent wish is to please their master."

"If you refer to him as their master, then they must be slaves," she objected.

"Not in the way you mean, and not by our standards. You must accept the ways of a different country here, Stephanie. Any young girl called to serve Prince Hali considers herself favored, and from the moment she's chosen, she lives inside the golden palace and is pampered for the rest of her life. Even when she is no longer considered suitable for the prince's needs, she is rested in separate apartments set aside for the purpose. There's no shame, either in being a present concubine or a retired one."

"Well, it wouldn't suit an Englishwoman to be so subservient," she burst out, horrified at all she was hearing. In her eyes, the sheer male arrogance and domination of Prince Hali made him a monster.

"Perhaps not. But even an Englishwoman has her price," he said insultingly.

She was affronted at once, but she was attuned to every nuance in his voice now. Was it unease, or just plain aggressiveness that made it suddenly harsh?

"Then what are the requirements of a new concubine, or am I not supposed to know?" she said, smothering her distaste, and wondering just how far she had come since her association with this man, to even ask such a question.

"She must be young and fresh and untouched, and her virginity will be ascertained by the court physician before she is even presented to the prince for his approval."

Stephanie felt her face burn and her skin prickle at the thought of this violation, and prayed that the men traveling behind them couldn't overhear what was being said. But she had asked for information, and she was obviously going to get it. Ross went on dispassionately.

"When she has passed the physical test, she will be bathed and perfumed, and attired in suitable garments to be acceptable in the presence of a prince. She will await instructions in the outer golden chamber, and at a given command, she will walk slowly to the four corners of the chamber, then return to the center. She will lower her eyes and speak a required passage of poetry, and then she will commence to dance to music."

"And where will Prince Hali be all this time?" Stephanie asked scathingly, shocked and yet shamefully fascinated by all she was hearing.

"Hali will be watching and listening, but he will not show himself at this stage. He will be seated behind a grille with his attendants, who will note his every comment on the girl's performance. If he is finally satisfied with all that he sees, he will clap his hands and the girl will be taken to the harem to be prepared for attending Hali that night."

"So he will see her, but she won't see him. That seems hardly fair," Stephanie was obliged to say. It was less than fair. It was barbaric, even though she had heard that in other eastern countries such customs were quite normal.

"None of the women see Hali until they are summoned to his bedchamber, and even then, they go through certain rituals before they are allowed to come within touching distance of the royal features."

"I remember," Stephanie said hastily, recalling the night on the *Princess Maria* when Ross had initiated her into the role of the concubine, and she had found it so erotic and sexually stimulating. But just how had he known it so intimately? she found herself wondering now. Had someone told him, or had someone shown him? She felt a burning jealousy at the very thought.

"Is there no love at all between the prince and his women?" she asked in a scratchy voice, finding the whole procedure unbearably shaming. In a loving relationship between one man and one woman, she agreed that such intimacies were acceptable. Hadn't Ross already taught her that nothing was forbidden or ugly between lovers? Or crude? But perhaps he had used the word in the mechanical sense only, she thought, her spirits plunging ever deeper.

"In this country, any prince of an ancient royal bloodline is akin to a god, and it was always forbidden for a god to love a human," he said. "Didn't your reading tell you as much?"

"I don't want to hear any more," Stephanie said feverishly. "In fact, I wish I was safely back in England, and didn't have to listen to such heathen tales at all!"

Ross's voice went several degrees colder. "I'll thank you not to voice such strong ideas when you're at Shaladd, Stephanie. To state such a fact is to insult your husband, and if it were overheard and I were not to treat you severely, I would lose dignity in Hali's court."

She could hardly believe she was hearing such nonsense. And yet she daren't suggest that it was nonsense, for at that moment Ross's face and demeanor was as dark and intense as that of any high-born Arab prince. He, too, had a flowing white scarf wound around his head and neck to keep out the ferocity of the sun, which he pulled up over his mouth and nose when they were not conversing, and it all had the effect of turning him into a dark and mysterious figure. Stephanie thought again that he had absorbed more than a little of Prince Hali Ahmed's ways and customs, and the nearer they got to Shaladd, the more she was aware of it.

She spoke more humbly. "Naturally, I'll keep my own counsel once we enter Shaladd. I would only beg you to remember that I had little knowledge of anything beyond the four walls of my stepfather's house—"

"Of course," he said distantly. "There was never any doubt on that score."

As if to show that the conversation was at an end, he pulled the scarf up over the lower half of his face, and dug his heels into his animal's side, encouraging it to move swiftly ahead of her.

Stephanie bit her lips hard. No matter how much she thought she knew him, he was still an enigma to her, and when he wasn't by her side, she was afraid of what the future held. He spoke so strangely at times, and he knew a different culture far more intimately than she had realized. She didn't want to hear these things, and yet she felt compelled to ask. There was a saying that understanding came with knowledge, but she would dispute that, for she could never understand such a lascivious personage as Prince Hali Ahmed, who apparently couldn't give love to even one woman, but needed so many to gratify his sexual needs.

They were within a few miles of Shaladd now, Ross told her some while later. The desert surrounding the valley basin was as inhospitable as ever, but she could already see the dark smudges of green that meant there were trees growing in the oasis princedom, and they were like balm to her tired eyes. She had long since given up wanting to talk at all, for her throat was parched and her senses were dulled from the traveling. She prayed that Ross's promise of more comfortable travel to the expedition site would be fulfilled.

If the sight of the trees was soothing, the domes and minarets of the princedom were not. Their marble and gilt were undoubtedly meant to be a testament to the wealth and power of the prince, but their brilliance dazzled and hurt the eyes, and Stephanie couldn't stare at them for very long. Perhaps that was the idea, to deter invaders, she thought.

When they entered the slopes of the valley, she could see that the entire oasis was bordered by a high, circular wall that was evidently intended to keep out those invaders. There were great wooden gates at intervals in the walls, and it was toward one of these that the camel train was progressing, and Ross rode alongside her once more.

"I shouldn't think Prince Hali could ever bear to leave such luxury to visit the outside world," she said for want of something to say.

"He never visits the outside world, as you call it. He may be persuaded to join us on the expedition, since it is in the burial area of his ancestors. He's highly intrigued by the work that we do, but that's all."

"You mean he never goes to Alexandria or any other city in Egypt?" she said in amazement.

"Never," Ross said. "He does not deign to do so. Here he reigns supreme, and he refuses to grace any other place with his presence."

Stephanie shook her head slightly. She had endured weeks of weary travel to be here, and her whole present situation had come about because of Prince Hali's wish to reward Ross with a gift of his women. She had constantly thought of Hali as the most arrogant man alive. And yet, he was also the man, whom she steadfastly refused to think of as any godlike incarnation, who refused to leave his princedom for fear it might diminish his powers.

Ross hadn't said it in those exact words, but that was exactly how it seemed to Stephanie. She could almost feel a little pity for someone whose high opinion of himself wouldn't let him unbend sufficiently to enjoy the everyday living of ordinary mortals. And then she remembered the concubines, and her pity vanished.

They had obviously been observed for some time, for she could hear the plaintive sounds of some kind of warning instruments as they neared the great gates, and as they approached them, they slowly opened.

At the sight that greeted her, Stephanie immediately felt as though she were in a kind of Arabian Night's fable. There were small dwellings and trees all around the circular shape of the oasis, but dominating the entire fertile area was one enormous building in the center, and crowning it was the gilt-and-marble dome Stephanie had glimpsed from afar. But now she recognized that not only the dome was made of marble, inlaid with gold and other precious metals. The entire palace was made of the same glittering materials, and its magnificence was nothing short of awesome.

They traveled on toward the palace, escorted now by black-skinned men on horseback, through streets lined with fountains and swaying palm trees. The others would have seen it all before, but Stephanie was completely dumbstruck by everything she saw. She had never thought such opulence existed outside of fantasy, and to think that it was all owned by one man was somehow obscene. But she knew better now than to say such a thing to Ross or anyone else. She was fast learning the sense of keeping such thoughts to herself.

"We shall be given our living and sleeping quarters in the palace," Ross told her. "Prince Hali will be informed of our arrival, and one hour after our arrival I'll be granted a short audience. Later, we'll be commanded to his presence for dinner this evening. The protocol never varies."

"Not even for such a valued friend as yourself?" she dared to ask.

"Not even for me," he answered gravely, seeing no irony in her words.

"And does everything at Shaladd revolve around his wishes?" she asked next.

"Naturally. The entire community is honored and privileged to be in Prince Hali's service. Not a move is taken anywhere without considering the effect it might have on him, and his advisers and astrologers are never far from his side."

Stephanie shook her head slightly. Surely not even the royal houses of England and France had ever commanded such servitude and loyalty. And she decided that Prince Hali must either be much loved, or a complete tyrant. Until she met him, she decided to reserve judgment.

Halfway to the palace, they heard shouts of welcome in English that were like music to Stephanie's ears. Four men emerged from one of the larger dwellings and the two groups greeted each other enthusiastically. Stephanie soon lost track of their names, but learned that they were the rest of the expeditionary team, already awaiting their arrival.

After assuring Ross that the trusted Arab guards at the tomb site had reported that all was well, Mac and Dawson dismounted and removed their baggage, and Stephanie realized it was only Ross and herself who were to continue to the palace. It unnerved her even more.

"I'd like to introduce you to Stephanie, my wife," Ross told the men before they continued on their way. "She will accompany us into the desert, and will ably sketch our discoveries to accompany my reports."

Seeing their startled expressions at all this, Stephanie knew she was a surprise to them, though they tried to hide it well enough. But she didn't mind their surprise. At least it told her that Ross had made no preconceived plan to seek a wife before he left Egypt, and that these men would be unaware of the true circumstances. As far as they were concerned, she and Ross were a normal married couple.

Once the greetings were over, the camel train continued onto the palace. They were ushered into a large stabling enclosure and relieved of their mounts, and a carriage took Ross and Stephanie to the wing of the palace that was reserved for honored guests. The Arab guides who had led them to Shaladd were then relieved of their duties.

Despite what Ross had said, she had still somehow expected Prince Hali to be there to welcome them, but servants quickly appeared to escort them to their quarters. She felt a mixture of relief and annoyance that Hali had not yet shown himself. She resented the very thought of him now. What if she hated him on sight, and was obliged to spend time in his company trying to disguise it? And just how soon could they conveniently begin the expedition and then go home? Already, she yearned for time to pass and for normality to return, despite knowing how foolish it was to wish time away.

She and Ross followed the silent-footed servants through what seemed like miles of marble corridors. The palace was full of twists and turns, and Stephanie couldn't help feeling that there were a thousand eyes watching her. There were so many doors and archways with golden-hued grilles, and she couldn't help remembering the story of how Hali chose his new concubines. As they passed one grille, she was almost sure she caught a movement behind it.

"How much farther?" she whispered to Ross.

"We're to be given the best of accommodation," he told her. "Just be patient, Stephanie."

Finally, the servant threw open a heavy, gilt-studded door, and Stephanie saw the most glorious bedroom she could ever have imagined. Everything in it was white. White carpets, white walls, white bedcover and drapes at the shuttered windows, white furniture, white robes hanging outside the closet, white towels laid out on the bed, white roses and other blooms that filled the room with an aromatic and sensual perfume in exquisite, almost translucent white vases.

"For Captain Sidi," the servant said deferentially. "And for lady—please to follow."

Stephanie stared at his retreating back. The bed in this room was huge, and was surely meant for two. The luxury of the room and the sensual perfume of the flowers was already reaching deep into her senses, and her swift reaction to it all was that here was surely a place meant for lovers.

"Does he mean I'm not to sleep in here?" she murmured in dismay as the man waited near the door for her.

"It's considered an indignity for a gentleman not to have his privacy," Ross told her.

She knew well enough that it was also the custom for many English couples to have separate rooms. But she truly felt the need for Ross's presence in this alien place. To Stephanie's heightened senses, it also seemed to imply that since Prince Hali only commanded a woman to his room when he needed her, it was assumed that the palace guests would behave in the same way. It was a humiliating thought.

The servant stood patiently near the door, his eyes fixed on a point somewhere ahead of him, clearly following instructions not to gaze at his betters. Stephanie was well used to the ways of servants, but this attitude was far more servile than most, and she found it humiliating on his behalf, not hers. She felt a sudden reckless defiance. In asserting herself, she might overcome some of the jitters in the pit of her stomach.

"Do you have a name?" she asked the man directly.

He still didn't look at her.

"I am simply called Nubian, from my country to the south," he said, without expression. "Please to follow, lady."

Stephanie swallowed. His skin was very black, like that of the guards who had escorted them to the palace, and unlike the other Egyptians she had met, whose skins were a bronze hue. She had no idea where or what Nubian was, but she made no further demur, and with a desperate look at Ross, she stepped forward.

"I'll call on you very shortly, Stephanie," he said encouragingly.

This time, Nubian darted a glance toward Ross, and to Stephanie's astonishment, there was a hint of contempt in the glance. It was gone in an instant, but if she had read the glance correctly, she interpreted it as meaning that the Englishman's esteem was lowered in his opinion, if he deigned to call on a woman, instead of commanding her presence.

"Your quarters, lady," Nubian said, as he opened a door along the corridor from Ross's room. To her relief, she realized they were not so far apart after all, and she gasped with pleasure at the sight of her own room. Here, everything was the most delicate blue. Blue tiles on the floor, blue rugs scattered around, blue bedcover and shuttered drapes, blue furniture and blue robes hanging outside the closet. The porcelain-blue vases contained delicately hued blue flowers, and whether or not their scent was real, they emitted a musky, sensual perfume. Except for the color, it was a smaller replica of Ross's room, and it was truly beautiful.

She realized that Nubian was already closing the door and retreating, his eyes lowered. And then she was alone. Her luggage had magically appeared in her room, and she felt a sudden relaxing of her nerves and lifting of her spirits, seeing this room as her sanctuary. She moved toward the window, and gazed out at the gardens below, where sparkling fountains played among the exotic blooms, and where trellises and arches glinted in the sunlight with the color of gold.

She was forced to acknowledge that Shaladd could truly be called a paradise in the wilderness of the desert. Whatever else was here, there was luxury in abundance. She gazed around her room, glorying in the silence after the constant movement and noise of the journey.

It occurred to Stephanie that she had hardly ever been alone since leaving England, and although her first instinct on realizing she and Ross were to have separate quarters had alarmed her, it had a certain erotic appeal for her now. Wouldn't it make their being together that bit more exciting? The place must already be affecting her, she thought faintly, for to be summoned to her master's bed like a concubine was both degrading and stimulating, yet she wasn't even sure now which feeling was uppermost in her mind.

She moved around the room, inspecting the toiletries laid out on the dressing stand. There were soaps and perfume bottles, hand and body lotions, combs and hairbrushes inlaid with shimmering mosaics, and all in the same delicate blue as the rest of the room. In the ceiling, several large fans moved silently, creating a pleasant circulation of perfumed air.

And where was the bathroom? There must surely be a bathroom connected to all this elegance. There was a door to the right of the room, to which Stephanie moved eagerly. After the dry, dusty journey to reach Shaladd, to soak in what she confidently expected to be sheer sensual luxury, was infinitely more inviting than any meeting with the fabled Prince Hali Ahmed.

When she opened the door, she paused in amazement. It was as she had expected, and yet it was nothing like she could have imagined. No bathroom in her experience had ever been fashioned with more attention to sensual pleasure. She saw at once that everything here was designed for self-indulgence and gratification.

There were piles of thick towels and bathrobes on a chest, and dominating the room was a huge, circular bath set into the blue marbled floor. The edging surround was made of gold-and-blue tiles. Above it, the ceiling was mirrored, with a fan in its center, which was presumably there to take the steam away and allow the bather the sense of being a voyeur.

The thought sent a tingling through Stephanie's whole body. It was something no English lady would ever do, and as a child she had been taught not to look at herself more than was necessary when she bathed, but in this place, she suspected that the rigid rituals of an English lady's life were as remote as the stars.

She leaned forward, and then she sprang back. Even as she watched, the bath began to slowly fill with scented, blue-colored water, from which steam rose invitingly into her nostrils. How it did that, she couldn't imagine and she hoped fearfully that it would stop when the bath was full.

Tentatively, she felt the water. It was incredibly soft, and at the perfect temperature, and she felt a great longing to be in its soothing embrace. Bath crystals were being dispensed from somewhere in the bath itself, and as they dissolved they produced an inviting foam. Clearly, no guest of Prince Hali Ahmed needed to lift a finger. It was pampering to a greater degree than Stephanie had ever imagined.

There was another door on the far side of the bathroom, and as she still gazed in fascination at the swirling bathwater, the door opened. Was this a servant, summoned by the very fact of the bath being filled, and sent to assist her? She turned quickly, and saw her husband standing there.

"Does it please you, my lady?" he asked softly, using words he had used before, and in a tone that always sent her desire soaring.

"It could hardly do otherwise," she said unsteadily. "But how—where—"

"It's protocol for guests to be given separate rooms, sweetheart, and naturally, since I have the largest guest suite I have a bathroom of my own. But we also have this communal bathroom, which is for the benefit of male guests who have a lady occupying the blue room."

"I see. And if a male guest doesn't bring a lady of his own, I suppose that one can always be supplied?" she said, trying not to wonder how many times Ross had been here before, and taken his pick of the concubines offered to him for his pleasure.

He came and took her in his arms. "You think too much,

Stephanie. What's past is past, and can never be changed, and it's a waste of the precious days of our lives to dwell on it. It's more important to look to the present, and to enjoy life now. And as you have so thoughtfully filled the bath, why should we waste more time merely looking at it?"

"Why indeed?" she murmured. "If you will leave me to attend to it, then——"

"You misunderstand me, darling," he said with a slow, animal smile. "This bath is designed for two to share. And we won't be disturbed unless we ring the bell for a servant's assistance. Is that your wish, or will you be satisfied with your husband's attentions?"

His voice had dropped to a note of pure seduction, and Stephanie shivered with a sensation of pure pleasure running through her veins. He was her husband, and nothing they did together was wrong. He had told her so, and she believed him.

"I'm sure you can do all that is necessary," she said huskily, already aware of the hardening of his body against her, although he was still fully clothed.

He tipped up her chin with his hand, and the scent of the dissolving bath crystals rose up between them, sweet and erotic.

"I'm sure I can," he said softly, and then he was tearing the clothes from his body with a feverishness that excited her, and helping her shivering fingers to remove the dress and undergarments until there was nothing left between them but the warmth of their flesh. He drew her close, kissing her mouth with a hard and urgent passion, and she felt the wild pulsing in her body, knowing what was to come, and finding no shame in knowing that she could arouse this virile man to such physical needs.

"We should bathe first," he murmured in her ear. "But I won't guarantee that I won't ravish you there and then, my sweet one. It's been a long while since the last time."

It was less than three days, but to Stephanie, too, it was a long time. He held her hand and they entered the huge bath together, sinking down into its pleasurable softness. As they did so, Stephanie became aware of tiny jets of water spurting out from various points in the bath, tingling on her skin like dozens of invisible fingers, and invigorating it. It alarmed her until she realized how enjoyable it was, and then she leaned back against the curved edge of the bath, closing her eyes for a few moments to let the invisible fingers touch every part of her with sensual eroticism.

But not all the fingers touching her were inanimate ones. She was aware of Ross's hands stroking her breasts and lingering over every curve and hollow of her body, and her breathing became shallower and quicker, as if she couldn't bear to let herself miss his slightest touch. She opened her eyes a fraction, and because she was still leaning her head back in the bath, her gaze was caught immediately by the reflection in the mirrored ceiling.

She caught her breath more sharply now. She was watching two lovers in a scene of sheer abandonment. The woman lay back in the foaming water, her arms outstretched along the marbled surround, her hair flowing freely over it. Her damply gleaming, perfectly proportioned breasts were lifted above the water by the man's hands, and he was leaning toward them, kissing each rosy peak in turn. She couldn't see his features at that moment, only his dark head and his powerful back and muscled arms as he leaned toward her, pleasuring her.

To see two lovers in such an abandoned pose was like viewing an erotic painting and yet, it was far more than that, because this scene was throbbing with life, and filled with a sexual energy that even the finest paintings lacked.

Ross was suddenly aware of her gaze, and he leaned back, too, spreading his own arms along the marbled surround. The bath was too vast for them to be linked completely, but he cradled one of her hands in his own.

"Do we not make a splendid pair, my Stephanie?" he said

softly. "You with your beauty, and me with my need to have you here and now?"

Before she could think what he meant to do, he had moved swiftly toward her, ignoring the waves of water that went coursing over the side of the bath. Someone else would clear it up. Someone else would attend to their every whim, if required, but some things could only be done by two.

He drew her onto him, and she felt a new heat invade her as they fitted together as perfectly as two halves of the same being. They always matched, but this was different. This was quick and urgent, and he held her head gently backward to see the images above them—to make her watch. He watched, too, and their combined image was one of total sexual completeness.

She accepted without question that there was nothing wrong in such voyeurism. They were one, and together they were invincible. Stephanie had no idea why that particular phrase should come into her head, but it seemed to epitomize all that was good in a loving relationship. And then she gave up thinking at all, and abandoned herself to pleasure.

Eleven

The time had come for the honored guests to be presented to Prince Hali Ahmed. The bathing was over, the baggage in their rooms had been silently and discreetly hung in closets, and Stephanie's most elegant gown had been newly pressed and laid out on the bed. It smelled of roses and some other, muskier perfume. A young girl had appeared to help her dress, and to arrange some of the jeweled combs in her hair, which she was told were humble gifts for the lady.

It was all too much. By the time they descended the great staircase led by escorting servants, Stephanie was simply petrified at being summoned to the Great One's presence. She fully expected an ogre.

"There's one last thing I must tell you," Ross said. He had already complimented her on her appearance, and declared, in an oddly formal manner, most honored to escort her to Hali's presence. "When we enter the Audience Chamber, you will walk three paces behind me."

"Oh, Ross, must I?"

He made a small moue of annoyance. "Haven't you been listening to a word I've been saying? You must observe the rituals here, and it's not seemly for a woman to walk beside a man. She must always defer to his superiority."

She felt a sudden anxiety. "Is this really the nineteenth century? Sometimes I feel as though we've stepped back into some ancient time—"

"Here at Shaladd, we have," he told her. "Time has virtually stood still here for a thousand years, and Hali has no intention of changing it. It's written in his stars that he should not, or disaster will befall him. Few outsiders are permitted to enter these walls, and we disobey the ancient rules at our peril. Hali will also greet me as if this is our first meeting, disregarding our private audience earlier."

He could still tell her things to astound her. Even now, when she thought she had heard it all, there was still more to know about this strange isolated place that was apparently held back in time to suit the selfishness—or superstition—of its prince. But there was obviously no point in arguing, and she just had to accept the fact that when they entered the Audience Chamber, she must walk three paces behind her husband.

"Very well," she said. "I'll do my best not to disgrace you, but I can't promise to remember every single thing, nor to pace my footsteps as you say!"

"There's no need. You'll be restrained at the door of the Chamber and led in at the appropriate time."

Mentally, she threw up her hands in despair. She still had the constant feeling that none of this was real, and that it was a dream from which she would soon awaken. Just as long as the reality still contained Ross Kilmarron—and providing the dream didn't become a nightmare.

The Audience Chamber was magnificent, ornate and shimmering. Great crystal chandeliers hung from the ceiling, and costly, deep-piled carpets replaced the usual tiles and mosaics. Presumably because the sound of footsteps might offend the princely ears, Stephanie thought, still trying to overcome her terror. The whole effect of the Audience Chamber was of soft green and white, very pleasing and restful to the eyes, but Stephanie didn't miss the fact that it was also lined with black-robed, watchful attendants, who all wore curved, sheathed swords at their sides.

At the far end was a gilt-framed throne, and seated upon

it— Stephanie drew in her breath in a small gasp of surprise. She had fully expected Hali to be a large, dominating figure, but the man who sat there in his green-and-gold robes and adorned with heavy and costly jewelry, was not of any great stature at all. He was certainly not as tall or well built as Ross, but he was handsome, and Stephanie could understand how any woman would welcome his attentions. Such wealth and charisma were powerful aphrodisiacs.

On either side of Hali stood several elderly persons, whom Stephanie assumed to be the attendant advisers and astrologers. She registered all these things quickly, wanting to be able to record her first impressions in her sketch pad, already anticipating the wonderful paintings she would create from seeing such exotic surroundings.

They were escorted toward the dais by two of the attendants. For one frightening moment, Stephanie blanched as a sheathed sword was thrust in front of her, obviously intended to restrain her from following Ross too closely. Then the sword was lowered, and her own escort permitted her to follow at the pace he dictated.

As they approached, she saw Hali's darkly intense features begin to relax, and before Ross reached him, he had risen to his feet and clapped his hands. The escorts withdrew a few paces, but Stephanie noted that they remained close enough to rush in if danger threatened the prince, keeping the visitors under scrutiny the entire time.

"So, my friend, you have returned to Shaladd," Hali spoke in almost perfect English diction. "It does my eyes and my heart good to see you. Come close, that I may embrace you."

Stephanie heard a sudden swishing noise, and the closest guards had unsheathed their swords in readiness, in what was presumably a normal procedure in case a guest should attempt an assassination. Yet this was Hali's *friend,* and the man who had saved his life, so heaven knew how vigilant the guards would be in a stranger's presence. But she knew now that few strangers were permitted in the palace, and neither Hali nor Ross seemed to see anything untoward in the action of the guards.

She saw the two men embrace, and then exchange a few brief pleasantries before the prince nodded and retreated to his throne. Ross turned toward Stephanie and smiled encouragingly into her pale face. She guessed from the way she was feeling that all color must have drained from it, and she just prayed that she wouldn't do anything as undignified as fainting clean away.

"Come closer, and keep your eyes lowered until you are requested to raise them," Ross told her quietly.

She took his hand and was brought to his side. She no longer questioned anything. She merely obeyed. She was drugged by the power and presence of the prince and by all she had learned of him. And by her husband, too.

"Prince Hali, I would humbly present my wife, Stephanie, and request that she is welcomed into your illustrious presence," Ross said with grave formality.

There was total silence for a few moments, and even with her eyes dutifully lowered, Stephanie was well aware that she was being inspected. God help the concubines who went through an even worse ordeal, she thought.

"You have done well, my friend," she heard Hali say eventually. "The woman is a worthy companion for you, and we give a gracious command for the woman Stephanie to look upon the royal features."

She raised her eyes to look steadily at him. His eyes were black in his narrow, sculptured face, but they held no expression at all. Now that she was closer to him, she knew that although he would be considered handsome by many, it was not in a way that appealed to Stephanie in the slightest. The face was too arrogant, too self-important, too reminiscent of those ancient god-kings in the illustrations she had studied, as to be almost frightening.

"You may speak, woman," he said graciously.

Her nerve almost deserted her. What in heaven's name did

one say to a prince, especially one who seemed to be hardly of this earth at all? She was unnerved by her own fanciful thoughts, and swallowed dryly, searching for the right words, and doubtful that any would come to her aid at all!

"I'm honored to be here, Your Highness," she managed to say huskily. "And I thank you for your hospitality."

It was obviously enough to please him. To her astonishment, he suddenly laughed aloud and his voice lost its pompous tone.

"Good. You please me greatly, and now I have a new friend. The three of us will dine shortly, and then we shall be entertained while I hear the plans for the expedition into the desert. You will wish to begin with all speed, I suspect, friend Ross, and if it pleases you, you may arrange a meeting for your team to converse in the palace tomorrow."

She was astonished at how quickly his attitude had changed. He was quite human now, and she thought his choice of words was significant, guessing that he had very few real friends. There were attendants and guards and advisers, but these were not the same as real friends. There were servants and concubines who obeyed his every whim, but these were not the same as a wife who was chosen out of love. She reordered her thoughts quickly. But if Ross Kilmarron was an enigma, how much more was the intriguing Prince Hali Ahmed?

She was quickly realizing something else. She was no longer quite so afraid of him. For all his power and riches, Prince Hali was still only a man. If it was a dangerously naive thought, it was one that helped to sustain and relax her as they were escorted into the great dining hall. Here, the three of them were seated at one end of the most enormous dining table she had ever seen.

It was already filled with great bowls of fruits and sweetmeats, and the first course alone would have fed an army. Later, there were choices of cooked meats marinated in exotic sauces, accompanied by succulent vegetables, and a variety of mouth-watering desserts to pamper the most jaded palate. They were waited on by male servants, and Stephanie was well aware that everything that was placed in front of Hali was first put to the test by a taster. If anything contained poison, it would be the taster who fell in agony, not Hali.

It dawned on Stephanie that as yet she had seen no other women in the palace except the maid who had helped her dress. It was strange, and sad. Where was the kind of closeness and companionship that one man and one woman gave to each other in this beautiful, yet somehow sterile place? Whatever the circumstances of her marriage to Ross, in the eyes of God and English law, their marital duty was to cherish and comfort each other, and Ross had never made her feel cheap in the way she had been coerced into marrying him.

She watched the prince covertly and curiously throughout the meal. The Prince Hali who ate with them was clearly more relaxed than the formal one who sat on the throne in the Audience Chamber. He and Ross continued to exchange news of each other since the last time they met, and he was clearly intrigued to hear of the style and custom of an English wedding.

"It's very strange for a man to take only one wife, and to be content to be tied to her for life," he said, giving a small shake of his head as though mystified by such an arrangement. He stared at Stephanie so thoughtfully that she began to feel as if she was under inspection, and there was a small sense of alarm in her head.

"You will know that each country has its own customs, and this is one of the most important ones in ours, Your Highness," Ross said firmly. Stephanie had thought Hali's comment was directed more toward her than Ross, but she knew she must not answer unless addressed by name. But the prince's words annoyed her. Was he perhaps wondering how this particular woman could hold a man to such fidelity?

He turned to Ross then, and began to address him in his own tongue. Instinctively, Stephanie knew he was talking about her, and that he evidently saw no discourtesy in shutting her out of the discussion. All was permissible for the Great One, and the normal courtesies of other people didn't apply to him. She resented it intensely, but there was nothing she could do about it.

She was immediately struck by the way in which Ross answered the prince. He, too, spoke in the Arab tongue, and she could understand none of it, but she knew Ross well enough to know from his clipped tone that he was angry, and that he wasn't trying to hide his feelings.

The prince spread out his hands that were so heavy with rings it was a wonder he could lift them, and shrugged his royal shoulders in disdainful unconcern. He glanced toward Stephanie and smiled, and for some reason that she couldn't explain, it was a smile that made her shudder. It was the smile of the predator sensing a kill and she quickly reversed her earlier thought of not fearing him because he was only a man. There was something in those glittering black eyes that told her this was the very thing that should worry her.

Once the meal was over, they moved again, this time into another room with a marbled floor in which musicians were awaiting them. This was the Entertainment Hall, Ross told her quietly. There were no chairs in it, only a vast scattering of large velvet floor cushions at one end of the room, on which they were expected to sit, or lounge, in what seemed to Stephanie to be the ultimate in decadence. The musicians began to play, and a group of sinuous long-haired girls appeared from the four corners of the room and proceeded to dance in a highly provocative manner for the prince's pleasure.

Stephanie had never seen such dancing before, and she felt the rich heat of embarrassment filling her cheeks. She was totally shocked at the way the girls flaunted themselves so shamelessly, and wondered just how their behavior was affecting the gentlemen. Surely no man could be unaffected by what he saw?

She darted a glance toward Ross, and knew that he was enjoying the spectacle immensely, and that he would have seen it all before on previous visits to Shaladd. The knowledge made her seethe with jealousy, for in England, only in the lowest establishments were there to be found women such as these, who saw no shame in baring their bodies for men's pleasure. Or so she had heard.

She glanced even more surreptitiously at Prince Hali. Was he, perhaps, singling out the woman who would share his bed tonight? Or were these women not part of the harem at all, but women-in-waiting for the call to higher things? To her surprise, she saw that Hali looked more bored than entertained, and was almost asleep after the gargantuan meal. She could only suppose that when too much of anything was constantly at your disposal, you quickly tired of it.

The dance ended, and the girls dispersed quickly. A magician then appeared, seemingly producing items out of the air, and then a flock of love birds from beneath his robes, at which Hali applauded loudly. He had so much, Stephanie thought, and yet this was the act that appealed to him the most, and he could still retain a child's delight in the mysteries of magic. He suddenly made a great belching sound, followed by a huge yawn. It was so unexpected, so disgusting and so rude, that she found herself staring, until Ross leaned toward her, and told her to lower her eyes quickly.

Hali then snapped his fingers, and the guards that stood around this room as in every room, opened a door, through which ten veiled young women appeared, to sink down on the marbled floor in front of the prince. Their painted faces could clearly be seen through the gossamer veils that revealed only their kohl-rimmed eyes. All of them were young, and all of them were beautiful. Hali turned to Ross.

"I have decided to accompany you on the expedition, friend Ross," he said. "And these are the women I have chosen to attend me for my pleasure. Since I have so many, you are still at liberty to take any one of them that pleases you."

"I thank you from the bottom of my heart, Your Highness," Ross said, while Stephanie's stomach seemed to be turning somersaults with fury at the offer. "But it will not be necessary. I have my own woman, and she will be sufficient for my needs. Besides which, I must abide by the laws of my country, as Your Highness will assuredly understand and approve."

It was so outrageous and flowery a statement that Stephanie was speechless with rage. How *dare* he refer to her as no more than a chattel in that demeaning way? And yet it was obvious that Hali saw nothing unusual in the words, other than his mystification that Ross didn't choose to take advantage of his generous offer. She burned to shout at the pair of them there and then, but she dared not. Those armed guards would as soon slice off her tongue as look at her if she dared to insult their prince. She was under no illusions about that now. With almost inhuman willpower, she held her anger in check until later, when she and Ross were alone.

"Very well," Hali said in a bored voice that said he would never understand the European ways, nor wished to.

He became bored very quickly, Stephanie thought, and no doubt the forthcoming desert expedition, so important to Ross, would be seen as just a jaunt to Prince Hali Ahmed, to break up the glorious monotony of palace existence.

He suddenly pointed a finger at one of the women, who came to lie prostrate at his feet, while the others moved just as silently out of the room. Hali rose to his feet, and the chosen woman did likewise, keeping her head bowed and her hands clasped in front of her. Ross stood up as soon as the prince did, and gestured to Stephanie to do likewise, for no one must sit while the prince stood.

"We shall meet tomorrow, friend Ross," he said graciously now. "And when the stars are favorable, our journey will begin."

He nodded to Ross, and strode out of the Entertainment Hall without acknowledging Stephanie at all, with the woman following demurely behind him. Above her veil, she glanced toward Stephanie for one brief moment. Her almond-shaped, startlingly dark eyes, were beautiful and shining, telling Stephanie in an instant how ecstatic she was to be the prince's chosen companion for that night.

They were escorted at all times between rooms in the palace, and Stephanie soon realized that there was always a servant outside each heavy bedroom door. But once in her own room, she stormed through the connecting bathroom to Ross's room without any invitation.

"Before you tell me I'm defying palace protocol," she raged, "I just want to tell you what I think of you for treating me like a chattel—"

He caught hold of her clenched hands and held them fast, his face filled with amusement.

"My God, you can be a little vixen when you choose, can't you? If I was of the same race and status as Hali now, you would risk being locked in irons, put into the deepest dungeon, and have the key tossed into the desert for the sands to devour."

She glowered into his arrogant face, knowing that her own burned with fury.

"But you're not, are you? Or has this association with your precious Prince Hali completely turned your mind so that you've forgotten the decency with which English gentlemen treat their ladies?"

She saw the matching anger in his eyes now.

"You still don't understand, do you? Did you think I enjoyed speaking about you in that way to the prince?"

"It certainly seemed like it!"

"And what do suppose would have happened if I had become shocked and affronted, and declared in some whining way that English husbands don't take more than one wife? The more you associate with those of a different race and customs, the more you learn the value of tact and diplomacy, and especially in this case, of allowing the prince to retain his dignity at all times. Is that so difficult for you to understand?"

"I don't know," she said, uncertain what he was getting at.

"Then I'll tell you," he said, still with the strong grip on her hands that was starting to hurt. "If Hali had thought for one moment that I was showing contempt at his customs, I would have insulted a royal personage by implication. In Shaladd law, that would have been a treasonable offense, and treason has only one punishment."

She stared at him with eyes that were large and round and frightened as the realization of what he was saying was drummed into her mind.

"I won't waste time on letting you guess the outcome," he went on brutally. "I would have been put to death by the sword, and all the males accompanying me would have been executed as a warning to all who dare to insult the prince."

At her gasp of horror, he went on relentlessly.

"As for you, my dear sweet wife . . ." He paused, and then his voice became insultingly mocking. He was aware that she had gone limp now, and he ran his fingers over her bare arms until she shivered. "You would have been absorbed straight into the harem, and it would be as though the party of English guests had never existed at all."

She had no doubt at all that he could only be speaking the truth. And the prospect he presented to her was too terrifying to ignore or to take lightly.

"So you only spoke the way you did to protect us all?" she said slowly.

"Of course. But it was also true. I have no wish to take another woman, when the one that I have fulfills all my needs," he said so objectively that she wondered if she had heard him aright. So coolly that she wondered if he could be the same man who had made such vigorous and passionate love to her on so many occasions.

Why couldn't he say that he loved her, she thought in anguish, since he found her desirable enough to resist the charms of any other? Surely such a situation meant that she was loved? And if it did, then it seemed that Ross simply couldn't, or wouldn't, say the words she longed to hear.

"Then I suppose I must submit to these indignities while we're here, even though they make me feel less than a woman," she muttered slowly, accepting the inevitable.

He took her in his arms, and she could feel the beat of his heart. It was the one warm thing in a world that was suddenly cold and alien and cruel, despite its beauty. He spoke deliberately, gazing deep into her eyes, wanting to appease her.

"No one could ever be more of a woman to me than you, Stephanie. No man could wish for a more passionate and responsive wife, and despite your occasional childish tantrums, I did well when I chose you."

"Oh, now you're insulting me!" she said, ignoring the compliments and only hearing the male arrogance of the hunter who had caught his prey. "How can you imply that our marriage was a normal one in any way? Or that you chose me for any reason other than a selfish one?"

She felt his mouth descend hard on hers, and she couldn't breathe for the viselike grip of his embrace. When the kiss ended, he still held her, and his voice was harsh against her mouth.

"And can you deny that some parts of our marriage are blessedly normal, my sweet? Or have you already forgotten the delights we shared earlier? If so, it's clearly time I reminded you of them again."

Before she could guess his intentions, he was carrying her to his bed. He lay her on the white coverlet and leaned half over her, while her breath came very fast in her chest.

"How shall I make you mine tonight?" he said, suddenly teasing. "After watching the erotic dancing earlier, and seeing how the girls are so eager for Hali's attentions, would you care to act the concubine for my pleasure?"

"No, I would not," she whispered. "I'm no concubine, Ross, and nor would I ever wish to be one. I've no wish to be any man's plaything, but only his wife and loving companion. Is that too much for anyone to ask?"

As he had become teasing, so she had become serious, and her lovely English eyes filled with unshed tears. *Was* it too much to ask? Was it so impossible that even now, something could be made of this marriage that had begun as such a sham? She felt him gather her up in his arms, and she was held fast against his heart.

"It's too much to have you look at me like that with those damnably expressive eyes," she heard him mutter. "Do you think I don't know that I had no right to take what was so innocent and so lovely? I should have paid a doxy to play the role of my wife and then be rid of her."

"Is that what you really think?" she whispered against his shoulder. "Am I such a failure then?"

He bent his head to kiss her lips in a kiss of such tenderness that her heart cried out for him to love and cherish her. It was a moment without the frenzy of passion, and yet it contained all the sweetness in the world.

"You're so much more than I deserve," he murmured roughly, "and that's the hell of it."

"I don't understand," she said, bewildered by the sudden savagery of his voice.

"It's far better than you do not, my sweet one. And since this discussion has made me lose the urge for lovemaking, I shall carry you back to your own room."

She was truly very tired and she was half grateful that he wasn't going to make love to her, and half aching for that special sensual and spiritual closeness that they shared. But the tiredness won, and she linked her arms around his neck as he carried her through the connecting bathroom to where her nightgown was laid out on the blue coverlet of her own bed. He lay her down beside it and she gazed up at him with the love she was finding it impossible to hide, even though he couldn't seem to see it. In some instances, love was truly blind, she thought.

"I won't risk suggesting that I offer to help you undress, or all my good resolutions may disappear," he said. "And I need to be alert tomorrow, when I consult with Prince Hali and the team."

"And what will I do all that time? I presume I won't be included in the discussions?"

He gave a slight smile. "I think you know the answer to that by now. Your time will come when we reach the site, Stephanie, and you begin to do your sketching. You will be invaluable to me then."

And not now? she desperately wanted to ask, but she merely nodded, and allowed him to leave her. And she still had no idea how she would fill the hours of tomorrow.

"Ross!" she called out to him as he reached the bathroom connecting door. "Something has been puzzling me all evening."

"What is it?"

"You spoke very forcefully to Prince Hali when he spoke you in his own language. I had a feeling it might have been about me—or am I not allowed to know?" she said defensively.

He leaned against the bathroom door, looking at her thoughtfully for a moment, and then he shrugged.

"I'm not sure that you would want to know, even though you're quite right, and it did concern you."

She sat bolt upright on her bed now, all thoughts of tiredness forgotten. Men could be so infuriating, so damned *superior,* she raged, but she tried to appear composed.

"I'm not a child, Ross, nor a simpering female who will faint away at the first unpleasant thing she sees or hears. Haven't you learned that much about me by now?"

She saw him grin, and wondered suspiciously just what

the two of them *had* said about her that had been too much
of a masculine preserve to be said in English.

"Very well, but I don't guarantee that you'll like what you
hear."

He didn't attempt to come toward her again, but continued to lean against the bathroom door with his arms folded
in what she considered a very arrogant manner.

"Tell me," she said, as imperiously as she could, "and then
let me judge."

"All right. Hali was testing the bathwater, to put it in col-
loquial terms."

"And just what's that supposed to mean? Will you please
stop talking in riddles to annoy me!"

"Very well." The grin faded. "He complimented me on
my silver-haired woman, and said that for an Englishman I
had very good taste."

"What cheek," Stephanie muttered. "And then?"

"And then he said there had never been a silver-haired
woman in his harem, and that if you were not spoken for,
you would make a welcome addition. And that if I were to
feel so inclined, he would still be willing to bargain with me
for you in exchange for six of his own women."

Stephanie's mouth dropped open with shock. It was a fla-
grant insult to all womanhood for a man to speak of bargaining for a woman in such a way.

"And I trust that you refused!" she raged at him.

"Naturally," Ross said, suddenly cool in the face of her
fury. "Even when he offered an additional five thousand
camels, or my choice of his fabulous jewels, I resisted the
temptation. I'll leave you to ponder on your worth to me."

He opened the bathroom door, and retreated quickly behind it, just in time to avoid the nearest missile Stephanie
could find to hurl at it. The bottle of scented body lotion
smashed against the door, sending slivers of glass across the
room and filling the air with a pungent perfume. In its in-

tensity, it was strong and violent, and in perfect keeping with this wild and barbaric country.

Almost at once, there was a knock on her door, and as if summoned up by magic, a maid glided in to clear up the mess. No words were passed, merely a series of small bows, but the maid's unerring presence when needed was one more thing to add to the unease Stephanie felt about Shaladd, and the conviction that wherever she went, and whatever she did, there were eyes watching her.

And remembering how abandoned she and Ross had been in the mirrored bathroom, she vowed that such a thing shouldn't happen again. The sooner they began the sojourn into the desert, the better. At least they would have some privacy in the marital tent then, and she was quickly deciding that this palace, so luxurious and vast, was no more than a prison to those who inhabited it. And where there were prisoners, there were always wardens. The strong always overcame the weak, and it did nothing to help her nervous state to know in which category she came.

Twelve

The following day Stephanie was woken by the sound of a gentle female voice bidding her a hesitant good morning in English. The maid she had seen on two previous occasions was smiling shyly down at her, as if unsure whether or not such liberties as smiling should be taken with an English lady. Stephanie didn't miss how the girl's eyes looked in some amazement and envy at the luxurious tumble of Stephanie's silvery hair, spread out on the pillow from its confining daily pins and combs. She sat up quickly, remembering vividly the events of the previous day and night, and blushing at the memory of her hot temper at flinging the lotion bottle across the room after Ross.

"I'm sorry I caused you such trouble last night," she said at once. "It was careless of me to spill the lotion."

"Oh, no, lady. It was my humble pleasure and duty to assist you," the girl said at once, catching Stephanie totally off guard at such humility.

"Do you have a name?" she asked, thinking at once that it was a stupid thing to say, for didn't everyone have a name!

"I am called Yasmina," the girl said, "and I bring you food. I will also be taster for you, lady."

As she stood aside, Stephanie saw that she had brought a trolley of breakfast food into the room, and a choice of tea or coffee for the English lady. She was shamed at the thought of expecting this girl to taste her food first, and shook her head at once.

"I'm sure that won't be necessary, Yasmina, but you may pour me some tea, please."

"I would much prefer that I taste the food, lady," the girl went on with a hint of anxiety in her voice. "My master bids it, and I must obey my master's wishes."

"Very well, then," Stephanie muttered, not liking the sound of this at all.

But the smell of food was making her very hungry, and she rose from the bed. Almost before her feet reached the floor, Yasmina was at her side, easing her feet into slippers, and holding a dressing robe ready for her arms to slip into. It wasn't necessary, and it was somewhat irksome to have the girl so attentive, but for the moment she let it pass.

Very soon now, she would have left this place and its overpowering luxury. She never thought she would be thankful to do such a thing, but she knew that it was true. The customs and rituals of a desert princedom were definitely not for the likes of Stephanie Wheatley Buchan Kilmarron!

"Does my husband also have breakfast in his room?" she asked Yasmina as she contemplated the dishes of poached fish and chicken, the toast and eggs. She would soon be as big as a house if she ate everything placed in front of her, Stephanie thought. As she watched, the girl daintily put a morsel of each food into her mouth, proving that nothing was poisoned, either by accident or design.

"Captain Sidi breaks his fast in the presence of Prince Hali, and then they will receive the English gentlemen for the meeting. This is how I am told, in case you should ask it of me. Captain Sidi will meet you again this evening."

"What!" So she wasn't even to see Ross that morning. "And what am I meant to do for the rest of the day?"

It was unfair to show her resentment toward this girl, for the palace protocol was none of her doing.

"I am instructed to invite you to the harem, if it is your wish, lady," Yasmina went on in her soft voice.

"Oh?" Stephanie said in some trepidation.

She quickly rearranged her face, lest the girl should think she was condemning the idea of the harem. Besides, by now, she was intrigued to know how exactly these women lived. English women notoriously thought of them as no more than downtrodden slaves, but the young women that Stephanie had seen so far were pampered and beautiful.

"Do you wish for your bath next, lady? I will serve you in whatever you desire."

"Thank you, yes," Stephanie murmured, for although the day was still young and the room was not overheated by Egyptian standards, the sun was already high in the sky, and she could feel the cool trail of perspiration on her skin.

When she had done no more than pick at the various breakfast dishes, she breathed in the fragrant scent of the bath oils Yasmina had poured into the bath. The girl stood patiently, as immobile as if she was made out of stone, awaiting her new mistress's wishes. It wasn't right, Stephanie thought with a burst of anger. It wasn't right for anyone to be so subservient to another. They were about the same age, yet her own life was so vastly different from this girl's that it filled her with embarrassment.

"I can manage perfectly well by myself, thank you, Yasmina," she said quickly as the girl went to help her remove her bathrobe.

"But my master, and the mistress of the harem . . ." she began, and Stephanie gave a swift sigh, realizing that the girl was totally under the control of these others, and that no western woman was going to change it.

"Oh, very well," she said, and allowed the girl to hand her into the soft, aromatic water. She proceeded to bathe her, using a sponge with feather-light strokes, her fingers adroitly avoiding the merest touch on Stephanie's body.

Even so, it could have been oddly sensual, but Stephanie's

nerves were too much on edge for her to be anything but relieved when the bathing ritual was over, and she was once more swathed in thick, warm towels.

"Has lady chosen her garments for the day?" Yasmina asked next.

"Yes, and I'll see to the rest of my toilet by myself, thank you. You've done well, Yasmina, and you may take the break-fast trolley away and come back in half an hour to escort me to the harem. I shall sing your praises, never fear," she added with a smile.

She wanted to be alone for a while. She wanted to throw open the shutters and her bedroom windows and breathe in the morning air, instead of the cloying atmosphere produced by the bath oils and lotions. Yasmina did as she was told, reassured by Stephanie's last words, and then at last she was alone. She was quite used to dressing herself, and did so with all speed, and stepping out onto the little balcony outside her window, where the clean scents of fresh flowers were less of an assault on her senses.

She leaned over the gilded filigree balcony and closed her eyes momentarily against the glare of the morning sun. As she did so, she heard the sounds of voices. They seemed to float upward from a room somewhere below, and she recognized her husband's voice at once, and then that of Prince Hali's.

"You're quite sure that you wish for your woman to ac-company you on the expedition, friend Ross?" Hali was say-ing in English. "You would not prefer to leave her behind in the protection of the harem?"

Stephanie held her breath. It was the very last thing she wanted. She gave no thought to customs and rules here. Ross was her husband, and he had promised to show her wonders beyond compare, and she was desperate to be with him as much as possible.

"I would not," she heard him say firmly. "I want my woman with me, as is the custom for a husband's comfort."

She heard his manner of address, like that of one Egyptian nobleman to another, and was insulted by the condescending tone of it. But by now, she knew that it was Ross's tactic to address Hali in a way he fully understood and accepted. And if she squirmed for a moment, she also accepted that any implied insult was of little consequence if it meant that she could remain by Ross's side.

"Of course. And I, too, will have my women with me," she heard Hali say with a laugh. "I had originally planned on only six, but as you saw last evening, I have decided on ten. There is even more comfort in numbers. When one woman has a sour face, there is always another, my friend. You know you are at liberty at any time to change your mind about including your choice from my harem. And in exchange—"

Stephanie drew in her breath in an angry gasp, guessing that the intended exchange was herself. To her relief, she heard Ross speak more sharply in Hali's own tongue, and then the prince's laughter became more indulgent as he placated him.

"Peace be among us, my friend! I know when I am thrashed. That is your English expression, I believe?"

"Something like that, Your Highness," Ross said with more of a smile in his voice than before.

"So, shall we take a stroll in the gardens before we join the advisers and your party to make our final plans?"

The voices became louder, and Stephanie shrank back against the wall of the balcony as the two men emerged from a room below and went off through the arbors together. She prayed that neither of them would look up, for it was one thing to be an eavesdropper in her stepfather's house, however traumatic the consequences; it would probably be considered the height of insult to have overheard Prince Hali's conversation.

She shivered suddenly, despite the heat of the day. However fascinating, this was still an alien land, and the culture was not as her own. She could never forget that. It would be brought home to her even more sharply when she was finally introduced to the women of the harem. But despite her reticence, she couldn't deny her curiosity about them.

"I take you now, lady," Yasmina said to her when it was nearing midday.

By then, Stephanie had frittered away an hour in the fragrant garden until it became too hot for comfort, and spent the next enjoyable hours on her favorite pastime, sitting by the open window in her room. Her sketch pad was becoming full already, but she had no doubt that Ross would provide her with more. And there was so much to transmit onto paper. So many things that she would never see again, that her deft fingers almost overtook themselves in her eagerness to record it all.

She had a natural ability, though she doubted if any of these scenes would be used in Ross's book. It was for her own pleasure—and her relatives' scepticism—that she sketched this fabulous palace and its occupants.

"I take you now, lady?" Yasmina said again when she made no move away from her room.

"Yes, I suppose so. You were going to show me the harem," she said reluctantly, and wishing that Ross was here by her side. Though he would not have been allowed into the women's sanctuary, of course. No men were allowed inside—other than those strange emasculated creatures her husband had told her about.

"Will there be any eunuchs in the harem?" she said now, and saw Yasmina's slanting dark eyes widen a little.

"Of course, lady. They tend the concubines, obeying every request. They are most devoted slaves."

"They sound like worker bees attending a queen, looking but never touching," Stephanie murmured almost to herself, remembering some of the more curious facts about nature from her schoolroom lessons.

"Lady will explain?" Yasmina said, puzzled.

"It doesn't matter," Stephanie said, rising from her seat. Yasmina obviously saw nothing wrong in the situation in the harem, and it was probably wiser to keep her opinions to herself. "Tell me, Yasmina, have you ever wanted to become a concubine yourself?"

The way the girl recoiled was as physical as if she had been struck.

"Oh, no, lady. I am not worthy. Only the highest and most alluring of women are chosen by my master to serve him in his Golden Chamber."

"I see."

Stephanie pushed aside the unsavory image of Prince Hali's choice for the bedtime ritual crawling beneath the sheets to reach his royal presence. Erotic though it had seemed at the time when Ross initiated her into the practice on the *Princess Maria*, it was far less so now that she had met the prince and had observed his way of selection last evening.

At the girl's obvious unease, she went on quickly.

"It's quite different in my country, Yasmina. A gentleman asks a lady to be his wife, and they remain faithful to each other for the remainder of their lives."

Yasmina spoke defensively. "It is so in my country, too, for those who are not highborn. But for a royal person, there are other ways, and other privileges."

"But what of the concubines' feelings?" Stephanie persisted. "Can they be happy to be just one of many, instead of being his only wife?"

Yasmina began to back away, and Stephanie knew she had gone too far in her probing.

"I take you to harem now, lady," she said, stubbornly ignoring the question. "The old one waits to greet you."

"The old one?"

"The lady Aletha, the first wife of my master, and mistress of the harem. She was given to him as a young boy. She awaits you now."

Silently, Stephanie followed the girl through the maze of passages in the palace of Shaladd. The information that Prince Hali had an older wife given to him as a young boy was distasteful to her, and Ross had not told her of it. The lady Aletha had not been presented to her, and she disliked the way Yasmina had referred to her as the old one. It seemed to underline still more just how subservient was the role of women here. They were surrounded by beauty and riches, and yet kept so very much in whatever place in his life Prince Hali had designated for them.

The twists and turns of the palace passages, with their richly decorated turquoise-and-gilt walls, their filigree arches and marbled floors, were beginning to disorient Stephanie. She would be totally unable to find her way back to her room alone, and she felt a stab of alarm. She had no idea where Ross was, and for all she knew she could be heading straight for danger, drawn into this beautiful web as smoothly and skillfully as a spider devoured a fly.

"Wait, please, Yasmina," she said with a little gulp as the girl glided on in front of her. She turned at once.

"Lady must rest a moment?"

"Lady is not happy," Stephanie said frankly. "How far away can the harem possibly be? We seem to have been walking around in circles."

Yasmina smiled slightly. "Lady right. The harem is in heart of palace, to keep safe from intruders."

Stephanie supposed that must say something. At least Hali cared about his women—or more likely for his continued self-gratification, said the cynical voice inside her head.

"So how much farther?" Stephanie said desperately.

"We here now."

They turned a corner, where Stephanie saw two enormously muscled men on guard. They were naked to the waist, and their skin was black and gleaming. They wore a kind of long skirt with the now-familiar curved sheathed swords at their sides. Their feet were bare. In appearance they were

magnificent and terrifying. They stood guard outside an exquisitely painted door, covered in artistry. Stephanie couldn't
make out what it depicted at first, until she realized with a
gasp that it represented naked couples in the act of love in
various and seemingly impossible positions, presumably
symbolizing the nature of this part of the palace.

She had leaned forward curiously to look at the paintings,
and just as quickly sprang back with hot cheeks. At the same
time, as if she represented a threat, the guards moved inward.
They unsheathed their swords in one swift movement, clash-
ing them together to form a barrier between herself and the
door.

Yasmina spoke to them in her own tongue, and they bowed
at once, sheathed their swords, and stood aside. Stephanie's
mouth was so dry she couldn't have spoken a word to defend
herself, if required. But she realized the girl was speaking
to her now.

"They are called the trusted eunuchs of the door, lady. We
go now inside the Hall of Beauty. Come. I show."

The door was opened at a touch, and Stephanie walked
through it. She drew in her breath at the sight of so much
beauty and elegance. She hadn't known what to expect, and
had formed no images of it in her mind. But even if she had,
nothing could have prepared her for this. The entire effect
was of soft pinks and golds, and was essentially feminine.

In the center of the vast area into which she was shown
was a huge round bathing pool, with shallow pink marble
steps leading into its pink-tinted water, to complement the
decor of the Hall of Beauty. The tiles surrounding it were
pink and gold, and there were little pink goldfish darting
about in its depths. Stephanie wasn't too sure about the sight
of them in the pool that was presumably meant for the women
to bathe, but she held her tongue and made no comment.

There were many more black-skinned eunuchs in the Hall,
some waving huge palm fans to keep the women cool, others
fetching and carrying whatever any woman wanted. It was

indulgence to the most wanton degree, thought Stephanie. Even though this was the heart of the palace, it was light and blissfully airy, and she could quite understand any woman's desire to live here—providing it didn't involve the other obligations.

There were probably fifty or more women, she assessed, all of them young, with exquisitely painted faces, and all beautifully dressed in the same kind of gossamer garments as the dancing girls she had seen in the Entertainment Chamber. They lounged on deep floor cushions or satin-covered sofas, some simply conversing together, others drinking wine from sparkling goblets, or eating grapes from the huge bowls of fruit scattered about on tables. Several were idly playing stringed instruments, and all of them were attended by the huge, powerfully muscled eunuchs, needing to do nothing for themselves.

Stephanie was intrigued and somehow repelled by these men. Surrounded by such blatantly voluptuous and painted females, the walls of the Hall of Beauty adorned with more erotic paintings like those on the outer door, how could they bear to remain unaroused, to have all their masculinity taken away from them, and to be rendered impotent? Must it not be the worst torture of all to be constantly in this place and reminded of all they had lost?

She realized to her embarrassment that she had been staring at one of the eunuchs with a surge of pity in her soul for that part of his body that should be the most potent of all. And he knew. As she raised her eyes to his face from that forbidden area, she could see by the small tightening of his lips that he knew.

To her relief she suddenly heard a clapping of hands. The women playing instruments stopped at once, and they all got to their feet and formed two lines.

"The lady Aletha comes now," Yasmina said behind Stephanie. "I wait outside until you ready to return."

"Don't leave me here—"

But Yasmina was already retreating, and two eunuchs were approaching her, sending her courage plummeting. Had this been a terrible mistake, after all? What was going to happen to her now? And how formidable was this first wife of the prince going to be? This old one?

The man stood silently by her side, motioning her to step forward. At the far end of the Hall she saw a very large, buxom woman seated on a pink throne, swathed in a mass of gossamer garments ranging in color from palest pink to deepest purple, her face hidden by a heavy veil. Rings glittered on her hands, and gold and jeweled bangles clanked on her arms, but Stephanie had no way of detecting whether or not the seclusion of the veil hid an ancient harridan.

She felt as though she was traveling a great distance, as the concubines moved back to let her through, smiling and giggling, their teeth showing startling white against their crimson mouths, their kohl-rimmed dark eyes and their honey-eyed skin. She felt as though she was going to a point where there was no returning, and there was no one to save her. No Ross, no anyone.

She felt a burning resentment toward her husband. How dare he leave her like this? There was a eunuch walking ahead of her, and another walking behind her.

She had reached the pink throne now, and the two eunuchs guarding her flanked her on either side, while the swathed and heavily veiled Aletha inspected her. Stephanie kept her eyes lowered, remembering Ross's instructions when she had first approached Prince Hali, and assuming that she must do the same in the presence of this woman who was the mistress of the harem.

She hated every second of it. She was not born to servitude, and in a gesture of defiance she jerked up her head and stared the woman right in the eyes. At the same moment, she heard Aletha laugh, and it was a sound that startled her out of her fear. It was raucous, good-natured, and the next moment Aletha had let the veil drop from her face, and was grinning broadly into Stephanie's astonished face. There was a heavy mask of kohl and face paint and rouge on the creased visage, but despite all of it, the eyes were as blue as Stephanie's own, and the face was unmistakably European.

"Surprised to see me, are you, pet?" she asked in a broad accent Stephanie didn't know, but which she could understand perfectly well.

"You—you're English, I think!" Stephanie stuttered, unsure whether or not she was abandoning protocol. The lady Aletha didn't seem to mind, and motioned her to sit on the pink velvet floor cushion beside her.

"Some call it English," she said cheerfully. "Others call it somewhere between the Scots brogue and the impossible. I'm originally from Northumberland, pet, nearer to Scotland than London, but one of your own, for all that. And it's more than pleasing to see you, lass, and to talk in my own language for a while. Though I've done me best to teach these charmers the rudiments over the years, and there's a fair sprinkling of them doing quite well at the English now."

Stephanie tried to stop her mouth from gaping open. Everything was going topsy-turvy in her mind again. She had expected the worst from this lady Aletha, and here she was, listening to this friendly woman's chatter.

"Away and bring us some tea, fellows," Aletha said briskly to the eunuchs now. "And none of your Egyptian muck, mind. The lady and meself want proper English tea, with milk and sugar. Isn't that right, pet?"

"That's right," Stephanie murmured. She swallowed. "Please forgive me for staring, but—well, you're not at all what I expected."

"I know, and I shouldn't have teased you, but it's a harmless little game I play on the rare occasions when we have visitors. And I daresay you'll want to know how I came to be here, and why I've stayed, since I'm sure that husband of yours didn't think to tell you."

"He did not," Stephanie muttered. "It was just one more of his little surprises."

Aletha laughed, waving the concubines away to go about their business of enjoying themselves, since there seemed little else that they did. Stephanie wondered just when it all began to pall, but it didn't appear to have done so for the woman seated on the pink throne.

"I came here many years ago with my father and a group of countrymen seeking new pleasures," she said. "Hali was a young lad then, and since I never had the countenance to attract men at home I was destined to remain unmarried, until Hali's advisers decided I could be the one to initiate him into the ways of love. It was quite mad, really, since neither of us knew what it was all about. Anyway, they bargained with my father for me. He was willing, and so was I, and I've been here ever since. As for the bedding, I was given highly detailed instructions in how to please a man, which I now pass on to the young ones. It's all very civilized."

It all sounded horrific to Stephanie, but Aletha seemed so serene and content with her life that she knew better than to make any adverse comment. Besides, she was all too well aware of the eunuchs standing nearby with their sheathed swords, and that the smile could probably be wiped off Aletha's face as easily as it had appeared.

When the tea came, she drank it gladly, relieved to find that Aletha's directive had been faithfully carried out. It could have been any little four-o'clock tea ritual at home, and as she thought it, Stephanie felt a wave of nostalgia rush through her.

"My master is interested in you, pet," the woman said casually after a few minutes. "It's the silvery hair that intrigues him the most, as well as the pale skin and the bright blue eyes."

She gave a small sigh before she continued. "My skin was once as pale as yours, and my eyes were just as bright, but everything fades in the end, even lust."

Stephanie spoke carefully. "My husband would never

agree to Prince Hali's wishes, and I could not, either. We're newly married, lady Aletha—"

"You may call me Alice. It will be a relief to hear my English name once more."

"Alice, then. As I said, we are newly married, and very much in love—" She bit her lip, wishing it were true, and that not all the love was on one side. But she dared not give a hint of the true circumstances to this woman. Friendly though she appeared, she was undoubtedly loyal to Hali, and Ross's reason for his hasty marriage to avoid the gift of six concubines would result in death for them both. She knew it now, as surely as she breathed.

"I can see it by the look on your face, pet," Alice said, nodding. "And do you please your husband?"

"I believe I do," she murmured, her face scarlet at this intimate turn of the conversation. Especially so with the eunuchs standing immobile, but within earshot.

"You only *believe* so!" Alice said, that raucous north country laugh emerging once more. "Then I must give you some secrets, and you will be *sure* so!"

"Oh, but it's not necessary, I promise you—"

Alice stood up from the pink throne, and held out a pink-tipped hand toward Stephanie.

"Come. We will go to my chamber, and I will give you the recipe for some oils and creams, for yourself and for your man. I will tell you of the most potent aphrodisiacs to make him lust for you. You will see that your cook prepares oysters on a bed of lettuce and a soup of garlic on the night that you wish to conceive, and the loving will be like nothing you have experienced before."

"Thank you," Stephanie said faintly, the very thought of such a concoction making her stomach heave. But she followed the buxom woman out of the Hall of Beauty, into a quiet room that was evidently the chief wife's domain, and was given detailed instructions on how to entice her man, how to feed him and tantalize him and make him pant with desire for her. And all of it went in and out of her head, as she wondered how on earth this Englishwoman had become so changed.

The more she thought of it, the more she resisted any idea of keeping any of her recipes in her head. She wanted none of it. She wanted to be away from here, to be back in the soft green meadows of the English countryside, and away from this cloying way of life that stifled and enveloped her.

Alice had finally finished with her instructions. By then, Stephanie had learned that the woman never left the harem now. She was no longer summoned to the Golden Chamber, and rarely saw Prince Hali, but she had graciously assumed the role of tutor and mentor to the young concubines. To Stephanie, it seemed an unutterably sad way of life, and even sadder that Alice saw nothing wrong in it.

She was escorted back to her room by the end of the afternoon, by which time she had taken lunch with the concubines, and reaffirmed that their sole purpose in life was to please their master. She felt degraded on their behalf, knowing that each of them was so eager to do Hali's every bidding. She finished off her daily diary entry quickly, adding little more to it, for there was nothing about this day's visit to the harem that she wanted to impart to anyone. She doubted that she could ever speak freely of it.

A while later, she turned eagerly when a knock came on her door, followed by Ross's voice. As he entered she rushed into his arms, uncaring that she was not meant to show such loving emotion in this arranged union, just wanting and needing the sanity of an English marriage so much.

"Well, if this is the treatment I'm to receive after a day apart, perhaps I should arrange it more often," he began with a smile, and then saw the tears she couldn't hide brimming on her lashes. "What is it? Didn't you enjoy your day, Stephanie?"

"You should have told me about Aletha, or Alice, or whatever she's called. Why didn't you tell me?"

He could feel her tension as he held her in his arms.

"Because I knew how much it would alarm you that an Englishwoman was Hali's first wife. He never mentions her now, and she's simply part of his initiation into manhood."

His words didn't altogether mollify her. "She implied that Hali's still interested in me, so what do you say about that? I kept wondering if he'd wanted me to see for myself just how luxurious and indolent a life the women lead."

"And did it make you want to share such a life?"

"It did not!" Stephanie said. "I couldn't bear to be one of those vapid creatures, just waiting on a man's pleasure, and knowing that I would be only one of fifty or so for him to choose from."

"I'm glad you think that way," Ross said, his arms tightening possessively around her. "It's the way I think, and have always thought, and not all the riches in this world would make me sacrifice you to Hali."

"You promise?" she said tremulously. "I couldn't bear it, Ross. I simply couldn't bear it. I would rather die—"

His mouth came down hard on hers, smothering the words, and it was so normal, so welcome, so masterful. Not in the degrading way of the harem, but in the way of a husband cherishing his wife. And she surrendered to his kiss, pulling him to her with a hunger that surprised him at first, and swiftly met a matching hunger in himself, until he swept her up in his arms and carried her to the bed.

A long while later, warmed by his lovemaking, she murmured into his bare shoulder.

"Is there anything in this world sweeter than total fidelity between husband and wife, Ross?"

"Nothing in this world," he said gravely, and she tried to believe that he truly meant it.

Thirteen

"There's a delay in our arrangements," Ross told her when he entered her room the following morning.

They had already eaten a good breakfast, and the servants had been to the rooms to pack up their clothes in preparation for the journey into the desert. There were only the toiletries and writing and sketching materials to be put into Stephanie's personal bag, and she spun around from the dressing table at his annoyed tone.

"What kind of delay?" she asked.

"Hali will go nowhere without consulting his advisers and astrologers, and they've now decided that today is not a good day for traveling. There was blood in the stars last night, which is considered to be a very bad omen. Hali has been advised to wait at least half of one more day and then see how the charts speak to him."

Stephanie stared at him. "Are you serious? Does he really believe in all that mumbo-jumbo?"

"You'd do well not to scoff in his presence," Ross advised. "You can't change a centuries-old way of life in a moment, and if the gods are against Hali's trek into the desert, wild horses won't drag him there."

"What gods?" Stephanie asked contemptuously, wondering how grown men could be so gullible.

"The gods of his ancestors, and of all the kings and princes that have gone before him. I thought you'd read enough ancient Egyptian history by now not to take them lightly," Ross said, clearly resenting her attitude.

"So I have, but it doesn't mean I believe in it all. And I never had much faith in astrology, anyway. Do these people really have enough influence to persuade Prince Hali not to travel when he pleases, Ross? And in any case, is there anything to prevent us starting out without him?"

"They have every influence on him, especially when he leaves the palace so rarely," Ross retorted. "If there's any hint of danger or of traveling under a bad omen, he will insist on waiting until the stars are favorable. He's urgently requested a second consultation at sundown, which could just alter things."

"Do you believe all this, too?" she said flatly.

He shrugged. "I prefer to keep an open mind. I've seen too many things in my travels to disbelieve anything. As to our going on alone, it would be seen as a great insult. And since there's safety in numbers, it would be far wiser to wait until Hali's ready, when we will have the added protection of his guards."

There seemed nothing she could say to prevent them spending one more frustrating day at Shaladd. She couldn't quite explain her need to get away from here as quickly as possible now. Far from seeing it as the rich and fertile oasis that it was, she could only see it as a prison for those young and nubile women who couldn't see beyond their beautiful noses to how captive they really were.

"So can we spend the day together, or is this another day when you'll be closeted somewhere with Prince Hali?" she asked, unable to hide her resentment.

Ross laughed. "If Hali is closeted with anyone, it will be his advisers and astrologers. I shan't see him again until later today. The rest of the team have been informed of the change of plan, and will no doubt make the most of a free day in the city. You and I may do likewise, if you wish."

"You mean it?" she said, her heart leaping with excitement at this unexpected outing.

"Why not? We'll visit the old marketplace, and you can try your luck at haggling for souvenirs. We could also make the climb to one of the lookout posts where the guards are still required to patrol the walls, and remain constantly vigilant for any hint of danger to Shaladd."

His words sent a little chill through her, reminding her that the oasis, seemingly so large and lush a stronghold within its stout walls, was still an isolated and vulnerable place in the loneliness of the desert. A place just waiting to be plundered by unscrupulous barbarians.

"You've no need to be anxious," Ross added, seeing her changing expression. "It's been many years since Shaladd was attacked, and the nomadic tribes in the vicinity are mostly peaceful ones."

"Mostly?" she said, a query in her voice.

"Stop worrying, Stephanie," he said, squeezing her around the waist for a moment. "Nothing will harm you while I'm here to protect you."

He seemed to hesitate, and for a wondering moment, Stephanie almost believed he was going to say something more. That he was about to say he loved and cherished her. But the moment passed without the words she longed to hear.

But once away from the palace in one of Prince Hali's smaller horse-drawn vehicles put at their disposal, she took deep, relaxing breaths, trying not to think too much about the women who never saw outside those palace walls, and whose families were happy and proud to relinquish them to the prince's demands.

"Why do you look so sad?" Ross inquired as they neared the sights, smells, and sounds of the bustling marketplace.

"I was thinking how thankful I am, not to be a prince's love slave," she said at once.

He looked at her quizzically for a moment, and she felt her fingers clasped in his.

"It would have been a tragedy for such a thing to happen," he said gravely.

She drew in her breath, waiting for him to say more, but he didn't. And yet she couldn't help feeling it was another of those "almost moments." He had told her that when they returned to England he would release her from this farce of a marriage if it was what she desired. But she knew now that it wasn't. And it tore her heart, knowing it was something that a lady could never tell him.

"So now that we've got that settled and out of the way, could you at least pretend to be enjoying yourself?" he said more briskly. "Let's see what the market sellers have got that would please your lady cousin. I don't imagine that you'll feel inclined to buy your stepfather a gift after the way he treated you."

"Probably not," she answered him coolly. "He wouldn't expect anything, but I'd certainly like to buy Cousin Claire a gift. She's never traveled anywhere, and I'm sure she'd love something that's typically Egyptian."

After exploring the tiny shops, crammed with goods, they settled for a small gilt statue of the Great Pyramid. The mysterious lion-headed figure of the Sphinx squatted in front of it, and the twin statues sat majestically on a marble plinth. Whether or not it represented a true likeness or was in the right proportion, Stephanie had no idea, but she knew it would please Claire.

They spent several lazy hours examining all the artifacts on display, and Stephanie was stunned by the variety of spices, whose aroma and color were more exotic than any she had seen before, and she promised herself to take some back for Claire on their return to Shaladd.

To Stephanie, the marketplace was nothing short of an Aladdin's cave. Beaten silver and brassware glinted in the sunlight, dazzling the eyes, along with a huge array of richly woven carpets, exquisitely made perfume bottles with close-fitting stoppers in all shapes and colors, and trinkets of every description.

"You seem especially taken with the perfume bottles," Ross said. "Which do you like best?"

"I love them all! The turquoise one reminds me of the slim minarets, so delicate and pretty—but so is the rose-colored one shaped like a bell. And the design of the gold-and-white one is so like the royal palace—"

"You shall have them all," Ross said. "Wrap up a dozen of my lady's choice, boy," he instructed the young Arab boy who was eagerly anticipating a sale.

Stephanie felt a surge of pleasure. The bottles could be used purely as decorative dressing-table trinkets, or filled with rose water or exotic perfume, or even bath oils. But, however and wherever she used them, they would always remind her of this magical place, and of being here with Ross.

"Now we'll go to the lookout post, if you think you can climb a hundred steps," he said, so prosaic that her own dreaming thoughts were dissipated at once.

"Of course. I'm quite used to taking exercise. And after that miserable camel ride to get here, I think I'm capable of anything," she added, though even as she said it, she was quite surprised to realize how quickly the slight bruises from the ride had gone, and the memory of discomfort had faded. She could probably get used to camel travel quite quickly, which was just as well, considering there would be plenty of it in the days ahead, she reminded herself.

All the same, climbing a hundred winding stone steps to the top of the high lookout post in the blazing heat was definitely something that she wouldn't recommend too often. She felt quite faint by the time she had reached the top, and hardly noticed when the robed guard on duty greeted her husband warmly. The lookout was a small, circular affair, with a walkway set into the walls, along which the guard was about to take his vigilant walk, meeting a fellow guard from the next lookout post before turning back.

But Stephanie wasn't overly concerned with the daily procedure of the guards. She was too busy leaning against Ross for a few moments to allow her heart to stop thudding. The climb had taken more out of her than she realized. When she felt able to open her eyes and look beyond the oasis walls to the infinite vastness of the desert beyond, she felt immediately giddy at realizing how high they had climbed, and she clung to him wordlessly.

"I think I must take you sightseeing more often if this is the response I get," he said in an amused voice. "It's quite endearing to have you hold on to me in that helpless way, instead of so frequently battling against me."

"I do not battle against you!" she said hotly, and then laughed wryly, knowing he had been baiting her, and that she had risen to the bait so easily. "I was just startled when I opened my eyes. It's foolish, I suppose, but I never dreamed there would be quite so much desert. It gives you a very different perspective, seeing it from on high rather than seeing it from the back of a camel."

"That's why I wanted to bring you here. I didn't want you to underestimate what we're about to do."

"What do you mean by that?"

She made no attempt to extricate herself from his arms, and apparently he saw no reason to let her go.

"I want you with me, Stephanie, make no mistake about that, but if you're having second thoughts about it, there's still time for you to say so."

"I'm not. I couldn't bear to be left behind. It's the very last thing I want, Ross, believe me."

"All right. There's no need to get so heated about it, my dear girl, but you must be aware that the desert can be a frightening place. The entire company of earlier expeditions have been found bludgeoned to death by rogue tribesmen. Sometimes it's been impossible to identify them, because their bones have picked clean by the buzzards. Others have been apparently swallowed up in the sands during a sand-storm, and lost forever."

"Why are you telling me such things at this late stage? Are you really doing your best to put me off?" she asked, her voice far from steady at the terrifying picture his words were producing in her mind.

"No. I just wanted you to know that you still have the choice of staying behind, or coming with us. I forced you into a life you didn't choose, and you should at least have the choice of remaining in the care of the lady Aletha or journeying on."

His offer made her curious, for hadn't she already heard him tell Prince Hali that he wanted his woman with him? She couldn't tell whether this caring for her safety meant that he also cared for her.

But she already suspected that he cared for her in a way. She wasn't stupid. He showed his feelings for her every time he made love to her. It might not be the kind of committed caring she craved for as yet, but it was certainly a kind of loving. And for now, she had to be satisfied with that.

"I go with you," she said huskily.

He folded her more tightly in his arms, and in the seclusion of the lookout post there was no one else to see the moistness in her eyes as she breathed in the scent of him. No one else to hear the pounding beat of her heart as she heard the sudden gentling of his voice.

"I wanted to hear those words, Stephanie, but I had to give you the choice."

They heard the sound of approaching footsteps, and broke apart as the robed guard came walking back toward the look-out post. They took their leave of him, and retraced their way down the stone steps once more. The oppressive heat seemed even heavier inside the enclosed walls of the city, and Stephanie felt more exhaustion than a whole morning's horse-riding in the country could produce.

"Would it be all right if I rested in my room this afternoon, Ross?" she murmured.

He glanced at her from his side of the small vehicle taking them back to the palace.

"Of course it would. You're free to do as you wish—within certain limits," he added, without actually saying what those limits were. He gave a slight smile. "I'd be more than happy to join you if I hadn't been summoned to Prince Hali's chambers later this afternoon, though I fear you might not get too much rest if I stayed with you."

His meaning was clear, and she felt her skin prickle. The color rushed to her face, and her blood sang. He wanted her. There was no denying the fact that he wanted her. However much this marriage had been forced upon them both—and she must never forget that he wouldn't have chosen it, either—there was never any doubt that physically they were entirely compatible. But it was far more than that to her.

The times when he made love to her were the most ecstatic and euphoric of her life. If she craved for his love, then at least at those times, she could pretend that she truly had it. *It wasn't enough,* said the small restless voice inside her head, but if it was all he had to give, then for now she must settle for it. Many women would settle for far less, Stephanie thought, remembering the torrid nights they had shared, and the intense pleasure he gave her.

"You have a look of deep concentration on your face, Stephanie," she heard Ross say in an amused voice as they neared the palace of Shaladd. "Have I offended you, or could it be that you're also wishing we could spend this afternoon together?"

She tried to give him some flippant reply, but the words stuck in her throat, and she found herself answering in a husky way again.

"Perhaps I was," she murmured. "It seems that I have little enough time to spend with my husband these days, and once we go into the desert, we'll always be surrounded by other people."

She saw his look of surprise at this frankness, and she bit her lip, wondering if she had gone too far. Pride wouldn't let her admit to him how much she loved him, and how devastated she would be if their marriage had to end, but even in the poorest of marriages there could surely be some show of affection from time to time. There must be *something* that held such couples together. His hand closed over hers, and as always, she tingled to the mere touch of his skin on hers.

"I can promise you many desert nights when we will be quite alone, my dove," he said. "And no matter how elaborate the prince's sleeping arrangements might be, no one will disturb us in the privacy of our tent. We'll be in a world of our own."

She swallowed at the imagery his words evoked, not knowing what he meant about the prince's arrangements, and not caring. But she couldn't help wondering about the preparation of Prince Hali's ten chosen concubines right now. They, too, would be awaiting the expedition into the desert, sleeping in tents that were far removed from the pampered luxury of the harem, and never knowing which of them would be summoned to Hali's tent for the royal lovemaking. She would never exchange her life for theirs, she thought fervently. She already had the best.

They returned to the palace in the early part of the afternoon, and ate the cold lunch that had been left ready for them in the dining hall. Ross was informed by a servant that Prince Hali would be pleased to receive him as soon as he had eaten.

"You see?" Ross said, as the servant withdrew. "Hali was quite amenable to our exploring this morning, but now he wants his pound of flesh from me."

"What an extraordinary thing to say," Stephanie said in alarm. "You make him seem like an ogre."

"Not at all. But even as his guest, I'm expected to be available whenever he demands my presence."

"It should surely be the other way around," she said uneasily, "though I can't imagine that any English host would demand a guest's presence."

"But this is not England, my sweet. Haven't you accepted that yet? Shaladd, above all places, has its own rules, and its ultimate ruler. None of his subjects ever questions Hali, and neither do wise visitors."

His voice held a small warning, and she realized he had eaten quickly, and was already preparing to go to his audience with Hali. Again, Stephanie knew how much she hated this despot who seemed to control everything he surveyed. Not that she believed Ross was the type of man to be controlled by anyone. He was too strong, too masculine for that, but he was also wiser than she, and she gave a small nod in answer.

"I understand, and I shall gladly retire to my own room for a couple of hours, or until you bring me any further news of our movements," she said.

And perhaps when he came to her room, he might decide to stay a while.

As he passed by her chair, he placed his hands on her shoulders, leaned forward and kissed the nape of her neck. It was so unexpected that she felt her senses leap with a glow of pleasure, and thought with a touch of shame how little it took for her to be aroused by him. But she simply couldn't help it. She was in love for the first time in her life, and every instinct in her begged to be loved by him in return. Without thinking, she leaned her head back a little, and for a moment she felt the warm caress of his hand on her cheek.

"In case I forget to tell you now and then, Stephanie, I want you to know that I'm well pleased with my beautiful wife," she heard him say in an oddly controlled voice. "And there would never be any question of my accepting favors from another."

"Thank you," she said faintly, for it was the nearest he had come to vowing fidelity to her, however temporary.

She accepted his comment now, and believed it. He intended being faithful to her for as long as they remained together, and it was a warming thought to keep in her heart when she retired to her room for a welcome rest in the hottest part of the day.

She hadn't intended to sleep. But no one would disturb her, unless she rang for a servant. The shutters at the windows were drawn to keep out the fierceness of the afternoon sun. She slid out of her dress and confining undergarments, and lay beneath the cool sheet in her petticoat, closed her eyes, and drifted immediately into sleep, and the dreams of fulfillment with the man she loved.

She awoke with the touch of someone's mouth on her own, wondering if she was still dreaming. Her dreams had followed a now familiar pattern. She and Ross had been passionately embracing, and his hands and lips had lovingly caressed every inch of her body while he whispered endearments to her. Their mutual pleasuring had been intense and erotic and beautiful, and as it mounted to a crescendo, she had lost what few inhibitions were left to her, vowing to love him for ever and beyond.

"Ross," she murmured faintly, opening her eyes to find his dark shape fractionally above her. The whole room had grown dusky now, and she knew the hours must have passed while she lay in rapturous dreams. And while the core of her throbbed and longed for him, she was sure that the sweet pressure of his mouth on hers hadn't been all dreaming.

Without thinking, she reached out her arms for him, and he held her for a moment and then gently put her aside. But the expectation that the dream was about to become reality was shattered when he spoke with barely controlled impatience in his voice.

"We go tonight, Stephanie. Hali has persuaded the astrologers to give in to him, although they are still arguing about the wisdom of it. But he got his way, since their opinions were divided, so the rest of the team will be told to assemble here at nine o'clock, when the conjunction of planets and stars are presumed to be at their most favorable aspect."

It was all so ludicrous to her, that grown men could change a vital course of action because of what was written in the stars! She'd never been able to believe fully in such things, and she wasn't at all sure that Ross did, either, but it was clearly to everyone's advantage to go along with Hali's beliefs.

"So we travel at night as before, but it seems very odd to be setting out so late," she said dubiously, sitting up slowly as she came more consciously out of her sleep.

"It's been agreed that it's the most favorable time," he repeated. "Everything is ready, so there's no point in delaying. The moon will be full and high, and the desert will be as bright as day for traveling, and at its coolest. You'll see the advantages when you remember our journey here."

She remembered the heat and the discomfort of daytime travel only too well. And she quickly realized that there was obviously no time for sharing special moments now. Ross was fired up with keenness for getting the expedition underway, and hardly noticed that she was in a state of undress, and still relaxed and drowsy. Such abruptness, coming so soon after the erotic dream that had seemed about to continue into blissful reality, made her sharp.

"I suppose I'd better dress then," she said crossly. "I presume we shall have time to eat before we leave?"

"Of course, but I've arranged to have our dinner sent to my room, Stephanie. Hali wishes to be alone for contemplation before we set out. And after we've eaten . . ." He hesitated.

"Yes? What then?"

Ross went to one of the wall closets, and returned with some robes over his arms.

"We shall both dress in Arab robes for traveling, Stephanie, and you will wear the veil at all times except when we're alone. This will give you protection from the sun and sand."

"And from Prince Hali's lecherous eyes?" she asked daringly. He gave a short laugh.

"From those, too," he agreed. "But there will be many others traveling with us, Arabs and Europeans, and the less conspicuous you are, the better it will be. We can do nothing about the color of your eyes, but it's wisest that you keep your hair covered by a long scarf, and you will secure the veil to it."

For a moment, he stretched out his hand and caught a silver tendril in his fingers, his voice truly regretful as if loath to cover up her glorious hair. But although she saw the sense of it, she felt a shudder of unease at being the object of men's lust. She didn't really care for the idea of wearing loose robes instead of her normal clothes, but she had to admit that they would be far cooler than the fashionably tight European garments.

"Do we take all our baggage with us?" she asked. "I'm sure there will be times when I long for my own clothes—"

"Not all," Ross said. "Just enough for comfort, but the rest will be waiting here for our return. It's all been arranged, Stephanie, and our belongings have already been put into two separate packages. You need do nothing, my sweet."

It sounded effortless, but to Stephanie, it wasn't right. Everything was being done for her, but everything was also being taken out of her hands, while she had no say in the matter. It definitely didn't feel comfortable. When she returned home to England, to the country estate in Oxfordshire that she and Ross would share, she would want to be mistress of her own household, with a say in everything.

"What's wrong now?" Ross said with an impatient frown at her indrawn breath.

"Nothing," she said quickly. "Just ghosts walking over my grave, that's all."

And she wished immediately that she hadn't even thought of such a thing. If she had been of a more imaginative and superstitious nature, it would seem the very worst omen to suggest, when they were on the brink of the great adventure. She swallowed hard. The great adventure. She must never forget that this was what it was, only somehow the thrill of it had become a little tarnished in her mind, and she simply couldn't explain why.

Dinner was brought to Ross's room in due course, and she was invited to join him there. It was so odd and formal an arrangement, when normal English couples would expect to share the intimacy of their bedroom at all times. Royalty didn't, of course, and that was probably why Prince Hali's household followed such protocol for his guests, since the few guests who came to Shaladd would be important personages, but surely none could ever be as illustrious as the prince himself!

"Do you want to share your amusement with me?" Ross said as she smiled into her dish of chicken and spiced vegetables, already duly tasted by a servant.

"I was only thinking what a poor life royalty must lead compared with we ordinary mortals, that's all."

"I hardly think royalty would agree with you, and I'm not sure what you mean, either," he said.

"Well, they can't do the simple things we can do, can they? For all their wealth, they can't travel about freely or go into a marketplace like we did today. They can't go to a theater without being on their guard in case somebody wants to assassinate them. They can't marry whom they choose. Don't you think those are enough disadvantages to be going on with?"

"You seem to have done a great deal of thinking about this," Ross said.

"Does the fact that I have an inquiring mind bother you?" she asked defensively.

"It does not. I prefer it to having a merely decorative companion without a thought in her head. But I thought we'd already established that. A sharp brain as well as beauty creates a very potent partnership, my dear, and I consider myself fortunate to have a wife with both."

"Even a wife whose tongue sometimes runs away with her?" Stephanie said.

"That rather depends on the journey her tongue takes," he answered. And although he wasn't given to ambiguity, she knew very well by the sudden hotness in his voice and eyes that his thoughts, too, had returned to the erotic nights they had shared. And the surge of excitement was back in her veins, in anticipation of all the romantic desert nights that were yet to come.

But by the time they were ready to leave their rooms to join the prince and his entourage, they resembled two strangers in their unfamiliar robes. And for the life of her, Stephanie couldn't recover that surge of excitement. It was the mode of dress, she decided desperately, or the time of night, or the knowledge that this was the last time she and Ross would be truly alone for heaven knew how long.

Or the fact that all his energies now would be concentrated on the job he loved the best, and this final expedition into the desert in the hope of finding treasures beyond price. She knew all about a man's addiction to a cause. Her stepfather's had been to the gambling tables; Ross's was more noble, but still an addiction of a kind. And she knew about a woman's place when a man had such an addiction, practically forgotten, pushed aside, very much a secondary consideration in the superior male order of things.

What in heaven's name is wrong with me? she asked herself angrily as she and Ross went down the wide curving staircase to join the rest of the party *When have I ever allowed myself to be so intimidated by anyone, even a prince!*

But she stepped out into the moonlight in her flowing robes, her hair completely hidden, and only her eyes visible above the linen veil, to where the princely caravan awaited them.

And then she knew she was only fooling herself. Not for Hali was there an undignified ride into the desert. All the camels were saddled for adequate comfort, but the royal beast had a deeply cushioned saddle across its back, containing a thronelike seat for Hali, while a gold-and-purple silken canopy above was designed to keep out the fiercest rays of the sun.

There were five camels for the ten concubines. Each animal had a seat on either side of its body, on which the heavily veiled girls were to ride. It didn't look too uncomfortable, and obviously Hali wouldn't want his women bruised and battered when they were summoned to his tent, Stephanie thought cynically.

She could hear them chattering nervously in their own language. She sensed that they would be feeling very apprehensive, remembering that it would be the first time they had left Shaladd since entering the harem. Other camels were laden with the royal tents and baggage, and all the expeditionary equipment was dispatched on the backs of the carrier camels.

There was so much noise and hustle, and so many Arab attendants to organize the entourage, that Stephanie began to wonder if they would ever get started. It was surely a more ridiculously formal procession than Ross would want, and she was relieved to see the presence of the Europeans, even Mac and Dawson.

But at long last they were about to leave and the stark, clear moonlight lent a certain glamor to the occasion. The great high gates of Shaladd were slowly opened wide to a fanfare of trumpets, and a swirl of stinging sand whipped into their faces from the vast desert beyond.

Fourteen

By the third day of traveling, Prince Hali had decreed that they must continue in daylight, since he needed his rest at night. Hali clearly needed his comforts, too, Ross told Stephanie, and this self-indulgence made her resent the royal personage even more. Daytime travel was a hundred times more uncomfortable than traveling at night. And if she had thought the desert was an alien place before, it became ever more evident to Stephanie now. As they slowly journeyed south, the blazing sun burned through her robes, and the influx of sand made her frequently desperate for water for her parched throat.

"Don't drink too much or too quickly," Ross constantly advised her. "We need to conserve all the water we carry. There are precious few watering holes to be found in the desert from now on."

"I'll try not to take more than my fair share then," Stephanie retorted, sharp with irritation.

But she knew she must abide by the rules. The longing for a bath, and to sink in the sheer, indulgent luxury of her bathroom at Shaladd, must be forgotten for the present. She tried to ignore her constant thirst, and instead, she concentrated on taking stock of every weird and wonderful dune for when she could get to her sketch pad.

To Stephanie, all of it simply screamed out to be recorded for British eyes to see, for comparatively few could have any idea of the stark natural beauty, the shapes and shadows, and the startling colors that went from palest ochre to deepest tan, and everything in between.

Ross might want her artistic ability for his records, but she would also want to show the more dramatic elements of this journey to Cousin Claire, and to anyone else who appreciated them. And in her mind, she already envisaged a romantic desert scene painted lovingly in oils, that would hang in the Kilmarron drawing room as a permanent reminder, and to show to their children.

She pushed such heady notions aside, and as they went deeper into the desert, she also questioned that word *romantic,* for there was less and less evidence of living things. There were occasional bedouin nomads on the horizon, but who could really tell where the horizon was? Was it that shimmering heat haze that suddenly and alluringly transformed itself into a place of unbelievable and tantalizing beauty, bearing life-giving water and trees and just as quickly disappeared?

"It's nothing but a mirage," Ross told her when she commented for the tenth time on the fact that they seemed to be nearing a small, lush oasis during the late afternoon of the fourth day.

By then, they had camped each night, and the performance of erecting Prince Hali's sumptuous tent would be expediently undertaken by the eunochs and attendants, while he waited impatiently for his food to be tasted, ate it with disgusting haste, and then commanded whichever of his concubines took his fancy, to attend him that night.

Stephanie had long since decided that he sickened her. He was the epitome of debauchery and self-gratification. And when the group settled down for the night, and the great yellow moon rose high in the heavens above them, spreading light and shade on the contours of the sand and turning it into a magical place for lovers, she did her best to close her mind to the subjugating rituals that would be being observed in the royal tent.

She was assured on that point. From the moment they closed the tent flap against the night, and were alone, Ross made no secret of his desire for her. The nights were far cooler than the days, but the two people inside the Kilmarron tent were filled with an inner fire that raged between them, and surfaced nightly. She was thankful that her husband shared their marital tent with her, and wanted no other.

Through the canvas of the tent, the moonlight lit herself and Ross in a soft, romantic glow, and she felt a surge of desire as she lay waiting for him to disrobe. She never tired of watching his elegant, powerfully built frame. There was not an ounce of spare flesh on him, and in the soft moonlight he was very beautiful to her, as beautiful as a sculpted statue. She wondered fleetingly why so few women ever thought of calling a man's body beautiful.

"Sometimes I wish I could be inside that lovely head of yours, to discover your thoughts, my sweet wife," she heard him say, as he saw her watching him so intently. "Does your womanly modesty like what it sees?"

He was shameless, she thought, quite shameless. And a sliver of answering mischief ran through her mind. He was so much the arrogant, virile male, preening himself for her approval, and she was just as wanton, lying there in her nakedness, awaiting her mate.

"Well, yes, it does!" She spoke quickly, before she lost her nerve, and reminded herself that refined English ladies presumably didn't compliment the sight of a man's virility. "Does it shock you that I should say so?"

He gave a satisfied laugh, and then he was swiftly inside the blanket with her, his hands warm on her skin, seeking and stroking and caressing, and bringing forth little muted sounds of pleasure from her throat.

"Nothing about you shocks me, sweetheart. I feel only delight that you revel in our joining the way that you do. It's an added bonus to our union that I hardly expected, nor had any right to."

He bent his head to kiss each of her peaked breasts, and no doubt assumed that her intake of breath was because of the sensual contact of his mouth on her rosy nipples. It was, of course, but not entirely so. It was a breath of pleasure bordering on pain, because it brought so sharply into focus the reminder of why he had married her.

It happened often enough for her to sense that he never fully allowed himself to forget, even in the throes of passion, that theirs was a union that was destined to end once this expedition was over and they returned to England. He had given her his promise. She would be handsomely rewarded for her services and presumably given an establishment of her own, to live in comfort for the rest of her days. She would be given her freedom, after doing her duty.

But she knew by now that there could be no comfort for her without him, and that she would never be free of him. She found herself clinging to him with more fervor than usual, gripping his powerfully muscled shoulders and pulling him fiercely down to her.

"Be patient, my lovely girl," Ross said with obvious delight at her eagerness. "We have the whole night ahead of us, and there are many ways of pleasuring one another."

And then she gave up thinking, as sheer sensation enveloped her, and there was nothing so important or so beautiful in all the world as being held and loved and possessed by this man who belonged to her in the eyes of God.

"You're so beautiful," she heard him say roughly, as his mouth and his every feathery touch set fire to her senses.

And she wanted to touch him, too, to hold and caress and kiss, while the eddying magic of passion held them both in thrall. It could surely be no different for him, for his maleness was so potent, so desiring of her, that it seemed to Stephanie that their bodies and souls were fused together in this sweet ecstasy.

Her wild, exalted love would let her believe nothing else in these precious times when no one else existed for either of them. There was only each other, two people becoming one, until life shuddered from him to her in the final pulsing moments of release that left her with eyes damp, and her hands clinging to him as if she couldn't bear to let him go. And if she felt a momentary sadness at such times, it was only because this perfect intimacy was now ended—until the next time.

"I'm sorry," she heard Ross mutter, still heavy on her, still a part of her. "I know I have no right to expect or demand such a response from you, but you have only yourself to blame, my love."

Stephanie's eyes opened slowly, without her ever being aware that she had closed them. She felt his fingers trace the soft tears of pleasure on her cheeks.

"I don't understand you, or this constant talk of rights," she whispered. "What have I done that's so wrong?"

His breath was warm on her cheek, and his mouth sought hers in a gentle kiss that belied the momentous arousal of passion that had just preceded it. It was one of the things she loved about him—his tenderness, as well as his passion. But there was less tenderness in his voice when he spoke.

"You're too delectable a wife for a gambling man who won you through devious means," he said in an almost angry, almost accusing manner. "You should be selfish and grasping and shrewish, then it would be easier—"

"Yes?" Stephanie said, holding her breath as he paused abruptly. Was this the declaration of love at last that she had waited so long to hear? She felt her heart thud beneath him, their bodies still damp and filmy with heat, still more one entity than two.

Please say it, she begged silently. *Tell me you love me, and will always love me.*

She heard him give a strange little laugh, and he eased himself away from her, though not too far, for their tent was confined, and the bed was small. But he moved far enough for her to feel his loss, and her disappointment was acute.

"It's not good for a young lady to be paid too many compliments, or it will turn her head," he said lightly.

She had drawn the blanket up to her neck to hide her nakedness by then, and was somewhat tangled up inside it. She was definitely at a disadvantage right now, when it came to showing anger. She found herself wishing she was wearing her most elegant gown and her best superior manner. And especially her stoutest outdoor boots so that she could stamp her feet and rage at him.

"That's just the kind of remark I heard in the nursery," she snapped instead. "Why shouldn't a child—or anyone else, for that matter—be paid a compliment? What possible harm can it do to hear something good about oneself?"

She could hear the teasing in his voice now.

"Haven't you had enough compliments since we've been together, minx? Do you really need me to keep telling you I think you're beautiful and desirable, and that I'm more than satisfied with my choice of bride? I thought my actions told you that well enough. Or maybe you haven't had enough?"

But she was no longer in the mood for this kind of teasing. The desert night was majestic and beautiful, and their lovemaking had been as wonderful as ever. Yet now it was all spoiled, because however many compliments he paid her, they meant nothing at all if he didn't tell her he loved her. Nothing at all.

She felt his hand caress the soft curve of her belly beneath the blanket, and resisted the temptation to shiver at his touch. She held herself rigid, not wanting him to know how desperate she was for even one crumb of affection that wasn't tempered by lust.

"I've had quite enough, thank you," she heard herself say primly. "I'd prefer to sleep, if you don't mind. And if you wanted a shrew for a wife, you should have married one."

There was silence for a moment, and then Ross removed his hand from her body.

"I'm beginning to think perhaps I have," he said coolly. "Or at least a wife who blows hot and cold when the mood suits her. It wouldn't do for Prince Hali, my dear."

"But it doesn't have to, thank heavens," she whipped out, and turned her back on him.

But the cold shiver running through her veins now had nothing to do with Ross's nearness. She was not unaware that the prince's entourage far outnumbered the Europeans in the expedition, and apart from themselves and their team, everyone else was Egyptian and loyal to the prince. She was perfectly aware that should the unthinkable happen, and Hali turn against his 'friend Ross,' she would be at his mercy, absorbed into the harem and never heard of again. There was even the impossible thought that Ross might even yet allow the prince to take one nightly fill of her, as a gift to a friend.

Her breath was ragged in her throat as the thoughts raced through her mind and wouldn't be stilled. She couldn't help wondering now just how foolish it had really been for her to accompany Ross into the desert. Although he had offered to let her stay at Shaladd, she had always felt the choice wasn't really hers to make, aside from feigning illness. Even then, they might have waited for her recovery, until the conjunction of the planets and stars was favorable for the success of the expedition.

She found herself thinking about the astrologers' warnings, and wished away such thoughts. And yet, through the jittering fears, she began to feel a strange calmness. As if she could hear their monotone voices reciting the words, she knew that those austere foretellers would have said it was her destiny to be here with Ross Kilmarron, and to live or die with him.

It was written in the stars, and the stars never lied. And if it was a philosophy with which any questioning person might disagree, it was still an oddly comforting one. And with that thought in her head, she slept.

They were due to reach the valley where the rockface tomb was situated in another wearying three days' time. By then, Stephanie was well aware of the vagaries of the desert sand, never still, always moving, the dunes constantly changing shape against the merciless cerulean sky. It hurt the eyes and stung the throat, and the scorching heat never let up for an instant during daylight hours. The nights were different, and Stephanie was doubly glad of Ross's embracing arms.

"The astrologers forecast a *khamsin*," he told her as they journeyed on. "But with luck, we'll have reached the valley by then, and our camp will afford us some shelter."

"What is this *khamsin?*" she asked suspiciously, unable to remember whether or not he had explained it to her once before.

"It's what they call the very powerful, hot desert wind. It may last for a day, or continue for more than a week before it eases. It's been known to bury whole villages—"

"And the astrologers forecast that there's one coming?" she said in a fright. Her eyes strained against the saffron sand, like a sea of shimmering waves where the slightest breeze rippled its surface, and she felt terror at the reported force of this desert wind. As far as the eye could see, there was nothing in its path to stop it, no trees or other vegetation, no buildings.

"But perhaps not for weeks, by which time we'll have returned to Shaladd."

"So they take care not to make their predictions too definite, do they?" she asked witheringly, to hide her sudden feeling of panic. "It could be tomorrow, or it could be next month! Or they could be completely wrong about it!"

"I doubt that they're wrong in their calculations, apart from the actual timing. But obviously I shouldn't have told you," Ross said shortly. "You have the female attitude to danger, wanting to retreat from it immediately."

"And what do *you* have, sir?" Stephanie said sarcastically, though it wasn't easy to be sarcastic from the back of a camel, while trying vainly to push away the confining veil from her mouth by unfeminine little spitting movements with her tongue, and finding her palate becoming ever drier in the process.

"I have the explorer's need to challenge danger," he said with maddening male superiority.

"Then I apologize for being a mere woman," she snapped, and heard him laugh as his hand reached out to squeeze hers for a moment.

"Don't ever apologize for that, my dove. The best day's work I ever did was finding you."

He rode on ahead as the man Dawson called out to him, his camel's feet scattering a fine spray of sand upward. But it wasn't only the sand that stung Stephanie's eyes at that moment. It was the sweetness of one of those unexpected remarks he sometimes made, which probably meant little to him, but meant all the world to her.

The caravan was halted while the final directions were discussed, and Stephanie was glad to relax for a few moments. She glanced back to the concubines' camels, where the young girls sat stiffly on their double seats, veiled and aloof, and she wished she could have made a friend among them. But none of them ever spoke to her, and she had no idea if it was from choice or because of royal protocol. She didn't even know if there was one friendly countenance among them, for it was impossible to distinguish any features behind the heavy veils.

The shining city of Shaladd, so luminous and beautiful against the emptiness of the desert, was no more than a memory now, and only the bedecked and bannered tent that was erected each evening belied the fact that a royal personage traveled abroad.

She sighed, wondering again why she had ever set out on this hazardous journey. But she knew why. She was Ross's wife, and her place was by his side. Nothing could alter that. There was also love, of course. Love meant being together, and it would take more than a desert wind to tear them apart, Stephanie thought resolutely. And she refused to heed the fact that she was probably thinking like a reckless, romantic fool.

They had reached the valley, where the encircling rock faces soared high above them. It was as hot as Hades within the sheltering rocks, and Stephanie wondered just why those ancient nobles had chosen to be buried so far from civilization. But it was probably to do with their beliefs, as she had discovered that from her reading. Here, they were in commune with nature and the gods, and well away from tomb robbers, or so they had believed.

Thousands of years ago, when fear and superstition had kept their tombs intact from prying eyes, it had been so, but time had proved them wrong, and Ross told her that many of the tombs had been plundered over the centuries.

"Well, isn't that what you're doing?" she asked him bluntly. "Aren't you every bit as bad as the grave robbers who reputedly exhume dead bodies and sell them for laboratory experiments?"

"Good God, how do you know of such things?" he exclaimed irritably.

"My stepfather did not care for me to read the newspapers, but he could never resist reading the more ghoulish reports aloud, to see my horrified reaction. So—are you not just as bad as those grave robbers?" she accused.

"Certainly not. This is a recognized expedition to recover the artifacts of a rich nobleman whom Hali believes to be one of his ancient ancestors. Most of the treasures we find will be presented to the museum in Alexandria, as I've already told you. Some will be retained by Hali himself, and with his permission a few will be allowed to be taken out of the country for the British Museum. My own reward comes from the fact that Hali has put extra expeditionary funds at our disposal, and the rest will come from the book I've been commissioned to write, for which your drawings will be of immense value."

"Then I'm glad to be of use."

He was so formal, so precise, and so was she in her reply. He glanced at her set face. She had been so thrilled by the thought of this expedition into unknown territory, traveling at Ross's side, two pioneers of the most romantic kind. But now they were here, and there was nothing to be seen but dreary rockfaces, sand and ever more sand, and the bustling activity of the bearers, the eunuchs, and the Europeans, as they set up camp.

"I promised to show you wondrous things, Stephanie, and so I shall. Just be patient a little while longer," he said more gently.

She was immediately irked by her own childishness. He would be showing her things of which her compatriots could have no comprehension, and she should try to exercise that patience that so often eluded her.

"Well, I'll try," she said quietly, and was rewarded by a generous smile that widened his well-shaped mouth and lit up his dark eyes. He was even more fabulously handsome now, Stephanie thought fleetingly. He had always been so to her, but in his powerful demeanor in his Arab robes, and his skin taking on the rugged hue of the desert sheik, he was everything a woman could desire in a man.

But this was no time for daydreaming. The tents were put up now for the two weeks they planned to remain in the valley. It could hardly be called a little home from home, but at least they would be stable for those two weeks, and establish some sort of routine. As an official observer and artist, Stephanie was to be allowed to enter the tomb, although Ross had told her this had met with much disapproval from the Egyptians, who were sure that a woman's presence in the tomb would bring bad luck.

Curiously, it was the astrologers who had declared that since gods and goddesses were buried in the royal tombs, there was nothing to prevent a woman of noble birth or patronage entering the sacred place, and to Stephanie's relief, Hali had given permission. It would have been galling and frustrating to stay outside, twiddling her thumbs while the great adventure went on below.

"Then does this mean that the concubines won't be allowed to enter the tomb?" she had asked Ross.

"Most definitely not, and it's a gracious concession from Prince Hali that you may do so, Stephanie. The women must remain in their tent a short distance from the site in the valley, until such time as Hali sends for them.

"I would prefer it if you remained inside the tent until later, Stephanie," Ross continued. "When we're ready for the evening meal, I'll call you, but there's much men's work to be done outside."

"Is that an order?" she asked.

"It's a request, and it's for your own safety that I make it."

She spent the time alone in her tent in preparing her sketching materials. Gradually, the renewed thrill of what she was about to see came uppermost in her mind, and she could forget any ruffled feelings about being treated as very much the inferior of the male species. She comforted herself with the fact that the human race wouldn't exist at all if it weren't for women.

The first entry into the tomb would take place the following morning, but later that evening, Ross suggested that they should take a stroll. The atmosphere of the valley, enclosed as it was by the high rockfaces, was more oppressive than the vast, orange-hued plains through which they had traveled, and Stephanie accepted gratefully. She was tired of constrictions, and the simple pleasure of strolling with her husband in the most romantic setting on earth was something to be savored.

The sand was soft beneath their feet, still warmed by the heat of the day, but pleasantly so. Above them, the great orb of the moon had replaced the bloodred rays of the sun that had bathed the entire desert in a flush of glory. It was so easy here, where the desert was limitless, to believe in eternity. And she hesitantly put her thoughts into words, praying that Ross wouldn't think her unduly sentimental.

His arm was lightly around her waist as they stood on a small ridge, looking down on the array of tents and equipment, the campfire and the resting camels, and where Prince Hali's tent stood supreme. From here, it was like watching a panoramic scene on canvas that hadn't yet come to life, and Stephanie's artistic eye appreciated every curve and shadow that softened the night.

"Do you believe in God, Ross?" she asked quietly.

"That's a strange question, and not one that's often asked among men—"

"But I'm asking it, and it's not too difficult for you to answer, is it?"

And it was vitally important to her to know that he, too, felt this magnificent, awesome power that was greater than themselves, that made all their lives so small and insignificant, even Prince Hali's. And there was no more spectacular place to feel it than here, in this vast, empty place, where there was seemingly no present, but which held all the mysteries of the silent past in its tombs.

"Then yes, I'm a believer," he answered. "I can't say I hold much faith in astrology, though I've heard too many predictions to dispute them out of hand. But I do believe in a greater power than we can see. Something created this wonderful world, and the universe beyond, and it was something far greater than the hand of man."

His words made the breath catch in her throat, for they

were so much more emotive than she had expected. For once, he was no longer the hard-headed gambler, or the ex-military man, or even the fearless expedition leader and friend of royalty. He was her dearest one, her soulmate, her dream lover.

The sudden cracking of a whip made her turn her head sharply, but it was only one of the Arabs turning one of the restless camels back into line and tethering it more securely to the rest by tying up one leg in the approved manner. But the sound had broken the spell, and she gave a small shiver as she heard the plaintive sound of an instrument, and knew it was the signal for one of the concubines to attend the prince.

As they watched, they saw one of the eunuchs approach the concubines' tent and call out a name. Tonight it was the turn of one called Tamsika, and as she glided across the sand toward the decorated tent, with her jewelry glinting in the moonlight, Stephanie felt an inordinate sadness in her heart.

"Don't be sad for her," Ross said quietly, hearing her small sigh. "She knows no other life, and it would have been her greatest wish to be chosen by Prince Hali. To their eyes, it's we western men who are the strange ones, to prefer one wife. Even the humblest of them will be scornful that a wealthy man does not choose many women to share his bed."

"But you do not think so?" Stephanie murmured, needing to hear it again and again.

She felt his arm tighten around her waist, and his lips brushed her cheek.

"Your husband is more than content," he said softly, the old-fashioned style of speaking giving her an unexpected little stab of pleasure. "And if my wife is happy to do so, and has had sufficient moonlight, I suggest that we retire to our tent without delay."

Seduction was in his voice and his embrace, and the glow in her heart became a flame.

"Your wife is more than happy to do whatever you wish,"

she said demurely, and knowing that the message in her words was a blatant invitation that wouldn't be refused.

The following morning, the camp was all activity once more, and the air of excitement was intense. There was no sign of the concubines, and Stephanie was given her instructions before she and Ross left their tent.

"Stay close beside me, or beside one of our team at all times, Stephanie. It must be seen that you're under our strictest protection. And remember that it won't be seemly for you to converse with any of the Egyptians, and such a breach of culture will cause them great embarrassment and unease."

"Will they think I've put a spell on them or something?" she asked jocularly, only to be repaid by a look of stern disapproval.

"They might," he said, taking her seriously. "Naturally, if Prince Hali speaks to you, you will be expected to answer him, but make no move to speak with him first."

She was more than impatient with all this formality, and wished to high heaven that the prince had remained in his oasis stronghold instead of accompanying them into the desert.

But she knew better than to say so to Ross, and she was well aware that there was safety in numbers. There had been no hint of danger at any time in their journey from Shaladd, but that was no guarantee that danger didn't lurk around the hump of some shadowy dune, waiting in the lee of the sleeping, golden, catlike shape, ready to pounce.

Fifteen

Now that the real work of the expedition was at hand, there was a sense of excitement over the whole camp. And Stephanie was unable to explain why her own excitement was mixed with a feeling of foreboding and a strange sense of wrongdoing.

This was not a royal valley, filled with the remains and trappings of royal personages. But the nobleman who had chosen this burial spot for himself all those centuries ago had confidently expected to rest in peace for all eternity, and not to have his secret tomb discovered and examined and pried into, by strangers of another age and another race.

The entry into the tomb was now imminent, and Stephanie was finding the whole idea distasteful, and she had more than a passing sympathy for the Arabs who still muttered that a woman's presence in the tomb would bring bad luck. There was a powerful sense of mystery and ancient rites here, and she had to wrestle with her own conscience as to whether she could actually face it after all.

"What's wrong?" Ross asked her quietly when she stood motionless at the site of the opening in the rockface. By now, the Europeans had donned their normal clothes for ease of movement, though they still wore the face-concealing scarves loosely around their necks. The Arabs were in their usual dress, but since Stephanie was a woman, she wore the concealing robes. It added to her feeling of isolation.

"I can't explain it properly," she said uneasily. "But I feel a great sense of trespass. Disturbing the dead is a violation of all dignity, and against all human rights—"

She gave a great shiver, praying that he wouldn't just see her words as cowardice. Although there was certainly an element of that, too, she admitted freely. Who could tell what awful mummified countenance they might see in the tomb?

"We shan't disturb Ben Rashid's slumbers, my sweet. When the tomb was first discovered and reported, the innermost chamber was sealed forever, on Prince Hali's orders, and on the orders of the government. The most precious artifacts that were intended to guide him into the next world must remain in the sarcophagus chamber where he was meant to lie. Only those of lesser value in the outer chambers, and those chambers not yet explored, will be taken away for display in the museums, as being of historical importance."

"Then we won't have to witness the unwrapping of the mummy?" she said in wild relief, and he gave a sympathetic laugh at her flushed face.

"We will not, for the simple fact that the sarcophagus remained empty. After all Ben Rashid's elaborate preparations, he was reputedly slain, but no trace was ever found of his body, and the tomb was never used as it was intended."

Stephanie was astonished. "Then what are we doing here? Surely no treasures were brought here without a body?"

Just saying it made her feel slightly ill, but she had to know.

"The wishes of the nobleman must be carried out, even in such circumstances," he told her. "He was not a man of high importance, despite Hali's conviction that he was one of his ancestors, but he was extremely wealthy, and he had no children. All that he owned was deposited here as he would have decreed, so that wherever he lay, he would be transported to that other world in peace. It was a precaution that many wealthy men made."

"How do you know all this?" Stephanie asked.

"From the detail in the hieroglyphs around the walls of the chambers and passages. The ancient Egyptians were talented artists, as you must know, and the colors and detail in the wall paintings were beautifully preserved in the constant atmosphere of the tombs."

"And will we not pollute this purified atmosphere?" she asked at once.

Ross shrugged. "It's hardly purified in the way you mean, and yes, we'll pollute it with our breaths and our clothes. But once we've completed our mission here, we intend to seal up the tomb again, and leave the ghost of Ben Rashid to rest in permanent peace."

"Until the next expedition comes along," she murmured, more disturbed by his words than she could say.

"They'll have to find it first, and it will be no easy task. There are hundreds of valleys like this one, and no charted map of the desert to guide the way. We stumbled on it quite by accident ourselves, while taking shelter from a sandstorm, and charted our own way back to civilization. The rest you know."

He didn't hurry with his explanations, and she guessed that it was done that way to calm her. It succeeded where impatience would not have done. He made this fantastic journey seem so logical, so sane, and so worthwhile. How could she think otherwise?

"Then I suppose I'm ready whenever you say the word, Ross," she said slowly.

Her sketching materials were in a special bag she kept for the purpose, and her intention had been to take her materials into the tomb and do her sketches on site. Instead, Ross had advised her, at least on this first day, to commit the scenes in the tomb to memory, since the atmosphere would become oppressive, and they wouldn't be able to stay inside it for very long.

She could see the sense in that, and her memory was good enough for to commit everything she saw to make a faithful recording of the scene once they emerged into the daylight again. But it was still with trepidation that she went toward the tomb opening that was cunningly hidden in a sliver in the rockface and hardly discernible at all to those who didn't know it was there. She could sense that the Arabs were eyeing her with less than pleasure. Hali himself ignored her presence. Having accepted the fact that she would be there, this was dignity enough to accord to the Englishwoman.

"First, we have to break down the outer seal that was put up before we left, and then the way inside will be open to us. Stay close at all times, Stephanie," Ross instructed. She waited while the men hacked at the seals on the entrance, and Ross and his team immediately wound their scarves securely around their faces as the dust and sand rose in a stifling cloud about them. Even behind the linen veil and the scarf she wore, Stephanie coughed and choked, and thrust a handkerchief inside the veil to cover her nose and mouth more tightly.

But once the initial dust dissipated a little, the team was organized to enter. She had no idea what to expect. A dingy, dusty place, she had no doubt, with whatever kind of unmentionable creatures could dwell in rarified conditions. Her expectation of a purified atmosphere was immediately dashed by the foul, almost putrid air of decay, and she kept her mouth and nostrils pinched as tightly shut as she could.

The Europeans were to go ahead, sheltering her as before, by keeping her well in the middle of their party. They had lighted flares to guide them, and she saw at once that there were steps leading upward. Once they had climbed them, they turned sharply into a long passageway, symmetrically cut out of the rock by what must surely have been an army of builders. There were many false doors and concealed passageways, as though Ben Rashid had been afraid that even in death, his privacy would be violated.

And then she gasped as the flares lit the walls and ceiling of the passageway. For here were colors and drawings that had never been destined to see the light of day, but which appealed instantly to Stephanie's creative instincts.

The panoramic pictures of a nobleman's life, his hopes and dreams, and his expectations of his entry into that other world, were depicted here in all their glory. But they were for the benefit of the dead and the gods, and no human eyes were ever meant to see them once Ben Rashid Omir's tomb had been sealed. And now these strangers were here, seeing it all, knowing it all, and she felt at once humbled and afraid, and stunned into silence.

"Is it not fantastic?" she heard Ross ask at her side as the flares lit up another and then another portrait of a man and his life in vivid colors of glinting golds and turquoises and reds that no sun had allowed to fade. Here were hunting scenes; women shown harvesting grapes; children playing—everything happy and pleasant to demonstrate to the gods that here indeed was a good man, who was worthy of his entry into eternity.

"It truly is," Stephanie mumbled through her muffling veils, so overawed that she was surprised that any sounds came out of her throat at all.

They went deeper into the tomb, through twisting passageways that all held the continuing story of Ben Rashid Omir in hieroglyphic writings or in vast pictures depicting his daily life. The smoke from the flares was making Stephanie's eyes sting, and the heat was overwhelming.

She wished she dared ask if they could pause and rest, while she took in more detail of the walls, but the main aim of the team was to go ever forward and recover the artifacts, and not to waste time on the aesthetics. While she ached to be able to decipher what the pictures meant, to linger, and to feel that she knew more about the man Ben Rashid through this intimate detail.

They had reached one of the outer chambers now, and again, there was much hacking to be done to break the seals. This was madness, Stephanie thought as the dust threatened to clog every orifice, and she found herself thinking that the effects of a *khamsin* wind could surely be no worse than this.

"Are you all right, Stephanie?" she heard Ross's rasping voice say.

"Yes," she muttered, saving her breath and privately thinking she would never be all right again. Her palms were clammy with sweat, and she felt an uncomfortable trickle of it slide down her back and between her breasts. What in heaven's name had persuaded her to come to this godforsaken hellhole?

And then they had broken through the seal, and the door was gradually being eased open, and she knew. For here were some of Ben Rashid's treasures, the silver goblets and ornaments, the gold plates and bowls, the trinkets and jewelry, that went to make up a nobleman's comfortable life.

"This is the first offering chamber to the gods," Ross said quietly. "If they are appeased by what he has to offer here, he will be escorted through to the next stage of his journey to the afterworld."

She no longer questioned anything. Enveloped by the ancient past, and walking in its dust, she was too overcome to speak. Others were not so mute. All around her, the Europeans were examining the finery on display, and the Arabs were alternately jabbering excitedly, or gazing about them in whispering wonder.

She glanced to where Prince Hali was fingering an especially fine piece of gold plate, and she wondered cynically whether he intended having it for himself. Such a thought helped to restore her scattered thoughts to something like normality. Ross and other members of his first team would have seen the like of this before, but Hali had not.

"We will take most of what's here," Hali declared. "There is no sense in leaving it to molder for eternity."

No one dared to argue with him, even though it was obvious that nothing here would molder. It had already been preserved with time, and by the fact that no tomb robbers had discovered its whereabouts before. But this was a reputable expedition, sanctioned by a prince and two governments, and Hali ordered that certain things must be left in the chamber. On no account must everything be removed, and Stephanie sensed that the old superstitions and beliefs were still a part of him. The gods must still see that offerings had been made.

Her logical mind questioned the sensibilities of those who couldn't see that if nothing here had been touched, then the gods hadn't done a very good job of accepting their precious offerings. But she knew she would only dare to say such things to Ross in the privacy of their own tent.

She watched silently as the men began to put the items into stout canvas bags, and again she felt as though it was a desecration of something sacred. No matter that Ben Rashid was no longer here in this place, or that he would never see his lovely things again. They had been part of his life, and they belonged to him, and these people did him a great wrong in stealing them, for stealing it was.

"We go no farther today," Ross said firmly. "Your Highness will accept that today's excursion is enough?"

"It is enough," Hali agreed. "I am in need of fresh air and to be bathed. You have done well, friend Ross, and we will do more tomorrow."

Stephanie listened to him in astonishment. *He wished to be bathed?* But surely they were conserving their water, and couldn't spare so much, even for a prince. She averted her eyes from the prince's face, lowering them at once when he became aware of her staring. She heard his tetchy voice.

"Something puzzles your wife, friend Ross. I trust it is not a feeling of faintness."

He didn't address her directly, and it was Ross who answered him quickly.

"She is understandably dazzled by all that she has seen, Your Highness. She is young and foolish, and I trust you will forgive her small lapse of manners."

It was so unlike Ross to be so servile that Stephanie looked at him sharply. But as he gripped her arm, she realized at once that he had been so for her benefit so that she would seem to be pleading with her husband not to make her pay for her misdemeanor. But what a misdemeanor! It was so small, so stupid, merely consisting of staring for a moment too long at a prince who was still only a man, and she could have laughed out loud at the incongruity of it all. That is, until she heard Hali's gracious acceptance.

"As you say, she is young, and so we will not press the matter further."

Stephanie was astonished and upset that so much had been made of so little, and could only surmise what punishment could be meted out for any larger error of judgment. She shivered, and the rivulets of sweat clung uncomfortably to her skin as she did so.

Eventually, they retraced their steps, and she gulped in great mouthfuls of fresh air once they were out of the tomb, pulling the veil from her face and uncaring who might see her do so. The air was still burningly hot, but it was not so oppressive as it had been inside the tomb. Ross and the men began to set out the artifacts they had reclaimed, ready for cleaning, numbering, and bagging. Prince Hali was escorted to the royal tent for his bathing, and she escaped to hers with a sigh of relief.

She washed quickly in the minimum of water, but needing to rid herself of the smell of the tomb, as if she was tainted by its very dust, and defiantly, she changed into one of her own gowns, feeling more human again as she did so. For some reason that she couldn't explain, she felt very afraid. She wasn't given to premonitions, but there was a strong presentiment in her soul about the wisdom of this venture.

She gathered up her sketching materials and sat outside, in the shelter of the canvas tent canopy, and began sketching, hoping that attention to the second love of her life might help to dispel her fears. Her memories of the passages, the twists and turns, and the colors of the wall paintings, were all vivid in her mind, and she made many rapid and faithful executions of the general contours of Ben Rashid's proposed resting place.

She was engrossed in her work when Ross called to her, saying that food was being prepared, and that she might join the Europeans for the meal. They habitually ate little, for the heat had lessened their appetites considerably, but nourishment was still required, and she scrambled to her feet thankfully. Ross had said nothing about her changed appearance. Instead, he looked through her drawings and nodded approvingly.

"These are good, Stephanie. We'll have broken through to the interior in two days, and when all the dust has cleared, you can take your materials inside to perfect these wall sketches. When we've eaten our meal, I would like you to sketch the artifacts we've brought out today, before they're bagged up."

"Yes, sir," she murmured, feeling that this was more of an order than a request. He looked at her thoughtfully.

"Am I going to have trouble with you, Stephanie?"

She flushed, feeling like a reprimanded child at his tone. It was hardly the way a man should speak to his wife.

"I don't know," she replied stiffly. "If you mean, do I intend to resist being swallowed up in the ways of ancient Egypt, or the demands of Prince Hali, then perhaps you are."

He smiled slightly. "The demands of Prince Hali, as you call them, are fortunately being competently dealt with by other females."

Her color deepened even more. "That's not what I meant. But I don't like him. He unnerves me, and I hate the absolute control he seems to have over everyone."

"Don't you know by now that you risk your life if you voice such things?" Ross said, his words chilling her. "Keep your opinions to yourself, my dear, and I would prefer it if you reverted to a loose robe and veil. It's unwise for you to be wearing European clothes."

"I can't breathe in the veil! I'll wear it in the tomb, but it's ridiculous to make me cover up at all times. I'm not one of Hali's women, so why should I be so humiliated?"

For a moment she thought he was going to strike her. He took a step forward, gripping her arms cruelly, and spoke in a grating voice.

"For God's sake, keep quiet. We're in Hali's country now, and if he should turn against us, we're vastly outnumbered. Haven't you got that into your pretty head yet?"

She stared at him numbly. It seemed as if all this talk of friendship then counted for nothing. Ross had already rejected Hali's offer of recompense for saving his life, and so he was owed nothing. And she was certain that Hali still resented the fact that an Englishman could be so unwilling to accept his offer of six extra wives. A shudder of fear, as cold as a knife edge, ran through her.

"I'll change my clothes then," she mumbled.

"Not now. Come to the fire and eat. Hali's well occupied for the next couple of hours."

But he was terse, and Stephanie was left in no doubt of how precarious was the relationship between them all. The eager, boyish prince, leaping on the heels of the Englishman's adventure, could so quickly turn into a fiend.

The pattern was set for the next week or so. Each day they entered the tomb, going deeper and deeper into the passageways and either recovering the artifacts or leaving them where they were, under Hali's direction. This was officially Captain Ross Kilmarron's expedition, authorized by the British government, and with the sanction of the Egyptian hierarchy, but there was little doubt who was dictating the terms of it now, and there was nothing they could do about it.

"It doesn't matter so much," he told Stephanie. "The fact

that Ben Rashid's tomb was found and recorded will be sufficient to fire the imagination of the British public. And with your work to add to mine, the resultant book will be a surefire success."

"But it must make you angry that Hali is becoming so dictatorial!" she said. Ross was a strong-willed, powerful man, and normally he wouldn't be dictated to by anyone. Which only made Stephanie suspect that it was on account of her own safety that he held his tongue on the many occasions when she was sure he'd have railed against the prince's dictums. If anything happened to Ross, there would be no help for her.

He held her in his arms in the sanctuary of their tent, and his lips found hers. But the urgency for lovemaking was oddly lacking between them in these tense days and nights when the exploration of the tomb held all of their thoughts and attentions.

"I told you, it doesn't matter. This is my last expedition, and when we return home I shall become the English gentleman, living on his laurels. There are plenty of universities and clubs who will welcome a knowledgeable speaker on the glories of ancient Egypt and its tombs."

He was never lost for words, but she was still convinced he said these things to calm her, rather than with any great wish to settle down to domestic life, sweet though it was to her to think of being the cherished wife of an English gentleman. But as always, the dreams came to an abrupt end at that point.

By now there was a great quantity of recovered artifacts, and many of Ben Rashid's personal effects stored in the royal tent for security. A few of the smaller ones were allowed in their own. But Hali was a jealous man, who obviously needed to be surrounded by his treasures, and Stephanie knew that he was becoming greedy for more.

* * *

"We should be ready to break into the final chamber tomorrow," Ross declared to the assembled company on the twelfth day, at which there was an immediate howl of discontent from the Arabs.

"They do not like the sound of the thirteenth day for such an important happening, friend Ross," Hali informed him. "And neither do my advisers, but I am tired of waiting, so instead, we will break through one of the many side doors in the final passages, to see what is concealed there."

"It's a very unwise move, Your Highness," Ross said sharply. "I suspect that the majority of them are false doors, and it could be dangerous to disturb any of them. They may even be trapped, and you will recall that the last one we forced open presented us with nothing but rubble."

Stephanie gasped behind the veil as she saw Hali's eyes grow cold at this opposition. She could see the greed in his handsome, fleshy face. And for once, he was ready to ignore his advisers' superstitious warnings.

"I would remind you that I have the last word here. We will break into the door and see whether or not it is false." He paused. "Sometimes I begin to wonder if you are not the false one, for constantly crossing me."

There was that petulant, dangerous note in his voice again. He simply couldn't bear to be opposed, and only his advisers and astrologers were permitted to put obstacles in his way. But accusing Ross of being a false friend? She caught her breath, as Hali's glittering eyes turned to her.

Was this ambiguous remark on Ross's so-called falseness also meant to refer to his hurried marriage? Had Hali somehow discovered the truth, or strongly suspected it? If so, it could spell disaster for both of them.

But he was adamant about the day's procedure now. He was eager to be the explorer, the child desperate to unwrap a new toy, and nothing anyone said was going to dissuade him. And since it would be the height of insult to refuse to go with him, the team assembled, the flares were lit, and the day's business began.

They reached the door in question without incident. By now, the twisting turns of the passages were becoming familiar to all of them, but there were always surprises. An unexpected door here, a narrow passageway there, leading them away from the main chambers into a false trail. It was as if Ben Rashid had fully expected some disturbance of his resting place, Stephanie thought, and had mischievously instructed his builders to include these red herrings.

Hali's men were instructed to begin hacking down the door at once. In their enthusiasm their picks shattered some of the brittle walls surrounding the door, and Ross and his team stood back silently as the workmen scattered dust everywhere, apparently uncaring that they desecrated the beautifully painted walls of the tomb still more. The cracks that began to appear in the walls alongside the door seemed not to worry them one jot.

Once the door was broken into, it seemed as if it hadn't been a false trail after all. There was a passageway beyond, instead of the usual pile of rocks and rubble. Hali was triumphant.

"You see?" he said to Ross. "There will be something here, I'm sure of it. You will please lead the way through, and I will follow."

"I beg you to reconsider, Your Highness," he began, but he got no further.

To Stephanie's horror, the prince raised his hand a mere fraction, and two of his guards sprang forward as if they were on springs. One minute their swords were at their sides, and the next they had clashed and crossed, and were poised at Ross's heart. She gave a strangled cry and made to rush forward, and was immediately snatched back. Hali looked at her as he spoke to Ross again, and it was a baleful look that made her blood freeze.

"Since your woman is so fearful for your safety, she will

go with you. The two of you will be first through the opening, and report if all is well for us to proceed."

The entire mood of the day had changed, Stephanie thought hysterically. Prince Hali was no longer the accompanying friend, ready to defer to the Englishman's superior knowledge of archaeological work. He was the tyrant, and his word was law. The clash of steel as the crossed swords were withdrawn from Ross's chest made her wince, and then her husband took her shivering hand in his.

"Certainly, Your Highness," he said in a clipped voice, and she knew at once how he was hating this. It was an affront to his manhood to be so shamed in front of her, but she knew that Hali wouldn't see it so. In his eyes, no man could be shamed in front of a woman, for a woman was nothing, other than being a vessel for his pleasure.

She lifted her head high, and stepped forward. The rest of Ross's team stood silent and watchful as the door was pushed inward by the workmen, and then she and Ross moved carefully toward the dark interior. The passageway inside ended after a few feet, seeming to turn at right angles into darkness. They could see nothing beyond, and Ross snapped out a command for a flare.

As he held it aloft, and they moved slowly forward, Stephanie saw that these walls were rough and unadorned, and though the place might once have been intended as another chamber, it had clearly been abandoned. The floor sloped alarmingly inside the rocky interior, which had probably contributed to its unfinished state. They went as far as the right-angled bend, to be met with a shalelike mass of rock.

"There's nothing here," Ross said shortly. "Let's go back and report."

They realized that Hali had followed them, too eager to see for himself to wait behind with his guards. He was practically breathing down Stephanie's neck, and the mingled reek of garlic and the perfumed lotions on his body made her pinch her nostrils tightly together.

Almost before the words had left Ross's mouth, they were aware of an ominous rumbling. Even as they watched, the walls of the disused chamber began to crack, and then crumble inward, weakened by the hacking excavations. Ross shouted out a warning to Stephanie to get back quickly, but she was totally unable to move. She stood as if frozen, seeing herself entombed forever, and only dimly aware of Mac and Dawson shouting to them to get back to safety, and of the guards reaching for Prince Hali.

Almost blinded by dust and flying rubble, she clawed her way back. The flare had been dropped and extinguished, and for a few panic-stricken moments she was in total darkness. She screamed, and then felt someone's hands pulling her to safety as more rocks fell about them. The smell of him made the identity of her rescuer unmistakable.

"The whole place is threatening to cave in!" Ross shouted. "We've got to get out fast. Where are the others?"

She heard Dawson swear vociferously.

"The rest of the Arabs have fled, squealing like stuck pigs that it's the woman's fault for bringing them bad luck, and refusing to enter the tomb again."

"It's more than likely that they won't be able to," Ross said grimly as the rumbling continued. "Quickly, Stephanie."

She was hustled back to the wider main passage, by which time Hali's guards had quickly surrounded him and drawn him away from her. Hali inquired abruptly if Ross and his woman were all right. But there was no time for chitchat now. As they went to quit the tomb, a roar like thunder seemed to chase them through the passage, and a cloud of thick red dust enveloped them, followed by more falling rubble.

Stephanie lost sight of Ross, and then she felt a great crack on her head. Her senses swam, and just before she lost all consciousness, she had the sure and fateful feeling that she was doomed to die here. It was as if all the gods in creation were angry, and concentrating all their wrath on the woman stranger, for the greatest violation of this sacred place.

* * *

"I think she's coming 'round," a voice said.

Was it inside her head, or somewhere in space? She couldn't be sure. She felt as though she were still floating somewhere above the ground. Nothing was real. She coughed dryly, and her mouth and lungs were filled with the centuries-old dust of the tomb. She felt as though she would never be rid of it. She retched, but was unable to vomit, because of the dryness.

Her eyes wouldn't open, and the dust was drying their sockets. She felt utter panic, and then she felt the soothing touch of cool water bathing her eyes and trickling into her mouth. After a few moments, she managed a weak swallow, and her eyelids flickered open.

She was lying on the ground outside the tomb in the heat of the afternoon sun, and Ross was cradling her in his arms, while members of his team stood silently by.

"Thank God," he said hoarsely. "I thought I'd lost you."

At least she thought that was what he said, but her brain was so muddled she couldn't really be sure of anything. She hadn't even realized that Prince Hali was nearby, until she heard his silky voice, and it was filled with a triumph he didn't try to conceal.

"So now we are truly even, friend Ross, and a bargain must now be struck."

She felt Ross's arms stiffen around her, though she couldn't understand his furious retort, since he answered in Hali's own tongue. But at a single command from Hali, she was aware of the guards lunging forward as before. The clash of metal from their crossed swords that were pointed directly at Ross's heart made her blood freeze, and the cold steel in the sunlight dazzled and shimmered in front of her eyes. And then she fainted again, and heard nothing more.

Sixteen

As she struggled to regain her senses, Stephanie realized she had been taken to the women's tent, and that she lay on a soft mattress. She felt bruised and sore all over, but as she looked around her through half-closed lids, she became aware that the concubines were attending her, gently bathing her face and hands, and applying soothing ointments and sweet-smelling salves to her skin.

"Why am I here?" she said huskily. "Where is my husband?"

The majority of the women stared at her blankly, and she realized they didn't understand what she was saying. Stephanie assumed these were not some of those who'd been schooled in the English language. At the sounds of shouting somewhere outside, Stephanie turned sharply, and immediately wished she hadn't, for her head swam alarmingly. She closed her eyes again and waited for the unpleasant feeling to die down.

"Please take me to my husband," she muttered. "I don't belong in this place. I want to be with Ross—"

She felt a soothing hand on her brow, and opened her eyes a fraction once more. A beautiful, almond-eyed girl was leaning over her, wafting a scent of aromatic perfume with every movement that she made. Her arms tinkled with jewelry and amulets, and there were glittering jewels in her ears and at her throat. Here, in the harem tent, the use of veils was dispensed with, and Stephanie could see the beautiful, unlined faces of these young girls, all so willing and eager to serve their despot prince in whatever act of debauchery he demanded.

"You will see him in good time," the girl attending her said in halting English.

Stephanie clutched at her arm in wild relief. At least they could converse. All this time, there had been another female on the expedition who could speak in her own language, and she had been unaware of it. But even as she thought it, common sense told her that any conversation between them would have been strictly forbidden. So why was she here now instead of being taken back to her own tent? A deep, dark suspicion was beginning to simmer in her mind.

"I am Tamsika, and I am at my master's pleasure for this journey," the woman said, parrot-fashion.

"I see." Stephanie swallowed, wondering if it made sense to converse in words that the girl would understand, even though it galled her to do so. She spoke with a bravery she didn't feel. "And I am at my husband's pleasure."

She saw Tamsika smile slightly. She became aware that there was a girl on either side of her now, and that they were smoothing aromatic oils into her arms, massaging them lightly and sending a wonderful, heady perfume into her nostrils. The whole procedure was unexpectedly sensual, and if she hadn't felt so weak, Stephanie would have snatched her arms away from the girls in embarrassment.

"My master desires the silver-haired one," Tamsika said softly.

Stephanie's heart seemed to leap right into her throat at the words. She tried to give a small, cracked laugh.

"I'm flattered," she said, finally freeing herself from the seductive attentions of the young girls. She sat bolt upright on the mattress, ignoring the floating sensations in her head, and was immediately besieged by the girls, who gently wielded lotion-damp brushes through the long tangle of her hair.

She heard them murmur among themselves, and guessed that her gleaming hair was the cause of much admiration and envy. She was different, and therefore desirable, and it was the very last thing she wanted. All she wanted was Ross.

"Please," she began desperately. "I'm quite well now, and I should like to return to my husband's tent—"

"It is not possible at present," Tamsika said calmly. "You are to accompany us to the tournament shortly."

Stephanie stared at her, sick to her stomach with an awful presentiment of what she was about to hear.

"What tournament?" she whispered.

"My master has claimed you as payment for saving your life, and your husband has insulted him by refusing to give you up to him." Her voice became scornful. "Prince Hali could simply take you, but he is a gambling man, and has challenged your husband for you, as a sport. They will fight by the sword to the death, and you are the trophy."

"No! I belong to my husband, and no one else," Stephanie said hysterically. "I will never submit to this barbaric ritual!"

Tamsika spoke rapidly, and before Stephanie knew what was happening, all the concubines had crowded around her. She was as penned in by their seductive, titillating beauty as if she was in a silken prison. She began to feel like the Queen Bee, surrounded by worker bees, being pampered and prepared for the inevitable.

"You cannot interfere with men's affairs," Tamsika said in a voice that chilled her. "My master has long wanted to add you to his harem, and was much displeased when your husband refused him. He will not refuse this tournament. To do so would reveal cowardice, and for that he would be slain."

"Dear God," Stephanie whispered. "Does Prince Hali twist everything to suit his own lustful needs? Don't you ever question such self-indulgence?"

Tamsika looked at her stonily, and then they heard the sound of a fanfare of trumpets outside.

"Come, silver-haired one. It is time."

She was lifted bodily from the mattress, and there was no escape from the hands that held her and bore her outside into the glaring daylight. The ointments had soothed her in the coolness of the tent, but outside in the heat of the day, her scratches and bruises burned and stung. But none of it mattered, compared with the sight in front of her.

A circular arena had been prepared by the simple method of a large sandy space being ringed by Hali's guards and his attendants. Behind this circle were the onlookers: the astrologers and advisers, the Europeans, the lower-class workers and the eunuchs. The opponents were already inside the circle: Prince Hali and Ross Kilmarron, each with an unsheathed sword at his side. Stephanie gave a cry of anguish as she saw them. All this was because of her, and whatever happened, one of them was about to lose a friend. If the worst happened, she would be lost to all decency and the civilized world she knew forever.

"Ross, please don't do this!" she shrieked, but she was held fast by the concubines' hands as she tried to rush forward. She heard Ross speak rapidly to Hali, who gave a gracious nod, allowing him to stride through the ring of spectators to her side, where she clung to him wordlessly.

"Trust me, Stephanie," he said steadily. "For honor's sake, I cannot refuse him."

"What does honor matter when I might lose you?" she said, weeping bitterly against his shoulder.

"Your loyalty does you credit, my darling, but it will make no difference here. Don't make things worse by making me appear chicken-hearted, I beg you. Stand tall and unflinching, whatever happens."

He kissed her mouth, regardless of the mutters from the Arabs at this unwarranted delay, and then the trumpets sounded impatiently once more. In seconds, he was gone from her side, and she was held in the grip of the women at a good vantage point. She wanted to close her eyes and wish this time away, but she dared not. If Ross was willing to fight for her, then she owed it to him to watch—and pray.

As soon as the sword fight began, the roaring of encouragement from both sides began. In the cocoon of the valley, it reverberated from all sides, and Stephanie found it both frightening and deafening. But nothing was as frightening as the battle being raged between two men who had once been close friends, and who now faced each other as enemies because of her.

It was obvious from the outset that they were well matched, and each time the swords clashed together there was a bellow of approval or censure from the spectators. Prince Hali was obviously an expert swordsman, Stephanie thought sickly, and this would be among his many skills that were taught outside the bedroom known as the Golden Chamber.

But Ross was skilled as well. As the battle progressed, it dawned on her that many of the Arabs were falling silent as Ross's superior military prowess began to overpower Hali. Both men were bleeding from nicks from the sword points, though no real damage had been done to either of them yet. But in fencing and weaving, Ross was gradually outmaneuvering Hali, and all the spectators were aware of it.

Finally, in one thrusting movement, the sword was knocked out of Hali's hand, and as he overbalanced, he sprawled on the ground in an ungainly fashion, trying to grapple for it. Ross swiftly kicked the sword out of his opponent's reach, placed one foot on the prince's chest, and held the point of his own sword at Hali's throat.

Stephanie almost swooned, but she dared not look away now, though it had become hard to see just what was happening with the flurries of sand. The two men had begun the small dust storm, but the wind had begun to strengthen now, and was beginning to swirl and whip the sand through the valley. But the entire circle of spectators was silent and watchful now, waiting to see if the Englishman had the nerve to slay the prince. Stephanie coughed a little at the influx of dust in the squally wind, and all her nerves began to jump, as one voice broke into the silence of the onlookers.

"Finish me, you British bastard. Do it quickly, and do it well" came Hali's screaming voice.

"I refuse to kill a man I've long regarded as a friend," Ross said harshly. "Whatever our differences, there must be another way—"

Even as he spoke, Stephanie was aware that many of the spectators were scattering and moving swiftly away from the arena. She looked around in bewilderment, and even the concubines were gathering up their skirts and abandoning her. A sudden ferocious wind had begun to tear through the valley, whipping the sand into the air and hurling about anything that wasn't fastened down securely. The turbulence was so sudden and so violent that she stood in total confusion for a moment, and then she felt someone grabbing her, and she heard Ross's voice close to her ear.

"Come quickly, Stephanie. The *khamsin* may have resolved the fight for the present, but I've no wish to be drowned in sand any more than I wished to bleed to death by the sword."

The sky had darkened considerably, and Stephanie could hardly distinguish anything through the blinding, stinging sand. It was worse than the worst London pea-souper fog she had ever experienced, but from the shouts and scrambling footsteps, she assumed that everyone was fleeing for the safety of their tents, just as they were.

The clash with Hali had been averted for now—but for how long? It seemed to her now that they constantly exchanged one danger for another, and she was sobbing with a mixture of fear and relief by the time they managed to reach the haven of their own tent. She clung to Ross, unable to speak for the sand filling her mouth and eyes, and hardly able to think for the relentless sound of the *khamsin* wind raging outside. The full, terrifying power of nature was upon them now.

"We're safe for the moment," Ross said, his voice grating from the grittiness of sand in his own mouth. "While the wind rages, no one will dare to put a step outside his own tent. We've got food and water, and a jug of honeyed cordial that Hali must have had sent to our tent. We won't starve, and we won't die of thirst, and we've still got each other."

She looked up into his eyes, hungry for a tender word, but it was a mere statement of fact, and nothing more. She looked at his face and arms, and the fine trickles of blood that oozed from his wounds, and knew that they must be stinging appallingly with the layer of fine sand covering them. The thought of it steadied her ragged nerves a fraction.

"Let me bathe your wounds to get the sand out of the cuts," she said huskily.

She had some soothing cream, too, that would stop the stinging. Ross shrugged, as if the pain meant little to him, but since there was nothing else to do but ride out the sandstorm, he agreed, and he lay on their bed while she ministered to him. She bathed the skin tenderly with a soft cloth, knowing that it must hurt abominably, but he didn't so much as wince until she had finished. Only when she was gently smoothing on the healing cream did she realize how covertly he watched her. Her face flushed, and she felt oddly defensive.

"I feel so damnably guilty," she blurted out, heedless of the unladylike words.

He stared at her. "What in God's name have you got to feel guilty about?" he said in genuine surprise.

"Don't patronize me, Ross! You know very well!" she said. She had to raise her voice to be heard above the screaming wind. It sounded like a thousand banshees now, but because of it, she was also assured that no one else could hear her.

"Since I'm not a mind reader, I shan't know until you tell

me, and I demand that you do," he said aggressively. "We might be holed up here for days, and I can't bear the thought of looking at such a sour face for so long."

She glowered at him. She loved him desperately, but sometimes he drove her wild with his masculine arrogance.

"I'm guilty because I've caused you pain," she muttered. "I'm guilty because I've lost you a valued friendship. And I'm guilty because we're bound together in a loveless marriage, and I seem to have been nothing but a trouble to you from the day we met."

"As far as my relationship with Hali goes, it was doomed from the moment I saved his life," he said to her surprise. "From that moment there was a debt between us that had to be paid, and the fact that I refused the offer of his wives, was something that Hali always resented. You were merely the catalyst to this final confrontation, my sweet."

She was kneeling on her haunches by his bedside, and although they both spoke more quietly now, they were close enough to hear each other's words perfectly. And when she didn't answer him, he pulled her down to him so that she was splayed over his body, and his arms were holding her tight.

"Do you hear me complaining about my lot, woman?" he went on, almost angrily. "And I don't ever recall saying I wanted to submit you to Hali's pleasure. If I had, don't you think I had the perfect opportunity when Hali demanded that we strike a new bargain with yourself as the prize?"

Stephanie felt her heart thudding fast at his words, and although she was sure his wounds must be hurting him, he never lessened his hold on her.

"I suppose so," she whispered uncertainly.

"Then doesn't that tell you something?" he demanded.

She felt a frisson of anger. Why couldn't he just say that he loved her, if this was what he was implying? What devilish male pride prevented him from saying the words she longed to hear?

"Perhaps it tells me that you have no intention of giving up what you consider to be yours," she said. "Perhaps it tells me that an English wife is as much of a chattel in her husband's mind as those poor deluded concubines who think the sun and moon shine out of Hali's eyes, and don't realize how imprisoned they really are!"

For a moment, he said nothing, and the howling of the wind took precedence over Stephanie's hammering heartbeats and then his muttered oaths.

"Good God, woman, don't you know me at all by now?" Ross said softly, pulling her down toward him so fiercely that she had no chance of resisting. He fastened her mouth on his, and forced it open with his tongue. She felt it thrust inside her mouth, as if he would possess her by this act of invasive intimacy that was such a crude and erotic imitation of love-making, and yet so frequently a loving prelude.

She wanted to respond. Normally, she found it impossible not to do so, but today was an exception. Today, she was bruised in body and mind. She was also overconscious of Ross's wounds, and that she must inadvertently be adding to their hurt. She twisted her mouth away from him with a great effort, and spoke in a low voice, close to his ear.

"Please don't. I would prefer it if you allowed me a little peace to recover from this terrible day."

"Then you don't want me to make love to you, to prove that I'm your lord and master?" he said, unable to resist taunting her. She felt her eyes fill with tears once more, and blinked them angrily away.

"Not now. Not while I feel so—so distressed. I don't expect you to understand, but for a while I thought you were going to lose the battle."

"And what would have upset you the most? Seeing me slain, or knowing that Hali would have taken the silver-haired woman back to Shaladd and into his harem?"

She swallowed, and it was a moment before she could

answer, her voice shaking. "I don't know how you can even ask such a question."

But of course he could ask it, because he had no idea that she loved him. She had never told him so, and had no intention of telling him now. It would only feed his male ego, and that was abundant enough already.

She heard him give a small sigh, and then he put her gently away from him, where she lay beside him on the mattress that was just big enough to hold them both.

"We've both had a traumatic day, Stephanie, and I suggest that we try to get some rest. The day is already as dark as night, and there's no knowing when the *khamsin* will abate, or what havoc we'll find at the end of it. We may well need to conserve our strength. And once we're away from this place, we'll return at once to England. It's no longer safe for us here, and Hali is an unforgiving enemy."

She had no idea how they expected to get away safely with so many of Hali's men accompanying them. She shivered at the seriousness in his voice. But she was suddenly, appallingly tired, and she saw the sense of his words. So much had happened in so short a time: the accident in the tomb, and her own injuries; the realization of being in the concubines' tent, and virtually being prepared for Prince Hali's pleasure; learning of the so-called tournament and being obliged to witness it; then the affront to Hali's honor when Ross refused to kill him, and the advantageous arrival of the *khamsin*.

Now all of them were trapped inside their tents until the furious wind ceased. At least they were safe for the time being, though there was no knowing what would happen when Hali confronted them again. But it was pointless to worry about it when there was nothing to be done. She realized the deep need for sleep, to restore her energies, both mental and physical. She turned away from Ross, her back against him, and closed her eyes with a weariness that seemed to touch her soul.

Although she was nearly deafened by the wind, it had the effect of dulling her senses, and she quickly drifted into an exhausted sleep. How long she slept, she had no idea, but at some point during the blackness of the night, she turned around restlessly, and slowly awoke to find herself in the circle of Ross's arms.

"Now?" she heard him whisper seductively in her ear.

Her heart jolted. But she knew from the close proximity of his body to hers that he was already aroused and ready for her. All around them the elements raged and stormed, but here inside this tent, there was love awaiting her, if she wanted it. It was more than she could do to refuse it, knowing it could be the last time, and wanting him with all her heart.

As she whispered her assent, she felt his hands begin to roam leisurely over her body, and as the familiar, sweet sensations began, she gave a sigh of pure pleasure. No matter what Hali or the world did to them, they still had this physical bond that held them together. They were still soulmates in her heart, however short-lived it was destined to be. And whether it was Ross who dissolved their partnership at some later date, or the cruel fates of nature, or the eventual slaying by Hali's sword, they still had this.

"My beautiful wife," Stephanie heard him murmur against her soft flesh. "You were meant for far better things than this. What have I brought you to?"

She tasted the skin of his shoulder as he lay half over her, and felt her heart soar with love for him.

"I wouldn't have missed one minute of it," she said softly. "Except perhaps the ugliness of the tournament, and discovering that your friend is now your enemy. I regret that with all my heart."

"I regret nothing," Ross said with a touch of his old arrogance. "To indulge in futile regrets is to look backward instead of forward."

"Do we have anything to look forward to?" Stephanie couldn't resist saying, though she was finding it hard to say anything now, for those marvelous hands were moving inexorably downward now to the source of her pleasure, and she caught her breath in a little gasp as she felt the warmth of those questing fingers gently part and enter her.

"You have a future," Ross said, and then he hesitated. "Before we left England, I made certain provisions, Stephanie. If we do not return within a certain time, and it's presumed that something has happened to me, someone will come after you and try to find you, no matter where you might be."

Her eyes filled with weak tears at this. She had known nothing of such contingency plans, and she couldn't find any words to answer. She couldn't speak, anyway, because her husband was covering her mouth with his, and kissing her with infinite sweetness. He lay heavily on her, and she gloried in the fact that he wanted her so obviously. She held him close to her, trailing her fingers down the length of his spine to cling to the hard-muscled buttocks and feel the strength in him. He gave a smothered oath against her mouth, and eased himself slightly away from her.

There was no light in the tent, for they hadn't bothered to light a lamp, and outside where the wind howled and raged, all was in pitch darkness now. But inside, they were cocooned in a private world where no one could invade, and sight was not necessary, for all was touch and sensation and sweetly erotic seduction. Neither of them spoke now, as if each was lost in this sensual world of exploration of each other, where fingers and tongues spoke far more eloquently than mere words ever could.

And finally, the ultimate sensations began. He filled her with himself, and she threw back her head in glorious abandon on the mattress as the rhythmic movements began, slowly and seductively at first, and then ever more thrustingly, and carrying her with him to a place akin to heaven.

He couldn't see her now, but he must know of her wanton response, just as she knew his. By now, they knew each other well, and they were as one entity now. They moved together in perfect unison toward the sweet climax of love, and as his seed gushed hotly into her, she gave a little strangled cry of pure ecstasy.

He gathered her into him, loath to let her go, and they rocked together for some minutes, still a part of each other, as they had been so many times before. And Stephanie's eyes were damp with the sheer wonder of it. No matter if they made love a thousand times, each time would be as the first time, new and wonderful.

He reached for the jug of honeyed cordial and poured them each a drink, saying that the night was still upon them, and that a soothing drink would help them resume their sleep. Dutifully, Stephanie did as he did, and drank deeply, and the oddly bittersweet taste that lingered on her palate was far from unpleasant.

"Sleep now, my lovely wife," he whispered into her ear. "For only God knows what we may have to face tomorrow."

She wished he hadn't used those particular words, but by now she had learned that a man's brain worked differently from a woman's. While she was still rapt in the euphoria of their lovemaking, he could think beyond the moment, even though his arms still encircled her, keeping her safe. At least, she was safe for the present. She could try to forget the insidious threat of being doomed to die beneath a mountain of sand, or at a despot's sword. In any case, she was suddenly too heavy in mind and body to worry about anything. She huddled ever closer to Ross, drawing his strength into her.

Stephanie had no idea how long she slept, but both of them were exhausted. So much had happened to dull their senses on the previous day, and it was she who slowly awoke first, her senses still unwilling to face the day, and still in her husband's sleeping arms. She leaned forward and gently kissed his mouth. It was still relaxed in sleep, and infinitely dear to her. He didn't stir, though normally he was roused in an instant, and it seemed to underline what yesterday's toll must have meant to him.

She moved carefully away from him, and then she found herself listening intently. She was listening to total silence, and she realized that the day was bright and filling the tent with the reflected sunlight through the canvas. The *khamsin* wind had gone, and if Prince Hali saw fit to resume the tournament from yesterday, they would be back in the same state as before, with their lives hanging in the balance.

In the silence, Stephanie could hear the wild hammering of her own heart. The silence began to unnerve her. In the normal course of things, she would expect to hear the everyday sounds of morning in the camp—the Arabs shouting to one another in their own language, the camels scuffling, and the smell of cooking wafting on the air from the campfires. Today, there was none of it, and she was very afraid.

Not wanting to disturb Ross yet, she crawled tentatively out of the blanket and lifted the tent flap a fraction. And a cry burst out of her lips.

At the sound, Ross was out of the bed instantly. Cursing his lassitude, he began pulling on his trousers and shirt and opened up the tent fully. The dazzling glare of daylight hurt their eyes, and they gazed out on a strange new world that bore no resemblance to the one they had left behind yesterday. It was a world of gigantic sandhills that had swept through the valley and piled up against the rockfaces in weird and wonderful shapes. It had completely obliterated the opening of the tomb. It would be impossible to locate its whereabouts again, and what remained inside it of Ben Rashid Omir's relics and treasures were now hidden from human sight forever.

It was right and proper, Stephanie thought with a rush of something like relief, and perhaps this *khamsin* wind had

been the gods' response for the violation of the tomb. She
passed a trembling hand across her eyes, wondering if she
was truly going mad for thinking such wild thoughts. But
these were days for wild thoughts. And the next one that
entered her head, was to wonder why no one else had
emerged from their tents.

Ross stepped outside, while she was still hastily donning
the Arab robes which were more comfortable to wear in the
oppressive heat.

"Dear God!"

"What is it?" she asked.

He didn't try to disguise the truth from her with kind
words. What he said was brutal and direct.

"They've gone, the whole bloody lot of them. At least
Hali and his entourage have gone. As for our people—"

Stephanie peered over his shoulder, and gasped at the sight
of the two crossed swords stuck in the sand a little way outside their tent. The silence in the valley after the violence of
the sandstorm was almost more terrifying than the *khamsin*
itself.

"What does it mean, Ross?" she asked in the lowest of
voices, yet in her soul she already knew.

"I means that all our people have been slain, and by now
the desert will simply have swallowed them up," he said
harshly. "The symbolically crossed swords are to inform us
of the fact, and are also Hali's way of rejecting our friendship
for all eternity."

She hated the sound of the melodramatic words, but she
recognized Ross's need not to underestimate the horror of
these moments while she took in all that he said.

"Then we're entirely alone?" she whispered.

Even as she spoke, she heard a strange yawing sound, and
a camel loped awkwardly into view from one of the newly
formed dunes. Its back legs were tied together, instead of
the usual one leg being tethered high behind him, allowing
him reasonable movement but not enough to race away. The

animal was roped to another one, and lashed across their backs were water bags and provisions.

Ross immediately captured them more securely, and tied them to a hastily dug stake. In leaving them food and water and transport, she supposed Hali had had some thought of humanity, and she said, as much to Ross. He gave a brittle laugh as he shook his head.

"He's fully aware of the dangers we face now, my dear, and this is merely a hollow gesture. Take note of the black crosses on the bags. It's a reminder that when the food and water run out, we'll be lost to the desert. Hali is a man of brutal methods and quick-changing loyalties. He'll feel only hatred for me now, and all who work with me. He'll have had the others killed swiftly and silently, but he'll be rejoicing in the fact that you and I face a lingering death."

She flinched, starting to shake all over at the grim words. But although hysteria was not far beneath the surface, she refused to give in to it. She was twenty years old, and terrified out of her wits, but this couldn't be the end. They had come so far, and she simply wouldn't believe it.

"Then let's prove him wrong," she said, hardly recognizing her own scratchy voice. "Let's fight this desert and get back to Alexandria and home. Let's do as you always intended, and publish the book about the expedition, and about Ben Rashid's tomb. There will be even more romance and intrigue in it now that the tomb's lost forever. And it will be the best proof we have that we didn't perish, and that Prince Hali Ahmed is not all-powerful. He's not God, Ross! And if he believes in omens and the like, then surely he'll see that we were meant to survive, and that we've honored his ancestor. His enmity will be over then."

She paused for breath, with the taste of the softly drifting sand in her mouth. She wasn't sure of the logic of her own words, but it was the best she could do in the circumstances. As long as they had a plan of action, and a goal at the end of it, then there was a purpose to their existence. Ross must see that.

He took her in his arms and held her close, muttering an oath that was as soft as a caress.

"This God of yours must have directed my footsteps well, when He led me to you, my sweet. And of course we'll go on. We can do nothing else, for no one in the world knows where we are, save Hali, and I have no intention of sitting here and waiting for the buzzards to pick our bones clean."

It would have calmed her more if he'd chosen different words to talk about their plight, but she knew them for the truth. And if all these past months had been one kind of exotic adventure, they were surely about to embark on a new and far more dangerous one than she could ever have envisaged.

Seventeen

There was a great deal of work to be done before they could make their move, but the determination to trek north across the desert to Alexandria was an incentive that kept them motivated. Stephanie already knew that it was the more perilous route, for it was virtually uncharted, and that was one of the reasons why they hadn't taken the more direct route in the early stages.

They could be in danger of assaults by rogue bedouin bands, and they had also lost the security of numbers, and of Prince Hali's protection. So much was against them, apart from the vast areas of desert they had to cross, but at the end of it all, there would be safety and home. Stephanie kept reminding herself of that fact, knowing it was the only thing that was going to keep her sane.

Before they left the valley, Ross insisted on making sensible plans, and to outline the things that were in their favor. Their main assets were the dried provisions and water, transport and shelter, and the fact that he was an experienced desert explorer. He avoided saying that no explorer's expertise could compensate for the changing desert produced by the *khamsin,* and that no two journeys could ever be exactly the same. But he didn't need to say it. Stephanie had enough sense to know it.

"First things first," he said, with a half-smile. "We'll eat breakfast, and then assure ourselves that the tomb's opening is truly hidden forever. Then we'll check the valley for anything left behind by Hali's men, though I doubt that we'll find anything."

"You don't think we'll find Mac and Dawson, and the others?" Stephanie asked in a swift panic. "Oh Ross, I couldn't bear it if we came across their bodies—"

"I was thinking more of any small artifacts that had been dropped, or weapons, or items of food," he said quickly. "We already have the two swords Hali kindly left behind, and you never know when they may come in useful. But we'll find no trace of anything human. Hali's men will have done their work well, and you can see by the new dunes all around us that if we hadn't been on a kind of ridge in the valley, we'd have been smothered, too."

She shuddered, wondering just what miracle had kept them safe. There was simply no trace that any human habitation had ever existed in the valley, save themselves. Apart from the ridges scuffed up by the camels' feet, the sand was as virginally smooth as driven snow.

"Are you coming with me to do the inspection?" he asked when they had eaten frugally of biscuits and a brew of hot tea, sweetened with honey to give them energy.

"Oh, yes!" she said. "Please don't leave me alone, Ross." She glanced around fearfully, as if expecting brigands to leap out at her at any moment, brandishing their evil-looking swords.

"My poor lassie," he said with quiet sympathy. "This is not the adventure you expected, is it?"

The term he used, and the unexpected reversion to his northern roots, was enough to make her eyes sting, but she wouldn't let him see it. The last thing Ross needed now was a clinging female on his hands. She was already drawing on reserves of strength she never knew she had, preparing herself for the vicissitudes that were still ahead. She told him she was ready for whatever came, and even though it was a downright lie, she didn't miss the admiration in his eyes.

They left the tent and moved down the length of the valley

slowly. In places it was difficult to gain proper footholds on the deep wells of sand. Stephanie found it unnerving to find her feet suddenly plunging into a foot of sand. It was frighteningly unlike wading through water, and she frequently had to wait for Ross to pull her out. The hard-packed ridges produced by so many feet in the past weeks were all obliterated now, and there were no clear paths to the area where the tomb had most likely been situated.

Ross was determined to assure himself that it would be impossible for other expeditions to find it. Unless, of course, some future sandstorm uncovered it again.

"We've lost it," he said at last, after a futile hour of moving up and down the valley. By now, Stephanie was feeling the strain of the search, and the heat of the sun was making her light-headed, despite the scarf around her head and the veil that covered most of her face but did little to divert the insidious sand from invading her eyes and nose and mouth.

"Then please let's go," she pleaded. "We can do nothing more here, Ross."

But despite the need to depart, and to return to safety as quickly as they could, she sensed that Ross was still reluctant to leave this place he'd discovered, and where he had invested so much of his life. But the longer they stayed, then the more that life was in danger.

"I know you're right, and although I feel overwhelmed with sadness for all that we leave behind, I also feel an urgency to get away from this valley. But there's little sense in our moving on too far until after dark, Stephanie. The stars will be our best guide, and our traveling will be more comfortable during the hours of darkness."

"But surely we don't have to sit here the whole day!"

Now that he had abandoned the ancient tomb, she was nervously aware that the valley was also the tomb of the Europeans who had been slain at Hali's command, and it conjured up all sorts of superstitions in her mind. In the silence in this valley of death, she could imagine anything.

"We do not," Ross said in a clipped voice. "We'll pack up and move on, but we need to plan our general direction, or we could end up like those poor fools who wander the desert aimlessly until they go mad."

She was chastened by his tone, and ventured to say something else that had been troubling her as they made their difficult way back to their tent.

"Will Prince Hali ever be brought to justice for his brutality, Ross? He's responsible for killing at least a dozen men, and he should be punished for it."

"It could never be proved," Ross said. "Even we aren't certain of the truth of it, but it's well known that desert princes never take prisoners."

"So he'll get away with it?" Stephanie asked, sickened at the thought.

"I'm afraid he will. But be thankful that he didn't see fit to slay me, too, or you would be finding life very different in few weeks' time."

The image of the harem, and the pampered, cocooned life of the concubines in their luxurious surroundings, swept into her mind at his words, and she knew this was what he meant.

"I'd far rather take my chance in the desert with you than submit to Prince Hali's excesses," she said feverishly.

"Someday I'll remind you of those words," Ross said, his arm tightening around her waist as she stumbled slightly in the slowly drifting sand.

Even now, when the *khamsin* had long subsided, the desert was never still, she thought. It constantly moved and rippled, like a gigantic ocean whose most violent storm had abated now, but which was still restless enough to remind unwary travelers of its ultimate power.

But they reached their tent at last, and to rid her mouth of the sand, she drank deeply of the last of the honeyed drink that remained. She was surprised to realize how exhausted she felt. It was barely midmorning, yet she felt near to dropping. The tension of the day, and the fight to keep her feet from slipping into the grasping sand, had all taken their toll, and she sank down wearily onto the mattress.

"May I rest for a while?" she asked weakly.

"Of course," Ross said at once. "I've much work to do, and you'll be no help to anyone if you're falling asleep all the time."

His smile took the sting out his words, but they made her feel guilty all the same.

"Should I really be helping?" she murmured.

He knelt beside her for a swift moment and pulled her into his arms.

"You should not. I want you strong and resilient for the days ahead, Stephanie. Lie here and rest while I see to everything."

She was so weary she simply let him take over, knowing that "seeing to everything" meant packing their personal belongings and her precious drawing materials, as well as the few artifacts that had been stored in their tent. She was sad for him, on account of losing so much that he had fought and strived to achieve.

There were so few relics to take back to England, to prove that they had done all that they intended. But there was enough. There were tiny terracotta fragments of oil lamps, mosaics, and coins, many remnants of beads and figurines, and a little gold plate inlaid with semiprecious stones. And there were the dozens of Stephanie's sketches that were a faithful accompaniment to the mass of Ross's notes.

When she awoke, she almost had to drag her eyes open, and her head spun when she sat up quickly, finding herself alone. Her mouth was totally dry again, but when she reached for the jug of honeyed cordial, it wasn't there. As she stared around dully, she realized that everything was now packed up and ready for them to move on. As she registered it all, Ross entered the tent.

"I'm sorry. I didn't mean to sleep so long—" she began, her mind oddly muddled. He gave an expressive oath.

"It wasn't your fault, sweetheart. Nor was it your fault, or mine, that we slept so long and deeply during the night when our friends were being slain. The cordial that Hali so thoughtfully provided was drugged."

Stephanie gasped, but of course it explained everything. She hadn't been able to understand how they had heard nothing of the killings and the departures, for it surely couldn't have all been done during the ferocity of the *khamsin,* when no one would have been able keep to their feet.

She hoped and prayed that the Europeans had also been supplied with the drugged honeyed cordial, but she didn't dare make the suggestion to Ross in case he dismissed it. She preferred to think that perhaps they had been so drugged that they had known nothing of their final moments.

"He's more evil than I thought," she whispered. "And I finished off the last of it instead of helping you—"

"Thank God you did, or I might not have guessed the truth until I saw how heavily you were sleeping. And one of the water bags Hali left for us contains more of the same, so I've been forced to empty it."

He was bitter now, and Stephanie could see how painful he found this final abandonment of friendship. He and Hali had once been so close, so rich in comradeship, despite one being a mere Englishman and the other a fabled prince, but in the end it had all counted for nothing. Hali thought himself akin to those ancient gods, but he was no more than mortal, after all, for only a man could abuse friendship so viciously.

"Then that means we're short of water," she said slowly as her senses began to recover from the drugging effect of the cordial.

"We have enough. Fortunately, we had our own supply in our tent, and it will see us through."

But she noticed that he didn't look at her as he spoke, busying himself with hoisting some of the baggage onto his shoulders to take outside to the waiting camels. She saw that he, too, had changed into the Egyptian dress now, for more comfort in the intense heat.

Each of them was to ride a camel, with the baggage loaded about each beast as evenly as possible. The tent was taken down and rolled as tightly as possible, and in a mood of defiance, Stephanie opened up her little parasol that had traveled with her from England. Ross gently took it from her hands.

"No, my dear. We need to be as inconspicuous as possible, and to appear at all times as though we are merely two nomadic travelers. You must put all your fripperies away."

"And will I ever see them again?" she said huskily in a sudden sweep of depression. "Will I ever wear ball gowns or bathe in scented water, or feel clean ever again?"

She was ashamed of her outburst, but it had been impossible to control it. Ross held her tightly, feeling the trembling in her body that went deep into her soul.

"I promise that I'll do all in my power to see that you do, Stephanie. When we reach the Cleopatra Hotel in Alexandria, you'll have the finest gowns that money can buy brought round to the hotel for your choice. I'll give you anything your heart desires to make you feel like a lady again, but believe me when I say that you'll never be more of a lady than you are to me now."

She bit her lip, almost stung to tears by this solemn declaration in the face of all their dangers. If they were brave and unlikely promises, she didn't care. It was enough that he'd made them, and that they had been said with all sincerity. She lifted her burning face to his, and felt his mouth touch hers in a brief kiss of commitment. At least that was how she interpreted it, and chose not to think of it in any other way.

It was well into the afternoon when they left the doomed valley, for it would have been sheer madness to start out when the sun was at its highest and most cruel. Stephanie never looked behind her once, but she was aware that Ross did so often, and although he said little about their fate, she knew how much he grieved for his friends who would remain their forever. Their own survival was of paramount importance now, but she knew from his shadowed eyes how much he regretted ever bringing the expedition here.

Yet it was a futile regret. They had done what they set out to do, and the historic record of an Egyptian nobleman's life would eventually appear in print for the world to see. There was a worthiness in that that couldn't be denied, and musn't be overlooked.

Stephanie was more than thankful when they had left the valley behind them, but she quickly began to revise that thought once they were away from its towering, protective rockfaces and walls of sand. Ahead of them was the limitless desert, vast, wild, with soaring mountains of sand that seemed to stretch into infinity. She was already choked with sand, and glad that Ross had quickly abandoned the idea of her traveling behind him with the camels tethered together. They were still linked, but she rode alongside him now, which lessened the flurries of sand that the camels' feet threw up.

At first, they kept up a conversation, with Ross detailing the path they were taking, but the talking soon dwindled into silence, as the enormity of what they were undertaking became more and more obvious. And as they plodded ever northward, uneasy questions began crowding into Stephanie's head.

They had supplies, but who knew how long they would have to last? They had their health and strength, but what if it failed, for one or both of them? They had the camels, but what if one of them bolted, or wilted? What if, even now, some of Hali's men were lying in wait for them, intent on killing the last witnesses to all that had happened? She was unable to control the small whimper of distress in her throat, and Ross looked at her sharply.

"Do you want to stop?" he asked quietly. "There's no

point in becoming faint, and I can soon erect a temporary shelter for you to rest out of the sun for a while."

"I'm all right," she answered. "I was just letting my imagination run away with me, and not enjoying what I saw."

"You should leave all that to the fortune-tellers and astrologers," Ross said, whipping the sluggish camels forward with his switch. "Imagination is not always the wonderful thing it's supposed to be. Sometimes it's better not to have any at all."

"But then you wouldn't dream of all the good things in life, would you?" she said, needing to continue this line of conversation, rather than admitting the gloomy thoughts that assailed her far too often.

"And what are the good things in life that my lady dreams about?"

He was humoring her, and she knew it, but there was no point in getting angry. Anger would only use up their precious energy.

"A luxurious bath in scented water," she managed to say through her dry lips. "A long cool drink of water suddenly means more to me than all the finest wines imaginable. The feel of silk against my skin, and a soft bed to lie on with fresh linen on it—"

She paused, realizing how sensual were the words she had unthinkingly chosen. She could have said so many things—the scent of roses in an English garden, a satisfying meal of roast beef and plum pudding, a theater visit in the heart of London; a gentle stroll through Hyde Park and a horseback ride up Rotten Row. All those dear, familiar things that brought a breath of home. Instead, it seemed as though she were deliberately being provocative, when it had never been her intention. She went on clumsily.

"I'm sorry. I didn't mean to say all that—"

"Why be sorry?" She could hear the amusement in Ross's voice. "Do you think it displeases me that you dream of silk against your skin and a soft bed with fresh linen? And especially the scented bath. Your dreams mirror my own, and make me long for those things, too—"

She suddenly gasped. The desert was an undulating place, and they had just traversed a steep incline and were at the peak of ridged dunes that had been tormented into weird shapes and saffron sculptures. Below them stretched them sand and more sand, and in the midst of a small plain—

"Ross, do you see it? There's an oasis within our reach! See how the water shimmers so invitingly, and how the palm trees sway in the breeze. I can smell the freshness from here! Oh, how clever you are to have guided us here!"

As she turned toward him, her eyes shone as blue as the watering hole in the oasis, and she clutched at his arm with a feeling of joy in her soul. They would be able to bathe and drink, and rest in the shade of the palm trees, and restore their strength.

"Stephanie, darling—"

Before he could say whatever he intended, she had turned back to the oasis, wanting to drink in every vestige of it with her eyes. And then her heart jolted with an enormous feeling of disbelief. Seconds ago there had been life and comfort awaiting them, and now there was nothing. No shimmering blue water, no swaying palm trees or wafting breeze. There was nothing but the wasteland of the burning sands, and she felt huge sobs of despair begin somewhere deep in her throat.

"It was a mirage, Stephanie," Ross said roughly, holding tightly to her shaking hands. "You'll probably see many more before we reach our journey's end, and each one will be more beautiful and enticing than the last. And each will be a bitter disappointment."

"How do you know this?" she cried out. "If this part of the desert is uncharted, how do you know whether or not any real oases exist between here and Alexandria? They may not all be mirages!"

She wanted him to agree with her, to say that yes, possibly there could be an oasis that was real, and something more than a figment of the imagination. She saw him shake his head sadly.

"It's best not to build up your hopes on that score, my love. Of all the explorers who have ventured this way before, none has ever returned to tell the tale of such a place. Other British explorers consider it Egypt's wilderness, and one that's to be avoided at all costs."

Her eyes were gritty with sand and bitter disappointment.

"Then just how foolish are we to be attempting to cross it?" she muttered.

"Very foolish, but with no other choice, we go on."

He whipped the protesting camels again, and after a moment's resentful silence, Stephanie spoke again.

"Why did we have no choice? Surely we could have gone back the way we came, but done a detour to the east to avoid Shaladd? That way, we would have reached the Nile, and sailed back until we reached the road to Alexandria."

"Trust me, when I tell you that you'd not have wanted to go anywhere near Shaladd again. It's what Hali will expect, and he'll have his guards on the lookout for us. If he found us, we'd be taken back to Shaladd, but it wouldn't be as honored guests a second time."

She didn't need to ask what he meant. "Then he won't expect us to be making this northern route?"

Ross shrugged. In his robes, he looked quite magnificent, she thought fleetingly, but what use was a powerful physique and handsome appearance to a man who was doomed to die? She pushed the hateful thought out of her mind at once.

"He'll expect that if we try to make our way by this route, we'll be doomed anyway, which will save him the trouble of disposing of us."

He was brutal and terse, and Stephanie gasped again. But although she might only be a woman, and a young and naive one at that, the sense of survival in her was strong, and she found herself giving an arrogant toss of her head.

"Then we'll just have to prove him wrong, won't we?" she snapped.

She clung on to her camel's neck as they began the slipping and sliding descent down the dunes, and Ross gave a short laugh at her words. The sound echoed and reechoed oddly in the silence surrounding them.

"I assure you I'm not laughing unkindly! I'm full of admiration for that sense of survival in you, Stephanie. You can't know how very uplifting it is to hear you speak with such defiance. It's a quality that any man would be thankful to recognize in himself, and I love you for it."

She held on to her senses, not daring to believe that he had meant those words in any romantic way. He was grateful for her strongmindedness, and that she wasn't collapsing like an ingenue in their dire circumstances. His words merely likened her to a male companion sharing and overcoming danger, when she loved him with all a woman's love. She knew that now.

"I'll try to be all that you want of me, sir," she said with a burst of sarcasm.

Ross grinned at her. "You already are," he said simply, letting her make of that what she would.

By the time the sun began its low descent toward the horizon, they had seen no sign of life other than themselves. It was a strange and unnerving feeling to know that they were so alone in this endless wilderness, and as the dying rays of the sun streaked the sky with all the colors of the rainbow, from palest gold to rich, deep cerise and magnificent purple, Stephanie felt the awesomeness of space all around her.

The desert took on a different perspective as dusky night descended upon them. There was no longer any chance of glimpsing the beautiful mirages that could tease and tantalize so heartbreakingly. Since that first one, there had been three more, and all had seemed so near, so real.

But now there was no longer the eye-straining effect of staring at endless sand, and the searing disappointment of knowing that the mirages were simply that and nothing more. Instead, there were shadowed shapes and mountains that resembled crouching monsters, or vast, ridged plains like gigantic and symmetrically furrowed fields, sculpted by the wind into a different kind of natural beauty.

As the burning heat of the day dissipated a little, Stephanie could find it in her heart to feel poetic about this desert that Ross loved so much. But apparently, he didn't feel the same right now. He eyed her anxiously as she seemed to droop over the camel's back in a kind of lethargy.

"We'll pitch our tent in the lee of the dune," he said. "We'll eat, and then we'll try to have a couple of hours' sleep. Then I suggest that we travel on under cover of darkness, guided by the stars. Do you feel strong enough to cope with it all, Stephanie?"

"Of course," she said. For a moment, her mind flitted back to the past, when the most vital thing in her life had been which gown to wear that day, and whether or not Cousin Claire was coming for afternoon tea. How facile it all seemed now, and yet, how wonderfully *normal.*

"We'll survive, Stephanie," Ross said quietly, hearing her small intake of breath, and recognizing her bravado for what it was. She was so young, and she still faced so much. Traversing the desert could tax the strength of the hardiest man, and there were times when he thought Stephanie looked fragile enough to break. If they made it to Alexandria, he would reward her handsomely, he resolved.

No matter what the future held, even if he had to let her go, as he had once promised, instead of being tied to him in marriage, she would have her every wish. He found himself staring at her, knowing a hollowness in his heart at the thought of life without this lovely girl. But if it was her wish that they should part, he wouldn't stand in her way. He owed her that, and so much more.

They had reached the dune by now, and Ross slid from the back of his mount and came to help her down.

"Why did you stare at me so?" she asked huskily, still in the circle of his arms.

"I was marveling at the strength that's in that seemingly frail body," he said, unwilling to give away all the private feelings surging in his heart. "They always say the strongest willow will bend but not break, and if I had to compare you to anything, it would be a lovely, slender willow branch, my brave, beautiful Stephanie."

He caught her unawares, and if she had thought there was no poetry in his soul as he ignored the beauty of yet another desert sunset, she knew there was poetry in it now. She felt choked by his words, and she leaned against him, feeling their heartbeats, strong and steady, and together.

"That's one of the loveliest things anyone has ever said to me," she mumbled, and she heard him laugh softly.

"And it takes so little to please you, my love," he said, half teasing.

He crushed her to him suddenly, as if he couldn't bear to look down into those wide blue trusting eyes a moment longer when he had brought her to this. For no matter how much he tried to bolster her spirits, there was a sense of impending doom filling Ross's heart that he couldn't shake off. The only way to hide it was to be brusque and business-like, and the next time he spoke, Stephanie knew that the magical moments were over.

"I'll tether the camels' legs so that they don't desert us, and once I've got a fire going, we'll boil some water for a brew of tea. It'll be just like home."

She bit her lips hard at his words. No place on earth could be farther from home than this, nor from the familiar, homely English custom of brewing hot tea whenever spiritual and bodily revival was needed.

She didn't need to know that once their meager supply of twigs for fire-lighting was gone, they would be reduced to drinking sips of water, and chewing the dried meats and biscuits. But she refused to let herself dwell on such things. Following the time-honored rituals kept their hands busy, and she was glad to help Ross erect the tent and spread their mattress down for a couple of hours' sleep.

There was no reason to unpack everything, and Stephanie fetched one of the water bags that Hali had left for them, grimacing at the sight of the black cross on the leather. The sooner they had disposed of this one, the less they would be reminded of him, she thought.

Ross had started the small fire by now, and she poured a little of the water into the cooking pot for their tea. She placed it over the burning twigs, and then drew back at once with a small scream.

"What is it?" he asked sharply, but he hardly needed to ask. The scent of the honeyed cordial hung on the air, sweet and sickly, recognizable now with the drugs that had been used to lace it previously. With an expressive oath, Ross grabbed the pot and hurled the liquid away from them, where it disappeared at once into the greedy sand. He snatched up the water bag Stephanie had used, and sniffed its contents before flinging it away from him in a fury.

"The bastard!" he grated. "So his final generosity was not all that it seemed, after all."

Stephanie shook all over. They had assumed that both bags contained water, but the deadly cordial had obviously been included as a cooling drink, and if they had drunk it cold they would have been drugged on their camels' backs in the blazing heat of the desert and probably died from exposure to the heat. Ross took the second bag, dipped one finger inside and tasted the contents, and then tipped it into the sand. It was like seeing their lives spill away.

"It was water," he said harshly. "But God knows what

was in it, and we daren't take any chances. I prefer to rely on our own supplies, and to eke them out more carefully."

But he didn't look at her as he fetched one of their own water bags, and she knew they were in dire straits now.

Eighteen

The next few hours, which had been intended for rest, passed all too quickly, but sleep didn't come easily to either of them. Inside the blanket, they held each other close, but each had private thoughts of their own that they were reluctant to convey to the other. It served to keep them apart, just at the time when Stephanie felt at her most vulnerable, and longed for Ross to open his heart to her about their plight.

But once the stark words had been said, he saw no point in repeating them over and over again. While she needed constant reassurance and explanations, he remained tight-lipped about their chances now. To her, it seemed as if their changing fortunes had forced him to revert to the military man that he once was. He was very much the officer in charge, while those under his command remained in blissful ignorance of procedures and maneuvers and merely followed orders. And knowing so little of the desert compared with his superior knowledge, she was very much the underling.

While she resented this apparent withdrawal from her, she had no idea of Ross's wretchedness at bringing her to such an appalling situation. In his mind, to admit it would be to admit failure also. And, despite everything, he wasn't ready for that just yet.

Stephanie was still drifting in and out of a troubled sleep when she became aware that he was gently rousing her and preparing to pack up the tent once more. The night was dark now, but there was a great yellow moon above, and the stars were bright and clear and would chart their way northward more accurately than any map.

"The stars were there before any manmade materials existed, and they've proved their worth to navigators on land and sea throughout the ages," Ross commented.

"But it took man to read them and understand them, didn't it?" she said, wanting to prove that she had sense enough to know it. "However wonderful something is, it's no real use to anyone unless it can be understood. It's like your old hieroglyphics in the tomb. They meant nothing until someone managed to decipher them, did they?"

"Quite true. And I should have remembered that you have a clever head on those pretty shoulders of yours that constantly feels the need to question and learn. If I seemed to be patronizing, then I apologize."

Stephanie felt herself flush. She couldn't understand why they were being so stiff and formal with each other, and in his attempt to be *un*patronizing toward her, it seemed that he only patronized her more.

"It doesn't matter," she said brusquely. "I was only talking for talking's sake."

And if *that* didn't sound like the talk of a feather-head, she didn't know what did, she thought in annoyance. But as they continued their preparations without further discussion, her ruffled feelings gradually died down. There was no point in being at loggerheads with each other, though Stephanie had to admit that it sometimes seemed as good a way as any other to keep their minds sharp and alert.

Once all was ready, they remounted the protesting camels and continued their journey by the light of the moon and stars. They plodded northward, saying very little, and by the time they had covered a few miles, Stephanie was aware of a strange and almost spiritual calmness filling her. She couldn't explain it, but if she had been able to stand outside herself and observe the robed and veiled figure riding the camel into the unknown desert, she would have sworn there was a certain aura surrounding her.

Was it blasphemy to feel that way? To feel so protected by something so good that it transcended all evil? She didn't know. All she knew was that if she had ever doubted the presence of God, she would never doubt it again. For here in this glowing emptiness was peace and tranquility of a kind that was surely rarely shown to man. They traveled side by side on biblical beasts, the woman and the man, hidden beneath Arab robes, and traveled in silence through the night.

She could even liken their present situation to that of Mary and Joseph, and prayed that the Lord wouldn't consider such thoughts as wicked. It was a deeply private sensation in her soul, too deep to be able to speak of it, even to the one she loved most in all the world, and so she kept her thoughts to herself.

But she knew that the darkness was their friend, and that the moon and the stars were guiding them as surely as that bright star had guided the shepherds and the three wise men. And the sense of hope and optimism was returning and giving her renewed strength. They would survive. Together they were invincible.

Three nights later, Stephanie was finding it very difficult to recapture those fine feelings. They camped every day at dawn, ate a frugal meal and sipped at their precious water supply before trying to sleep inside the tent. But the heat was abominable now, burning through the canvas and making sleep near impossible until sheer exhaustion and the growing threat of dehydration overtook them.

Their lips were cracked and dry, their skin parched and drawn, and their eyes had begun to sink into their sockets. The camels walked at their slow, unerring pace during the night, but by then the two riders were almost too weary to care where they went, and only Ross's diligence kept them going in the right direction.

On the fourth day, they lay together in the tent, barely touching, unable to dredge up enough strength to talk for more than short bursts at a time. Stephanie was sure that death was near now, and in her heart she raged bitterly at the God whom such a short time ago she had gloried in so completely. She was often held in the grip of hallucination, and hardly able to heed any of Ross's words to her.

"Stephanie, there's something I want to say to you." She didn't even turn her head as his scratchy voice drifted toward her from his side of the blanket.

He was so near, and yet his voice seemed to come from a long distance away. Her head floated so much whenever she turned it, as if it was no longer part of her body. She felt his hand reach for hers, and he caressed it briefly before holding it loosely within his palm.

"What is it?" she said hoarsely.

Was he going to put into words the thing that she knew only too well? That they should begin to count their time on earth in hours rather than days? Was he even going to suggest that he should slay them both, instead of waiting for the ever-hovering buzzards to swoop down toward their tasty meal? Not that there would be much of her for them to pick, she thought with a faint attempt at humor, for there was little flesh left on her bones now. What the lack of food and water took from her, the relentlessly sapping heat finished.

"I won't lie to you, my love," Ross went on haltingly. "You must know that we're in a very serious position now. There was always a vain hope of coming across a small water hole, but it seems as if we're out of luck."

"I know," she murmured. "So it's hopeless, isn't it?"

"Nothing's ever hopeless, but our chances get slimmer all the time. If we don't find water soon—"

He didn't finish, but he didn't need to. They could exist a little longer without food, but not without water. As for finding it, they barely had the strength to go on. And the desire for a drink of water had become a feverish obsession that never left her now. She craved it as she had once craved his love, and neither seemed remotely possible.

"So the time has come for honesty between us."

Stephanie heard his voice as if in a dream. She couldn't concentrate properly on anything he was saying. She was somewhere in space, in a world of fantasy where all the colors of the spectrum were dazzling and beautiful. It was a world that enticed her ever nearer, where all things were held in a blissful and suspended state of stupefaction, and where she need never think or feel again. And she longed for it.

"Honesty?" she repeated thickly, as if the word was something in a foreign language.

"Honesty." Ross spoke softly through his own dry lips. "You see, I lied to you, Stephanie. Ever since I've known you, I've been living a lie."

Her brain was too befuddled to understand, or even to care. What did it matter now if he told her he already had a dozen wives, and that he had always intended handing her over to his friend Hali? What did anything matter since they were doomed to die? She thrashed out feebly with her free hand, as if to say it didn't matter.

He caught at her hand and raised it to his lips. Stephanie could feel the swollen dryness of that passionate mouth she had once loved to kiss, and she had just enough comprehension left to register sorrow at what had become of the vigorous lovers they had once been.

"The lie was in the way I married you," he stated.

Well, didn't she know that? Hadn't she always known it? This marriage, made in the sight of God, had been a desecration, a sham, and a lie. She *knew* that.

"I don't want to hear it," she whispered, the tears beginning to trickle down her dry cheeks and smarting where they ran into the cracked and burning skin.

"You *will* hear it," Ross said with a sudden burst of energy in his voice. "I won't let you go to your God without letting you know how much you were loved—how much you've always been loved!"

The air above her head was starting to swirl in front of her eyes now. The canvas sides of the tent seemed to wave about as if in a storm at sea, and the weird sensations were filling her with nausea. But she couldn't vomit, because there was nothing inside her stomach to expel. She could hardly think, because her teeth were chattering so much, and she was convinced that her last moments had come.

"Do you hear me, Stephanie? Do you understand me?" She heard Ross's voice close to her ear, and his face floated above her as he leaned over her, darkening the space in front of her eyes still more.

"I hear you," she said faintly, because it seemed it was what he wanted her to say.

"I love you, my darling girl. I've loved you from the moment I saw you. If you can take nothing else with you to your Maker, then take the memory of my love."

He leaned over her, touching her mouth with his, their tender and swollen lips scratching together in a semblance of a kiss. His face blotted out the light, and for one last, sweet moment, she closed her eyes, wishing herself far away from this dreadful place, wishing time backward, wishing with all her heart for the strength to tell him how much she loved him, too. But there was no time left, and no strength left, and she felt everything ebbing away from her as the darkness deepened, and the beautiful, floating, fantasy world turned into nothing but blackness.

She coughed uncontrollably, feeling the unexpected coldness of something pressed hard against her lips. It was forcing them open, hurting them and cracking them still more, as the thing tried to make her swallow. But she couldn't swallow, because her throat had swollen so much, closing sufficiently to make her retch painfully, and she was vaguely aware that someone or something was trying to push liquid down her throat. She couldn't open her eyes yet, and they felt as though they were permanently stuck together. But she began to realize that someone's fingers were prising open her lips, and trickling the water down the rasping chasm of her throat.

Her dulled senses took a few moments to register the taste. Water! Someone was trying to make her drink water. At the blessed realization, she tried to open her mouth greedily, but the action only made the skin at the corners of her lips crack even more, and she tasted blood as well as water.

She had no idea where she was, for she still couldn't see. Was it night or day? She couldn't tell, and she felt a terrifying panic at the thought that she might be blind for the rest of her life. Had God saved her from one hell, only to put her through another?

But gradually she became aware of sounds all around her where before there had been only silence. There were voices that she didn't know, jabbering in a tongue she didn't understand, and none of them was Ross's voice. Ross. She recalled his name, but she couldn't picture his face, and she needed to see him so desperately, to know that he was safe, too. That they were both safe.

With a great effort she allowed the probing finger to prise her mouth open a little more, and convulsively she swallowed a few drops of water. At the same time, her sticky eyes opened a fraction, and as she gazed straight up at the glare of the sun in a relentless blue sky, the pain in her eyes was sharp and needlelike.

She lowered them at once, and stared instead at the dark, hooded faces hovering over her. There were half a dozen of them, all wearing black robes, and she was convinced that they were the messengers of death, who had come for her. And then the abortive attempt to swallow became a curdled scream as she realized that it was one of these black devils whose finger was halfway down her throat. She was near to madness when she heard a hoarse voice that she knew.

"Stephanie, it's all right! It's all right, my love."

She twisted her head, thrusting the alien hand away from her face with what little strength she had, and saw that Ross was half sitting beside her. She had no idea why they were both prostrate outside their tent, when they had been preparing to die inside it, but as he pulled her close, she clung to him weakly, and gave way to wracking, releasing sobs.

"What's happened?" she croaked when she could finally speak. "Where are we, and who are these—these people? Where have they taken us? Are we at Alexandria?"

"So many questions," Ross muttered, then shook his head slowly at the faint flare of hope in her eyes. "Look around you, my love, and you'll see where we are."

Their final camp had been in the open, since they'd had no strength to go on any farther, and her strained eyes told her at once that they were in exactly the same place. They were no nearer to home, and these people must have come across them while they were unconscious. It was a bitter, cruel disappointment. But if they hadn't . . .

"Who are they?" she whispered, hearing them still jabbering, and realizing that they had pitched their own temporary camp some small distance away, where their camels lazed. She became aware that something delicious was cooking on a campfire. The smell of the food masked the now familiar smell of dried camels' droppings, baked hard by the sun and used for fuel, which they themselves had finally been forced to do when the twigs ran out. As Stephanie took in the aroma of the food, she felt the dormant juices in her mouth straining to react to it, and vying with the threat of nausea.

"They're desert bedouins," Ross said. "A band of nomads who took pity on us instead of killing us outright. We should be thankful for that, at least."

One of the men was still pushing the water bag toward

her, and as she accepted it, she drank too deeply and too fast. The next moment she had thrown up all over herself.

"You must take it very slowly, my love," Ross said.

He had obviously had his own fill of water before she came round, and he was remarkably revived, she thought with a start of irritation. How could he seem so much in control, when she still felt so close to death, and so very fragile? Her own mortality had stared her in the face, and she couldn't get over it that easily.

"I'm so hungry," she whimpered. "Are they going to give us food?"

She heard him speak to the bedouin crouching beside her. He spoke in a tongue she didn't know. The bedouin didn't seem to understand it, either, and for a moment she felt renewed despair. But with many gestures and halting words they seemed to make themselves understood, and the man nodded and pointed to the cooking pot, making scooping gestures with his fingers toward their mouths. Stephanie tried to nod in agreement, but all she could think about was that finger trying to force its way down her throat with the life-giving water. Rescuer or not, she could still taste the rancidity of that finger, and it was enough to make her nauseous all over again.

But she couldn't allow such ungracious thoughts to color her gratitude. Without these nomads, she and Ross would almost certainly be dead by now, or as near as made no difference. They owed them their lives, and they had virtually nothing with which to repay them. She only had a little jewelry, apart from her wedding ring. Ross had some of the expeditionary equipment, and the relics of Ben Rashid Omir's tomb, but she knew that those would be as precious as life itself to him now. They were the only evidence that this trip had not been a waste of government-sponsored money. She wondered swiftly if these nomads had already robbed them of their possessions while they were insensible, but now was not the time to worry Ross with such queries.

But the thoughts went spinning around in her head as the food was brought to them. She was so extraordinarily light-headed, and she could remember nothing of what had happened before lying down with a sigh of something almost akin to relief as she awaited the final sleep.

"What is this?" she asked, but she hardly cared, and since eating utensils were obviously not part of the bedouins' equipment, she hungrily dipped her fingers into her bowl of meat and vegetables in a kind of spicy sauce. She didn't recognize the taste at all, but it tasted so good after the ravenous days that it could have been shoe leather and she would have relished it.

"It's best not to know," Ross answered.

"But I'd like to know," she said with her mouth full.

Ross spoke rapidly to one of the bedouins, pointing to the meat with an obvious question in his voice. The man drew his sword from its sheath, and Stephanie gasped with fright, scrambling back toward Ross and wondering if he had said something to insult their rescuers.

Then she saw that the man intended acting out a little charade for their benefit. He strode toward one of his tethered camels, brandishing his sword, and made as if to slit the animal's throat, while Stephanie felt her eyes dilate in horror. Surely he wasn't going to kill the beast in front of them.

"Don't show your disgust, whatever you do," she heard Ross hiss in her ear. "He's merely demonstrating his source of food supply, and the way it was obtained."

Her stomach almost revolted then.

"You mean we're eating camel?" she spluttered out.

"Just thank the Almighty that they don't understand English," Ross rasped at her. "Do you want to insult them totally? For God's sake, smile and nod, give a small bow, and then continue eating."

She gaped, unable to move a muscle for the moment, until he nudged her sharply, forcing her to do as he said. And she saw that the watchful bedouins were expectantly waiting for her reaction. It was as much as she could do to force the morsels of meat down her throat then, but common sense told her that if it was her one means of survival, it would be madness to let feminine sensitivity get in the way.

And it was only meat, after all. She allowed herself the luxury of pretending it was beef or lamb, or her favorite chicken, and played her own private charade to get her through the ordeal. In any case, it wasn't so bad, if a little tough. In fact, it was rather sweet-tasting, and the spicy sauce complemented it well.

Despite her initial horror, she made herself react to it with a gourmet's palate, and although it filled her with self-disgust to do so, she reminded herself that in more uncivilized parts of the world, she could have been a victim of cannibalism. At least, it hadn't come to that.

"Well done," Ross said, when she had finally emptied her bowl. "Be ready for the next course."

Her heart sank, wondering what awful delights were coming next, and felt a surge of relief when she was handed a slab of coconut to gnaw, and a dish of coconut milk. Wherever the bedouins had traveled, they had obviously found these food supplies, and the thought gave her renewed hope that they, too, would find them.

The refreshing taste of the coconut meat, washed down by the milk, also sweet-tasting, began to revive her spirits as well as her body. She was warned not to eat or drink too quickly, but it was difficult to resist when her stomach cried out for nourishment after the last days of deprivation.

While she and Ross were eating their fill, Stephanie realized they were being watched intently by the bedouins, and she tried to smile gratefully, even though she wasn't altogether easy with them. There was no way of knowing whether or not these were enemies or friends, although surely an enemy wouldn't have offered food and precious water.

"Do they know where there's a water hole?" she mur-

mured to Ross. "They must know where to find water, and
perhaps they could direct us to it."

"I doubt it," he said. "Such places will be a well-guarded
secret. They may take us there, but they would never give
us clear directions."

"What's the difference?" she asked with a burst of her old
sparkle now that her stomach was full and her spirits revived.

"The difference is that they would take us by a devious
route that we would never find again so that we would be
unable to pass on the secret to their enemies."

Stephanie stared at him stupidly, not understanding the
logic in this. A water hole in the desert was surely there for
everyone who needed it, but even at the thought, she knew
it was more precious than gold, and the group who knew of
its existence would hold the power of survival in their hands.
A cold, clammy trickle of sweat ran down between her
breasts, just as it had done in the tomb.

"You speak as though they're bad men. But how can you
be certain of it?" she said slowly, very aware of the group's
excited babble now. They spoke in guttural voices with many
gestures, and she noticed how often their hands were raised
to their heads.

"I'm not certain of anything, but it pays to be always on
your guard," he said grimly, and she saw him finger one of
Hali's swords that he always wore at his side now. She shuddered, wondering if their safety was to be so very short-lived
after all.

A small breeze swirled about the sand, and the fine silvery
strands of her own hair blew across her face. Hastily, but too
late, she pulled the disguising scarf around it, guessing in
an instant that the bedouins had been discussing her, and
especially the strange lightness of her hair.

"Ross, I don't like the way they keep looking at me," she
mumbled. "They frighten me—"

"If you've finished eating, replace your veil," he ordered.

"Always keep as much of your face and hair covered as possible."

She knew then that she hadn't been imagining things. The bedouins were intrigued by the very sight of her, and if they turned ugly, there were too many of them for Ross to dispose of. It would be a slaughter, and without him, she would be helpless in the bedouins' hands . . .

The men had been sitting cross-legged on the sand, but now they got to their feet, as if preparing for a confrontation, and came very close to them. Ross pulled Stephanie to her feet also, and she stood as still as possible, while a kind of silent inspection went on.

Then, to her annoyance, several of the men began to prod her arms and cheeks, and when Ross swore angrily at them in English, his reward was a sword point at his throat. It happened so swiftly that Stephanie had hardly drawn breath to cry out, before she heard him shouting to them in that strange tongue that they seemed just about able to follow. She heard the word Alexandria, and the men glanced at one another, talking among themselves for a moment.

The apparent leader of the group, the one whose finger had forced the water down Stephanie's dry throat, finally answered Ross, pointing straight at Stephanie. She had no idea what he said, but it was clear enough to Ross, whose arm went protectively across her body at once. And even if she didn't understand the words, she understood the lascivious leers, and the gestures.

Dear God, she thought, *they're bargaining for me.* She turned her frantic eyes toward Ross.

"They're offering to show me the way to Alexandria in return for my woman," he said harshly. "You would be a rare prize and win them much admiration from their tribe."

Stephanie gasped, feeling the blood leave her cheeks. She swayed with sudden faintness, and Ross held her firmly and continued speaking rapidly in a low voice.

"Say nothing, and keep very still with your eyes down. I'll deal with this."

She didn't know how. Even with all his cleverness and ingenuity, she saw no way out of it. They would die if they were abandoned once more, and the last few nights had been a severe taste of how dreadful a lingering death would be until the sweet oblivion came. They had had some food and water now, and if they were left to the desert once more, the agony of starvation would begin all over again. Maybe the bedouins had done them no favors after all—it would have been better if they had been left for the buzzards.

She realized that Ross was speaking in that strange desert language in a stern, very aggressive manner now, though she had no idea what he was saying. He had to repeat some of the words several times to try to make the men understand. When they did, she was startled to see them huddle together. Their eyes became wild with unease, and their voices were higher pitched than before as they argued among themselves.

"What have you said to them?" she whispered.

The leader of the group was scrubbing his finger against his side now. She was astonished at the movements. Was he afraid she had defiled him, when she had been the one to be revolted at the taste and stink of that unholy digit?

"I'll tell you in a moment," Ross said quietly. "Meanwhile, keep your eyes lowered. Don't look at them, and don't look at me."

Stephanie hated every moment of this. She didn't know what was happening, but she felt very much that her status as a woman was diminishing in a man's world. They humiliated her, and she didn't know why. They shamed her, when she saw no reason to feel shame, simply because of her gender. She longed to hold her head high, and inform them that she was the stepdaughter of an English lord, but even if they understood her, what good would it do?

She realized that the other men who had touched her were gesticulating as well. She didn't look up, but out of the corner of her eye, she was well aware of their agitation and anger. Ross was holding her hand tightly, willing her to remain silent and docile, and she knew that there was no other course she could follow as she awaited her fate.

After what seemed like an interminable time, the leader of the bedouins came striding toward them, and with a strident gesture, he drew his sword and stuck it into the hard-packed sand a few feet in front of Stephanie. She smothered a little scream as it quivered there, and she quaked from head to foot when he addressed Ross as if she didn't exist.

Ross replied swiftly, and the Arabs retreated to their own camp without a backward glance at them.

"What's happening now?" she stuttered. "Are they leaving us?"

"No. They've agreed to act as guides until we're within sight of Alexandria."

She stared at him, but he didn't look at her. A terrible suspicion began to dawn on her. All she could think about was that he'd said the nomads would only guide him to the city in return for his woman. Some kind of agreement had obviously been reached, and since she couldn't understand a word that had been said, she could only think the worst. But surely he hadn't—he *couldn't* have sold her out? After everything they had gone through, had she meant so heart-breakingly little to him after all?

Nineteen

Ross almost dragged her inside the shelter of their own tent and lowered the flap to conceal them. By then, she could no longer control her tears. They ran down her cheeks and into the painful cracks of her dry skin, and she tasted them on her sore lips. She tore off the veil and the scarf that had covered her hair, and she literally shook from head to foot as she faced her husband.

"Tell me what you've done," she begged. "Tell me to my face that you've sold me out to these devils for the sake of your own salvation!"

She felt his hand across her mouth, stifling the words, and her eyes were full of anguish as she stared at him through the mist of tears.

"Be silent, woman, or we shall lose everything just when I've gained the advantage," he snapped.

She felt her heart plummet. Dear God, but he was Prince Hali incarnate, she thought. He was no longer her dear, her powerful, sensual lover, who could take her to the heights of ecstasy, but an alien, frightening figure, born of the desert and inducted into all its rites. She felt herself wither, and if his arms hadn't reached out to hold her up, she would have crumpled to the ground.

"Then tell me what's going to happen to me," she whispered. "I have a right to know."

She was held close to his heart, and as she felt its throbbing beat, her eyes closed, knowing that no matter what he did, she would always love him. She despised herself for being so weak at a time when she believed the worst of him, but she had always known that true love forgave everything.

"What's going to happen, my love," she heard him say in a surprisingly gentle voice now, "is that, hopefully, once darkness falls, you and I will be traveling on to Alexandria, and eventually home to England."

Slowly, she lifted her face toward him, feeling a wild surge of hope and disbelief in her heart. But there was no sign of deviousness in *his* face. There was only the steady, loving look of the man who had once promised to love and honor her. She gave a muted cry, and leaned heavily against him again, too full of emotion to think of anything but the homeland she had never thought to see again. And too ashamed of her moments of doubt to say anything more.

But she was still so weak, and her legs didn't want to hold her up any longer. After a few moments, they sank down on the blanket together, and he told her how these bedouins had come across them, dragged them out onto the sand, and tried to revive them.

"I wonder why?" she whispered. "They owed us nothing. Why didn't they just leave us to die?"

"It was probably more from curiosity than fine feelings," Ross agreed. "They may have taken me for an Arab like themselves, now that my skin's become so dark with the sun. But when they saw you—"

She shuddered. She had once been shamefully vain about her silvery hair, but in this alien country it had caused her nothing but trouble. And she hadn't missed the lascivious gleams in the eyes of the bedouins when they saw it.

"But you told me they were willing to guide you in exchange for me," she said uneasily. Though her nerves still shook, her brain was beginning to function more acutely now that she had received water and nourishment. "Why are they letting us both go?"

He leaned over her, and something stirred in her mind. Just before she had swooned for the last time, she had seen him above her like this, his eyes tender and loving, and she was sure he had said something that was vitally important to her. But no matter how she tried, she couldn't remember what it was. It was like a lovely, elusive dream that she couldn't quite recapture.

But there would be time enough for recollection. Her memory played strange tricks with her in the desert, and perhaps Ross had said nothing of importance at all. She was simply allowing her thoughts to wander, like a mirage of the mind.

"I had to tell them something that would ensure our safe passage, Stephanie," Ross was saying now. "You must understand that it was vital for our survival, and that there was no other way."

"I understand," she said, for of course she did. Whatever he had said, she knew it had been necessary, and she would surely have agreed with it. What she couldn't understand was his reluctance to tell her what it was.

"They have many superstitions, and one of them is a great fear of the woman's curse," he said abruptly.

Stephanie stared at him. Aside from the indelicacy of the statement, she could almost have laughed at the absurdity of it, for in her dehydrated state, no such natural event had occurred in weeks. She gave a small sound of frustration, as she seemed momentarily incapable of counting back the days and weeks. She felt Ross seize her hands and hold them tight.

"Do you understand what I'm saying, Stephanie? It was the only way. I had to inform them that you were in the unclean state, and that they might be already tainted by touching you—"

"No!"

She snatched her hands away from him in deepest humiliation. For a moment she felt totally irrational and outraged.

She was beyond caring or believing that these devils could be persuaded to leave them alone because of such an explanation. To Stephanie, it was something so personal, so much a violation of her intimate self, that she wanted to bury her head in the sand forever. She never wanted to look at any of them—or Ross Kilmarron—ever again.

She could hear herself sobbing with humiliation, and then he was shaking her furiously until her teeth rattled. Before she could stop him, he had struck her across the mouth, and she lay whimpering on the blanket, wondering if she was to be at the mercy of men forever. He lunged over her, his hand fastened tightly over her mouth, while her wild, frightened eyes implored him not to prolong this agony, but to end it now, if that was what he had in mind.

"Listen to me, my darling," he breathed into her ear. "It's vital that you go along with this plan or we're doomed. If they once suspect that I've lied to them, they'll have no hesitation in killing me, and I don't need to tell you what your future will be, do I? You'll be a prize worth a king's ransom at any marketplace from here to Morocco. Now, will you keep quiet if I take my hand away?"

She nodded, scrambling to sit up as he removed his hand, and moving as far away from him as possible with her legs curled up beneath her. Her arms hugged her body, and she still shook as though with the ague. She had never been truly afraid of him before, but she was afraid now. He was as barbaric as the desert tribes. In her mind, they were the same.

She seemed to crouch away from him, as if she would melt into the tent canvas if she could, and she heard him give a vociferous oath.

"Dear God, when you look at me like that, I rue the day I ever set eyes on you," he muttered. "That I could have brought you to this—"

"I rue it, too," she said shrilly, the tears starting to fill her eyes despite herself. "I've known little peace of mind since the day we met, and if I could turn back the clock I would have sold myself to the devil rather than marry a man I despise! No gentleman would do what you have done, however desperate the circumstances."

He stared at her, and she could no longer read the expression in his eyes.

"So, perhaps at last your true feelings have emerged, my dear," he said quietly. "But I fancy that a lady of such sensitivity as yourself wouldn't have cared to be at the devil's every command. In time, I trust you'll believe that you still had the better bargain."

"You flatter yourself, sir!" Stephanie said bitterly. "And what makes you think that being in the devil's clutches would be so very different from being in yours?"

"My lady has a very sharp tongue in her head, and I see that food and drink has quickly restored it," Ross said with an edge to his voice now, and Stephanie knew she had riled him. "Just offer thanks to that God of yours that we shall be receiving more sustenance in due course."

"What do you mean?"

"Do you really think I would have deliberately demeaned you to our captors if there had been any other way to save our necks, my sweet?"

"I don't know—" she began uncertainly.

"You know very little about this country and its people. For all your book-reading, you've only scratched the surface of tradition and superstition and violence that has enabled the people of this land to survive at all."

"And you understand them so well, I suppose—"

"No European can ever understand them fully. Who can understand how a close friend could turn on a man who once saved his life, and leave him to fend alone in the desert?"

"I cannot," Stephanie muttered, knowing at once that he was thinking of Prince Hali, and hearing the bitterness in his voice.

"So will you listen sensibly now?" Ross asked quietly.

She nodded, flinching a little as he leaned toward her until she felt the soothing coolness of a cloth dipped in water placed against her mouth.

"I'm sorry I struck you, but an hysterical woman is comparable to a madwoman, and—"

"Are the bedouins afraid of madwomen, too, then?"

"No. They just kill them and cut out their hearts to feed to their animals," Ross said brutally.

Stephanie gasped as the terror of what he was saying seeped into her brain. Then it was all too much, and she couldn't take any more of such atrocities. She felt as though everything inside her was turning to water, and she curled up on the blanket, looking up at Ross without speaking. She just couldn't fight anymore. Whatever was to happen to her would happen, and she had no strength to fight it. Fate always had its way in the end. The astrologers believed it, anyway.

"The only saving grace I could think of was to tell them you were in an unclean state, by way of the woman's curse," Ross repeated. "I knew they'd be terrified because their leader had touched you, even to forcing your mouth open with his finger. He was therefore in danger of being contaminated, and of contaminating the whole camp.

"Superstition is both a handicap and an asset, my love. What one group believes will damn them forever, another will see as the greatest gift on this earth. But no matter what the superstition, where it exists, one can always twist it to advantage."

"You mean they will leave us alone because they think that I—I have the woman's curse?"

Just saying the words, even to her husband, was enough to make her cheeks fill with color. It just wasn't done in genteel circles. At the ironic thought, Stephanie knew how ludicrous it was to have such thoughts in such a place and in such dire circumstances.

"They will, and whatever food and water we require will be brought to within a few feet of our tent and left for me to bring inside. They will also keep their distance from us when we travel—"

"When we travel? You mean they're going to guide us to Alexandria after all?" she asked, with a great leap of hope in her heart.

Ross gave a rueful smile, the first real smile in ages, it seemed to Stephanie, and she could see how the wind and sand had added extra creases to his fine-boned face. If he was so ravaged, with his superior strength, then how much more so must she herself be? But there was no time for such vanity, when survival itself was at stake.

"Have you lost all faith in me, woman?" he asked mildly. "I was able to persuade Shalikan, their leader, that the ancient gods would look more kindly on those who had touched an unclean woman and her companion were they to guide those same strangers to their destination. As nomads themselves, they understood the laws of strangers helping strangers, and I 'believe we struck a kind of truce."

"But you can't be sure?" Stephanie asked thickly, quick to notice every nuance in his voice now.

Ross shrugged. "It's in the lap of the gods now, and the bedouins will be holding council to decide whether or not they accept my story. We have to sit tight until sundown. If there's food and water outside our tent then, we'll know I succeeded. If not—"

He shrugged again, and Stephanie ran her tongue around her parched mouth. Moments ago, she had felt such hope, but even now, nothing was certain. If the bedouins didn't agree to Ross's request to act as guides, and simply vanished overnight, then this could be the last sundown they would ever see in their lives.

She felt the prickle of those damnable tears behind her lids, and dashed them back. From somewhere deep in her soul, she was fiercely aware of the primitive desire to survive all of this, to be able to tell their children such a tale of fantasy, one that had been a mixture of the bizarre and barbaric, and the utterly beautiful. Her eyes closed briefly against the sting of tears, and she swallowed hard.

"I want to see the sun go down with you, Ross," she said huskily. "Just in case—"

But she couldn't finish, and she felt him take her hand and raise it to his lips. After all the traumas and torments, it was an act of simple tenderness that tore at her heart. So much so that she had to snatch her hand away before she burst into noisy tears. But together with the need to survive, a semblance. of pride had returned.

"Please don't," she whispered tightly. "I can't stand any more."

If he'd taken her in his arms right then and told her he loved her it might have made these last hours bearable. But he didn't. He nodded, taking her at her word, and, instead, she watched in disbelief as he turned away from her, to take out his writing materials from his pack. He began to write in some detail, presumably in preparation for the book that he fully intended to write when they returned to England. For a moment, Stephanie wished she had his faith, no matter how blind it seemed.

For the rest of that interminable day, they had only the one container of water and the food that had been given to them earlier. Neither dared to set foot outside the tent, and Stephanie didn't know whether to be glad or sorry when the shadows began to lengthen. The nomads had been arguing noisily all day, and there had been frequent clashes of metal, as though weapons had been drawn. But now all was silent, and the aroma of hot cooking was beginning to drift toward the tent again, making Stephanie's mouth water and her stomach muscles contract painfully.

"I can't sit here any longer, just waiting for whatever death they could be planning for us," she said in a sudden feverish panic. "I have to go outside in the air, even if it's the last time I shall see daylight."

She thrust open the tent flap before Ross could stop her

and stepped outside into the comparative cool of the early evening. Night came swiftly to the desert, and the sun was already low on the horizon, filling the sky with all the unearthly colors of the universe. Outside their tent there was no more food or water. There was only a deep, wide circle around their camp, etched in the sand so that the outer ridges gave it the semblance of a waterless moat. Keeping them in, and keeping the nomads out. But for how long?

Stephanie could see them now, grouped around their cooking fire in their black robes, frightening and alien, and even darker in the dying light. She felt Ross try to pull her back as weakness threatened to make her stumble as she moved toward the edge of the circle. She shook him away.

"I have to feel the sun on my face, Ross," she said. "It's been our enemy for so long, but now I long to feel it on my skin for one last time—"

"For pity's sake, will you stop behaving like the messenger of doom?" he said. "But all right. We both need to stretch our legs, and we won't be disturbed providing we don't go anywhere near the nomads. If they're planning to kill us, we'll do half their job for them by walking off into the desert, anyway."

"Well, that's cheered me up no end," she muttered, with a small burst of her old spirit.

But she saw that it was true. The bedouins gave no more than a brief glance in their direction as they stepped outside the circle and away from the transitory camp, to where the crouching desert dunes seemed to gleam like hillocks of gold dust in the dying sunset.

Stephanie caught her breath, stunned as always by such beauty, no matter how treacherous she knew it to be.

"A person could spend their last hours gazing at worse places than this," she said huskily, and knew from the way Ross silently folded his arms around her that he understood.

She breathed in the dry, dusty air, coughing a little as a soft breeze swirled the ever-moving sand into their faces and leaned back against Ross. If these indeed were to be their last hours on earth, then at least they were spending them together.

As the sun dropped behind the horizon in one final, magnificent fiery moment, she felt the weak tears stab her eyes again. She was not a woman who was normally given to tears, but she felt as if she had cried a lifetime of them in these past despairing days.

"It's time to go back, Stephanie," Ross said gently. "Lean on me, and don't underestimate your weakness."

Oh, but she didn't! She had never felt so weak or helpless in her life or that she had no more substance than one of these grains of sand beneath her feet.

She moved forward, hardly knowing how she put one foot in front of the other. Her head was bent, and she was beaten. She had never felt less of a woman than she did at that moment, unless it was to feel the briefest empathy with those servile Arab women of the desert.

"Thank God," she heard Ross grate in her ear, and her head jerked up to look at him, knowing from his tone that he, too, had been unsure that this moment would come, or that his ruse would work.

But as Stephanie opened her sand-weary eyes wider, she realized they were standing just outside the etched circle around their tent. And placed inside the small moat of sand were dishes of food and containers of water.

"Does this mean they'll definitely guide us to Alexandria?" Stephanie spoke huskily against Ross's chest when her crying was done. But these were tears of relief and sheer exhaustion now, knowing that for the moment, at least, they were going to live. She didn't dare to think beyond the moment.

"It does," Ross said gravely. "Did you ever doubt me, my darling?"

He attempted to tease her, but she couldn't respond to teasing, not yet. Eternity had come too close, and she shuddered to think what her fate would have been without Ross's quick thinking. The little matter of shaming her femininity in front of these nomads seemed of such little consequence now. It had saved their lives.

"I'll try never to do so again," she said in a muffled voice. To her surprise he gave a harsh laugh.

"Don't make promises you're unlikely to keep, love. "You've doubted me from the moment we met, and with good cause. Let's not pretend otherwise."

She stared at him. He was being brutally honest about the beginnings of their association, and to her heightened senses, it seemed as if he was offering her no hope for their future together.

"So are we going to eat this food, or do we insult our hosts by leaving it to the buzzards?" she heard Ross continue.

He had insisted on leaving the tent flap open, and now that the swift darkness had replaced the daylight, the glow from the campfire threw long shadows between the watching nomads and themselves. They had to be seen to eat and drink, and to accept the terms of the transaction Ross had made.

Once they began to eat, Stephanie devoured the food hungrily, uncaring that she had to scoop it around the dishes with her fingers, until Ross told her to slow down or she would just as quickly lose all the contents of her stomach. She obeyed meekly, knowing he was right, and it only took a very little of the food to make her feel bloated.

Long before they had finished, Stephanie realized the nomads had lost interest in them. It was true, then. They would have insulted their so-called hosts if they hadn't eaten when they did. There was so much to learn and accept, and it was all so different from the simple rudiments of life in England.

For a moment, the sweet, sweet memories of other days, of taking afternoon tea with Cousin Claire, of thin cucumber sandwiches and properly brewed Indian tea imported from the best plantations to a gentleman's table, swept over her in waves. She gave a long, shuddering sigh, and at Ross's questioning look, she spoke in a strangled voice.

"Tell me what you really think, Ross. Will we ever leave this place? Will we ever see home again?"

She had no chance to know what his answer might have been, because the guttural voice of Shaikan, the bedouin leader, was calling to Ross from outside the moat of sand. Fearfully, Stephanie stood behind him in the shadow of the tent as he strode outside, keeping the moat between him and their captor. Stephanie found it impossible to think of the man as anything else.

She saw Shalikan gesticulating toward the sky and pointing in what she hoped was a northerly direction, the direction of Alexandria. He continued speaking in the strange desert patois that was still only half comprehensible to Ross. But after what seemed like an age, each man held up an arm as if in salute, and Ross returned to the tent. By then, Stephanie's heart was thudding wildly, and she could hardly wait for his explanation.

"Well?" she demanded. "What did he say? Did you understand him? Is he going to honor his agreement, or does his word mean nothing?"

She couldn't seem to stop babbling. She was desperate to know what had been said between them, and yet she was almost too afraid to know. And the longer she babbled, the longer she would keep away whatever it was Ross had to tell her. She simply couldn't believe it was going to be good news.

"We leave for Alexandria as soon as the good omen of the moon is directly overhead," he said calmly.

For a second, she couldn't believe her own ears. And then she simply melted against him, clinging to him and laughing and crying at the same time.

"It's nearly over, darling," she heard him say roughly, his hands caressing the silver of her hair. "In a few days from now, we'll be able to put all of this behind us."

"A few days?" she said hoarsely. "It will take that long to be rid of the desert?"

His hand was stilled for a moment. "Perhaps the desert isn't all you want to be rid of, Stephanie."

She shivered, thinking of Prince Hali and the killings, and the evils that men could do to one another.

"Perhaps not," she muttered, never thinking that he could be putting another interpretation on her words.

They traveled by night, a trailing camel caravan, strung out against the desert moonlight with the strangers some distance behind the bedouin group. If they came too close, there would be shouts and curses, and the clash of metal as swords were drawn. They were not welcome in their midst, and by now Stephanie was well aware that it was only the fear of superstition that gave them safe passage.

They set up their tent each morning as the dawn sky burgeoned the heavens with blue and gold. And by then, Stephanie was only too thankful to crawl inside her blanket for a few hours' sleep. Days and nights began to merge into one another, and only the necessary exercise she and Ross took away from their tent in the late afternoon was keeping her sane. Even then, there were constant shimmering mirages on the horizon, tantalizing and luxuriant, and ever out of reach, until they vanished into the sand as quickly as they appeared.

She began to wonder secretly if they would ever reach their destination. For all they knew, these nomads could be leading them round in circles, or to an even worse fate. They could be taking them to some native village where they would get a good price for the silver-haired woman, and the man would simply be swallowed up by the ever-encroaching desert sand. Her morbid imagination wouldn't let her be, and she often cried out in her daytime sleep, to find herself damp with perspiration and being rocked in her husband's arms as he bathed her face with some of their precious water.

"Hold on, my sweet girl," he breathed against her fevered cheek. "Hold on just a little while longer, and then it will all be over, and I'll make it all up to you."

"Will you?" she cried out through cracked lips. "Will you give me back my girlhood? Just how will you give me back these past terrible months? Are you God?"

She didn't know why she felt the need to lash out at him. He held her close and she loved him, but the urge to hurt and wound was as much a compulsive need in her as it had once been for her husband to ravish her so delightfully. She had lost his desire, and so she resorted to the word-lashing of a shrew.

Though, of course, she knew why he never attempted to make love to her. He had explained how deeply it would offend their captors, if they became aware of a man fornicating with an unclean woman. He had explained all that in the crudest terms for her education, but perversely, she had never wanted him more. And now, when she needed him most, it was the thing that was most denied her.

Twenty

On the third morning, when the sun was coming up over the horizon in a glory of red and gold, Stephanie was sprawled half insensibly over the back of her camel. She ached in every limb, and all she wanted was to lie down and rest. She didn't care where she lay her head now. Even here would be heaven, in the softly swirling sand. Just to sink down into its depths, letting it fold over her and bury her forever, would be such a sweet and effortless way to die.

"They're going on," Ross's scratchy voice came back to her as if through a mist. "It must mean that we're getting near to Alexandria at last."

She was completely unable to raise her enthusiasm to the level he expected. She could hardly raise her tired lids against the overwhelming glare of the sun. Where else in the world did it emerge so quickly from the hours of daylight, and vanish at night so abruptly? It gave no time for the brain and the eyes to adjust, and she couldn't think why they didn't just stop this endless traveling and let her sleep.

"Drink some water, Stephanie," Ross ordered sharply. He handed her one of the leather water bags they carried. She obeyed him dully, taking the bag from him, her limp fingers fumbling for the stopper. But as she pushed it open, it slid out of her hands, and the precious water dwindled away into the sand. She stared at it in horror, hearing Ross's muttered oath as he leapt down from his camel's back and retrieved it.

"Thank God there wasn't much left in that one," he snapped. "Next time, try to be more careful. We won't be popular with the bedouins if we waste their water."

She wanted to laugh out loud. What did she care if they were popular with them or not? It was a stupid word to use, and Ross was stupid if he couldn't see it. She hated them, and she hated him. He must hate her, too, since she had caused him nothing but trouble ever since they set foot in this land. If only she had been born a man, none of this would have happened. Their entire calamity was her fault.

"You'd better try again."

She realized Ross was handing her a second water bag. "I've taken out the stopper, so hold on to it tightly this time. Just take a few sips and leave some for later."

She obeyed automatically, wondering why it mattered whether they left some water for later or drank the lot at once. By now, she knew they were getting nowhere, and she had her own ideas about why the bedouins had decided to travel on in daylight. They must be nearing the village of her nightmares, where she would be sold into slavery to the highest bidder, who would gloat over the prize of the silver-haired one. To Stephanie, Ross was the gullible one for thinking differently.

They didn't even stop for breakfast or to make morning camp. They were only given just enough food to survive, and no more. Stephanie was constantly aware of the gnawings in her stomach, but she had no option but to move with the camel's plodding gait, mesmerized by the heat and the sun and the oppressive shielding of her concealing veil and scarf.

By the time the sun had begun to climb to its midday level, she wondered how much longer she could go on. Why didn't they stop and let them rest in the comparative shade of their tents, as on previous days? Or had it been their intention all along to let them scorch to death beneath the relentless sun?

"Ross, I can't take any more," she burst out in real anguish. "If we don't stop soon—"

She didn't know whether or not the black-clad group ahead of them had heard her gasping cry, or if they even cared about her distress, but they halted their camels, shouting to one another. Even as she strained her eyes to see what they were doing, the shimmering heat-haze threatened to distort everything in her vision, and she heard Ross mutter angrily.

"Now what are the devils about?"

Stephanie realized they had spread out in a line in front of them, so that she couldn't see past them. She was dry-mouthed with fear. If this was truly the end, and they were about to be slain, then she prayed to God to let it be quick.

The men were moving slowly toward them now, and the shaking in Stephanie's limbs wouldn't stop. She tried to be strong, to sit upright and to remember her dignity, but what did any of it matter anymore?

Shalikan spoke rapidly to Ross in the words she couldn't understand. Before she could ask him what was happening, and even before he could reply to the bedouin leader, the group had moved forward, swarming around them in a circle for a few heart-stopping moments, then racing their camels back to the desert. Stunned at the swiftness of the action, Stephanie swiveled around to watch them go, and within minutes the swirling dust and sand had taken them from their sight and hidden them among the dunes.

"Have they abandoned us?" she whispered.

The sun burned her eyes and skin, and she hardly cared what happened to them now. But Ross had come quickly to her side. He reached for her hand and held it tightly, as if afraid she would fall from the camel's back from sheer exhaustion and resignation.

"Look into the distance ahead of us," he said, his voice scratchy.

She looked and blinked, and tears of misery filled her eyes, because there was surely the most beautiful, cruelest mirage of all. Ahead of them, far away in the distance, a city seemed to shimmer and glow in the sunlight, and Stephanie knew that only a miracle could make it real. If she watched and waited just a few moments longer, it would surely disappear, just like all the rest of them.

"It's Alexandria, my darling girl," Ross said quietly, raw emotion in his voice. "We're almost there."

She gave a loud cry, and it was the cry of an animal that had suffered for too long, and couldn't take the kindness that was suddenly offered it. The cruel sky and the greedy desert melted and merged into one, and she slid off her camel's back in a dead faint.

When she came around, it was to find herself lying on the blanket inside their open tent, and the blessed shading of the canvas gave her some relief from the blistering sun. She also discovered that she was alone.

"Ross," she said huskily. "Ross, where are you?"

There was no answer, and she bit her trembling lips, knowing she must have been dreaming, and not wanting to wake up from such a beautiful and impossible dream. They had almost reached the city of Alexandria, and they had been feted and welcomed back like conquering heroes, and she had bathed in warm, scented water that was scattered with rose petals, and then lain between soft sheets with her beloved.

But it had only been a dream, of course. If she looked outside the tent, it would be to find the bedouins still motionless, still watching the silver-haired woman, and waiting to claim her as they had always intended.

The thought of it sharpened her nerves, but she was unwilling to lie here awaiting her fate. she had to *know*. Tentatively, she crawled across to the open tent flap and peered out. The sun constantly hurt her eyes now, though it was lower in the sky than she remembered, and she guessed that the day had moved on while she had lain unconscious. There was no sign of anyone at all, and it seemed as if she was entirely alone in the whole universe. For a wild moment she panicked, then, as she stood upright, swaying a little in her weakened state, she saw a lone figure etched against the sky.

"Ross— "

In her head she was screaming out his name, but no more than a croak emerged from her tired throat. Her normally melodious voice deserted her, and as she swallowed, vainly trying to bring some saliva to her aid, she realized how vulnerable he looked on the ridge of the dune alongside them. She had never thought of him as being vulnerable before. He was too strong, too much a man in every way, yet if only she hadn't felt so weak, she would have run to him and put her arms around him and told him everything was going to be all right now. It was a pitiful urge, she told herself, when she wasn't sure of any such thing, but it was part of her nature to comfort where comfort was needed.

He turned, as if aware that she was watching him, and came swiftly back to the tent.

"Thank God," he said with a crooked smile. "I was beginning to think I would have to travel on to Alexandria alone after all."

She stared at him. Even now, she was finding it hard to comprehend what he was saying. But she ignored the implication that he had believed her to be near to death, in the all-importance of something else.

"Are you telling me I didn't dream it then?" she asked hoarsely. "Are we nearly there?"

"Look into the distance, Stephanie, and believe it. It's no mirage, my love, and if it is, then it's the most substantial one I've ever seen. Shalikan and his men refused to take us any nearer to the city, so from now on, we're on our own.

We'll rest until nightfall, and then we'll begin the last part of the journey."

She still swayed on her feet, but she needed to stare fixedly at the distant shadows that were vaguely assuming the shapes of minarets and buildings, as if to assure herself that they wouldn't vanish from her sight within seconds. When they didn't, she felt the surge of life returning to her veins. She clung to Ross, and gave a thin laugh of sheer disbelief, and the unfamiliar laughter muscles stretched taut as she did so.

"Can't we go right now?" she said thickly.

"I think not," Ross said. "You've surely been in the desert long enough by now to know the foolishness of daylight travel. You need food and water and rest before we move on, and you've been near to delirium these past hours, my love."

He brought her a drink of water, and she sipped it slowly, feeling its coolness slide down her throat as if it was the nectar of the gods.

"Have I really been so out of touch with reality?" she asked. She hated the thought, and she prayed that her strength would soon return with the incentive that they were so close to safety at last. "I can't remember much of what happened at all. Have those men really gone for good?"

"Oh, yes. There's only you and me and the desert now, my sweet," he said lightly. "A perfect setting for seduction, wouldn't you say?"

She stared at him. He surely wasn't serious! In her almost emaciated state, and their desperation to reach Alexandria where they would be safe, he surely couldn't mean what he was saying! Didn't he know that she couldn't think of anything so primitive now as making love? She heard him give a short laugh.

"You needn't look so worried, Stephanie. I doubt that even I could raise the energy for such delights, and we should reserve them until we reach the Cleopatra Hotel. But it's been a long while, and by then I shall be hungry for my wife."

She turned away. She couldn't bear to see the flicker of desire in his eyes right now. She couldn't think of such things, nor believe that such normality might yet be theirs. For her, it was enough that they had survived, and she wouldn't debase these God-given moments with lustful thoughts.

The need for physical love must wait until later, she thought, and then she gave a sudden shudder. She felt so empty, so devoid of all emotion, that she began to wonder if such feelings would ever return, or if these weeks of knowing only despair had robbed her of the capacity to love at all.

"I see that my natural desires aren't welcome," Ross said, seeing her shudder. "It's no matter. A wife's duty is to obey her husband, and I'm sure you would not choose to be lacking in such duties."

For a moment, a flare of anger lit Stephanie's eyes.

"Don't speak to me of duty as if I'm no more to you than one of Prince Hali's concubines!" she said hotly. "You once told me they mean no more to him than vessels to feed his desires and to bear him sons. An Englishman's wife deserves more respect from her husband than that!"

"And gets it," Ross retorted. "How quickly you react, my sweet, but it's no matter. In fact, I'm thankful to know that your spirit hasn't been entirely smothered by the desert."

They were half lying inside the tent now, taking the necessary rest while the daylight hours lasted, and Stephanie was slightly mollified by his words, even though she was always suspicious of him when he agreed with her so readily. But she couldn't deny that she had promised to love, honor, and obey him. She found it so easy to do the first, sometimes difficult to do the second, and frequently impossible to do the last!

She was not exactly the perfect English wife, she thought guiltily, but then, in no way could this be called a perfect marriage. One that was procured through deceit stood no more than a poor chance of success. And love that was all one-sided could only be a bittersweet love.

She swallowed, pushing such thoughts away, and tried instead to think ahead. If they were to return to Alexandria so soon, perhaps they should arrive looking less like tramps of the desert, and more like the Europeans they were. Or would that be wise? She looked down at herself, knowing how slight was her figure beneath the enveloping Arab robe. Wouldn't their own clothes hang on them now, their hair so lank and unkempt, and their skins so weathered by the sun and wind that they would look even more disreputable than a band of desert nomads?

As she drew in her breath, she felt Ross's fingertip raise her chin to make her look at him.

"What's going through that beautiful head of yours now, I wonder?"

"I'm wondering how you intend our arrival to be. Do we sneak into the city under cover of darkness as we are now, or do we return in a kind of triumph at surviving at all, and wearing our own clothes?"

Ross laughed. "I'm glad to see that you haven't lost all your feminine vanity—"

"Don't mock me, Ross! I'm serious. I know I look terrible—" She bit her lip, for what he said was true. Even though death had stared her in the face, it hadn't taken long before the thought of wearing soft, feminine garments and indulging in the simple luxuries of a lady's life that she had always taken for granted were tantalizing her senses again.

Was she really so shallow, that she could forget so soon? But she knew she would never forget. Every experience of these last weeks was etched sharply on her memory, and would eventually be transmitted onto paper and canvas through her talented fingers.

"I'm not mocking you, my love. I'm only too glad that you can think of such things again. It's been so long since you were permitted to behave like a woman."

She hadn't been looking at him. She was weak and tired, but now there was a great ache in her soul to do normal things again. To sit in an English garden with her drawing materials, and sketch an English sunset, in a place where there were little silvery streams, an abundance of trees, and rolling green meadows.

She wasn't looking at him, but as she became aware of the quickening of his breath, his meaning slowly penetrated her brain. It was so long she had been permitted to behave like a woman, and it was so long since he had performed like a man.

Slowly, she lifted her head toward him, and he was her dark, her own beloved prince. She caught her breath in her throat as she felt his hand cover her breast. The coarse cotton robe was still between the touch of his palm and her flesh, but it did nothing to lessen the swift surge of longing for him that filled her like a flame. She felt her nipples react to his gentle touch, and it seemed like the first normal bodily reaction she had experienced in weeks.

"So. Perhaps making love to my wife would not be such an unacceptable occupation after all," he said in a gentle voice.

"Perhaps not," Stephanie whispered.

"But would I be welcome?" Ross asked, his sensitive fingers still circling the buds that seemed to yearn toward his touch.

"When have I ever said that you were not welcome?" she murmured, unable to beg for his favors but becoming ever more feverish for these preliminary moments to end, and for the loving to begin.

"That's true," Ross said thoughtfully. "I don't believe you ever have. In that respect, you've been a dutiful wife, sweet Stephanie."

Her eyes suddenly flashed at him.

"Will you please stop speaking of duty! You debase what should be something very special between two people—"

"But we're not two ordinary people, are we? We're the lovers who came together because of circumstances, rather than through woman's love and man's desire."

She felt his hand move lower over her body, palming and kneading, and her limbs relaxed and parted involuntarily. The warmth of his caresses was filling her with a different kind of heat, one that she had hardly thought to feel again, and one that cried out for fulfillment. Hot, surging sensations filled her veins, and her breathing was short in her chest.

"Do you not think a woman capable of desire as much as a man?" she said, her voice tight as the sensuously shooting feelings began to overwhelm her. She ached for him, and he seemed determined to keep her waiting.

"I think my woman is capable of anything," he said softly, covering her mouth with his own.

"Then why do you bait me so?" she whispered when she had breath enough to speak. "Why not do what you intend to do? It's not as though there's anyone to see us. We're alone in the world, and it will be soon enough when we're surrounded by other people."

Why she said such improper things she didn't know. But she was suddenly nervous, and nervousness always made her more talkative. She was nervous of making love again after so long, and even more nervous of reentering the world of people and normality again.

They had created their own private world here in the desert. They had shared moments of the rarest beauty and total despair, but all of it belonged to them alone, and in a sudden ludicrous flight of fancy she knew it was a part of her life that should be cherished, for it would never come again. She wanted to jealously guard all the good, and all the bad, and she wasn't even sure that she wanted it recorded for the world to read about.

She felt the coolness of the air on her skin as Ross gently removed her robe, and she felt an urge to cover her body with her hands, sure that because of the weeks of hardship she would be less comely than before, and she was ashamed at knowing she must appear that way to him. As if he could read her mind, he gently removed her hands.

"Do you think you're any less beautiful to me now than you ever were, my love?"

"I don't know."

"Then let me reassure you."

He leaned over her, kissing every inch of the flesh that was exposed to him, and seeking out what wasn't. She arched toward him, her body crying out for him, and the next moment he was inside her, filling her with that sense of glory and excitement that only he could give her. For a few moments they simply lay together, joined as one, and then she clung to him wordlessly as he began to move within her. The movements were slow, for exhaustion was never far from either of them now, but for all that, it was a sensual, erotic commitment of all that had gone before, and which bound them together.

The climax came swiftly, and the energy each of them produced was as quickly diminished, and long afterward they lay in each other's arms until the heat forced them apart.

"Even the elements are against us," Ross murmured wryly. "I never thought I'd envy those lovers who are probably shutting out the wind and rain of an English night right now and keeping a huge fire burning in the bedroom fireplace to keep them from freezing!"

The sweet imagery of it made Stephanie draw in her breath.

"I never thought I'd long for rain, either," she said wistfully. "But when we get home, I shall run outside in the first downpour, and just revel in it!"

Ross laughed. "And I'll join you! Who cares if the whole country will think we're mad? If too many garbled reports of our expedition going awry and us missing have already reached the newspapers, they must think so already."

Stephanie spoke sharply. Such a thought had never occurred to her before.

"Do you think that's possible?"

He shrugged. "It's more than possible, it's highly likely. There was a time limit for us to return, or at least to send back reports to the newspaper link at Alexandria. It was part of the contract that I would deliver current reports as often as was reasonable. Our continued silence all these weeks will be seen as very grave indeed, and I doubt that Prince Hali will have contributed to the outside world's knowledge."

"But if such newspaper reports have reached England, then my stepfather and cousin Claire might well believe that we're dead!" she said, appalled. "Why haven't you told me any of this before?"

"What good would it have done?" he said curtly. "We've had enough to worry about, without your added sniveling over something that couldn't be changed."

She glared at him in anger. It was undeniable that he had been as worried as she during these past weeks. But to reduce her feelings to *sniveling* was too much to take. The euphoria of the last moments, when she had been so rapt with love for him, quickly evaporated, and she struggled to don her robe once more and to cover herself from his eyes.

"How dare you!" she snapped. "I never snivel, and I had every right to know about these newspaper reports. I can just imagine that my family will be at their wits' end, wondering what's become of me."

"I seem to remember your stepfather was only too ready to hand you over to my care, and as for your stepbrother, I assumed there was little love lost between the two of you."

She ignored his smarting remarks about the lack of affection from the male members of her family.

"But you forget my cousin Claire, who was always kind to me, and will be mourning me—"

"For God's sake, Stephanie, there's no need to speak as

though we're already dead! We're within sight of safety, so don't let your morbid imagination drag you down."

"Then I insist that we leave right now!" she said, leaping to her feet and swaying horribly for a moment. "I refuse to wait here for one single moment more, fretting over whether or not some other band of heathens is going to descend on us. '

"I doubt that," Ross said dryly. "We're too near to the city. That's why the others left us when they did. Nomads don't care too much for civilization—"

But she was past listening to reason.

"I want to leave *now,*" she said, in her most imperious voice. "I demand that you take me to Alexandria, Captain Kilmarron, and that once we're settled, we send word with all possible speed to my family to inform them of our well-being. And if you won't take me," she added, "I'll go on alone."

He stared up at her thoughtfully. If she hadn't been so slight and so fragile, she might have resembled a colossus, standing over him with her elbows stuck out at right angles to her body in washerwoman fashion, and her hands fastened firmly on her hips.

"God, but you're still beautiful when you're angry," he said mildly, and so insultingly that had she had the strength, she would have pummeled him into submission with her bare hands. Instead, she resorted to staring him out, with those melting blue eyes that had always had the power to fascinate him so.

"All right," he said abruptly after a few minutes when their eyes seemed to be locked. "We'll get everything packed up and leave as soon as we're ready. The sun is on the wane, in any case, so it's time we made a move."

When she looked outside she could see that the shadows were lengthening, and it would probably only have been a little more time before Ross decided to move, in any case. Instead of which, she had used up more of her precious energy in baiting him. She moved around the tent silently, gathering up the belongings that had been shielded from the heat of the day, and helping him to pack them onto the camels' backs. Suddenly, she could think of nothing to say to him. They were nearing the end of the great adventure, and instead of being awash with eagerness and joy, Stephanie could feel nothing inside but emptiness.

They left the place that had been their final camp without a backward glance. They allowed the camels to make their regulated pace, and Stephanie stared steadfastly ahead, to where the walls and outlines of the city were coming ever nearer and more defined.

Even Ross seemed oddly subdued now, when she would have expected him to be overjoyed that he could begin the next stage of his work. The discoveries in the tomb of the nobleman would be recorded for posterity, and Captain Ross Kilmarron would be hailed as one of Britain's famed Egyptologists, his services as lecturer and adviser widely sought.

There was no explanation for their mutual disquiet. It was as though, with the culmination of reaching safety, all feeling for each other had vanished. They were two strangers, riding side by side into a city of strangers. Ross had made no mention of changing the robes for their own clothes, and Stephanie had felt disinclined to risk any snide reference to her vanity in mentioning it. So they rode in silence, like two nomads, through the quickly descending night.

She tried to push aside all the uneasy feelings that gripped her, and tried to remind herself that of course they would not be strangers in Alexandria. The staff at the Cleopatra Hotel would welcome them warmly, and their rooms would be readily available for them. Even the clothes they had left behind would still be hanging in the wall closets. A flicker of relief flooded through Stephanie at the thought. The clothes might hang loosely on her now, but at least they would be her own, and she could wear them with all the grace of an Englishwoman, instead of covering herself from head to foot in the concealing garments of an Arab.

Much of the city was in darkness by the time they reached the environs, and the shanty dwellings of the wretched. They were obliged to travel through areas that were rank and unsavory, and the howling of the city's many wild dogs constantly unnerved Stephanie. She held on tightly to her camel's rope, thankful that Ross had lashed them together, for if the darkness or other terrors were to have separated them, she knew she would probably have died from sheer fright.

"Hang on, Stephanie," she heard his quiet voice say as she gasped at the sudden guttural shouting and wild barking from one of the hovels. "Once we're through the alleyways, we'll only be a short distance from the hotel."

It was almost impossible to believe, but she knew well enough that in places like these, very little distance separated the affluent from the poverty-stricken. So she gritted her teeth, and hung on. And surely—surely there was a faint smell of the sea among all the other indescribable smells, against which she tried so hard to pinch her nostrils. And where there was the sea, there would be a ship to take them home.

"We're here, my love," she heard Ross say as her eyes blurred with weak tears of hope.

She blinked her eyes blindly. She hadn't even realized they had left the stinking alleyways behind and had reached the fragrant grounds of a hotel built of redbrick, adorned with the splendor of tall white colonnades. She hadn't even noticed that they were already approaching the impressive front door, where the sign of the Cleopatra Hotel above it was faintly illuminated by the glow from the interior.

And then the great surge of thankfulness in her heart was brutally shattered as furious voices shouted at them, and several white-robed men emerged from the hotel, angrily waving their arms and barring their entry.

She couldn't understand the language, but the message

was plain. They were being turned away, because they appeared to be shambling vagabonds. And despite the fact that Ross was shouting back in a mixture of English and Arabic, it suddenly became all too much for Stephanie to bear.

Even so, her last sensible thought as she slumped over her camel's back was that she must try to hold on to her senses at all costs. She had surely done enough swooning in these last weeks, and to do so again would hardly be the dignified entry into Alexandria she had envisaged.

Twenty-one

By sheer willpower alone, Stephanie forced herself to stay as alert as possible, and all the shouting quickly aroused other hotel staff. More white-robed figures appeared as they heard the commotion, while others rushed inside to relay the arrival of the apparitions to the hotel manager. Eventually the door opened wide, letting out a stream of light onto the weary travelers, and a familiar robed figure came toward them with outstretched arms. His melodramatic gestures were matched by his flowery welcome.

"My dear Sidi Captain Kilmarron and lady! Can it really be your noble selves! We had given up all hope of seeing you again, and for you to be received in such a way will be to my eternal shame and damnation—"

Ross slid down from the camel's back and held out his hand to assist Stephanie. She moved stiffly. She ached in every limb, but she held her head up high as she was escorted into the hotel, leaving the duty boys to unload the camels of their burdens and presumably to send them off into the night. She didn't care what became of them now. Let some poor Arab take them and make good use of them. They had been good servants to herself and Ross, but she prayed that she need never sit on such an animal's back again as long as she lived.

"Your accommodation still awaits you, Sidi Captain Kilmarron," Calid said, handing him a key with a flourish. "The

Alexandria bank has sent regular payments for its availability, and everything is still in apple-pudding order, as you say, just as you left it."

"Good," Ross said briefly. "Then, since we seem to be attracting more attention than we would wish at this moment, we will retire to our room at once, and perhaps you would have a hot meal and some tea sent up as soon as possible."

"It will be attended to immediately," Calid said with a little bow.

Until Ross's words, Stephanie hadn't realized that there were other guests in the hotel who were peering at them curiously through the glass door of the dining room. She blushed furiously, seeing that there were well-dressed Europeans as well as some affluent Arab guests who were obviously wondering who these disreputable-looking newcomers could be who had aroused such interest from the staff.

Their identities and nationality might be completely obscure, and thankfully so for the moment, Stephanie thought, but it was obvious to the other guests that they were commanding the highest attention from the hotel staff.

"Can we go to the room at once, Ross? We're being stared at, and I feel horribly conspicuous," she muttered.

"Of course," he said. "But I'm sure that a hot bath and some proper food will soon aid your recovery. You have nothing to fear from now on, Stephanie."

The duty boys came behind them with all their baggage, placing it quickly down on the floor, as if the touch of the assorted dust-laden canvas bags was going to contaminate them.

Stephanie smiled faintly, for little did they know that inside several of those bags were the treasures of a nobleman who had lived and loved and died thousands of years ago. The bags contained the clues to their own past.

But at last the duty boys had left the room and she and Ross were alone. She couldn't think of a single thing to say to him, and in desperation at the sudden silence between them, she went quickly across to the wall closets and threw them open.

And there were the gowns she had left behind, still hanging in the closets, the gleam of shot-green taffeta and glowing amber satin, more alluring to her touch than all the seductively silken garments of a harem. She trailed her fingers over the sensual fabrics, reveling in them, and remembering how they had been made for her alone by an English seamstress who had stitched far into the night in readiness for a honeymoon to surpass all others.

"Have you missed wearing your own clothes so much?" she heard Ross say.

"I suppose you think I'm being vain. It's just that I long to feel like myself again, and I haven't known who I really am for such a long time. These clothes were made especially for me, and they're part of my personality. Not that I expect you to understand—"

"Of course I understand," he said roughly. "I understand far more than you think."

"Do you?" she murmured. *Do you understand how I ache for a normal relationship with the man I love? For a home and children, and just to go about our daily lives serenely and happily together?*

"This has been a terrible time for you, Stephanie, but I'll make it up to you, I promise. You'll want for nothing when we get back to England."

She looked at him mutely, wishing she could say that what she wanted most dearly in all the world was to have his love, until the end of time. She took a step toward him, and she might have burst out with all that was in her heart had there not been a discreet tap at the door. The next moment, the serving boys had arrived with trays of food and hot drinks, and almost before their eyes a table had been laid with a damask cloth and they were being invited to eat.

"I hadn't realized I was so hungry," she said to Ross, when the attendants had left them and they had begun to eat the delicious food. "I had expected to have a bath first and then a rest, and then to change into some of my own clothes, and to feel more civilized."

"Instead of which, your stomach is relishing good food that's been prepared in a hotel kitchen, rather than over a desert fire."

Although he said the words matter-of-factly, it seemed to Stephanie like a small censure.

"Have I been such a disappointment to you, Ross? I did try, truly I did."

She stopped, hardly knowing what she was apologizing for, and annoyed with herself for sounding so feeble.

"Don't be ridiculous," he said. "You haven't been a disappointment to me in the slightest way. No one could have complemented me more. But if you're hoping to hear anything more flattering tonight, I suggest that you let it wait until the weariness leaves us and we're more refreshed."

She heard the tension in his voice, and knew that this journey had been an immense ordeal for him. Not only the partial failure of the expedition and the loss of his team, but the betrayal and loss of his friend, Prince Hali, too. For the first time, she pondered on how much of the prince's part in their troubles Ross intended laying at Hali's door.

"Will you accuse Prince Hali of murder?" she said huskily, putting it into words for the first time.

As she did so, she began to wonder just what repercussions such an accusation might have on Ross. It would be only his word against that of a fabulously wealthy prince, whose loyal supporters would surely form a stronghold around him. And who knew what dangers lay in store for an Englishman who dared to denounce a prince? Around every corner, there could lurk a dark stranger who would strike in the night. Stephanie shuddered, clattering her knife and fork onto her plate at the thought.

"There are some things that are best left unsaid," he said quietly. "There's no proof of what happened during the *khamsin,* and it would be a foolish man indeed who suggested a crime that may never have happened."

"But isn't that betraying Mac and Dawson and the others?" Stephanie said.

"They would have done the same for us," Ross said calmly. "There was an unwritten code among us that says that if a crime can't be proven beyond all doubt, then we don't arouse undue suspicions."

"But it's so unfair, and it means that Hali gets away with it—"

"What good would it do to try to bring Hali to justice, when the desert has taken all the evidence? Who will search in that vast wilderness for the remains of bodies long since swallowed up by the sand, or eaten by the buzzards?"

"Our men had families," she muttered. "They have a right to know what happened."

"None of my team had wives or children, and they were handpicked for that reason. They knew the risks, Stephanie, and any next of kin will be informed that the men were lost in the desert in the course of the expedition during the *khamsin,* and must now be presumed dead. They will receive a handsome compensation."

She felt her face burn with indignation at this callous dismissal of men's lives. The ways of men could be very brutal, she thought.

Without warning, Ross brought her hand to his lips, and kissed the tender skin of her palm, where the desert winds had coarsened it.

"Trust me to do what's right, Stephanie. I know this country better than you, and the ethics must be observed. When I write up my reports, I shall give due credit to all the members of my team, but the manner of their disappearance must remain a mystery. It will also be recorded so in my book, and any speculation on my part will not involve Prince Hali."

There was a slight warning in his voice that she didn't miss. He was telling her that she, too, must not voice her suspicions. It was wrong, and she knew it was wrong, and yet, it was the only thing they could do. The had no proof, except for a gut feeling that Hali had brutally slain all the rest of their team and left them to fend for themselves in the desert. By now, he probably thought they had perished from hunger and thirst, and the madness of dehydration.

"Very well," she said slowly.

She clasped her hands tightly in her lap. The whole world was full of treachery in one form or another, and there wasn't a single thing that one lone voice could do about it.

"Finish your meal," Ross said, as if nothing had happened.

"I can't eat any more. It would choke me."

Besides, she had begun to eat too fast and too well when the food was first put in front of her, and her stomach wasn't used to such quantities. She sipped the hot, refreshing tea, and felt unutterably tired.

"Do you mind if I have a bath and go straight to bed?" she murmured. "I can't take any more conversation tonight."

"And I shall have half an hour's consultation with Calid. I need to send messages as soon as possible to the bank and the British consul as well as the newspaper office and the Egyptian authorities, and to arrange meetings with them all in the next couple of days."

She stared at him, her heart sinking. "You mean we're not going to leave for England right away?"

"I doubt that a ship is waiting in port especially for Captain Kilmarron and his lady," Ross said dryly. "Certain arrangements must be made, Stephanie, and I must inform the necessary authorities here that we're safe and well, as well as getting permission to take the relics from the tomb out of the country. They have to be registered here, and their future in British museums assured."

She listened to him numbly. How naive she had been to think they would simply slip out of Alexandria tomorrow and be on their way home. Now it seemed there were all kinds of legalities to be cleared up before they could even think of such a thing. She was bitter with disappointment.

"Go on then," she said with all the petulance of a child. "Go and talk to Calid, and please don't disturb me when you come back to the room."

"I had no intention of doing so," he said calmly. He pressed a kiss on her forehead before he left her, still swathed in the Arab robes that sat on him so well, and leaving her even more frustrated and annoyed.

A short while later she lay back in the soft, warm water of a real bathtub, with the fragrance of aromatic bath crystals washing through her senses. She had never felt so grimy in her life, and for one who was normally so fastidious, the feeling of having been unclean for so long was especially abhorrent to her. She began to scrub at her skin, and then realized how foolish she was being, for much of the darkness on her limbs was as much due to the heat of the sun as to the abrasive ingrained sand.

When she had bathed for long enough, she stood up carefully, knowing how weak she still was. In the mirrored panel on the bathroom wall, she could see her pale, thin body, so changed from the voluptuous curves of her blossoming womanhood. How could any man desire her now? she thought in desperation.

Her gaze roamed slowly upward over herself, finally reaching her face, and she gasped with horror. Her face was a deep, honey-gold color. It was a very attractive hue in other cultures, but not on an English lady's face. And she could have wept for the revered peaches-and-cream complexion that was no longer hers. She gasped, too, at her lank hair, its silvery strands dulled and stiff with sand.

She washed and dried it as best she could, and then wrapped herself in towels, no longer wanting to look at herself, though she was thankful to feel clean again for the first time in weeks.

There were creams and lemon-scented lotions on the marble washstand, and she smothered her face and hands in them in an attempt to whiten them a little. Then she covered herself in one of her nightgowns and crawled into bed. The last thing she wanted was for Ross to see her like this, she thought incongruously, forgetting that he had seen her in far worse plights, and she was fast asleep long before he came back to their room.

She awoke slowly, knowing that it must be nearly dawn, for she could see that the nighttime darkness had lifted, even behind her half-closed lids.

"We're in Alexandria," she murmured as memory rushed back at her. "Oh, thank God—"

She turned her head, and by the beginnings of daylight that filtered through the shutters of their room, she could see a darker head alongside her on the pillow.

"You look more rested, my sweet," Ross said softly. "I hardly knew what to say to you last night. You looked so exhausted, and so distraught, and I knew you needed to be alone."

He stroked her hair, and she felt a stab of gladness that it was no longer a dried-up tangle. As he ran a gentle finger around the contour of her cheeks, they, too, felt a mite softer after the application of the creams and lotions.

Stephanie recognized the touch, and with a rush of returning warmth in her veins, she welcomed it feverishly. Perhaps he understood her feelings of doubt in herself better than she knew. She yearned so much to feel like a woman again, to be loved and wanted, so that when his arms reached out to pull her close, she went into them willingly and eagerly, returning his kiss with a passion that took him by surprise.

"My beautiful girl," Ross murmured. "Don't ever think that a little loss of weight will make you anything but desirable to me!"

"And am I desirable to you?" she asked huskily. "Despite

everything? Despite the way I came into your life, and the disaster of all that's happened?"

She felt his hands slowly run the length of her body, and she shivered as her responses began. She knew how helpless she was in resisting him when he began the sweet seduction that bemused her senses, but still she felt the need to question, to be sure.

"If you hadn't come into my life in the way that you did," he said, deftly avoiding the disharmony of their arranged marriage, "you would have come into it some other way. Two lovers such as you and I were destined to meet and be together. I thought your romantic heart would have told you that."

And while his hands and mouth were doing such delicious things to her, how could she ever doubt him? Somehow he had removed her nightgown without her even being aware of it, and for a moment she covered herself with her hands, ashamed that she wasn't as perfect for him as when they had first met. The shining girl with the silver hair who he'd seen in the portrait at her stepfather's house was not the same as the woman in his arms at the Cleopatra Hotel, and for a moment she mourned the loss of that young girl.

But only for a moment. Ross removed her hands from her breasts and gently circled their tips with his tongue. The sensual contact sent shooting waves of desire coursing through her, and she gasped aloud at the sweetness he evoked.

"Don't ever cover yourself from me, sweetheart. There's nothing about you that I don't find beautiful, and always will," he said, his voice thick with desire.

And then he had covered her with himself, sliding into her with all the sensuality of a lover, and all the finesse of a husband. He knew what she liked, and wanted, and needed. His hands cupped her breasts as the rhythmic movements began, and she reveled in possessing and being possessed.

But knowing that neither could bear to wait too long for fulfillment, their loving quickly reached its climax. She gasped against him as she felt his seed gush hotly into her, and he lay heavily against her while she strove to steady her erratic heartbeats. They lay, spent, for some time afterward, and then Ross moved away from her.

"Much as I'd like to spend the day in bed with you, Stephanie, I have meetings to attend," he said regretfully. "I've asked Calid to arrange for a seamstress to come to the hotel this morning to make any necessary fitting adjustments to your gowns, and to supply you with any new ones that you desire. I may be gone all day—"

"All day!" She could think of nothing else. "Oh, don't leave me here alone, Ross!"

"Please don't be difficult, my dear. I told you about the people I must meet today, and I shall also see about a passage home as soon as possible, so I hope to have good news for you when we meet for dinner this evening."

She saw that he was dressing quickly now, and in his normal clothes. The dashing sheik of the desert was gone, but in his place was a man that no one could ever call ordinary. He was too tall, too powerful, too much a man in every way, with a man's business to attend to, and she swallowed her disappointment at being left alone all day.

She washed and dressed quickly, wearing one of the day gowns that hung on her now. She bit her lip, dreading to try on anything more graceful, and resolving to eat every morsel of breakfast in order to gain weight as soon as possible.

It was a mistake, of course. She ate too much bread and too many eggs, and felt overfull and uncomfortable, but still the day gown looked as though it had been made for someone two sizes larger than herself. She could have cried with frustration, and when the young seamstress arrived in her room, she almost fell on her with relief.

She begged the girl to say and alter every one of her gowns. She spoke a smattering of English, but enough to understand that the Saïda Kilmarron needed everything to be done immediately. She nodded in agreement, and set to work on the alterations while Stephanie dutifully wrote in her diary and did some quick sketches of the hotel environs.

By the time Ross returned, she was impatient to show him that the gowns now fitted her new, slender figure. With a little powder applied to her cheeks to tone down the tanning, she looked more willowy than gaunt.

"You have a strong heart, Stephanie," Ross told her. "I wouldn't have expected anyone to revive so quickly after all you've been through."

"I also have the incentive of going home," she said. "Have you seen about a passage home for us?"

Suddenly, nothing else mattered. Oh, she knew he had to see certain officials, and to sort out the affairs of business and legalities, but the all-important thing in her mind was going home.

"There's a ship leaving for England in three days' time—" he began, but he got no further, because by then she had thrown herself into his arms, and his own automatically closed around her slender waist.

He looked down into her shining eyes, and without warning he felt the increasingly familiar tug of remorse for all he had put her through.

It was alien to Ross Kilmarron's virile nature to think himself incapable of holding a woman's affections, but he was well aware that this woman was different from all the others in his life. What he felt for her was love as he had never felt it before. He had told her so, but she had never referred to it since that time in the desert when they both thought their last moments were imminent. Knowing the eagerness of any woman to enjoy hearing the declaration of love repeated, he had expected that she would, and it disturbed him that she didn't seem to care.

Impatiently, he shook off the nagging feelings, wondering what the devil was the matter with him. He held his wife in his arms right now, but it was that very innocence, that very sweet, trusting nature of hers, that could make him feel such a rat for changing her life so dramatically.

"You must be patient for three more days, my sweet," he said coolly, taking her arms from around his neck before he crushed her to him. And she was so thin, seemingly almost ready to break.

"And then," he went on, "once we've returned to Oxford-shire and shown ourselves to be utterly respectable, you may relieve yourself of any obligation toward me, and go where you will—if you so desire."

He spoke mockingly and stiffly, unable to resist the urge to torment himself still more. She had done her duty, and he would release her from her marriage vows if she wished. He owed her that much.

"Is that what you want? To be rid of me so soon?" Stephanie said in a strangled voice. "What about your book, and my illustrations? I've an interest in it, too, and I want to see it through to the end. That is, if you have no objections."

She listened to herself discussing the wretched drawings as though they were the be all and end all of her life, when he was the one who was all that, and more. But it seemed to Stephanie that he was making it very obvious that he wanted to be rid of her as soon as possible, and she wouldn't beg for any more favors.

"Of course I want you to work on the book with me," Ross said, his voice rough. "We set out on this expedition together, and we'll see it through together."

And after that? But Stephanie refused to look that far ahead, unable to contemplate the emptiness of a future without him.

Twenty-two

They were feted at the hotel on the night before they joined the ship for England. Calid was proud that they had spent their time at his hotel, and provided a sumptuous dinner that left them feeling uncomfortable, for they were still unused to such ample portions of food.

There were many goodwill wishes when they were finally ready to leave the next day, but at last they arrived at the dockside, and all their baggage and the precious tomb relics were safely stowed in their cabin. Stephanie had never felt so relieved in her life as when she boarded the English ship *Felicity* and heard the crew speaking in English voices.

They were greeted by Captain Strong, and invited to join him at his table for all their meals, an honor indeed. But Ross's name was well known, and already news of their recent exploits had begun to circulate.

"How do they all know of it?" Stephanie said in amazement, when she had inspected their comfortable cabin.

"News travels fast," Ross said. "I sent messages to your family and my home to let them know we were safe, and I alerted the newspaper agency In Alexandria with brief details, so some of it will have appeared in British newspapers long before we get there. I'm afraid we must be prepared to be inundated with reporters for a few days, my dear, but I've no doubt it will only be a nine-day wonder."

"Do I sense that you hope it won't be?" she said with a smile.

He shrugged. "I haven't spent half my life studying Egyptology, and frequently almost perished through my love of it, to be able to dismiss it all so quickly."

Stephanie shivered. Could he ever dismiss it at all, this love that was only second to the way a man loved a woman? Wouldn't the tug that Egypt had on his heart always be there to pull him back? If it did, he would go alone, for she had vowed never to set foot in that country again.

"Don't fret," she heard him say. "You needn't be present at any of their press conferences if you prefer to stay in the background. I'm quite adept at fending off any probing questions I don't want to answer."

"It might be best," she murmured. "I'm not used to such occasions, and I wouldn't want to say anything to embarrass you. Supposing I should inadvertently say anything untoward about the disappearance of the men, for instance—"

He looked at her thoughtfully.

"You know, Stephanie, it might be that I have to keep you after all. A wife can't speak out against her husband in a court of law, should it ever come to that, so I might yet have second thoughts about letting you go!"

She gaped at him, wondering if he was serious, but by now he was answering a knock on their cabin door. A steward passed on the request that Captain Kilmarron would meet several gentlemen from *The Times* and other newspapers, who were on board and who would be most interested to hear his story after the evening meal.

"So it has already begun," Ross commented. "For a while, our lives will no longer be our own."

And perhaps it was better so. While Ross was being interviewed by all and sundry, it might give them both time to stand back and examine their lives, and decide what was to be made of it, together or apart. But the comment Ross had

made about perhaps not letting her go after all seemed nothing more than a mockery.

The long voyage home progressed in some style. Stephanie soon discovered that they were being treated like very
important passengers indeed. The fact that the rest of the
team had so mysteriously vanished and the saga of the perilous journey back to Alexandria of Captain Kilmarron and
his wife lent an air of dangerous intrigue and romance to the
whole episode. Sometimes it was too much so for Stephanie's
taste, especially from certain newspaper people who scented
the possibility of a sensational story.

"I can't believe people can be so callous," Stephanie ex-
ploded one evening toward the end of the voyage. "They try
to wrench every gruesome detail out of us, whether it's true
or not!"

"Yes, and we must be on our guard to tell them only what
we know," Ross said sharply. "We don't guess, and we don't
surmise. We describe the terrors of the *khamsin,* and how it
can blow for days and change the landscape beyond all recognition, and we leave it to their imagination to provide the
rest. They'll get enough taste of adventure from learning
about our time with the bedouins."

She shivered, knowing that some of the more unscrupulous
scandal rags could make a tasty tale out of nothing. Their
private suspicions about Hali and the fate of their team was
their secret, and must always remain so.

"You're cold," Ross said as she silently prepared for bed,
lost in thought. "Would you like me to warm you?"

She looked at him mutely, not knowing whether he meant
he wanted to love her physically or merely wrap his arms
around her. And for once, all she wanted was to be comforted,
to feel safe and secure, and not to have to think about tomorrow.

"If it's not too little to ask, I'd just like to feel your arms around me until I sleep," she whispered, hoping she wasn't offending his masculinity.

She couldn't read the inscrutable look on his face, shadowed by the dim lighting in the cabin. But she could hear the tenderness in his voice, and, as always, her heart swelled with love for him.

"Then if that's what my lady wants—"

He slid into the narrow bunk beside her. There was hardly room for two, and she was squashed against the cabin wall, but with his arms wrapped tightly around her, it was a comfortable squashing. And with her husband's hands resting lightly on her breasts, and his steady breathing in her ear, she fell into a dreamless sleep almost at once.

She awoke before dawn had really broken, aware that there was a subtle change in the movement of the *Felicity,* a slowing-down. There was no sign of Ross in the cabin, and she jumped out of bed and peered through the thick glass porthole. At first she could make out very little, and then her heart leapt. There were flickers of light ahead, and surely, surely that was a smudge of land instead of the endless ocean. Thinking back quickly, Stephanie realized they must have sailed through the English Channel during the hours of darkness, and they were now within sight of Tilbury. They were nearly home.

The emotion of the moment was almost too much to bear, and it was a moment she needed to share. Quickly, she donned her clothes, remembering to put on several more layers of her warmer garments now. The English morning would be chilly, but she felt a surge of unmitigated joy run through her at the ironic thought. Who ever thought she would be welcoming a chilly English morning!

Ross entered the cabin, and she turned to him eagerly.

"It *is* Tilbury, isn't it, Ross? Oh, please don't tell me I've been dreaming, and that we're about to dock at some miserable French port!"

"It's Tilbury, my love," he said quietly. "It's nearly over."

She looked up at him, happiness spilling out of her, and he shook his head slightly. Even in this half-light, with her hair still tumbling and uncombed, she looked ravishing to him. And he still didn't know what to do with her.

"But not for us, surely! We've got so much work to do! Your writing—and my sketches—"

She paused, wondering if she was being too forward in including herself in his plans. He had said it was nearly over. Was there an ambiguity in his meaning? Was he telling her it was over for the two of them as well? Her happiness drained away, and she turned away from him.

"Of course there will be work to do," he said brusquely, "and I shall value your help, Stephanie. You know that. Now, let's go and have some breakfast before we prepare to disembark."

She followed him, aware that something wasn't quite right. The constraint between them wasn't of her making, but she knew she would add to it, for whenever he went away from her in spirit, she retreated, too. While love held them together, they were like two immovable objects, but when it didn't . . .

The time for disembarkation came quickly, and at the rush of excited newsmen on the quayside, Stephanie's heart sank. News of their arrival had clearly preceded them.

"Stay calm," Ross murmured. "I'll speak to them all, and then we'll be on our way home."

"But not quite yet!" Stephanie said suddenly, seeing two familiar figures struggling through the crush of people.

She could have wept at the sight of Cousin Claire's homely red face, and even Lord Buchan's embarrassed kiss on her cheek was not wholly unwelcome. But Claire's exclamations of dismay on her appearance were not so welcome.

"My dear child, thank God! But you're so thin! And that dreadful darkness in your complexion is most unbecoming."

"On the contrary," Ross said quietly. "With the contrast of her silver hair, I think it makes her even more beautiful, if that were possible."

Before Stephanie could register her astonishment at this statement, he was swept up by the newsmen with more questions, but eventually the four of them were able to retire to an inn to take refreshment, before a hired carriage took Ross and Stephanie home to Oxfordshire.

"You're to come to town for a visit very soon," Cousin Claire said when the moment of parting came. "There's so much I want to hear about, Stephanie, and you need properly feeding up—"

"Why don't you come to Oxfordshire to visit us?" Ross said politely. "We shall be burying ourselves in work for the next few months, to record our trip while the memories are still fresh, but in a month of so, I know Stephanie will be aching to see you."

"Why, thank you, Captain Kilmarron," Claire said, as flushed with pleasure as Stephanie at the unexpected invitation.

"And meanwhile, I promise to write to you very often," Stephanie said. "I kept my diary as faithfully as I could, and I have so much to tell you."

It was as far as she could go right now, and her stepfather might not have been there at all, for all the interest he took in them, but none of it mattered a jot to Stephanie. There were more hugs and kisses and tears before they were on their way at last, where the lanes and byways of leafy Oxfordshire beckoned them home.

"I had forgotten how beautiful it was," Stephanie murmured when the thin sunshine of the late afternoon revealed the outlines of the mansion on the Kilmarron Estate. The undulating green hills and the darker green of the distant forest were like balm to her tired eyes after so much endless desert, and she felt an almost irresistible urge to kneel down and kiss the sweet young grass of the early English springtime. The seasons had moved on, and she had moved with them, though just how far, she didn't yet know.

By the time they reached the house, excited word had

spread that they were coming, and the lineup of servants she remembered from when she had entered this house as a bride was there to greet them again. How different she was now from that time. How changed, and how much more worldly.

Their baggage was taken up to the master bedroom, and when they entered it to change out of their traveling clothes, everything looked exactly the same. The thick Persian carpet, the costly draperies and furnishings, the large, lace-canopied four-poster bed, the delicate toiletries on the dressing table.

Everything was the same, and only they had changed, for no one could go through the experiences they had without being changed in some way.

"Perhaps it will be too quiet for a young lady brought up in the town," Ross commented tersely. "I wonder how long it will be before you yearn to be back among the theaters and soirees, and to be the toast of London, which I've no doubt you could be without even trying."

She stared at him. "Is that what you want? To send me back to London, now that you've done with me?"

"Of course not. I told you, we've got work to do, and you promised to help—"

"And so I shall. You'll get your pound of flesh, never fear," she snapped, hardly knowing how her bland remarks could have stirred up such a hornet's nest of anger inside him.

"I'm sorry," he said after a moment. "I'm feeling boorish, and I shouldn't take it out on you. It's the usual reaction. When you've climbed a mountain, it takes time to readjust to the lower slopes."

And in times past, he'd never had a wife around on whom to vent his spleen, Stephanie thought.

"I do understand, Ross," she murmured.

"I doubt that you do," he said. "But just promise me this. If my moods become too much for you, just keep out of my sight, for you don't deserve my tongue-lashing."

It wasn't what she wanted to hear at all. Surely a wife should be there to soothe and placate, and be a helpmeet in all things, but she reminded herself that she wasn't an ordinary wife, and that Ross was far too proud a man to bare his soul to a mere woman.

Her brow puckered for a moment, trying to remember a time when it hadn't been like that. Trying so hard to recapture a moment when she had had her heart's desire, and she had felt so overwhelmed with love that she had been dazzled by it. But the memory was always too elusive to recapture, always swimming in and out of her senses as if it was no more than a lovely watercolor dream, when she so desperately wanted it to be real.

"I'm sorry if I offend you," he said, seeing her frown. "But that's the way it has to be, Stephanie. Now, I want to speak to my estate manager and various others, so I shall leave you for a while. Just ring the bell for a maid to help you unpack."

"After all I've had to do these past months, I'm sure I can manage by myself, and perhaps I, too, prefer to be alone," she snapped. And seconds later he was gone, leaving her staring at the bedroom door, her clenched hands at her sides.

It should have been so wonderful, the unwinding from all the tension of the desert and the pressures of the newspapermen to get a story. But to Stephanie their marriage was still a hollow sham, and the colorful and romantic reports the newsmen concocted about the couple who had braved the desert and come home unscathed left her with a bitter taste in her mouth. They were depicted as a true hero and heroine, sharing adventures and love, and nothing seemed further from the truth in the emptiness of her life now.

After several weeks of business meetings, interspersed with his solitary walks or rides into the forest, Ross declared that they must start planning their book. Stephanie had already begun. In her own solitary hours, there had seemed little else to do. She had made many sketches of the relics that had now been handed over to a pompous official of the British Museum.

"You've done well," Ross remarked, looking through the folder. "I had no idea you'd been so busy."

"What else has there been for me to do?" she said, trying not to sound petulant. "You're always so busy seeing people nowadays, and you don't have much time for me."

"I know I seem to be neglecting you, Stephanie. But I promise you I'll make up for it later."

But when? He always had demands on his time that didn't include her, and by now she was seriously considering going up to London for a week or so to stay with Claire. The one thing stopping her was that Claire would be just as likely to ferret out her unhappiness in London as anywhere else. So she stayed where she was, feeling that she was simply marking time until their joint work in the book was begun and finished, by which time Ross would have no further need of her.

She allowed herself the luxury of feeling thoroughly sorry for herself, and her depression wasn't helped by the oppressive nature of the weather. Early spring in England was notoriously unpredictable, and this one was no exception. It was damp and cold, with a frequent sting of drizzle in the air. But Stephanie didn't object to the rain. After the burning heat of Egypt, she had promised herself that one day she would walk and run in the rain, and revel in its life-giving properties.

And today was the day, she decided recklessly. Ross was ensconced in his study, sorting out his many papers, and she would take that walk in the rain that she had been promising herself, and perhaps the sheer sensual pleasure of it would cleanse the misery from her soul.

An hour later, she was asking herself what possible pleasure there was in such a reckless undertaking. She was a mile from the house, soaked to the skin in a sudden heavy downpour, her shoes were sodden, and her silvery hair hung down in rat's tails. She shivered as she pulled her ineffective woolen shawl around her shoulders, knowing she should have worn something far more substantial.

"What the devil do you think you're doing, Stephanie?" She jerked up her head as she heard Ross's angry voice. He reined in his horse sharply, disregarding the animal's protesting whinny, and she glared up at him, her eyes smarting from the rain, and from her mortification at appearing like a scarecrow.

"I'm walking in the rain. Don't you remember how we once said we'd do it together—" Her voice trailed away, for their homespun dreams all seemed so long ago now, and such plans were for children.

"Get up on the horse before you catch your death of cold," he snapped. He slid down, bundling her onto the horse's back, and mounting the animal quickly behind her. Within minutes they were approaching the stables. Ross called for a stable lad to give the horse a rubdown, and he and Stephanie hurried toward the front of the house.

"You need locking up," he told her roughly.

"It wasn't raining so hard when I went out," she said defensively. "I just wanted some fresh air. I feel so stifled indoors. You wouldn't understand."

They entered the house, where the housekeeper gaped at them in astonishment. She was in the act of putting together a magnificent floral arrangement in one of the valuable jardinieres on a side table. Trying not to look too shocked at Stephanie's appearance, she asked quickly if there was anything she could do for Madam.

"Madam is going to take a hot bath, and later we'll have some tea and brandy sent up to our room," Ross said tersely. "I'll send for it when we're ready."

"Yes, sir," the housekeeper said without expression.

She turned back to her floral artistry, unaware that for those past few moments Stephanie had stood motionless, watching the deft hands as the woman combined fresh spring blooms with carefully prepared sprays of dried flowers and ferns, and the delicate, waxy, paperlike spheres of honesty.

Honesty. Like a mantra, the word went over and over in Stephanie's mind, knowing it was desperately important to her to remember why. For a blurred moment longer she struggled, and then she knew.

"Honesty," she said thickly. She turned her luminous eyes toward Ross. He didn't understand, but some sixth sense told him that something momentous had occurred in her mind, and without a word, he put his arm around her waist and took her up the curving staircase to their room. She turned toward him slowly, her heart in her eyes.

"Please tell me the truth, Ross," she whispered through trembling lips. "Did I dream of a time when you said there must be honesty between us?"

"It was no dream," he said, just as quietly. And then she was stumbling toward him and caught in his arms, both of them ignoring the rainy dampness that steamed gently between them.

For gradually the mists of memory were clearing, stripping away the layers that were as fragile as the gossamer veils of the harem girls, revealing clarity and truth, and love. She drew in her breath, able at last to visualize herself lying in Ross's arms, so near to death in the blistering desert heat, while he told her that he had always loved her, and that he wouldn't let her go to her Maker without the knowledge of that love. The memory became more crystal clear with every breath she took.

"Oh, Ross, then you *do* love me?" she burst out, her heart so filled with emotion she could hardly speak. "Let me hear you say again that you love me as much as I love you, and that we'll never part—"

His answer was to pull her wildly to him, and to crush his mouth to hers in a kiss that said everything. But still she needed the words.

"I've always loved you, and I always will, my darling girl," he said. "And if Hali and all the fates in hell didn't have the power to part us, then I swear that nothing will ever part us now."

They were the sweetest, most precious words on earth to her. And for long afterward, the sensual enactment of love endorsed what the words had begun as she lay in her husband's arms in the lace-canopied bed that she knew now would see their lives continue, and their children born.

But for now, as Ross's fingers delicately traced her inner thighs and caressed her into shuddering and exquisite responses, she drew him eagerly and wantonly into her, glorying in the fact that only love made them truly one flesh. And she was free to speak the words of love at last, and to know that they were wanted and reciprocated for all time.

Much later that night, they lay entwined together, sated by love, and with a golden future ahead of them. And as she gazed through the window at faraway stars in the heavens, she thanked God for all He had given her, vowing never to forget the past.

It had shaped all their tomorrows, and together she and Ross would relive all the magic of the good memories they had shared. They had a fabulous tale of fantasy and adventure to tell the world, and their children, for in the way of storytellers as old as time, she knew that in the telling, everything still lived on.

ROMANCE FROM JO BEVERLY

DANGEROUS JOY   (0-8217-5129-8, $5.99)

FORBIDDEN   (0-8217-4488-7, $4.99)

THE SHATTERED ROSE   (0-8217-5310-X, $5.99)

TEMPTING FORTUNE   (0-8217-4858-0, $4.99)